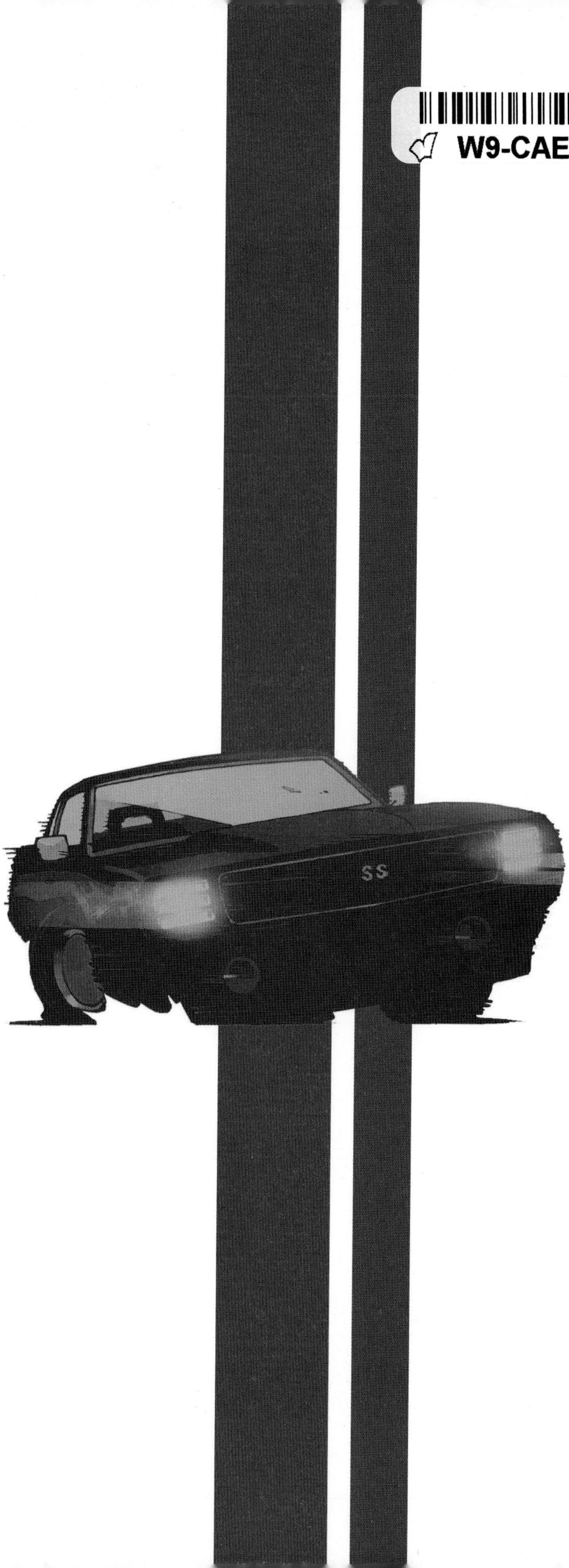
SS

IMAGE COMICS, INC.

Robert Kirkman • Chief Operating Officer
Erik Larsen • Chief Financial Officer
Todd McFarlane • President
Marc Silvestri • Chief Executive Officer
Jim Valentino • Vice President

Eric Stephenson • Publisher/Chief Creative Officer
Corey Hart • Director of Sales
Jeff Boison • Director of Publishing Planning & Book Trade Sales
Chris Ross • Director of Digital Sales
Jeff Stang • Director of Specialty Sales
Kat Salazar • Director of PR & Marketing
Drew Gill • Art Director
Heather Doornink • Production Director
Nicole Lapalme • Controller

IMAGECOMICS.COM

COLLECTION DESIGN JEFF POWELL

DEATH OR GLORY, VOLUME 1: SHE'S GOT YOU. First Printing. October 2018. Published by Image Comics, Inc. Office of publication: 2001 Center Street, 6th Floor, Berkeley, CA 94704. Copyright © 2018 Rick Remender and Bengal. All rights reserved. Originally published in single magazine form as DEATH OR GLORY #1-5. DEATH OR GLORY™ (including all prominent characters featured herein), its logo and all character likenesses are trademarks of Rick Remender and Wes Craig, unless otherwise noted. Image Comics® and its logos are registered trademarks of Image Comics, Inc. No part of this publication may be reproduced or transmitted, in any form or by any means (except for short excerpts for review purposes) without the express written permission of Image Comics, Inc. All names, characters, events and locales in this publication are entirely fictional. Any resemblance to actual persons (living or dead), events or places, without satiric intent, is coincidental. PRINTED IN THE U.S.A. For information regarding the CPSIA on this printed material call: 203-595-3636 and provide reference #RICH–815924. For international rights inquiries, contact: foreignlicensing@imagecomics.com.
REGULAR: 978-1-5343-0858-9
FORBIDDEN PLANET EXCLUSIVE VARIANT: 978-1-5343-1173-2
KINOKUNIYA EXCLUSIVE VARIANT: 978-1-5343-1178-7
MCM LONDON EXCLUSIVE VARIANT: 978-1-5343-1185-5

WRITER **RICK REMENDER**

ARTIST **BENGAL**

LETTERER **RUS WOOTON**

EDITOR **SEBASTIAN GIRNER**

PRODUCTION ARTIST **ERIKA SCHNATZ**

LOGO **VINCENT KUKUA**

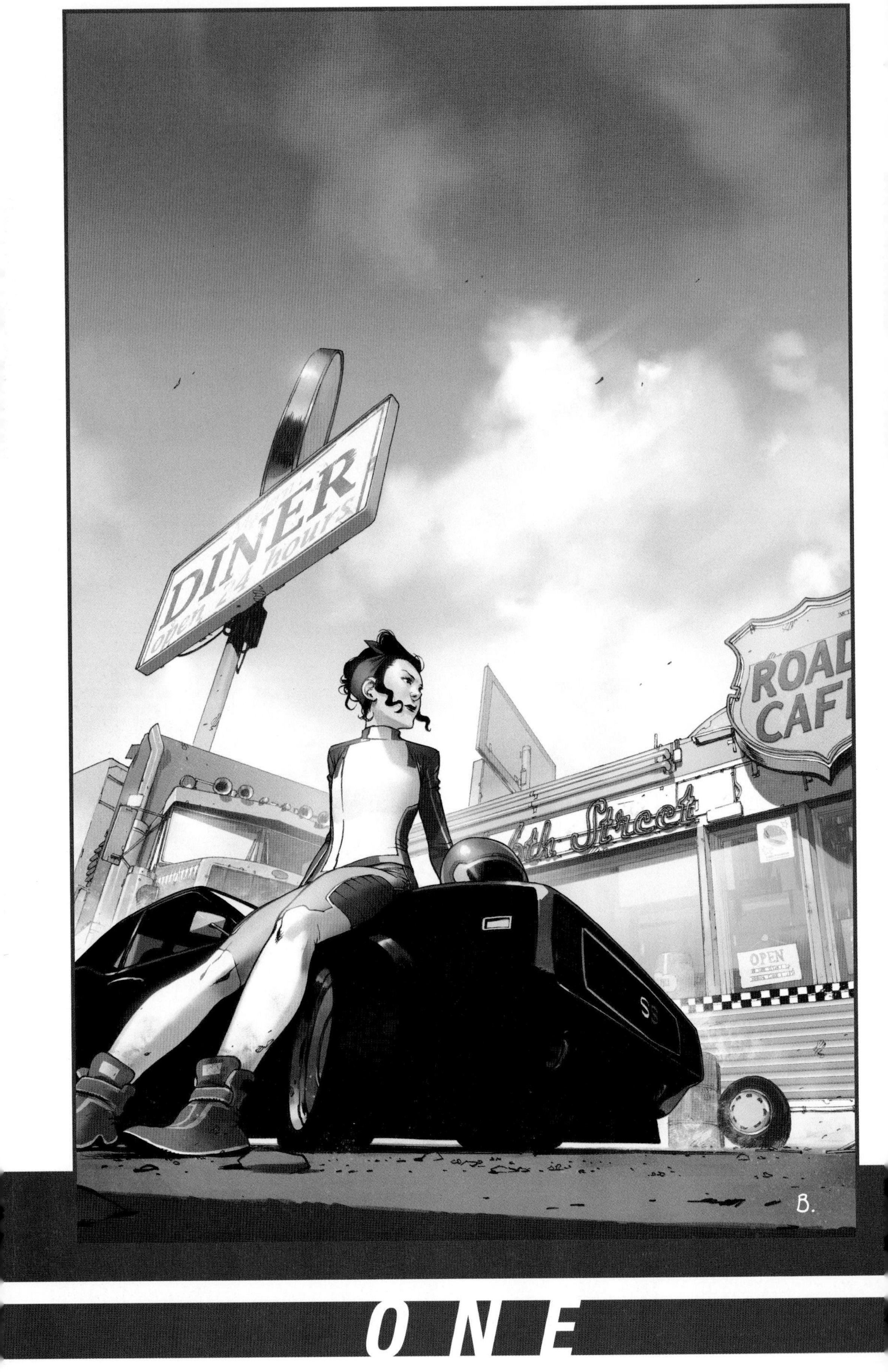
DINER
open 24 hours
ROAD
OPEN
B.

ONE

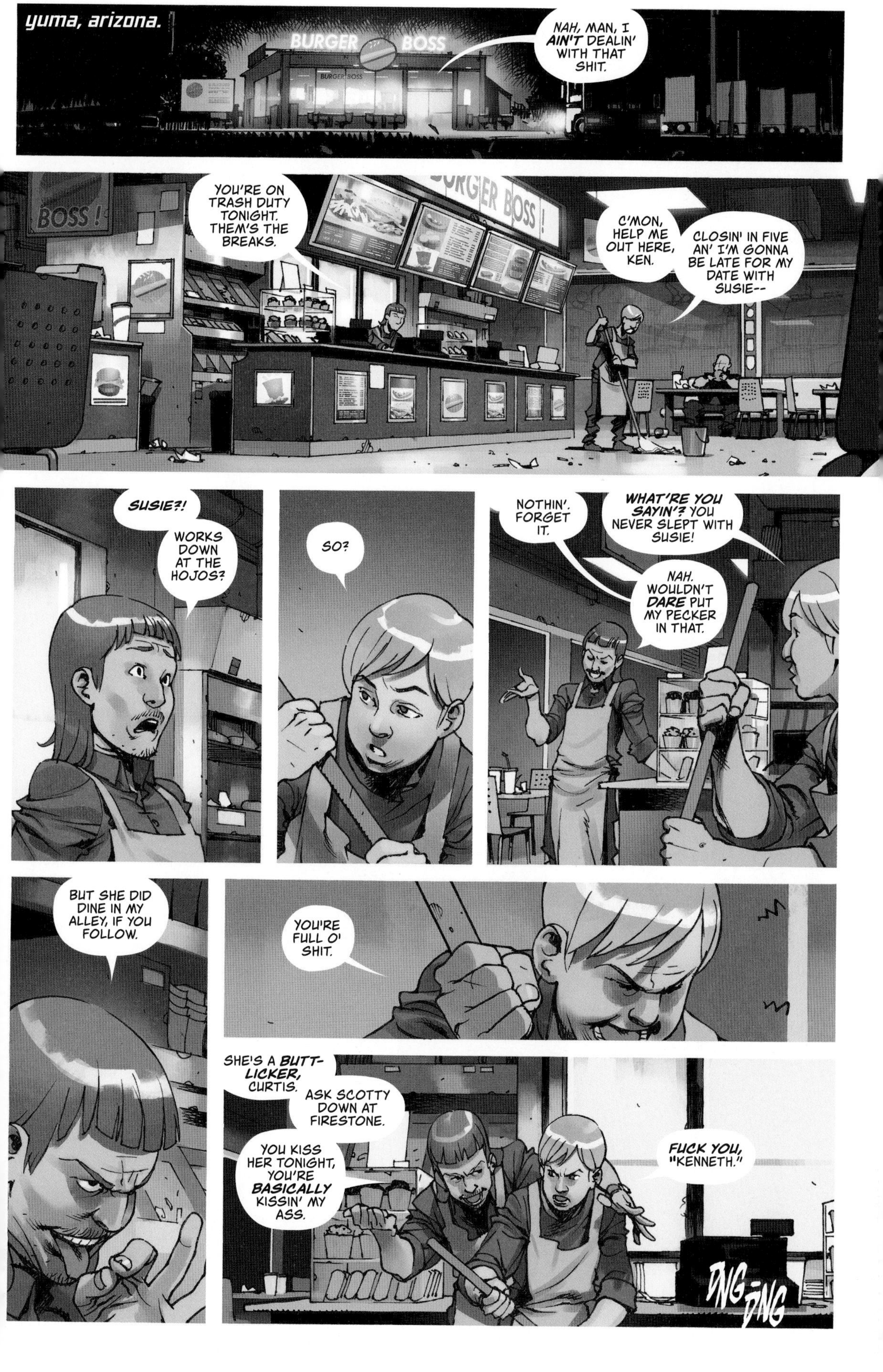
yuma, arizona.
BURGER BOSS
NAH, MAN, I AIN'T DEALIN' WITH THAT SHIT.
YOU'RE ON TRASH DUTY TONIGHT. THEM'S THE BREAKS.
C'MON, HELP ME OUT HERE, KEN.
CLOSIN' IN FIVE AN' I'M GONNA BE LATE FOR MY DATE WITH SUSIE--
SUSIE?!
WORKS DOWN AT THE HOJOS?
SO?
NOTHIN'. FORGET IT.
WHAT'RE YOU SAYIN'? YOU NEVER SLEPT WITH SUSIE!
NAH. WOULDN'T DARE PUT MY PECKER IN THAT.
BUT SHE DID DINE IN MY ALLEY, IF YOU FOLLOW.
YOU'RE FULL O' SHIT.
SHE'S A BUTT-LICKER, CURTIS.
ASK SCOTTY DOWN AT FIRESTONE.
YOU KISS HER TONIGHT, YOU'RE BASICALLY KISSIN' MY ASS.
FUCK YOU, "KENNETH."
DNG-DNG

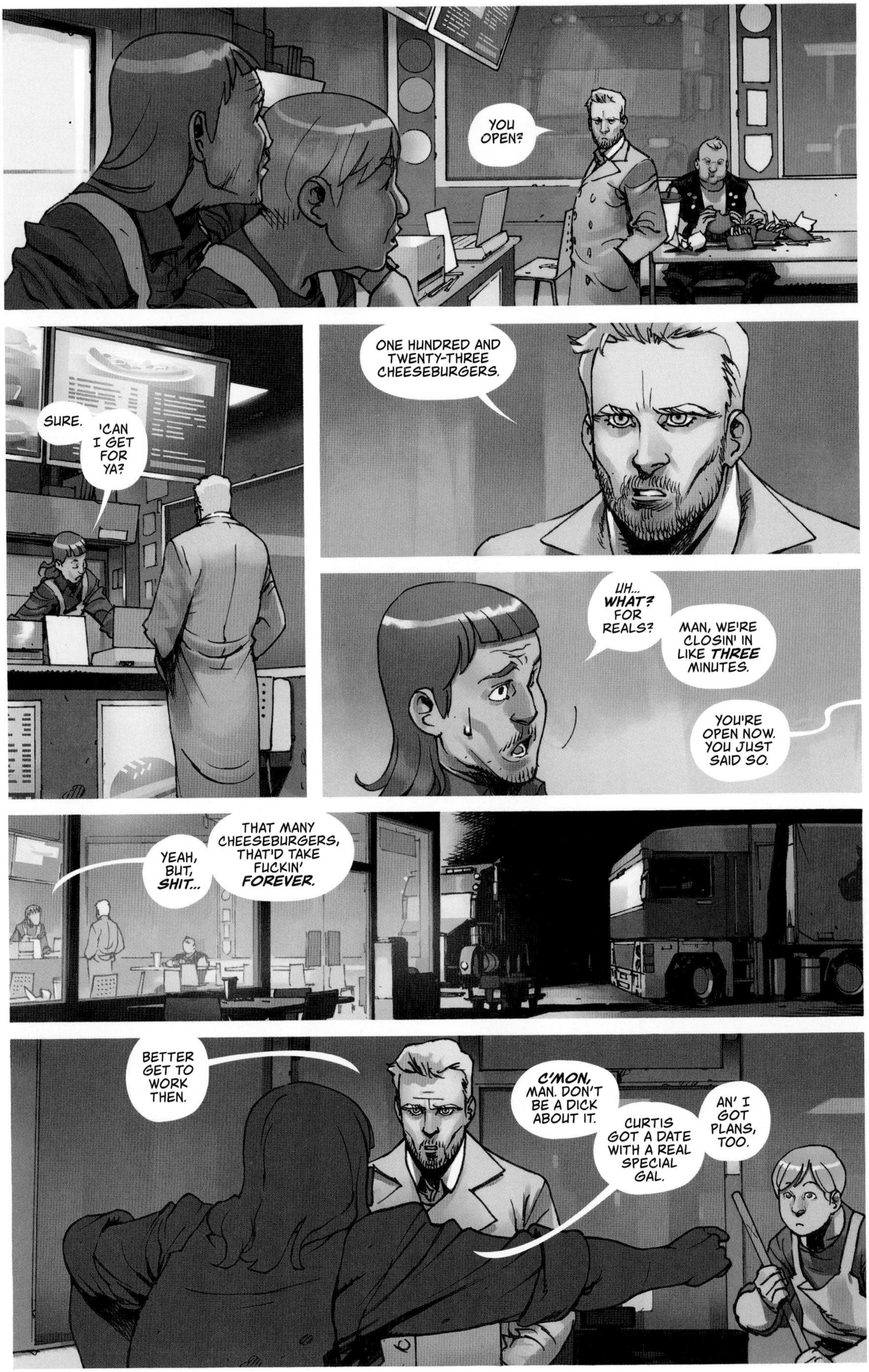
YOU OPEN?
SURE.
'CAN I GET FOR YA?
ONE HUNDRED AND TWENTY-THREE CHEESEBURGERS.
UH... **WHAT?** FOR REALS?
MAN, WE'RE CLOSIN' IN LIKE **THREE** MINUTES.
YOU'RE OPEN NOW. YOU JUST SAID SO.
YEAH, BUT, **SHIT...**
THAT MANY CHEESEBURGERS, THAT'D TAKE FUCKIN' **FOREVER.**
BETTER GET TO WORK THEN.
C'MON, MAN. DON'T BE A DICK ABOUT IT.
CURTIS GOT A DATE WITH A REAL SPECIAL GAL.
AN' I GOT PLANS, TOO.

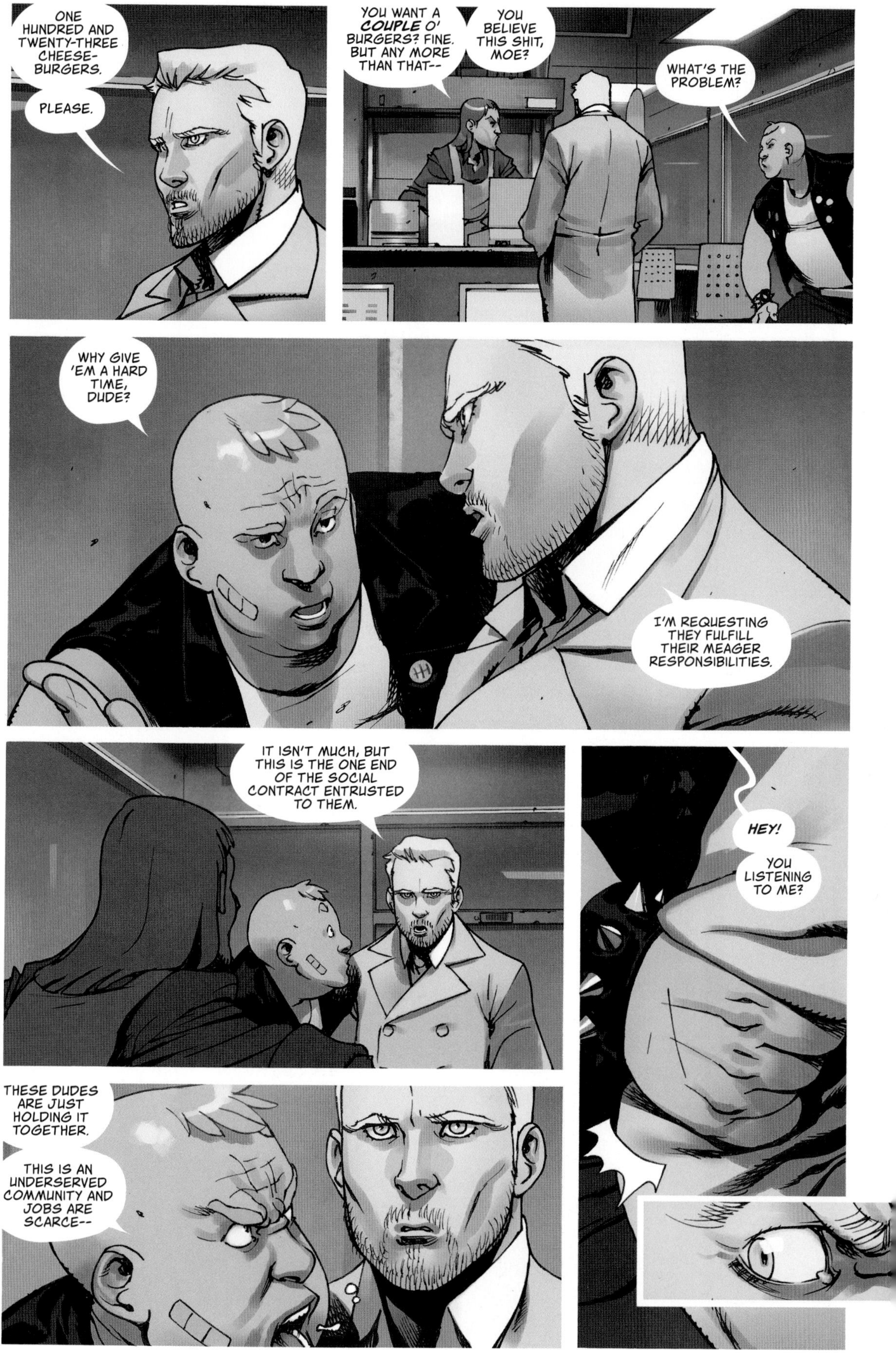
ONE HUNDRED AND TWENTY-THREE CHEESE-BURGERS.
PLEASE.
YOU WANT A COUPLE O' BURGERS? FINE. BUT ANY MORE THAN THAT--
YOU BELIEVE THIS SHIT, MOE?
WHAT'S THE PROBLEM?
WHY GIVE 'EM A HARD TIME, DUDE?
I'M REQUESTING THEY FULFILL THEIR MEAGER RESPONSIBILITIES.
IT ISN'T MUCH, BUT THIS IS THE ONE END OF THE SOCIAL CONTRACT ENTRUSTED TO THEM.
THESE DUDES ARE JUST HOLDING IT TOGETHER.
THIS IS AN UNDERSERVED COMMUNITY AND JOBS ARE SCARCE--
HEY!
YOU LISTENING TO ME?

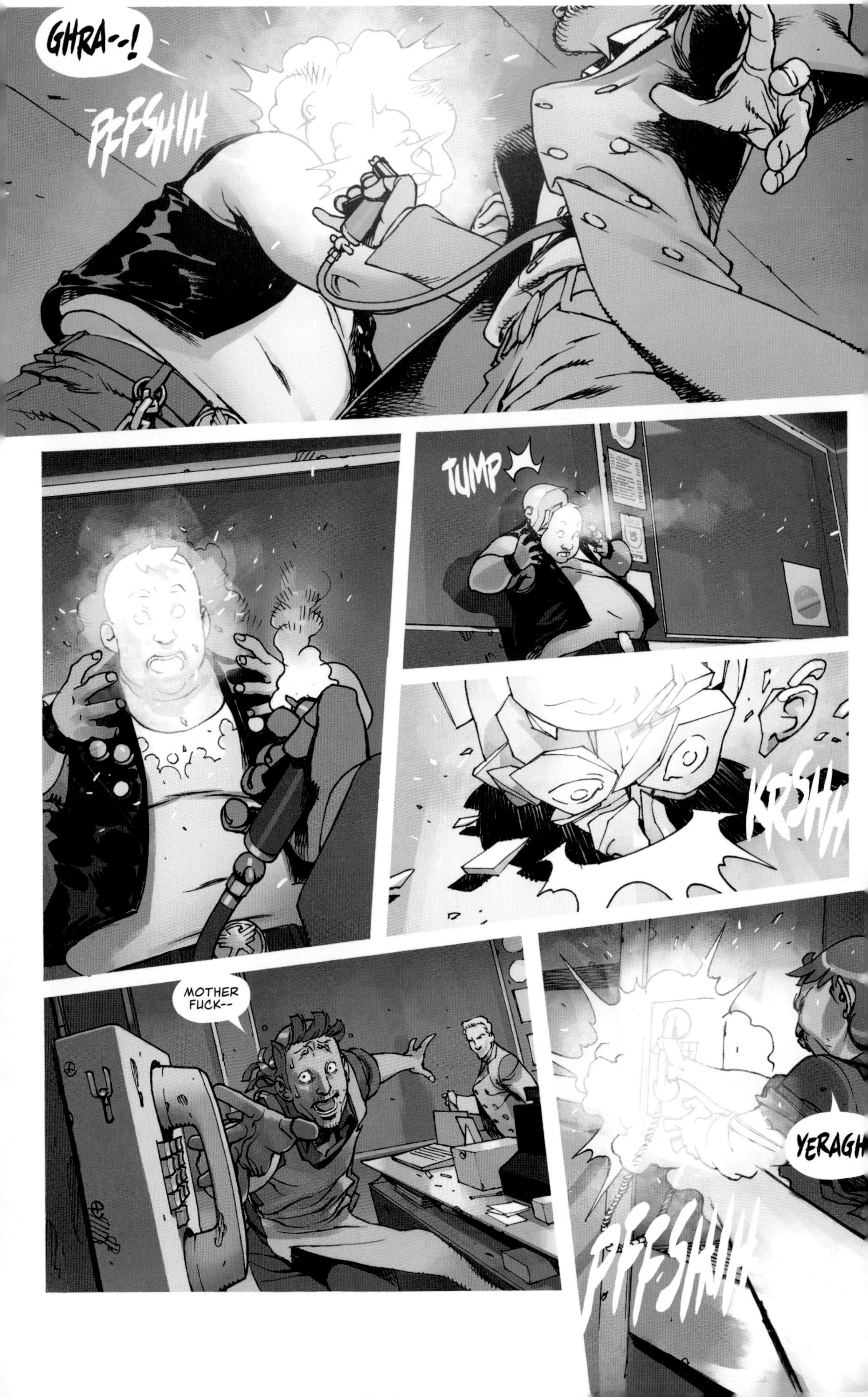
GHRA--!
PFFSHH
TUMP
KRSHH
MOTHER FUCK--
YERAGH
PFFSHH

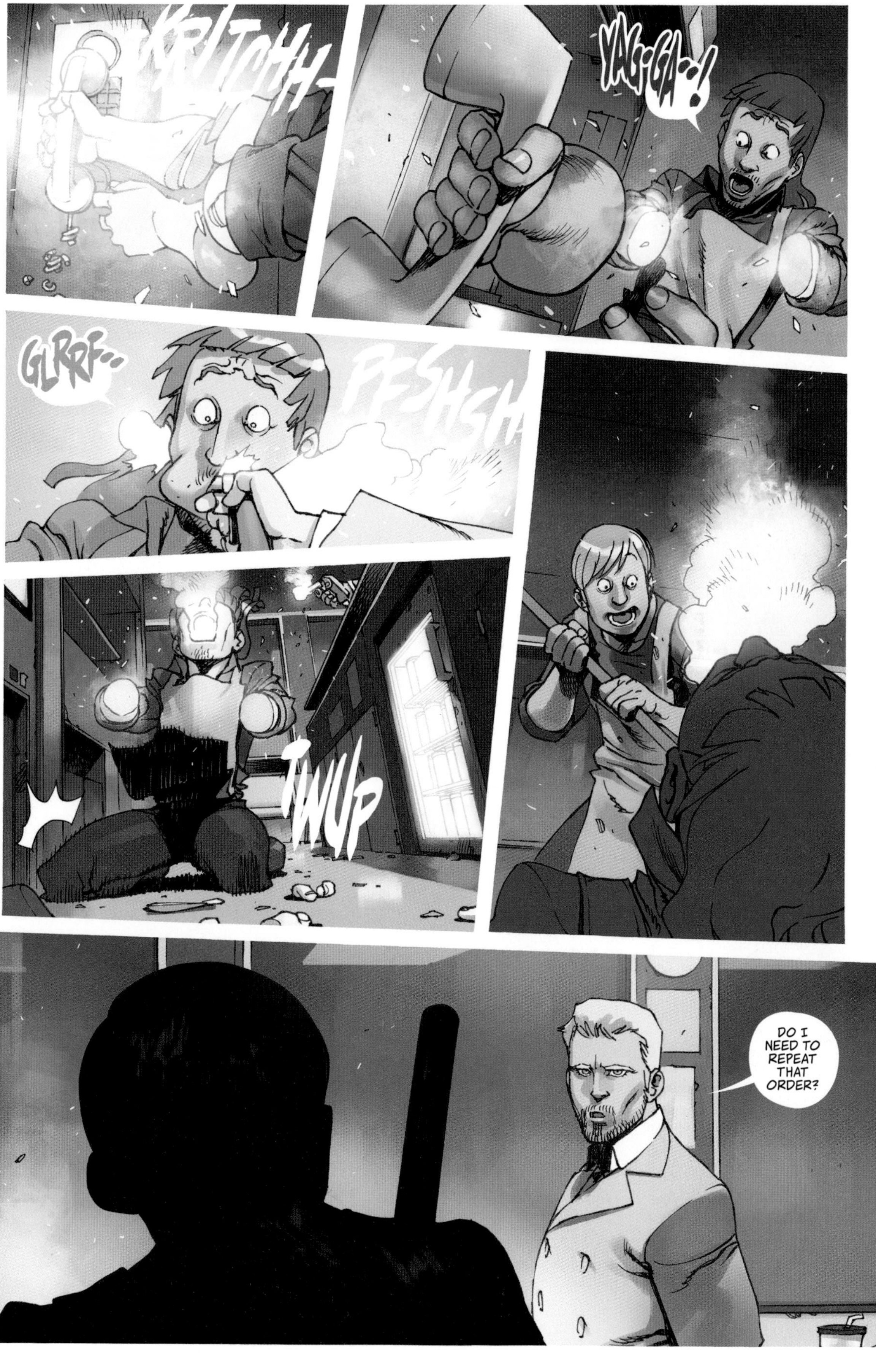
KRITCHH-
YAG-GA..!
GLRRF..
PFSHSH
TWUP
DO I NEED TO REPEAT THAT ORDER?

"SHE'S GOT YOU"

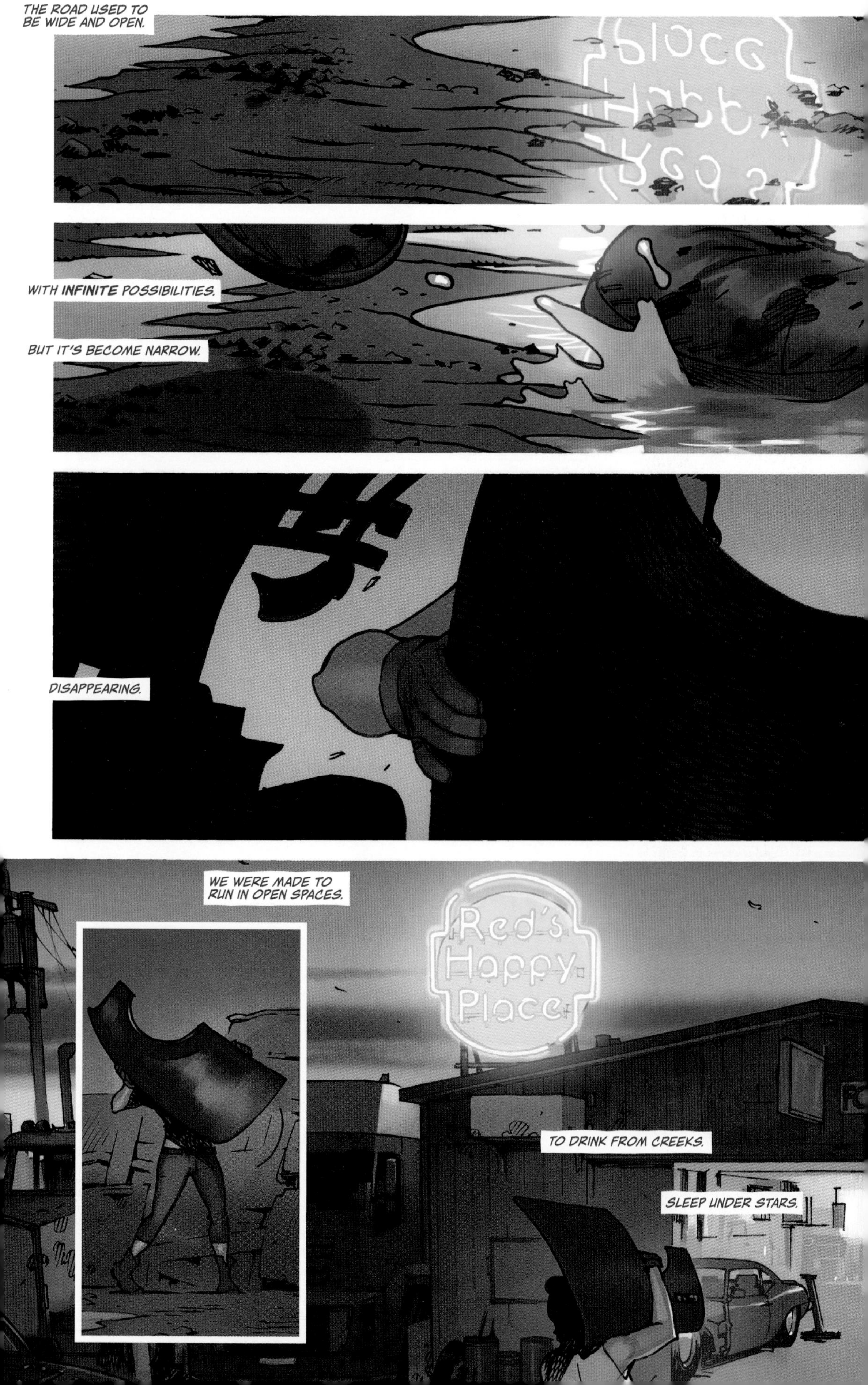
THE ROAD USED TO BE WIDE AND OPEN.
WITH **INFINITE** POSSIBILITIES.
BUT IT'S BECOME NARROW.
DISAPPEARING.
WE WERE MADE TO RUN IN OPEN SPACES.
Red's Happy Place
TO DRINK FROM CREEKS.
SLEEP UNDER STARS.

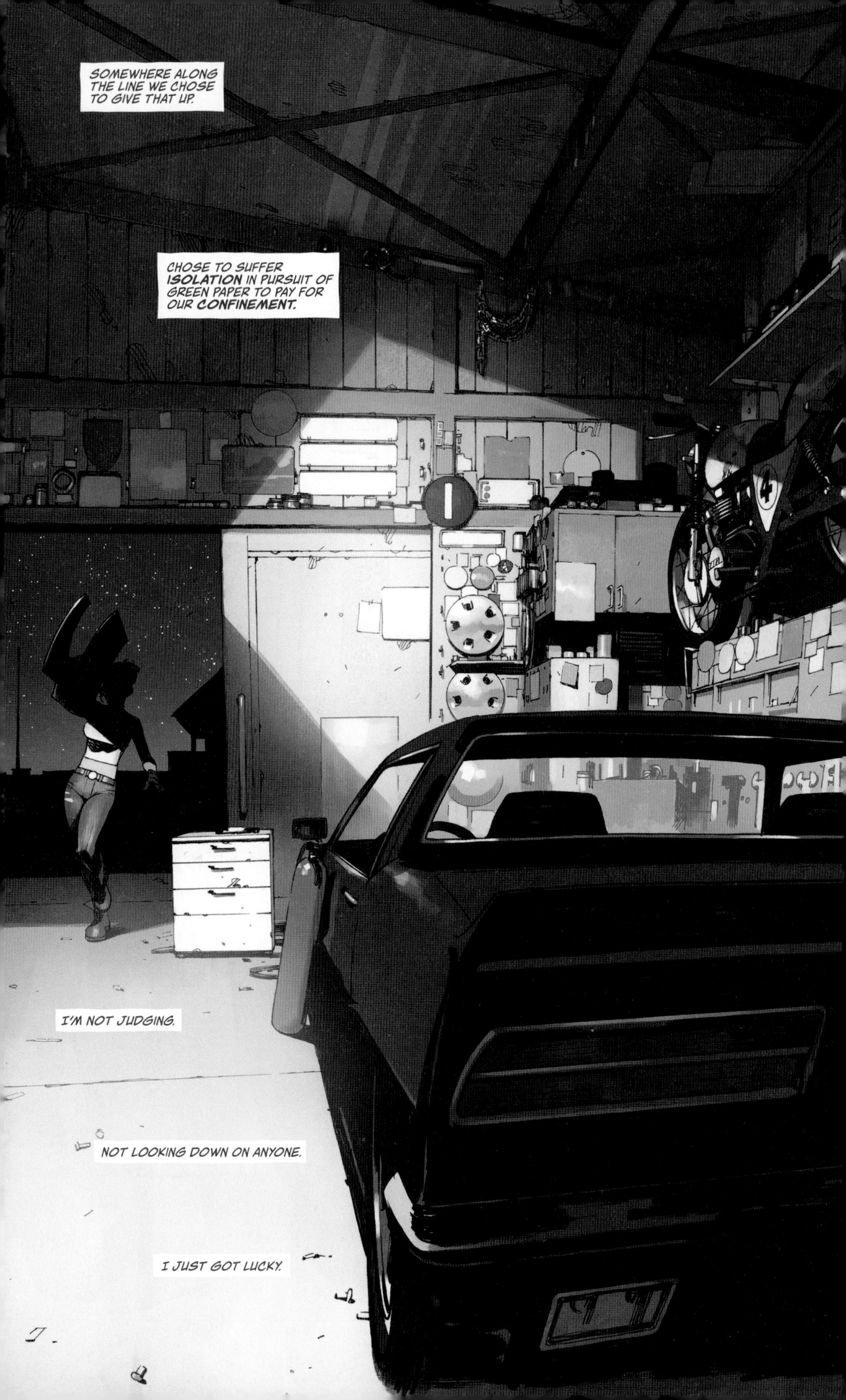
SOMEWHERE ALONG THE LINE WE CHOSE TO GIVE THAT UP.
CHOSE TO SUFFER **ISOLATION** IN PURSUIT OF GREEN PAPER TO PAY FOR OUR **CONFINEMENT**.
I'M NOT JUDGING.
NOT LOOKING DOWN ON ANYONE.
I JUST GOT LUCKY.

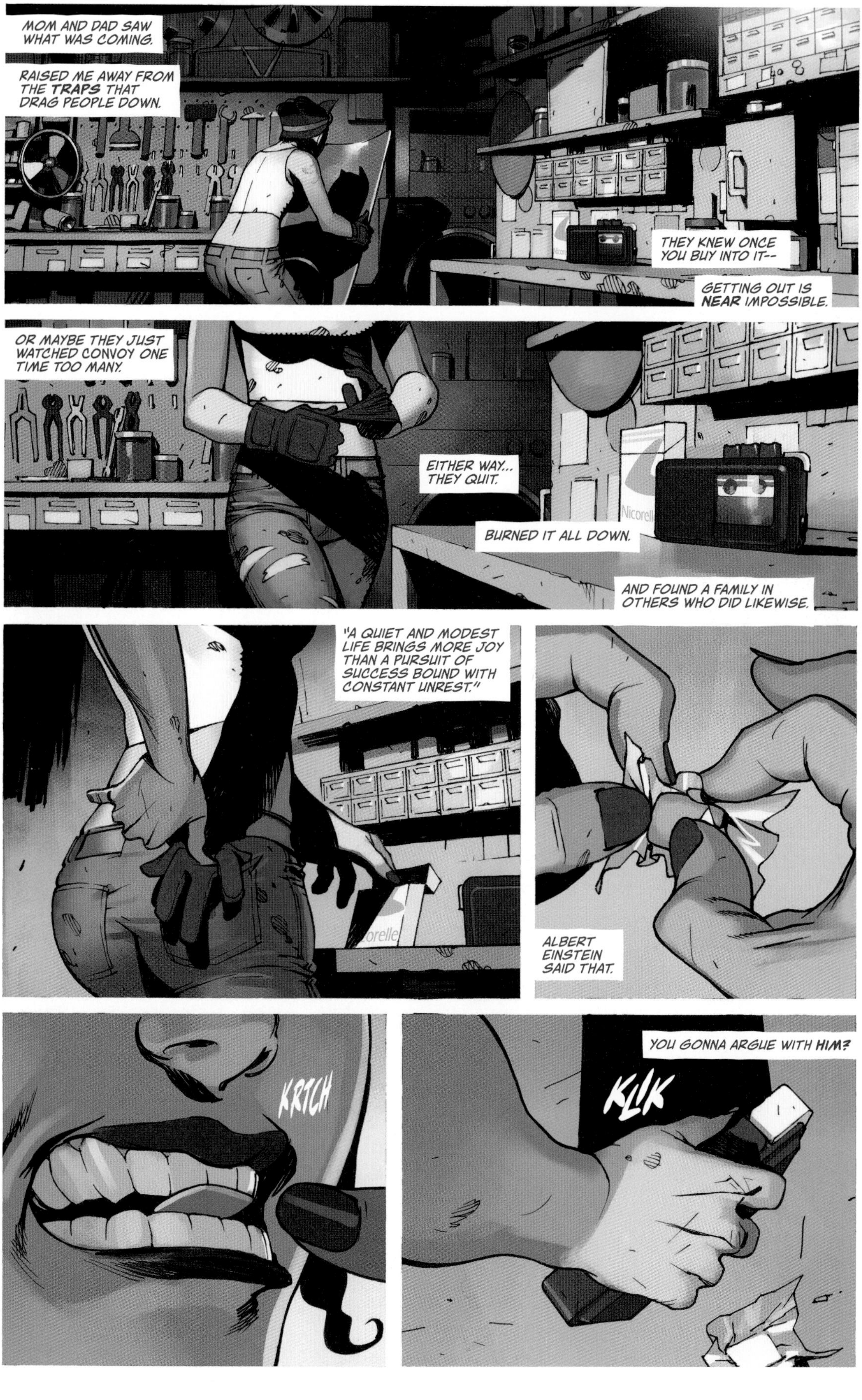

MOM AND DAD SAW WHAT WAS COMING.
RAISED ME AWAY FROM THE TRAPS THAT DRAG PEOPLE DOWN.
THEY KNEW ONCE YOU BUY INTO IT--
GETTING OUT IS NEAR IMPOSSIBLE.
OR MAYBE THEY JUST WATCHED CONVOY ONE TIME TOO MANY.
EITHER WAY... THEY QUIT.
BURNED IT ALL DOWN.
AND FOUND A FAMILY IN OTHERS WHO DID LIKEWISE.
Nicorelle
"A QUIET AND MODEST LIFE BRINGS MORE JOY THAN A PURSUIT OF SUCCESS BOUND WITH CONSTANT UNREST."
ALBERT EINSTEIN SAID THAT.
KRTCH
YOU GONNA ARGUE WITH HIM?
KLIK

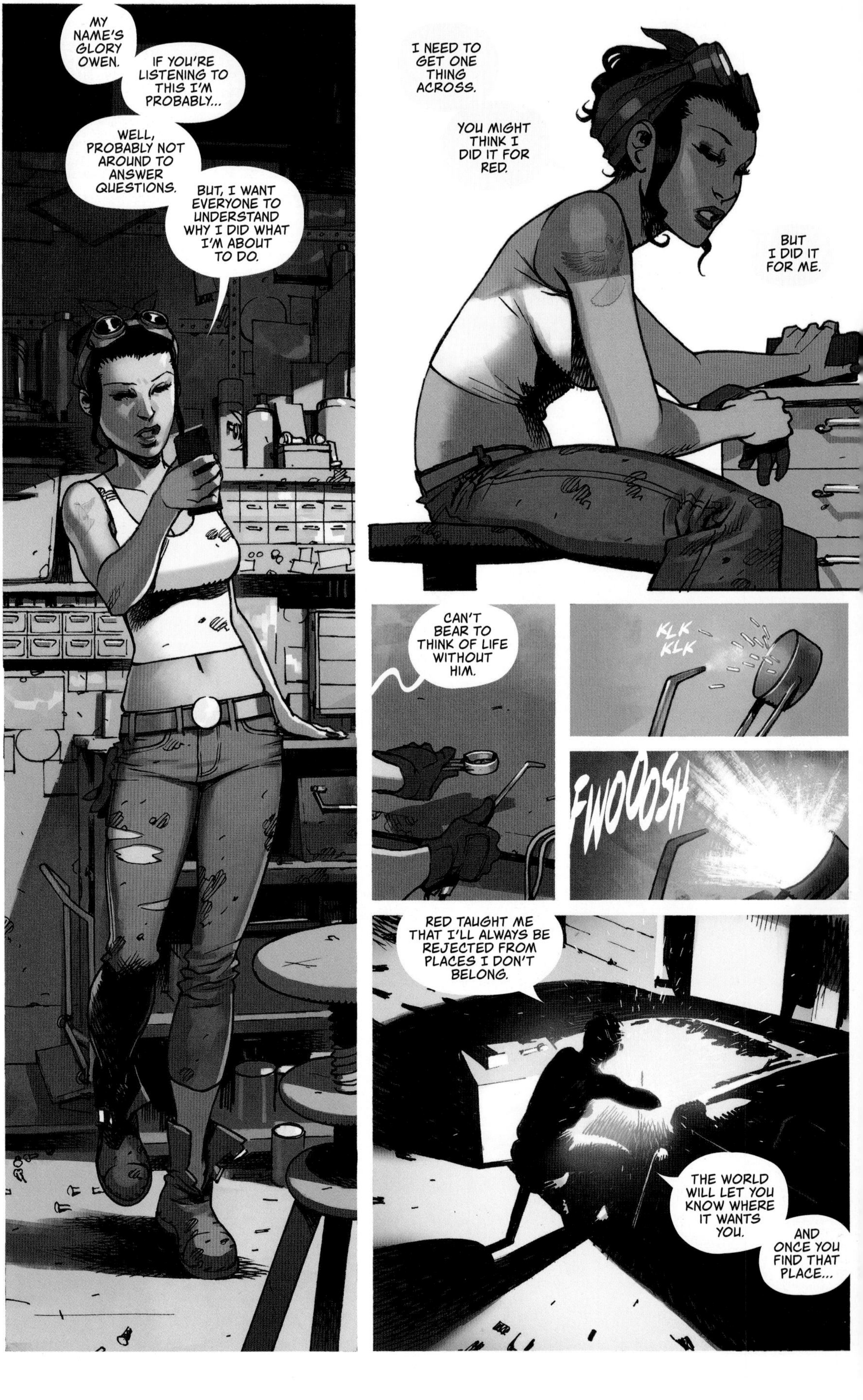
MY NAME'S GLORY OWEN.
IF YOU'RE LISTENING TO THIS I'M PROBABLY...
WELL, PROBABLY NOT AROUND TO ANSWER QUESTIONS.
BUT, I WANT EVERYONE TO UNDERSTAND WHY I DID WHAT I'M ABOUT TO DO.
I NEED TO GET ONE THING ACROSS.
YOU MIGHT THINK I DID IT FOR RED.
BUT I DID IT FOR ME.
CAN'T BEAR TO THINK OF LIFE WITHOUT HIM.
KLK KLK
FWOOOSH
RED TAUGHT ME THAT I'LL ALWAYS BE REJECTED FROM PLACES I DON'T BELONG.
THE WORLD WILL LET YOU KNOW WHERE IT WANTS YOU.
AND ONCE YOU FIND THAT PLACE...

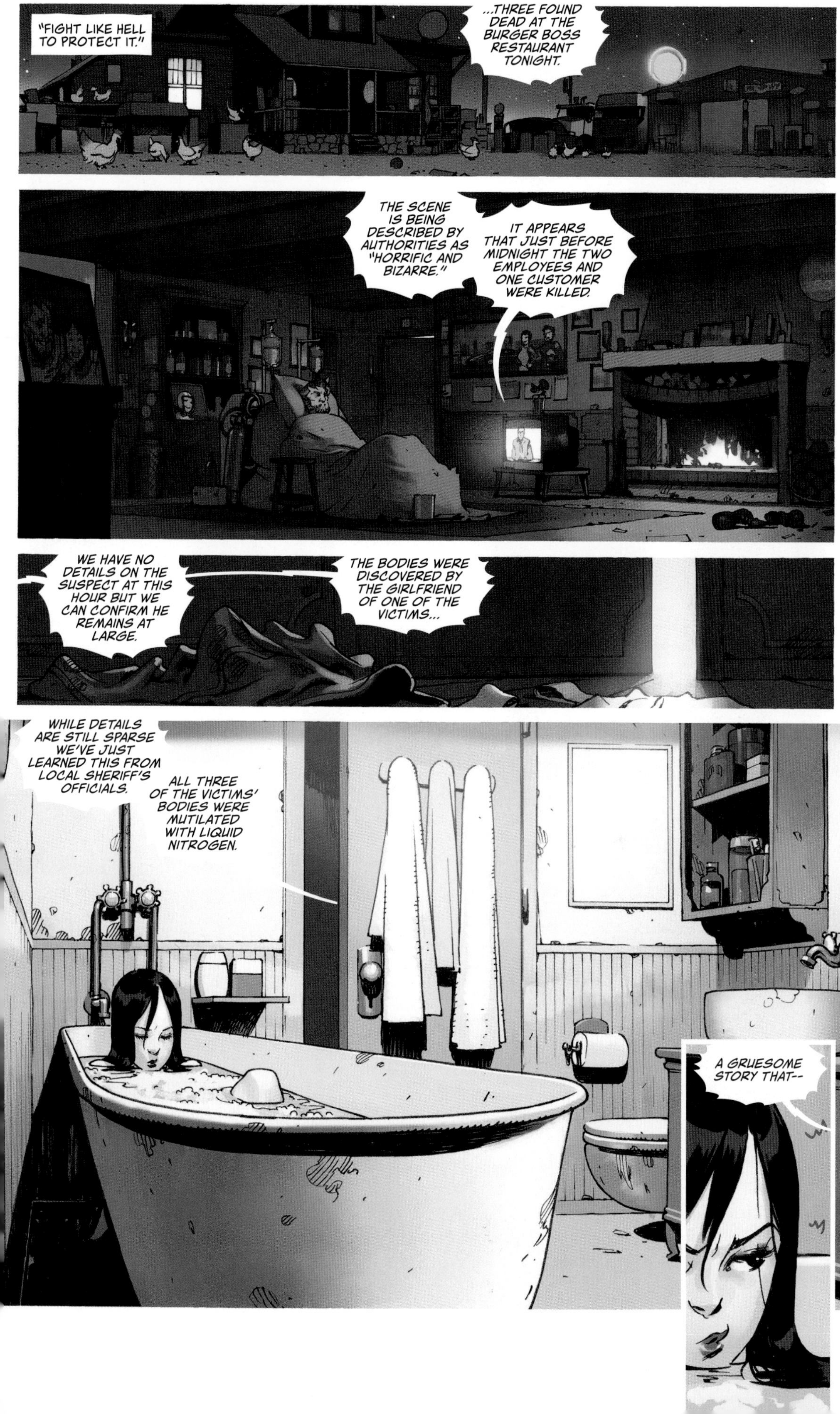
"FIGHT LIKE HELL TO PROTECT IT."
...THREE FOUND DEAD AT THE BURGER BOSS RESTAURANT TONIGHT.
THE SCENE IS BEING DESCRIBED BY AUTHORITIES AS "HORRIFIC AND BIZARRE."
IT APPEARS THAT JUST BEFORE MIDNIGHT THE TWO EMPLOYEES AND ONE CUSTOMER WERE KILLED.
WE HAVE NO DETAILS ON THE SUSPECT AT THIS HOUR BUT WE CAN CONFIRM HE REMAINS AT LARGE.
THE BODIES WERE DISCOVERED BY THE GIRLFRIEND OF ONE OF THE VICTIMS...
WHILE DETAILS ARE STILL SPARSE WE'VE JUST LEARNED THIS FROM LOCAL SHERIFF'S OFFICIALS.
ALL THREE OF THE VICTIMS' BODIES WERE MUTILATED WITH LIQUID NITROGEN.
A GRUESOME STORY THAT--

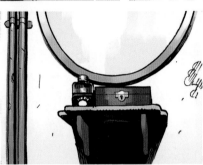

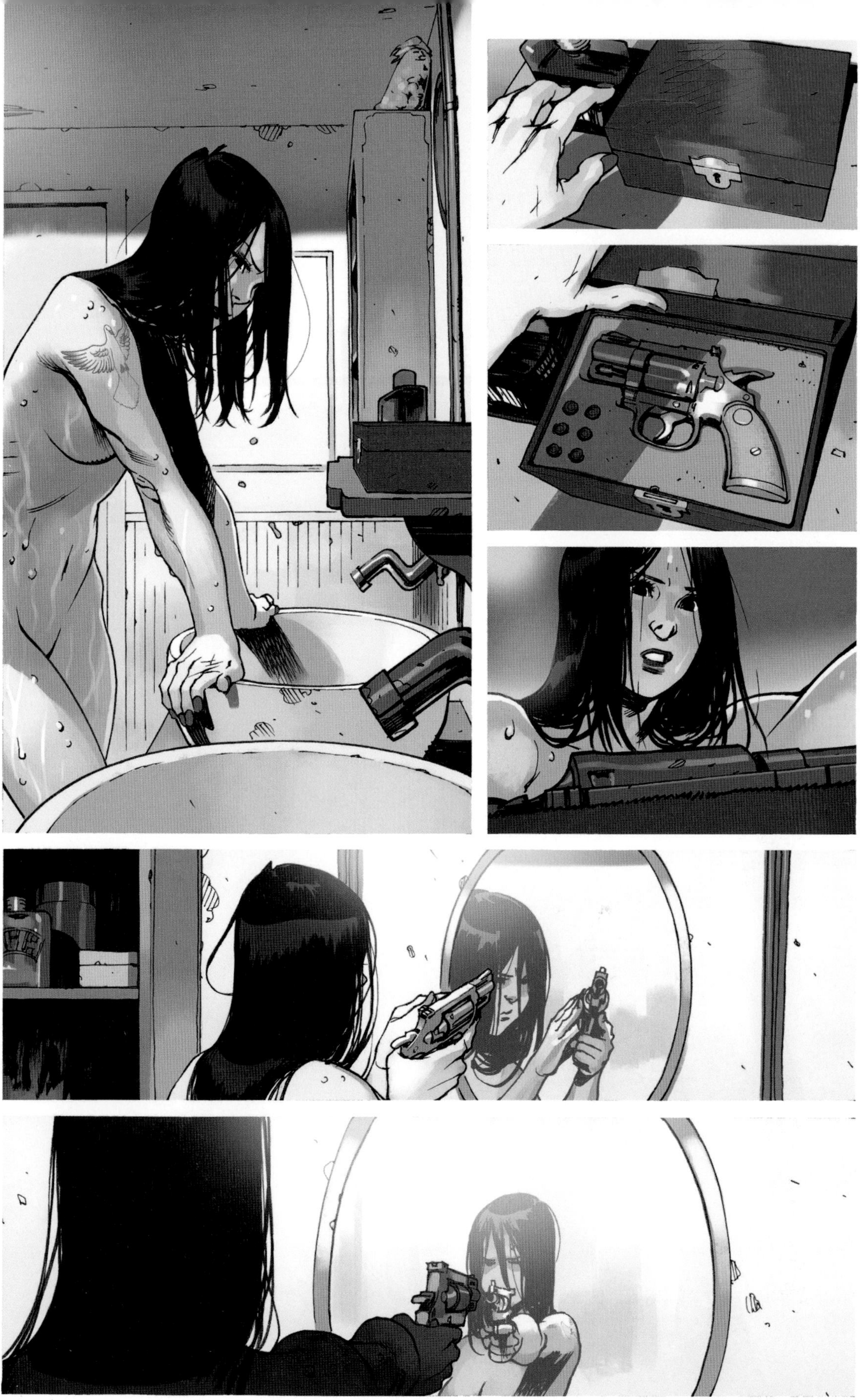

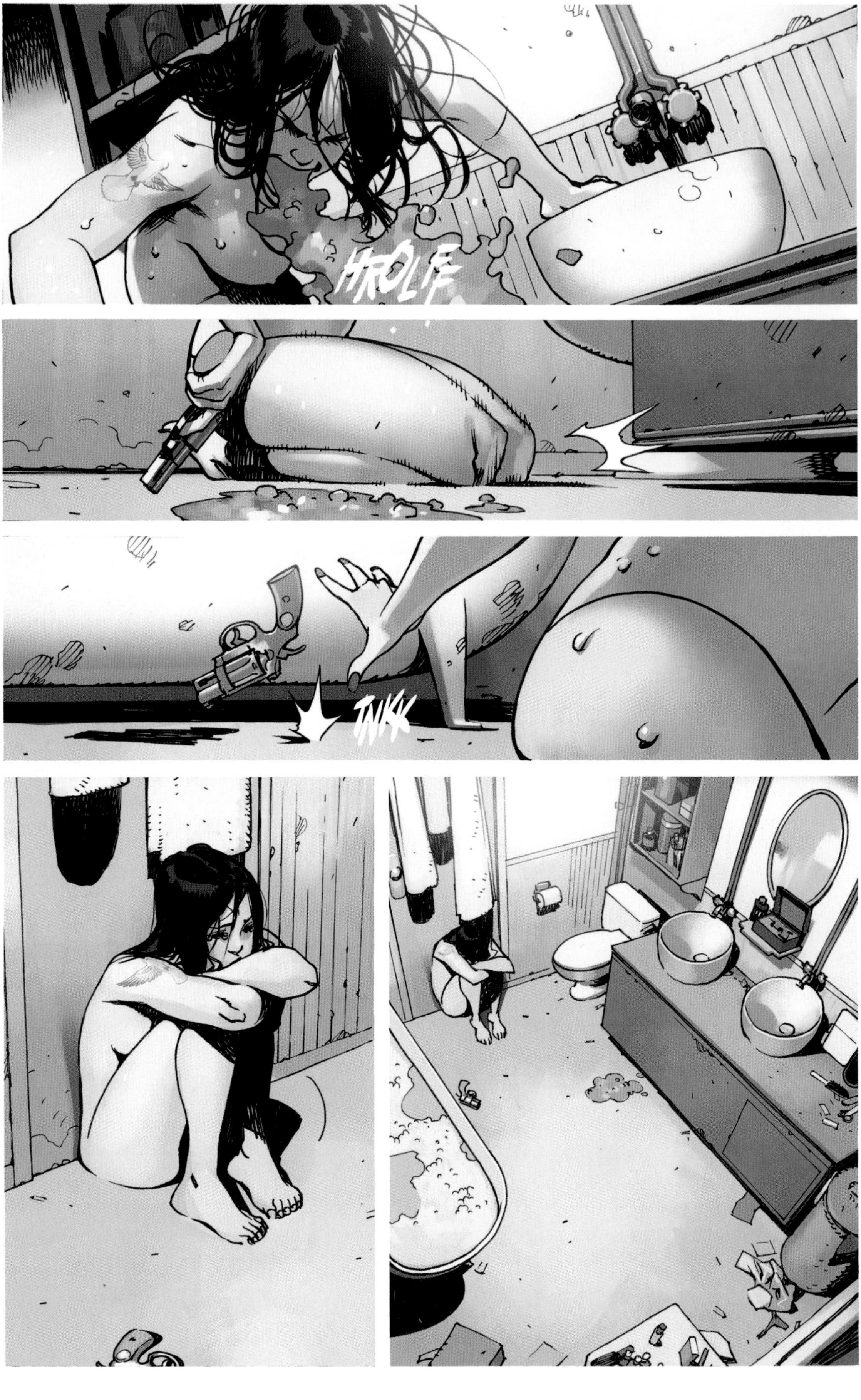
HROLFF
TNKK

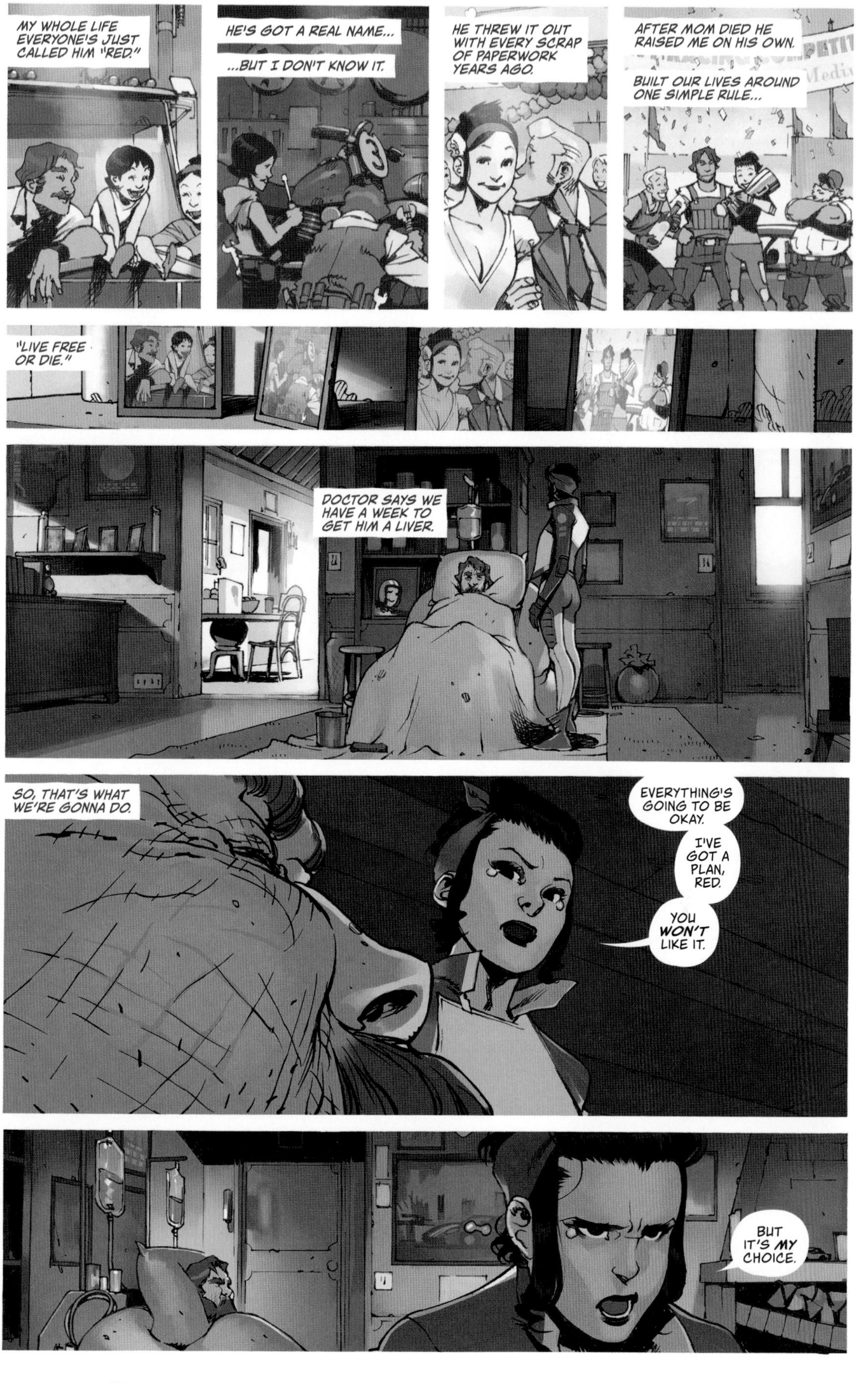
MY WHOLE LIFE EVERYONE'S JUST CALLED HIM "RED."
HE'S GOT A REAL NAME...
...BUT I DON'T KNOW IT.
HE THREW IT OUT WITH EVERY SCRAP OF PAPERWORK YEARS AGO.
AFTER MOM DIED HE RAISED ME ON HIS OWN.
BUILT OUR LIVES AROUND ONE SIMPLE RULE...
"LIVE FREE OR DIE."
DOCTOR SAYS WE HAVE A WEEK TO GET HIM A LIVER.
SO, THAT'S WHAT WE'RE GONNA DO.
EVERYTHING'S GOING TO BE OKAY.
I'VE GOT A PLAN, RED.
YOU **WON'T** LIKE IT.
BUT IT'S **MY** CHOICE.

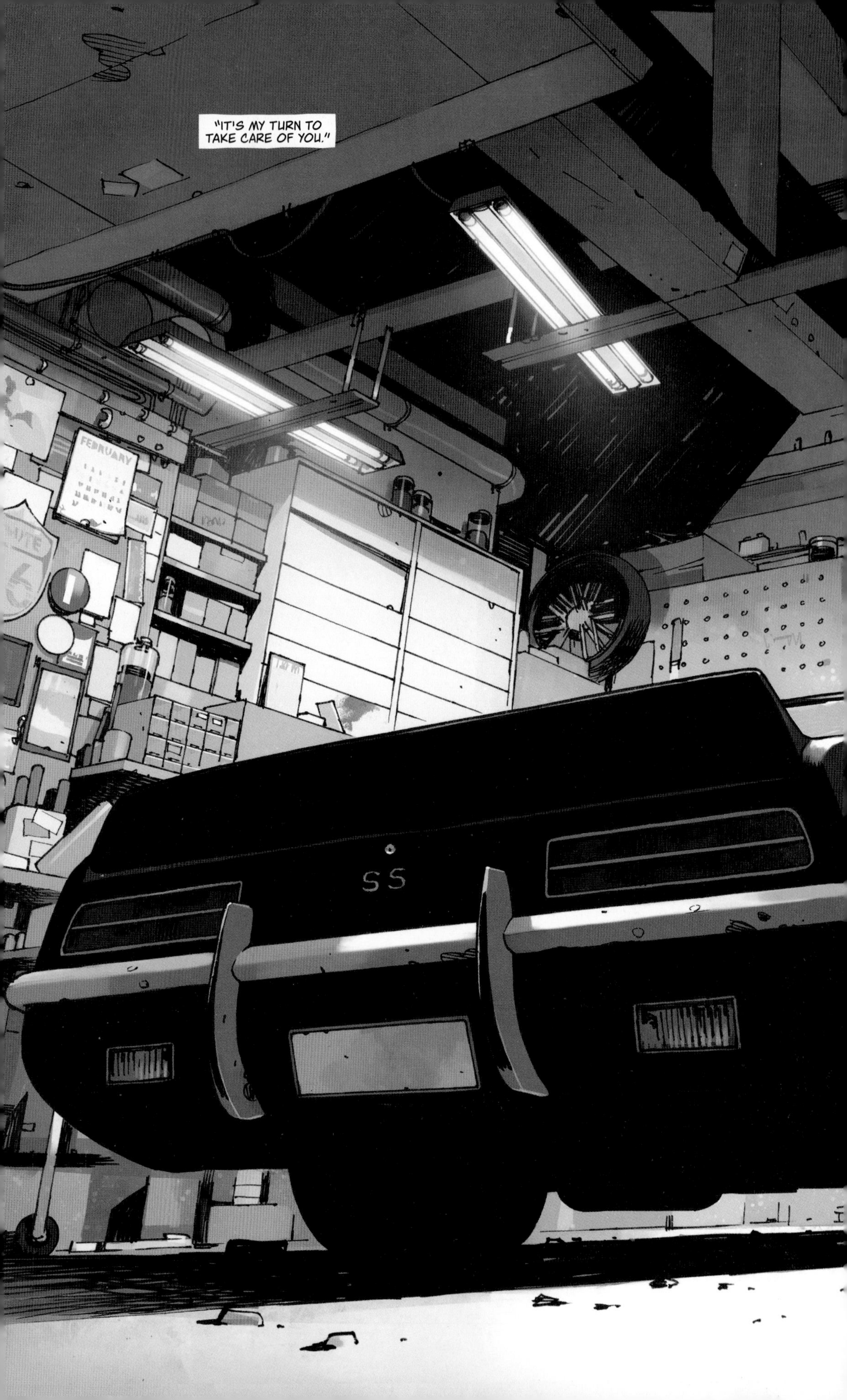
"IT'S MY TURN TO TAKE CARE OF YOU."
FEBRUARY
SS

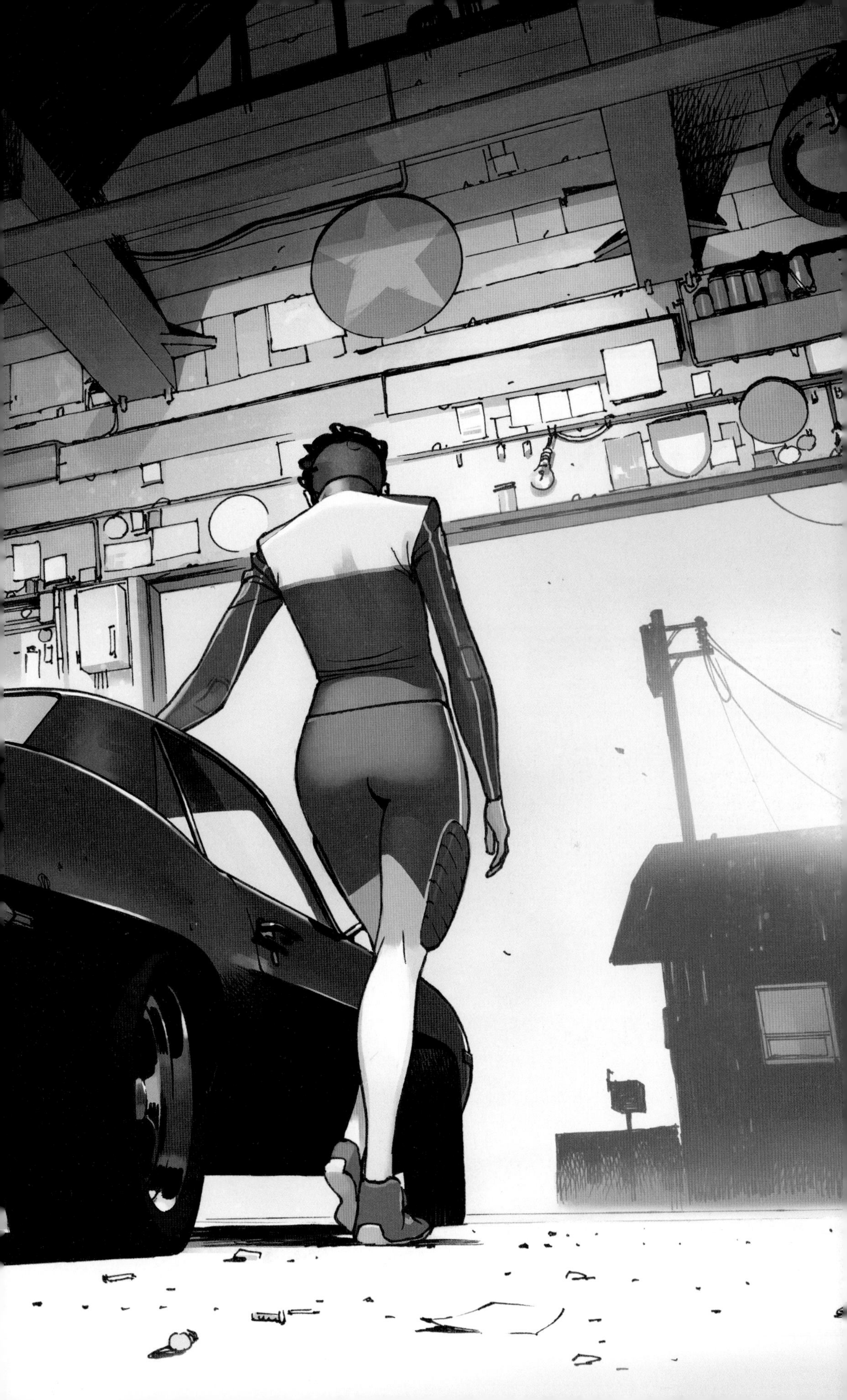

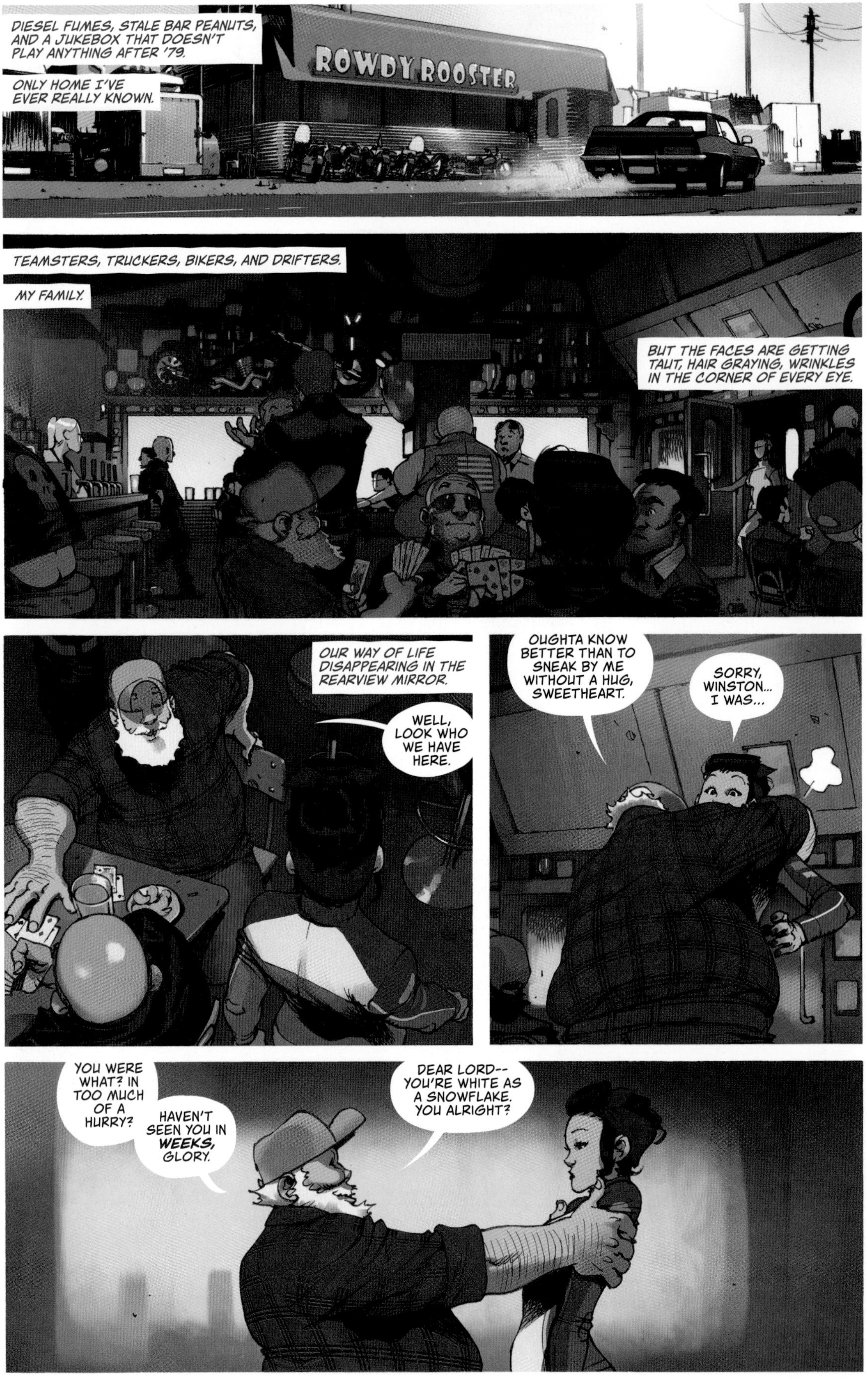
DIESEL FUMES, STALE BAR PEANUTS, AND A JUKEBOX THAT DOESN'T PLAY ANYTHING AFTER '79.
ONLY HOME I'VE EVER REALLY KNOWN.
ROWDY ROOSTER
TEAMSTERS, TRUCKERS, BIKERS, AND DRIFTERS.
MY FAMILY.
BUT THE FACES ARE GETTING TAUT, HAIR GRAYING, WRINKLES IN THE CORNER OF EVERY EYE.
OUR WAY OF LIFE DISAPPEARING IN THE REARVIEW MIRROR.
WELL, LOOK WHO WE HAVE HERE.
OUGHTA KNOW BETTER THAN TO SNEAK BY ME WITHOUT A HUG, SWEETHEART.
SORRY, WINSTON... I WAS...
YOU WERE WHAT? IN TOO MUCH OF A HURRY?
HAVEN'T SEEN YOU IN **WEEKS,** GLORY.
DEAR LORD-- YOU'RE WHITE AS A SNOWFLAKE. YOU ALRIGHT?

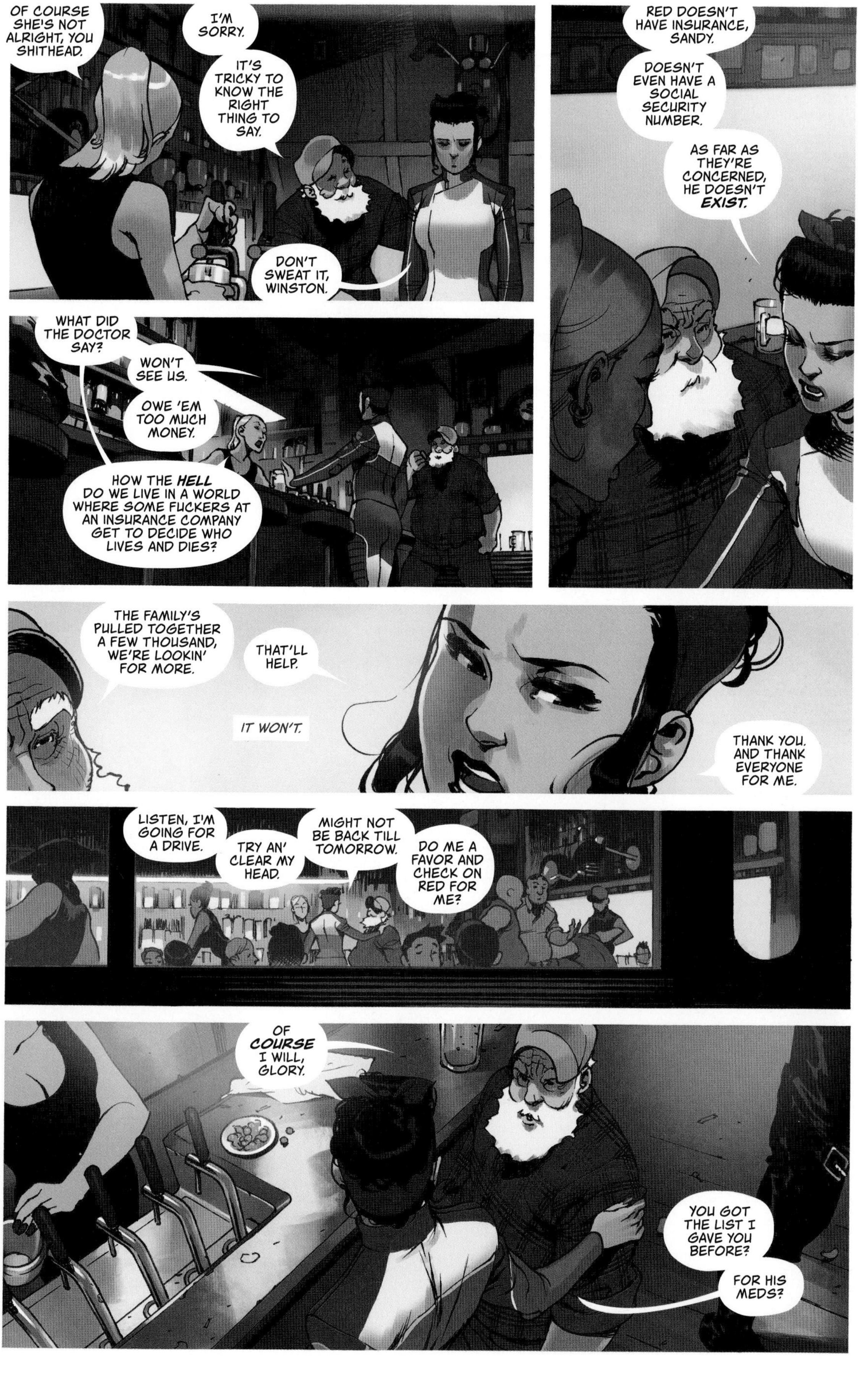
OF COURSE SHE'S NOT ALRIGHT, YOU SHITHEAD.
I'M SORRY.
IT'S TRICKY TO KNOW THE RIGHT THING TO SAY.
DON'T SWEAT IT, WINSTON.
WHAT DID THE DOCTOR SAY?
WON'T SEE US.
OWE 'EM TOO MUCH MONEY.
HOW THE HELL DO WE LIVE IN A WORLD WHERE SOME FUCKERS AT AN INSURANCE COMPANY GET TO DECIDE WHO LIVES AND DIES?
RED DOESN'T HAVE INSURANCE, SANDY.
DOESN'T EVEN HAVE A SOCIAL SECURITY NUMBER.
AS FAR AS THEY'RE CONCERNED, HE DOESN'T EXIST.
THE FAMILY'S PULLED TOGETHER A FEW THOUSAND, WE'RE LOOKIN' FOR MORE.
THAT'LL HELP.
IT WON'T.
THANK YOU. AND THANK EVERYONE FOR ME.
LISTEN, I'M GOING FOR A DRIVE.
TRY AN' CLEAR MY HEAD.
MIGHT NOT BE BACK TILL TOMORROW.
DO ME A FAVOR AND CHECK ON RED FOR ME?
OF COURSE I WILL, GLORY.
YOU GOT THE LIST I GAVE YOU BEFORE?
FOR HIS MEDS?

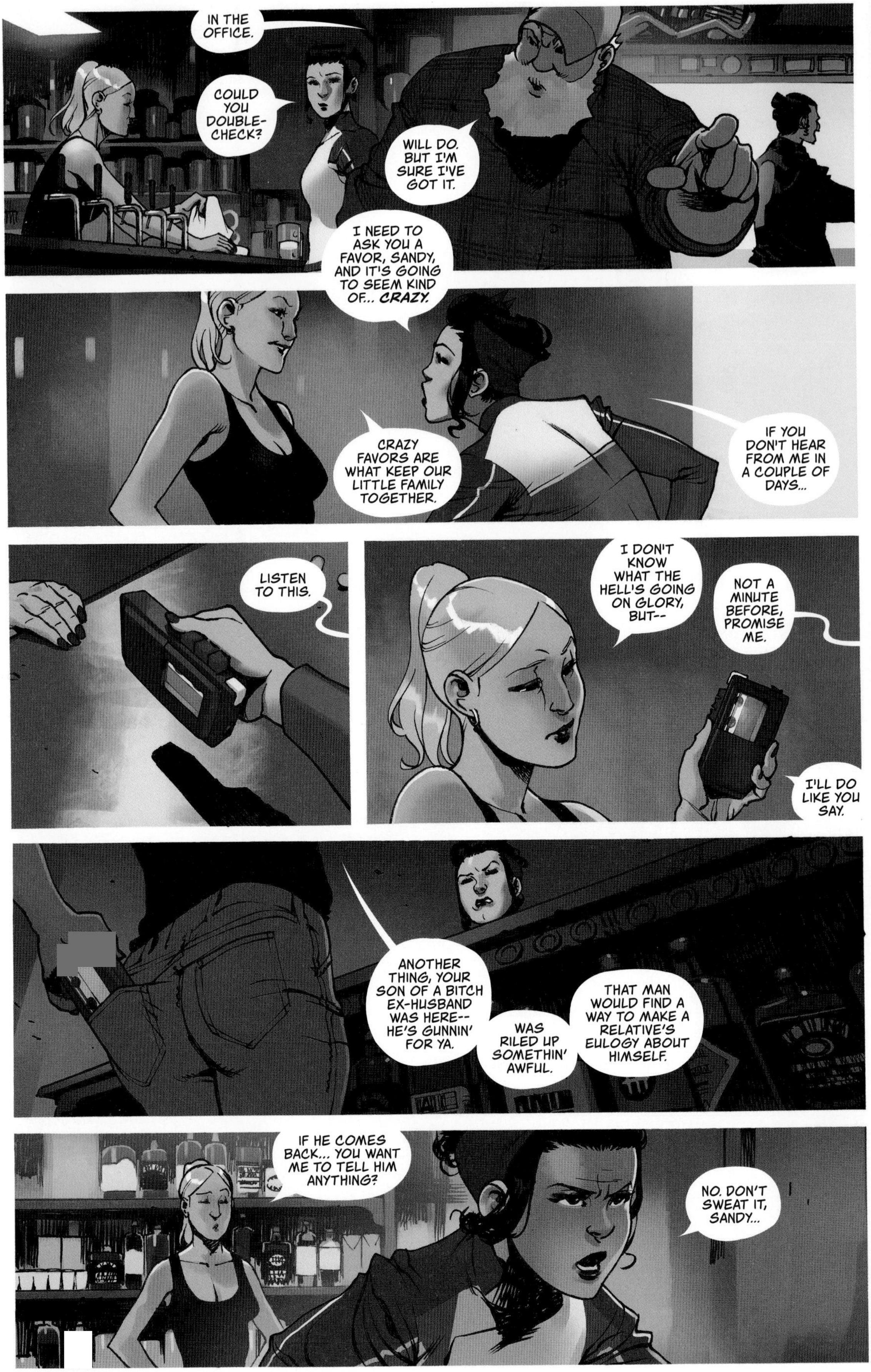
IN THE OFFICE.
COULD YOU DOUBLE-CHECK?
WILL DO. BUT I'M SURE I'VE GOT IT.
I NEED TO ASK YOU A FAVOR, SANDY, AND IT'S GOING TO SEEM KIND OF... CRAZY.
CRAZY FAVORS ARE WHAT KEEP OUR LITTLE FAMILY TOGETHER.
IF YOU DON'T HEAR FROM ME IN A COUPLE OF DAYS...
LISTEN TO THIS.
I DON'T KNOW WHAT THE HELL'S GOING ON GLORY, BUT--
NOT A MINUTE BEFORE, PROMISE ME.
I'LL DO LIKE YOU SAY.
ANOTHER THING, YOUR SON OF A BITCH EX-HUSBAND WAS HERE-- HE'S GUNNIN' FOR YA.
WAS RILED UP SOMETHIN' AWFUL.
THAT MAN WOULD FIND A WAY TO MAKE A RELATIVE'S EULOGY ABOUT HIMSELF.
IF HE COMES BACK... YOU WANT ME TO TELL HIM ANYTHING?
NO. DON'T SWEAT IT, SANDY...

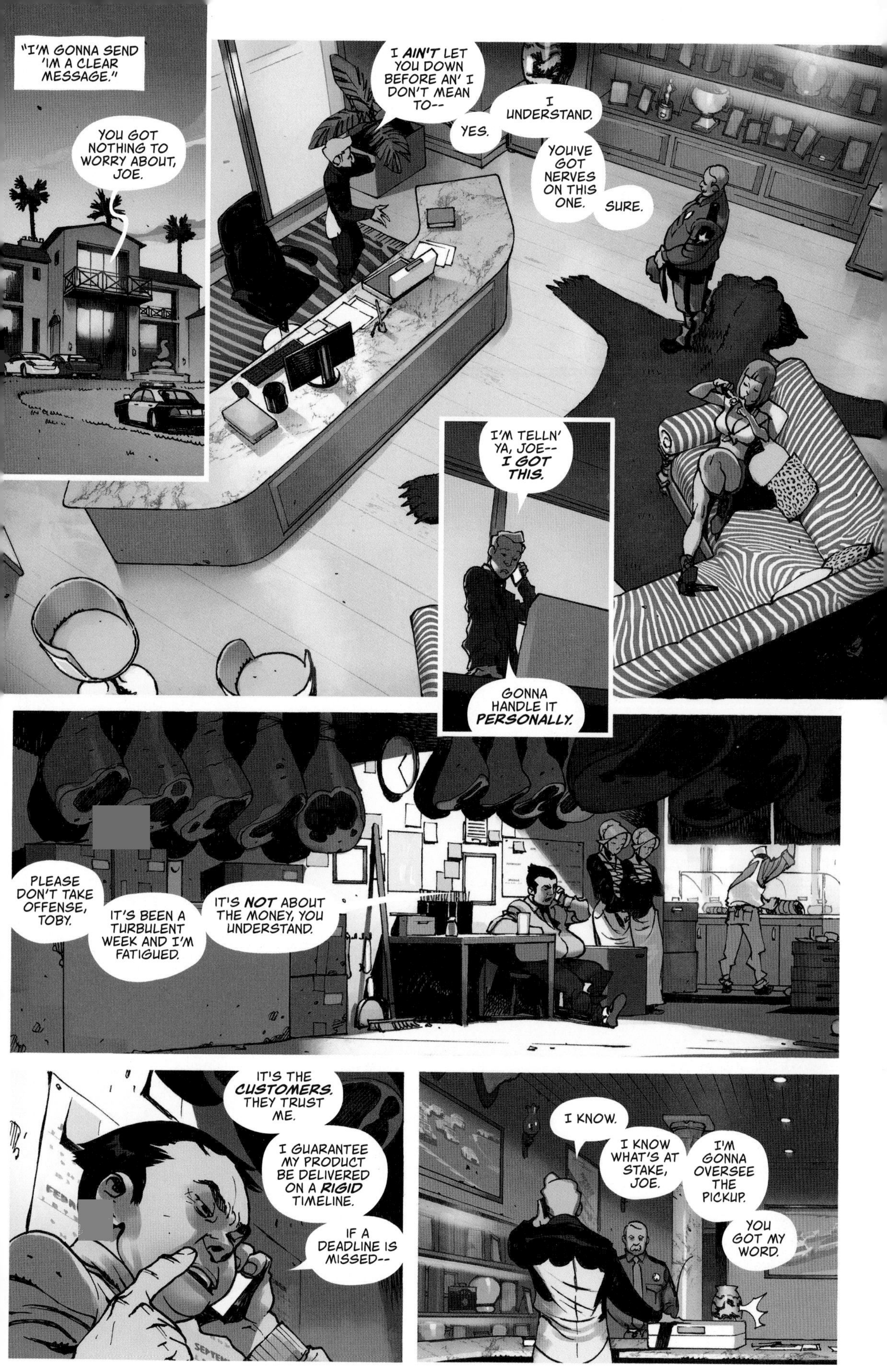
"I'M GONNA SEND 'IM A CLEAR MESSAGE."
YOU GOT NOTHING TO WORRY ABOUT, JOE.
I AIN'T LET YOU DOWN BEFORE AN' I DON'T MEAN TO--
YES.
I UNDERSTAND.
YOU'VE GOT NERVES ON THIS ONE.
SURE.
I'M TELLN' YA, JOE-- I GOT THIS.
GONNA HANDLE IT PERSONALLY.
PLEASE DON'T TAKE OFFENSE, TOBY.
IT'S BEEN A TURBULENT WEEK AND I'M FATIGUED.
IT'S NOT ABOUT THE MONEY, YOU UNDERSTAND.
IT'S THE CUSTOMERS. THEY TRUST ME.
I GUARANTEE MY PRODUCT BE DELIVERED ON A RIGID TIMELINE.
IF A DEADLINE IS MISSED--
I KNOW.
I KNOW WHAT'S AT STAKE, JOE.
I'M GONNA OVERSEE THE PICKUP.
YOU GOT MY WORD.

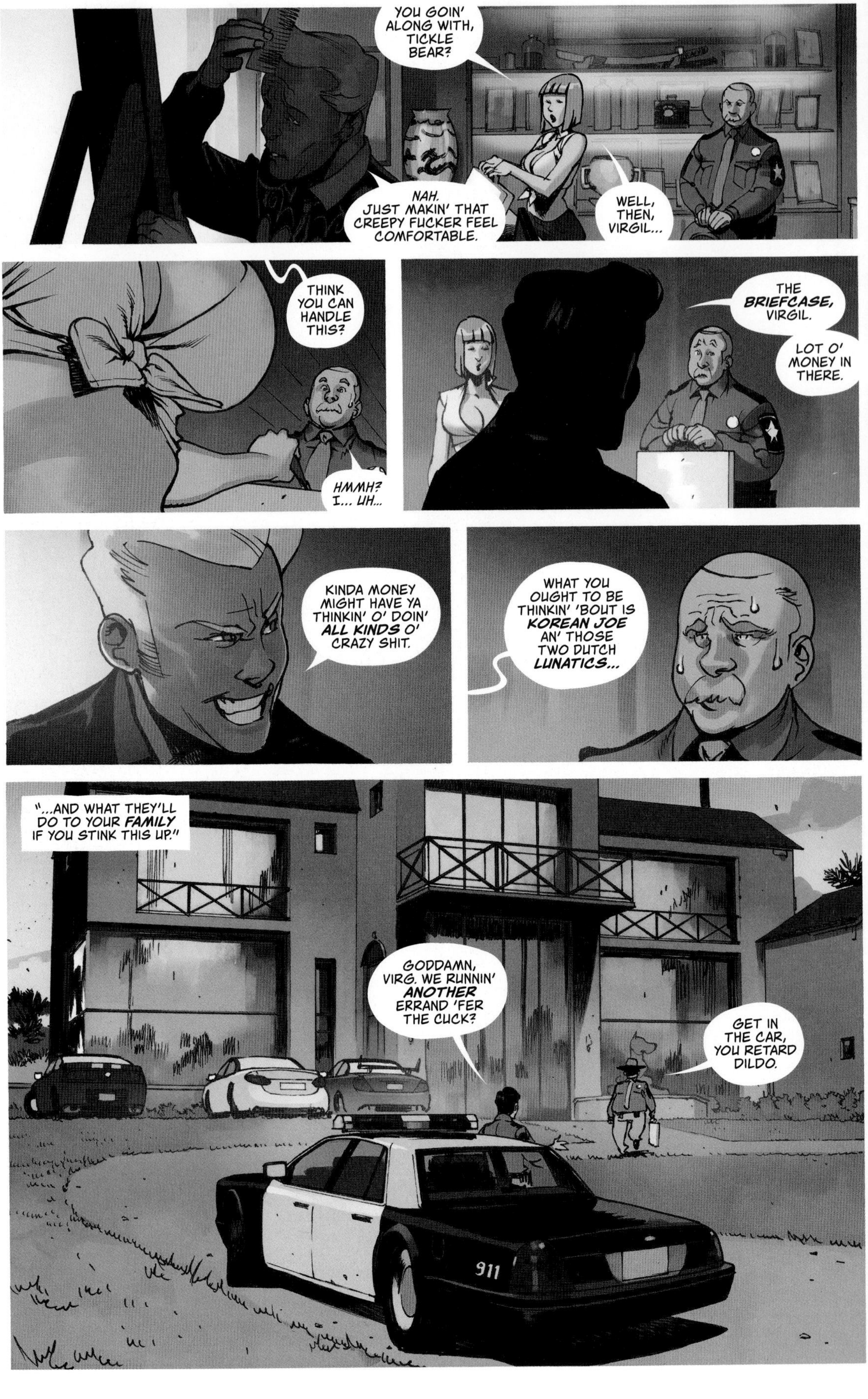
YOU GOIN' ALONG WITH, TICKLE BEAR?
NAH. JUST MAKIN' THAT CREEPY FUCKER FEEL COMFORTABLE.
WELL, THEN, VIRGIL...
THINK YOU CAN HANDLE THIS?
HMMH? I... UH...
THE BRIEFCASE, VIRGIL.
LOT O' MONEY IN THERE.
KINDA MONEY MIGHT HAVE YA THINKIN' O' DOIN' ALL KINDS O' CRAZY SHIT.
WHAT YOU OUGHT TO BE THINKIN' 'BOUT IS KOREAN JOE AN' THOSE TWO DUTCH LUNATICS...
"...AND WHAT THEY'LL DO TO YOUR FAMILY IF YOU STINK THIS UP."
GODDAMN, VIRG. WE RUNNIN' ANOTHER ERRAND 'FER THE CUCK?
GET IN THE CAR, YOU RETARD DILDO.
911

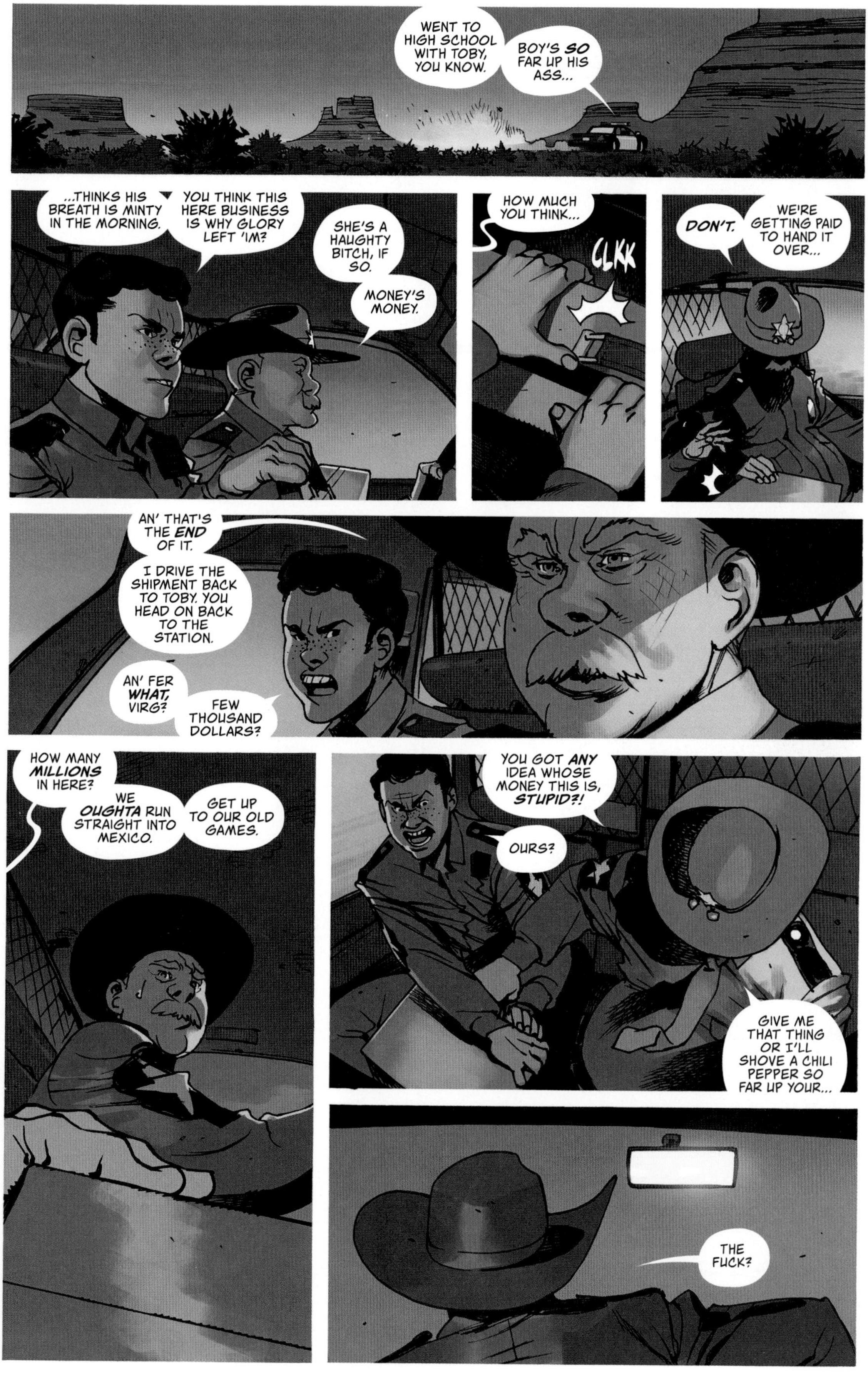
WENT TO HIGH SCHOOL WITH TOBY, YOU KNOW.
BOY'S SO FAR UP HIS ASS...
...THINKS HIS BREATH IS MINTY IN THE MORNING.
YOU THINK THIS HERE BUSINESS IS WHY GLORY LEFT 'IM?
SHE'S A HAUGHTY BITCH, IF SO.
MONEY'S MONEY.
HOW MUCH YOU THINK...
CLKK
DON'T.
WE'RE GETTING PAID TO HAND IT OVER...
AN' THAT'S THE END OF IT.
I DRIVE THE SHIPMENT BACK TO TOBY. YOU HEAD ON BACK TO THE STATION.
AN' FER WHAT, VIRG?
FEW THOUSAND DOLLARS?
HOW MANY MILLIONS IN HERE?
WE OUGHTA RUN STRAIGHT INTO MEXICO.
GET UP TO OUR OLD GAMES.
YOU GOT ANY IDEA WHOSE MONEY THIS IS, STUPID?!
OURS?
GIVE ME THAT THING OR I'LL SHOVE A CHILI PEPPER SO FAR UP YOUR...
THE FUCK?

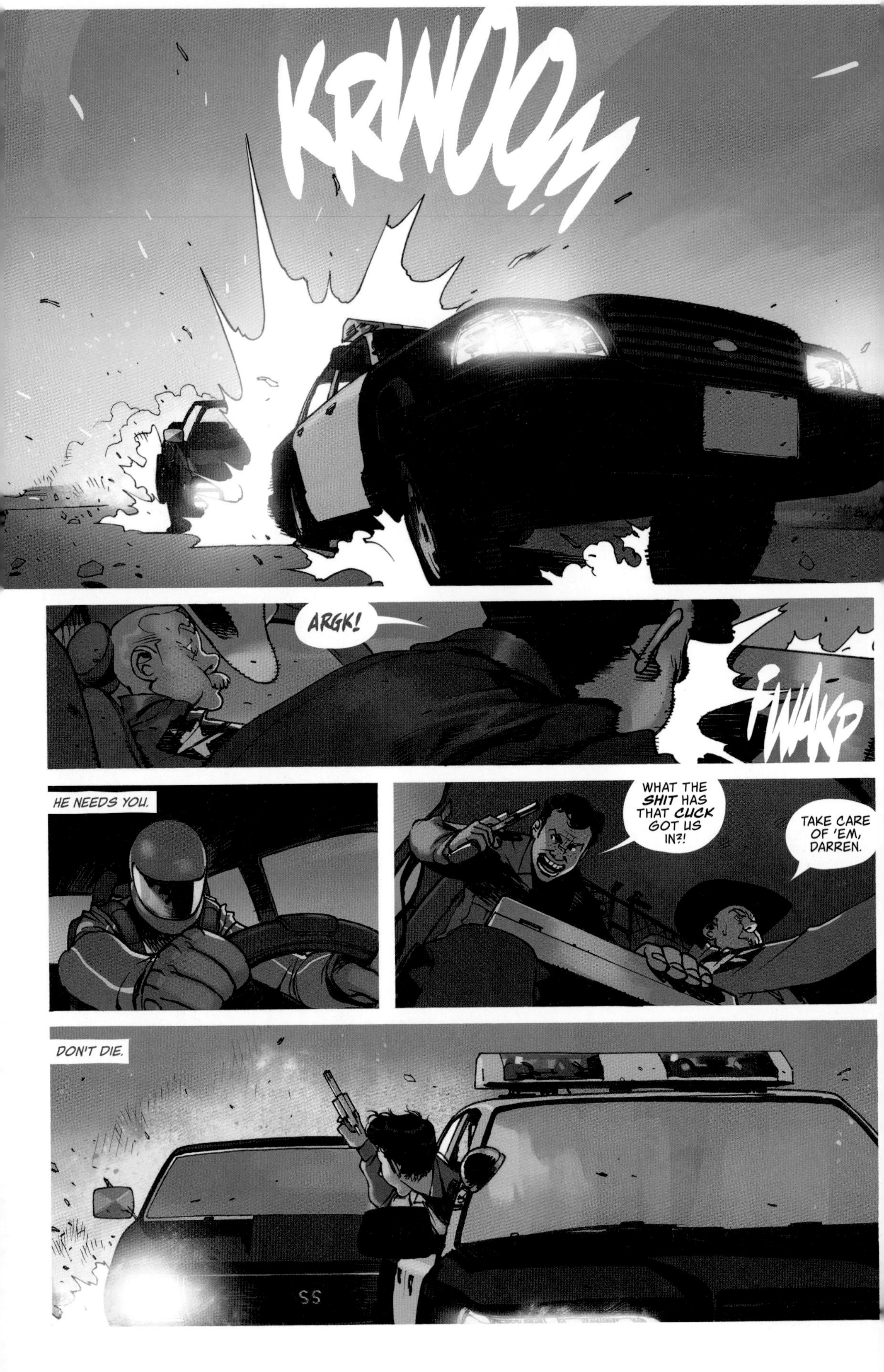
KRWOOM
ARGK!
FWAKP
HE NEEDS YOU.
WHAT THE SHIT HAS THAT CUCK GOT US IN?!
TAKE CARE OF 'EM, DARREN.
DON'T DIE.

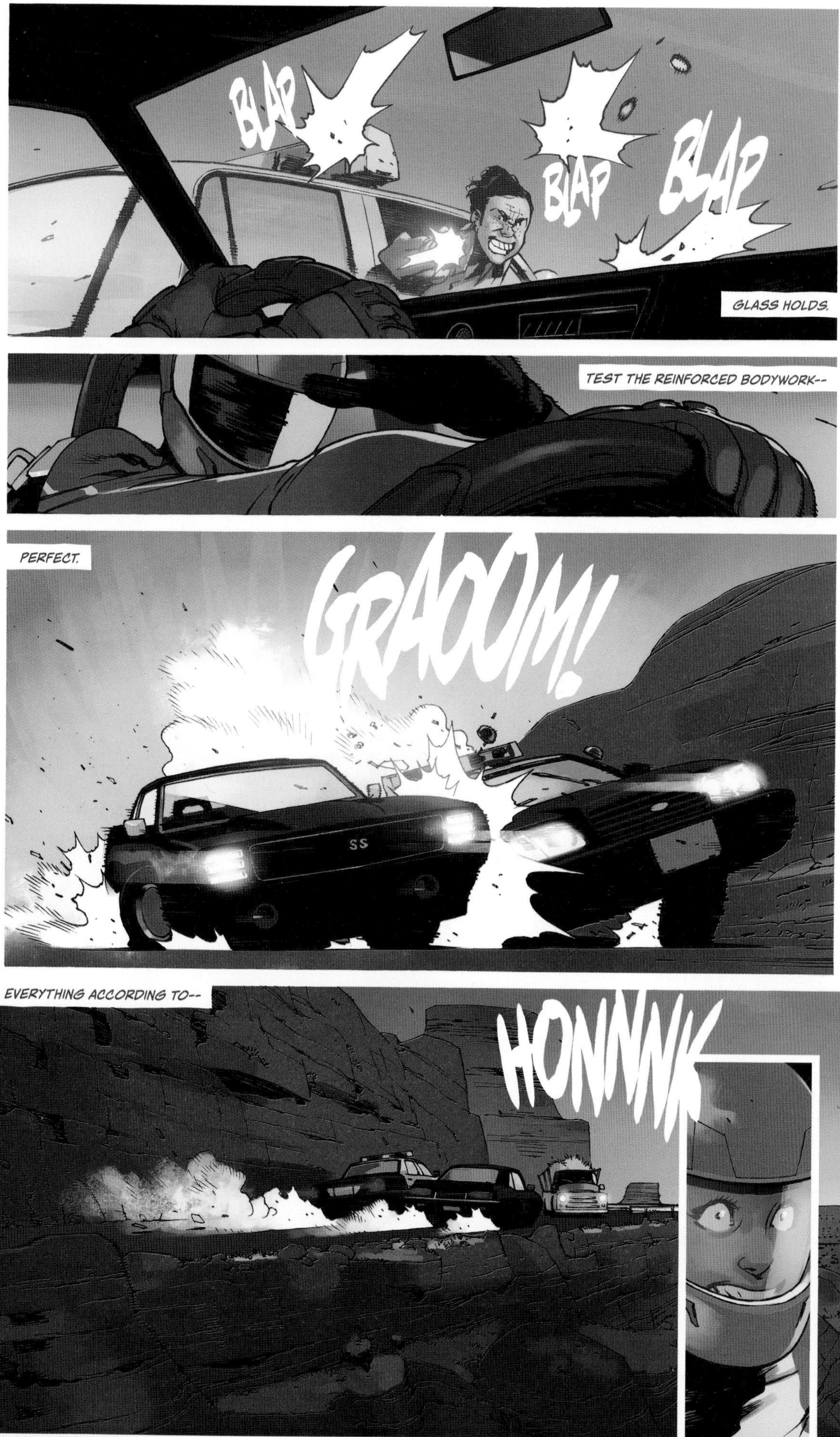
BLAP
BLAP
BLAP
GLASS HOLDS.
TEST THE REINFORCED BODYWORK--
PERFECT.
GRAOOM!
SS
EVERYTHING ACCORDING TO--
HONNNK

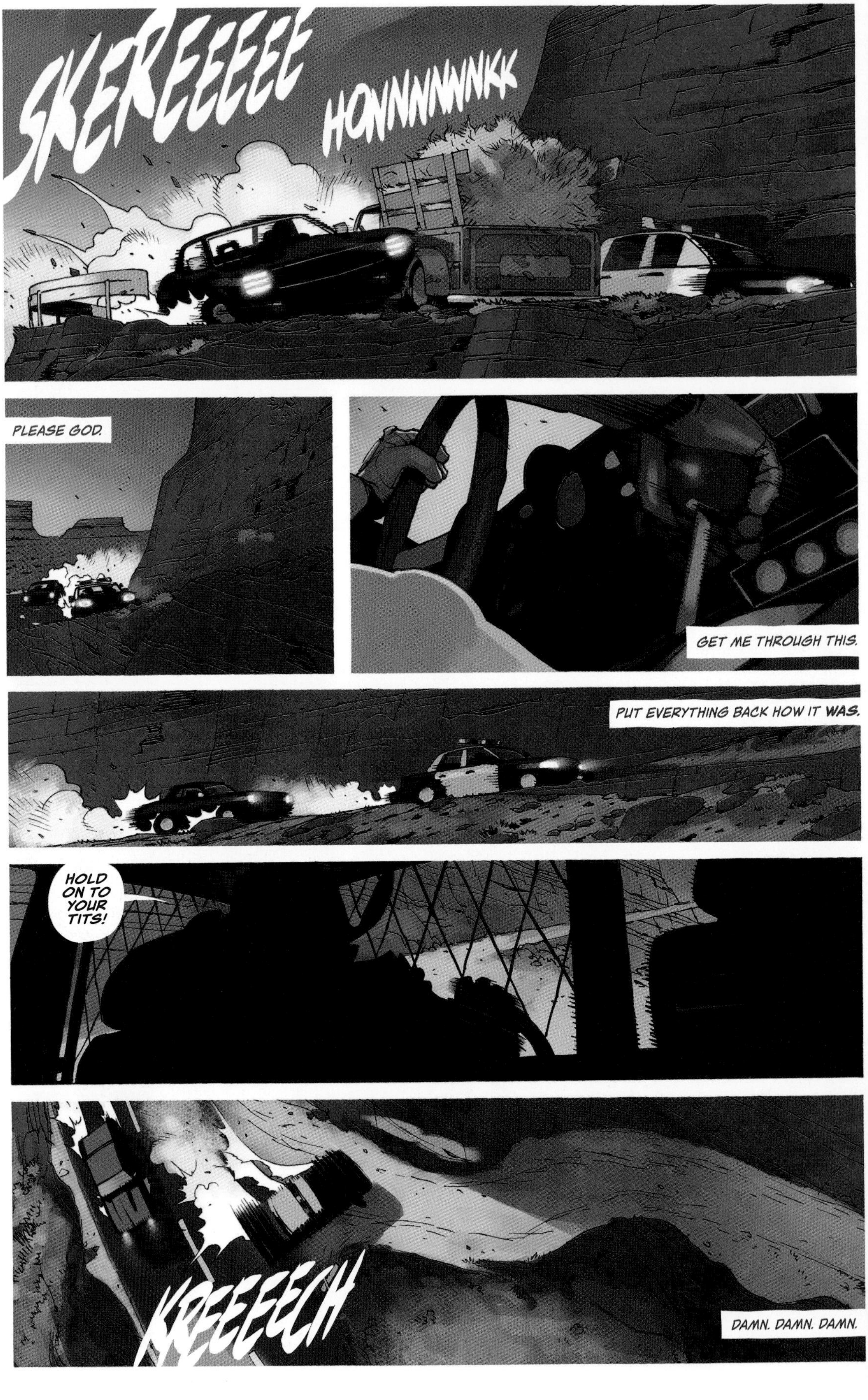
SKEREEEEEE
HONNNNNNKK
PLEASE GOD.
GET ME THROUGH THIS.
PUT EVERYTHING BACK HOW IT **WAS.**
HOLD ON TO YOUR TITS!
KREEEECH
DAMN. DAMN. DAMN.

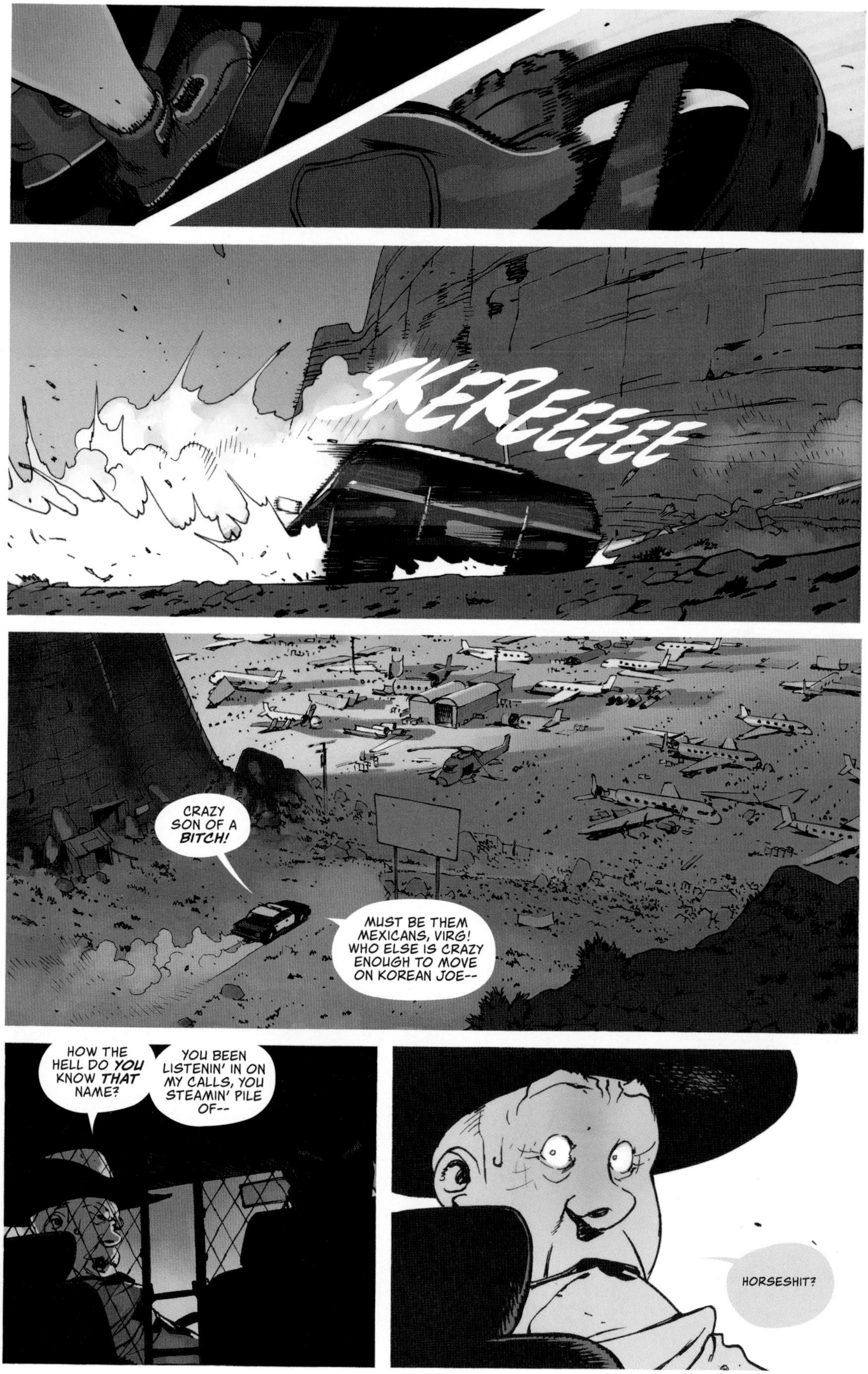
SKEREEEEE
CRAZY SON OF A BITCH!
MUST BE THEM MEXICANS, VIRG! WHO ELSE IS CRAZY ENOUGH TO MOVE ON KOREAN JOE--
HOW THE HELL DO YOU KNOW THAT NAME?
YOU BEEN LISTENIN' IN ON MY CALLS, YOU STEAMIN' PILE OF--
HORSESHIT?

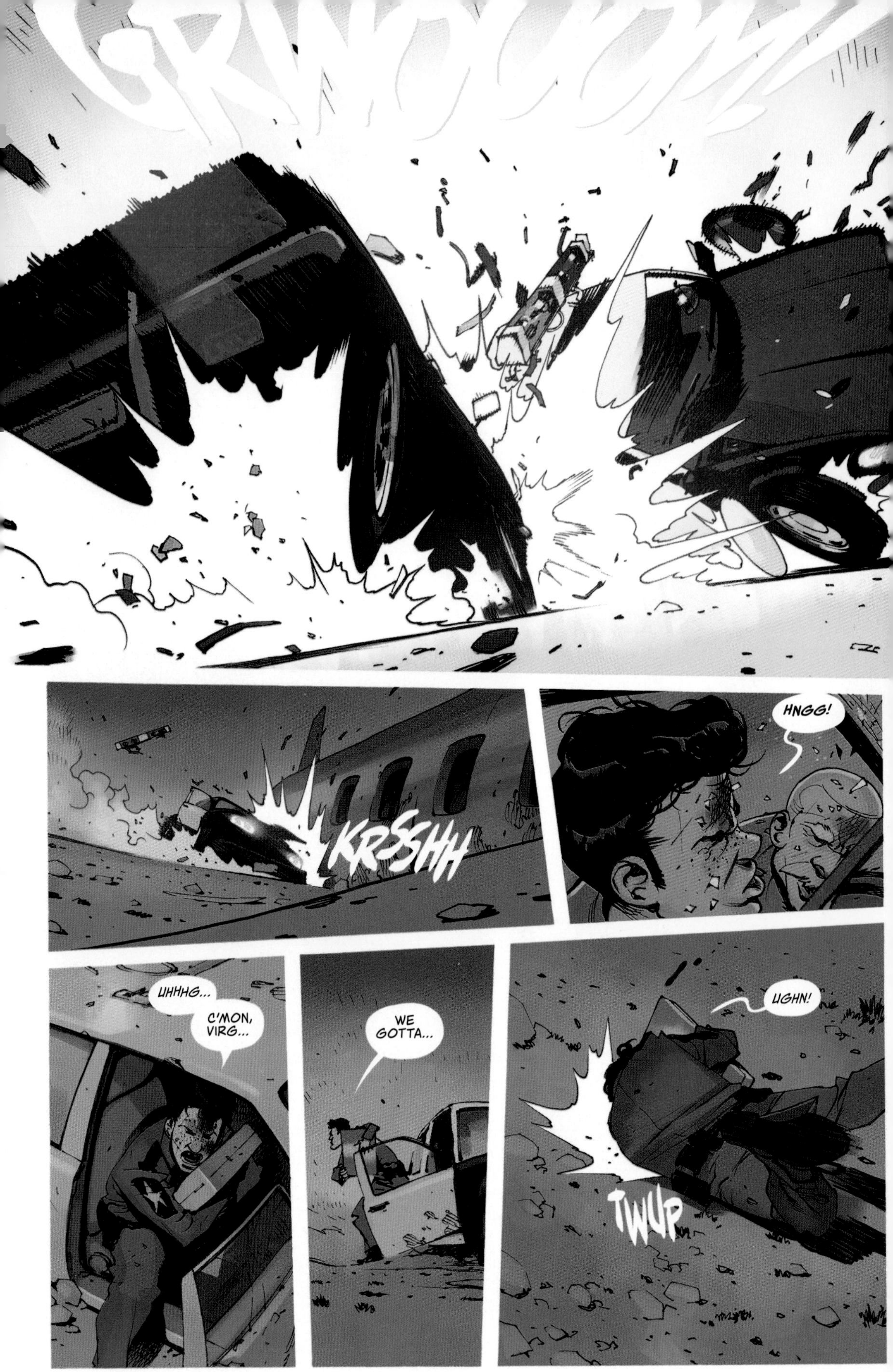
KRSSHH
HNGG!
UHHHG...
C'MON, VIRG...
WE GOTTA...
UGHN!
TWUP

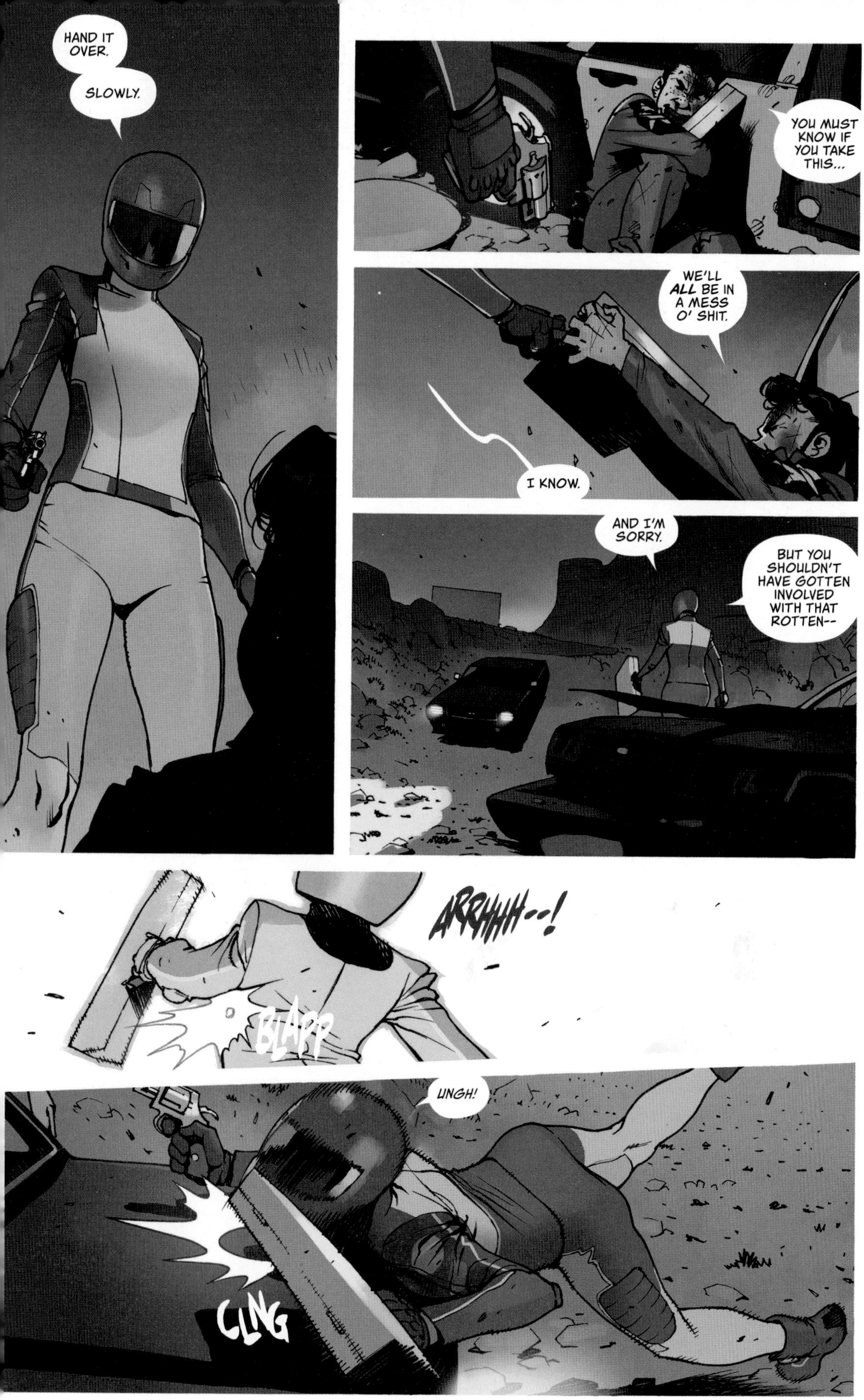
HAND IT OVER.
SLOWLY.
YOU MUST KNOW IF YOU TAKE THIS...
WE'LL ALL BE IN A MESS O' SHIT.
I KNOW.
AND I'M SORRY.
BUT YOU SHOULDN'T HAVE GOTTEN INVOLVED WITH THAT ROTTEN--
ARRHHH--!
BLAPP
UNGH!
CLNG

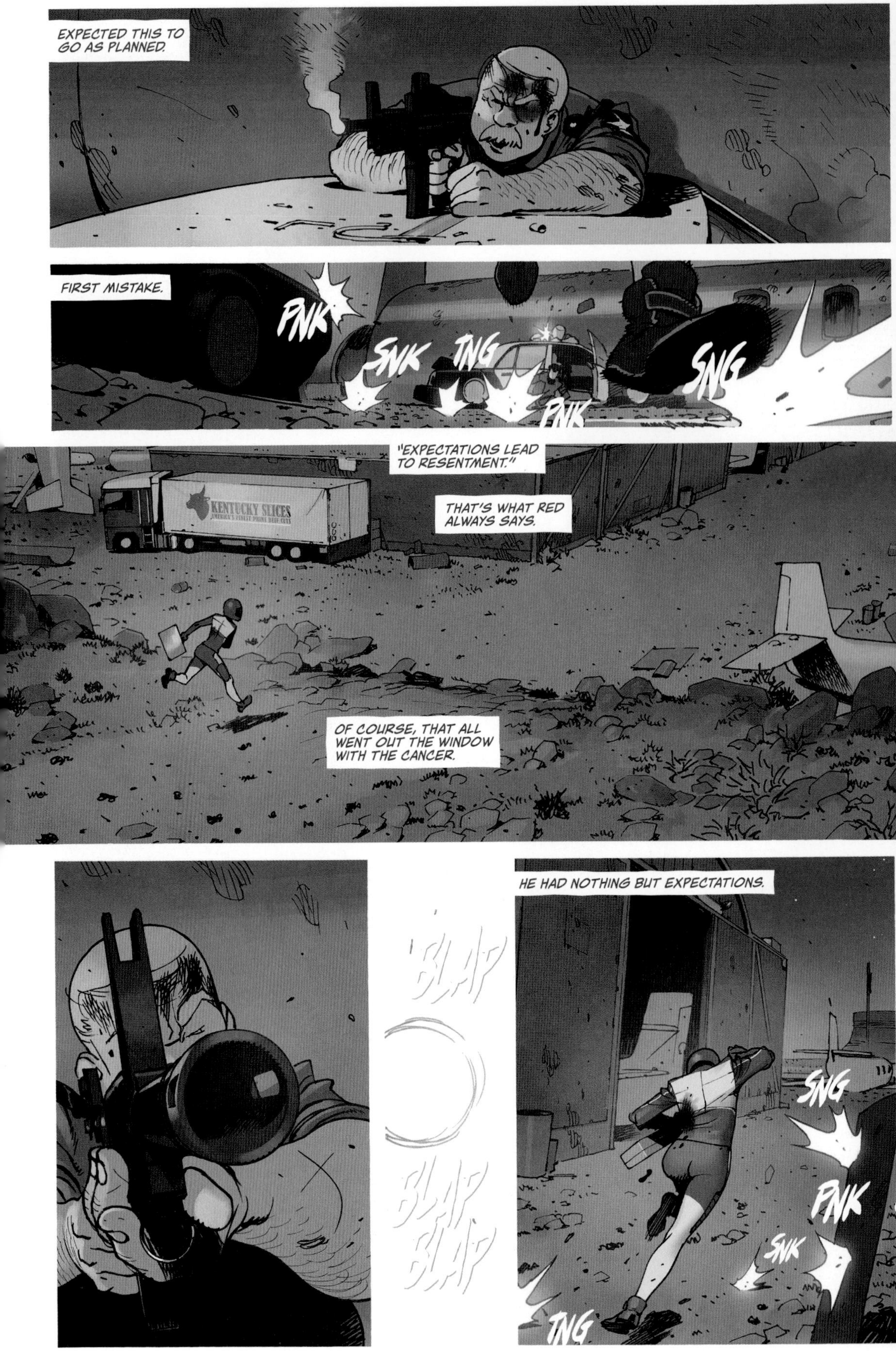
EXPECTED THIS TO GO AS PLANNED.
FIRST MISTAKE.
PNK
SNK
TNG
PNK
SNG
KENTUCKY SLICES
"EXPECTATIONS LEAD TO RESENTMENT."
THAT'S WHAT RED ALWAYS SAYS.
OF COURSE, THAT ALL WENT OUT THE WINDOW WITH THE CANCER.
BLAP
BLAP
BLAP
HE HAD NOTHING BUT EXPECTATIONS.
SNG
PNK
SNK
TNG

IT'S HARD TO KNOW YOU'RE DYING OF SOMETHING WHEN THERE'S A TREATMENT ON THE OTHER SIDE OF A WALL.

RED'S EXPECTATIONS WERE **BORN** AS RESENTMENTS.

WOULDN'T LET ME GET A BANK LOAN.

AS IF I COULD.

ALL THOSE YEARS TELLIN' ME HE'D RATHER DIE THAN JOIN THEIR WORLD.

BLAP BLAP

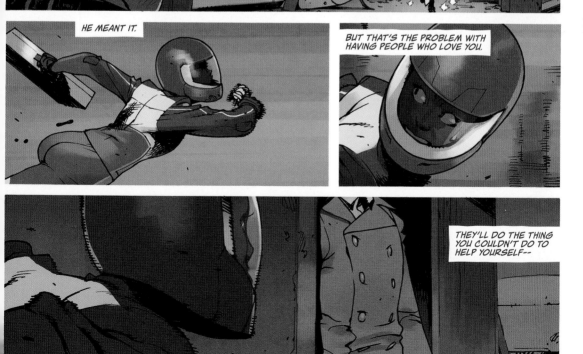

HE MEANT IT.

BUT THAT'S THE PROBLEM WITH HAVING PEOPLE WHO LOVE YOU.

THEY'LL DO THE THING YOU COULDN'T DO TO HELP YOURSELF--

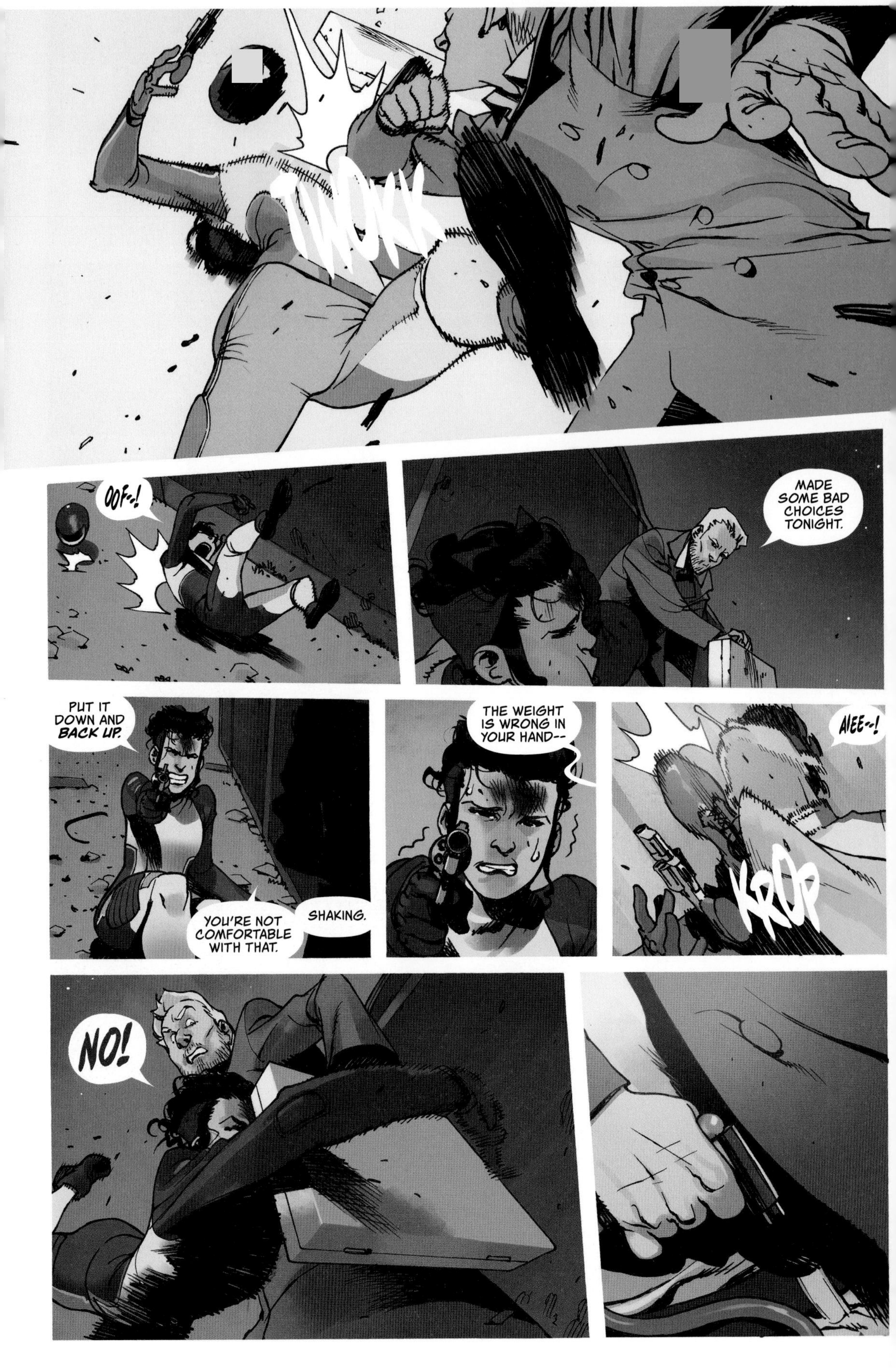
TWOKK
OOF--!
MADE SOME BAD CHOICES TONIGHT.
PUT IT DOWN AND BACK UP.
YOU'RE NOT COMFORTABLE WITH THAT.
SHAKING.
THE WEIGHT IS WRONG IN YOUR HAND--
AIEE--!
KROP
NO!

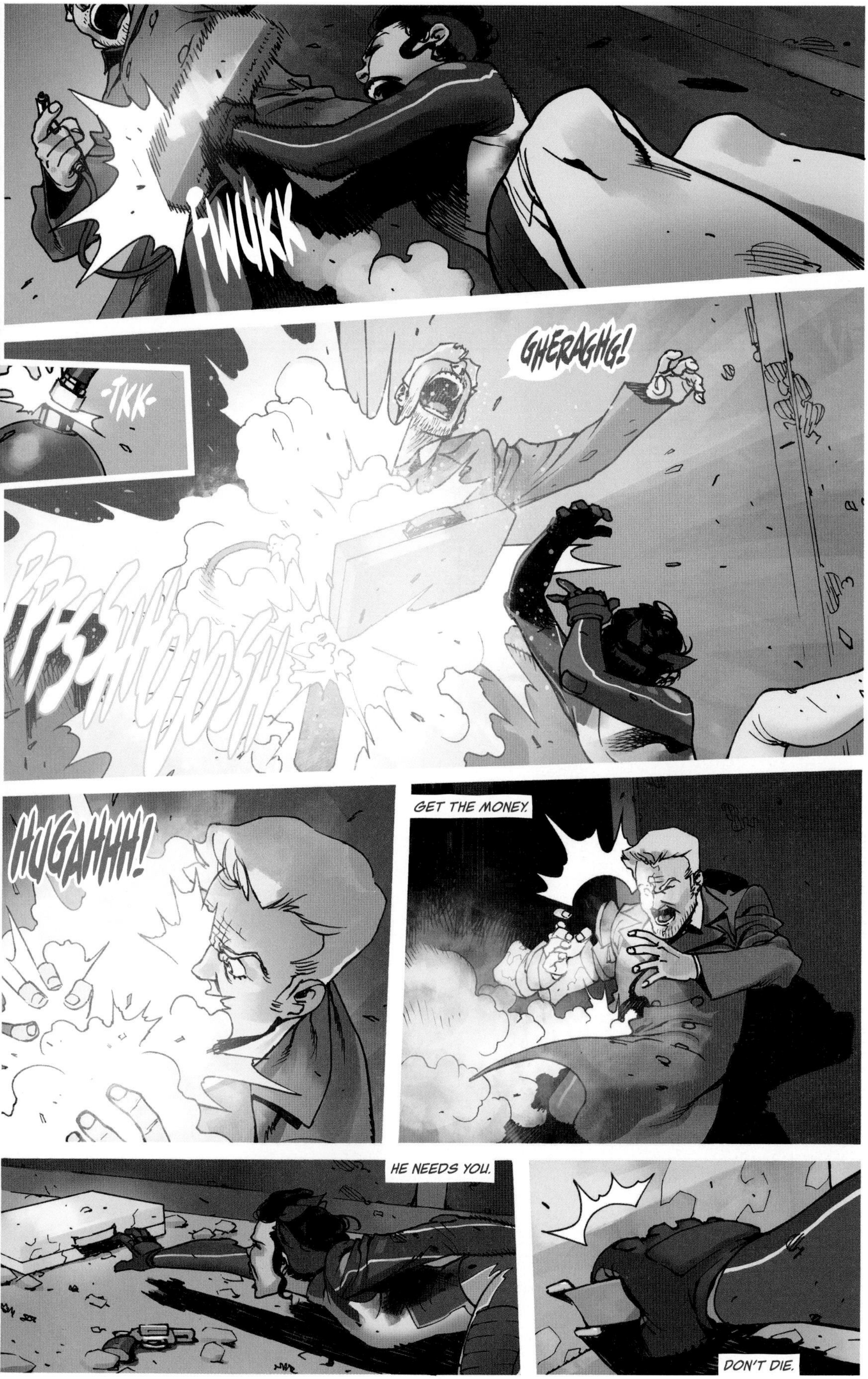
FWUKK
GHERAGHG!
-TKK-
PPSHOOOSH
HUGAHHH!
GET THE MONEY.
HE NEEDS YOU.
DON'T DIE.

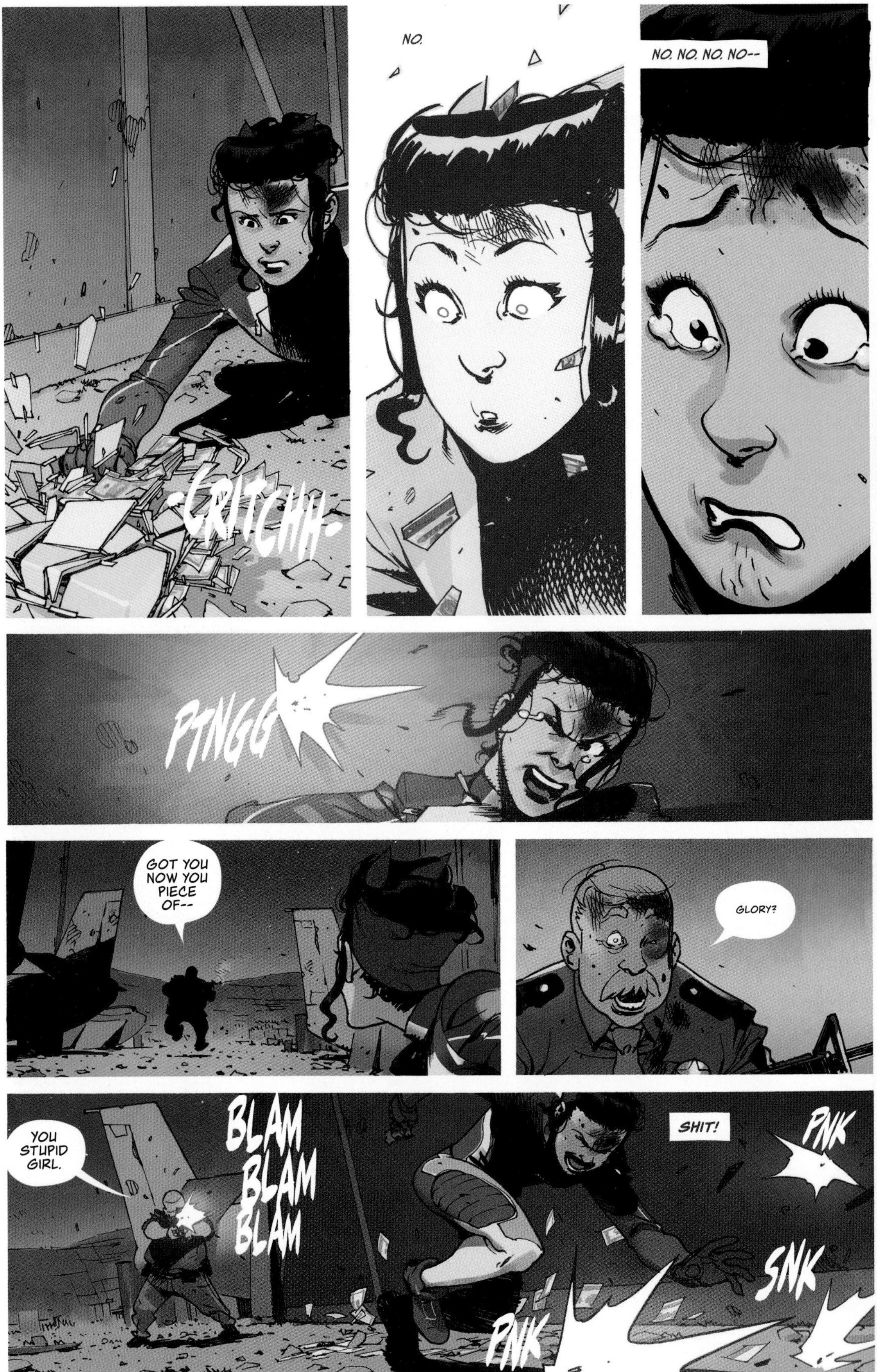

-CRITCHH-
NO.
NO. NO. NO. NO--
PTNGG
GOT YOU NOW YOU PIECE OF--
GLORY?
YOU STUPID GIRL.
BLAM BLAM BLAM
SHIT!
PNK
SNK
PNK

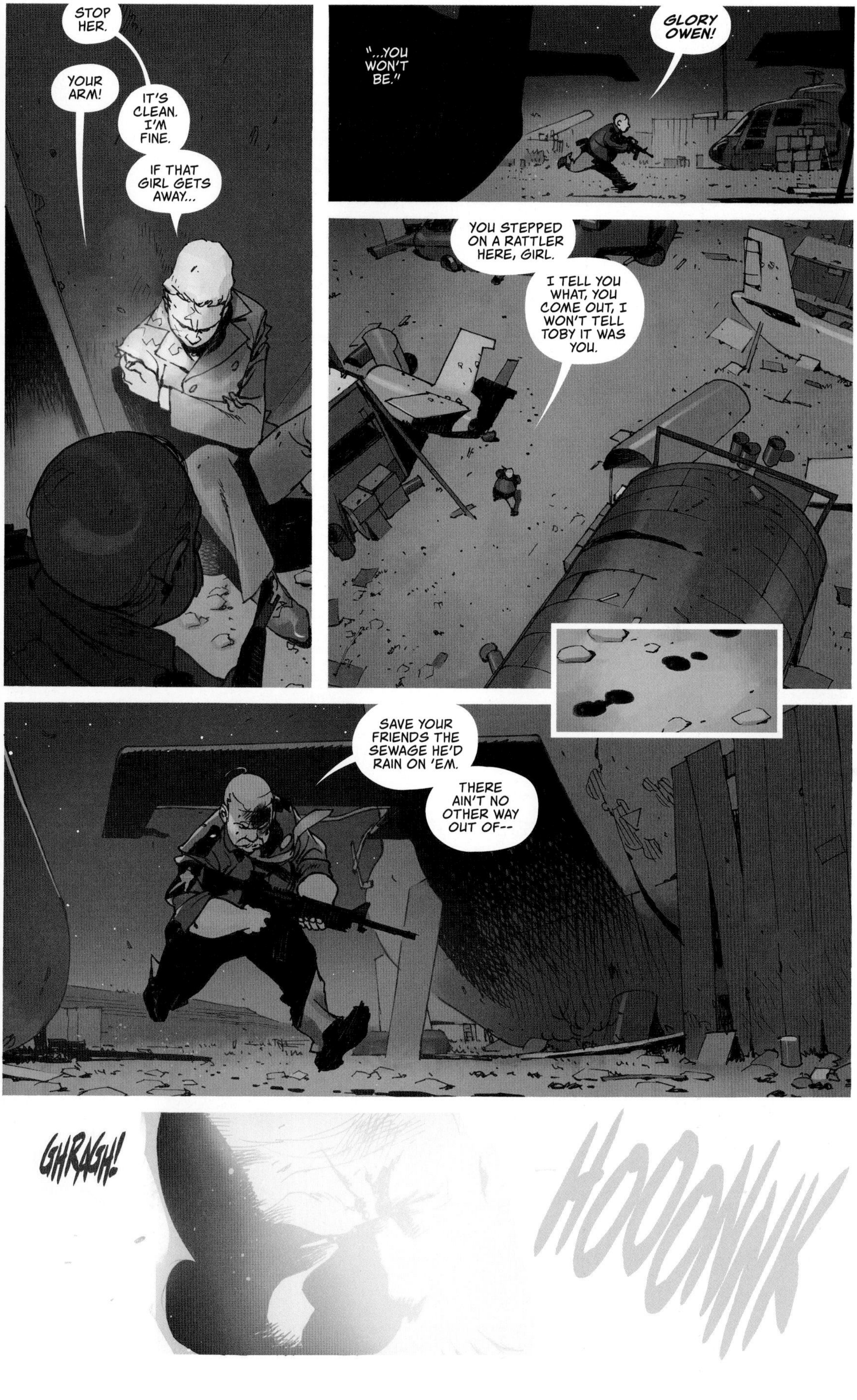
STOP HER.
YOUR ARM!
IT'S CLEAN. I'M FINE.
IF THAT GIRL GETS AWAY...
"...YOU WON'T BE."
GLORY OWEN!
YOU STEPPED ON A RATTLER HERE, GIRL.
I TELL YOU WHAT, YOU COME OUT, I WON'T TELL TOBY IT WAS YOU.
SAVE YOUR FRIENDS THE SEWAGE HE'D RAIN ON 'EM.
THERE AIN'T NO OTHER WAY OUT OF--
GHRAGH!
HOOONK

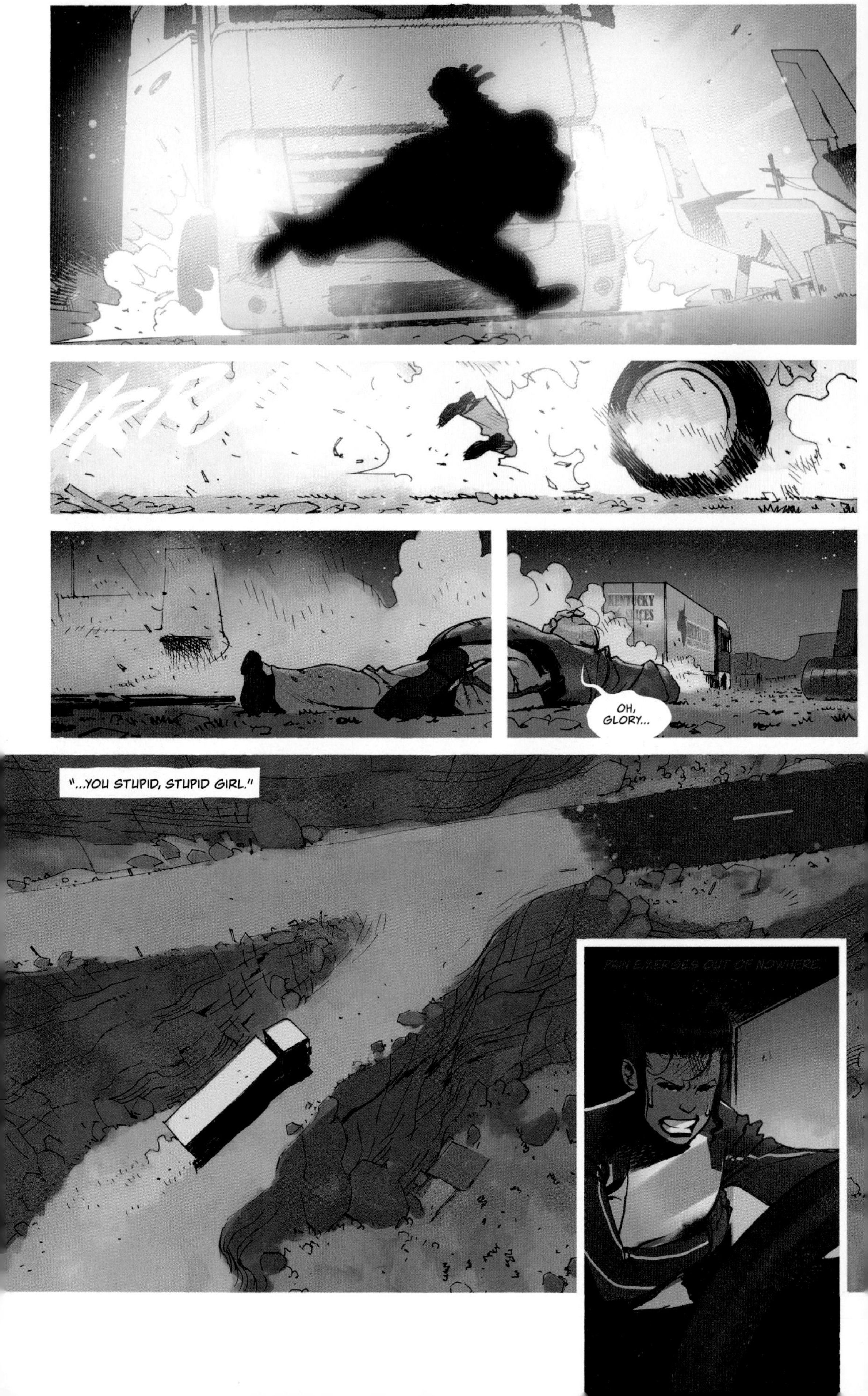
OH, GLORY...
"...YOU STUPID, STUPID GIRL."
PAIN EMERGES OUT OF NOWHERE.

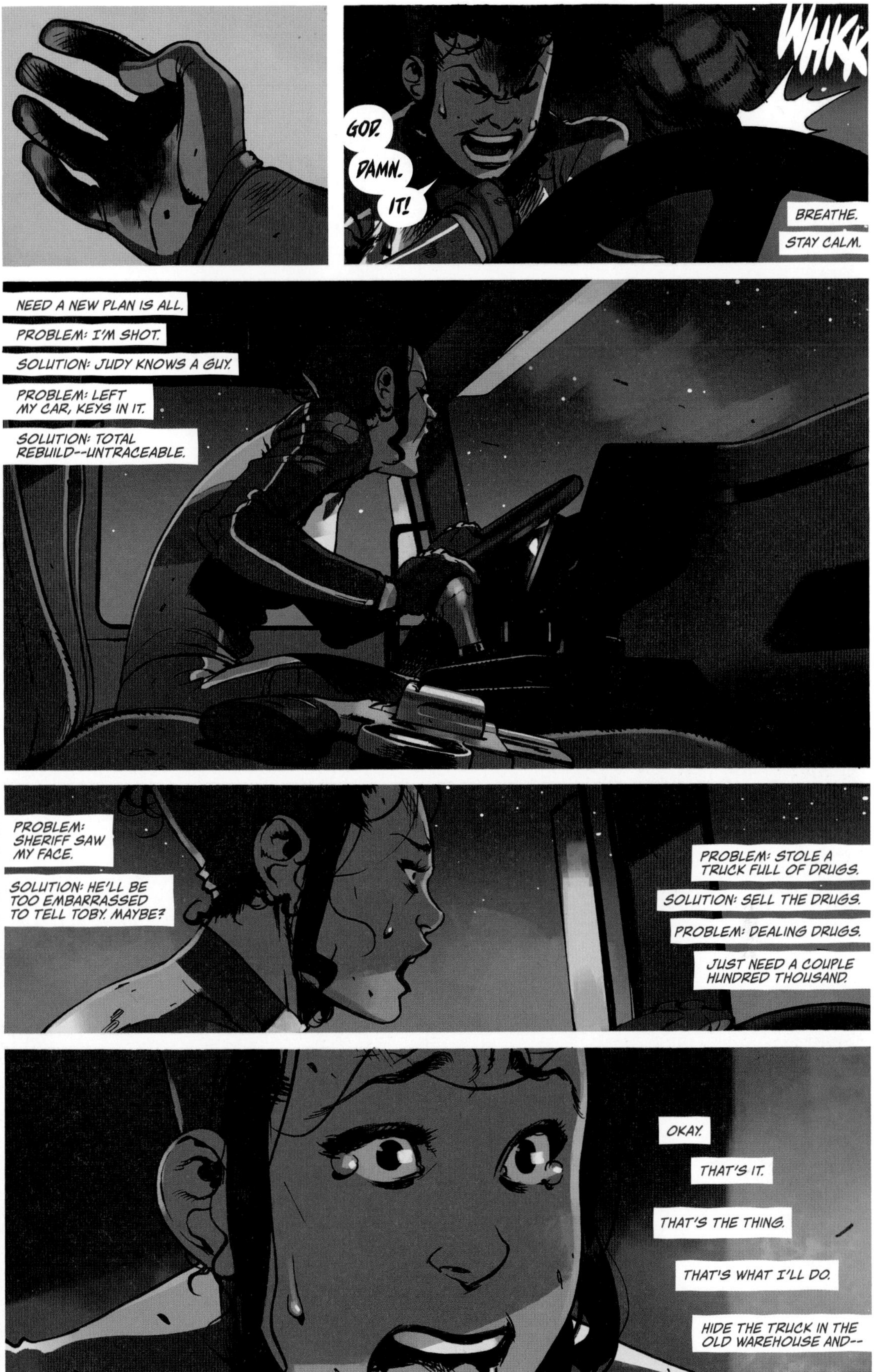
WHKK
GOD.
DAMN.
IT!
BREATHE.
STAY CALM.
NEED A NEW PLAN IS ALL.
PROBLEM: I'M SHOT.
SOLUTION: JUDY KNOWS A GUY.
PROBLEM: LEFT MY CAR, KEYS IN IT.
SOLUTION: TOTAL REBUILD--UNTRACEABLE.
PROBLEM: SHERIFF SAW MY FACE.
SOLUTION: HE'LL BE TOO EMBARRASSED TO TELL TOBY. MAYBE?
PROBLEM: STOLE A TRUCK FULL OF DRUGS.
SOLUTION: SELL THE DRUGS.
PROBLEM: DEALING DRUGS.
JUST NEED A COUPLE HUNDRED THOUSAND.
OKAY.
THAT'S IT.
THAT'S THE THING.
THAT'S WHAT I'LL DO.
HIDE THE TRUCK IN THE OLD WAREHOUSE AND--

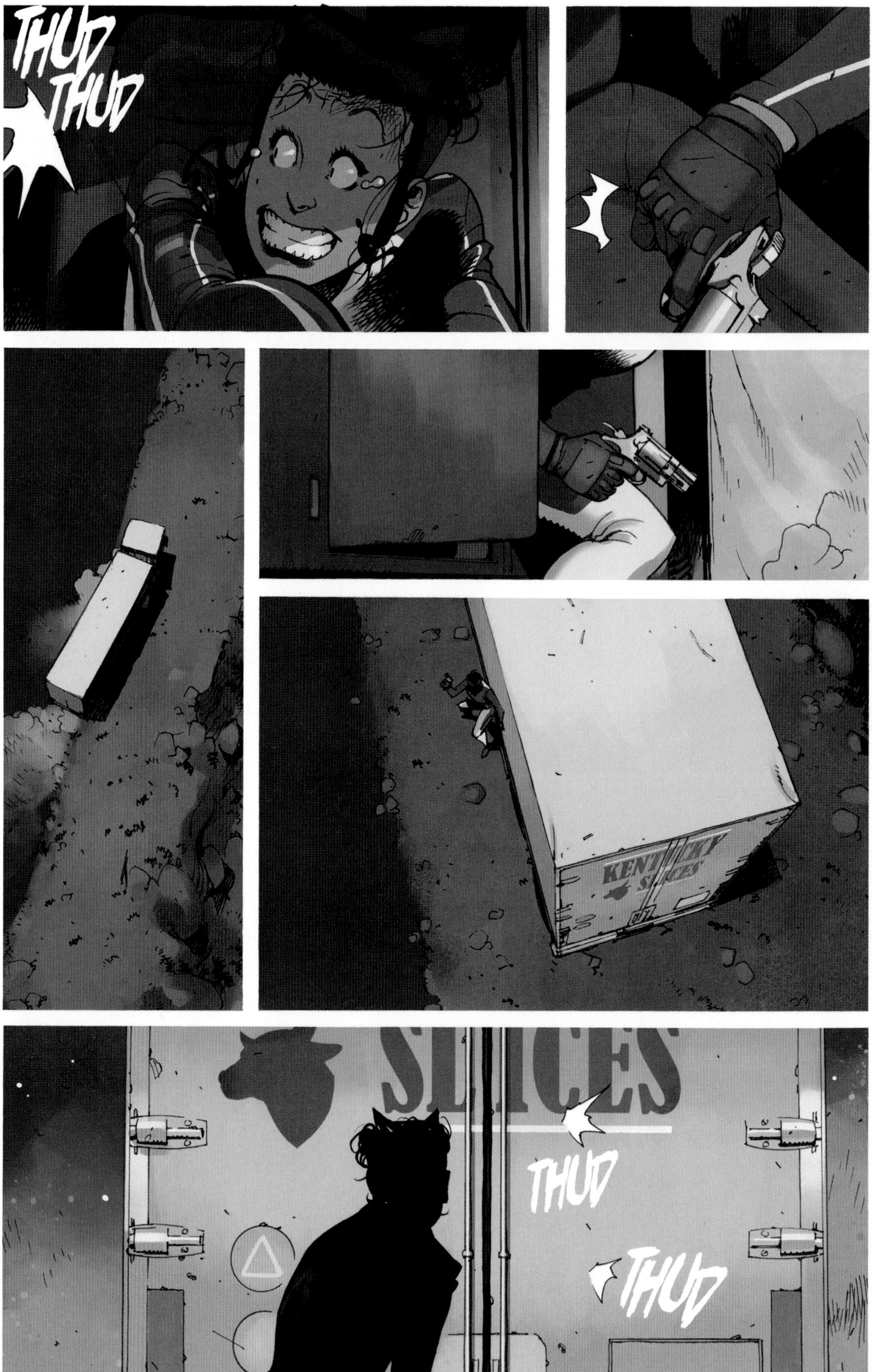
THUD
THUD
KENTUCKY SLICES
SLICES
THUD
THUD

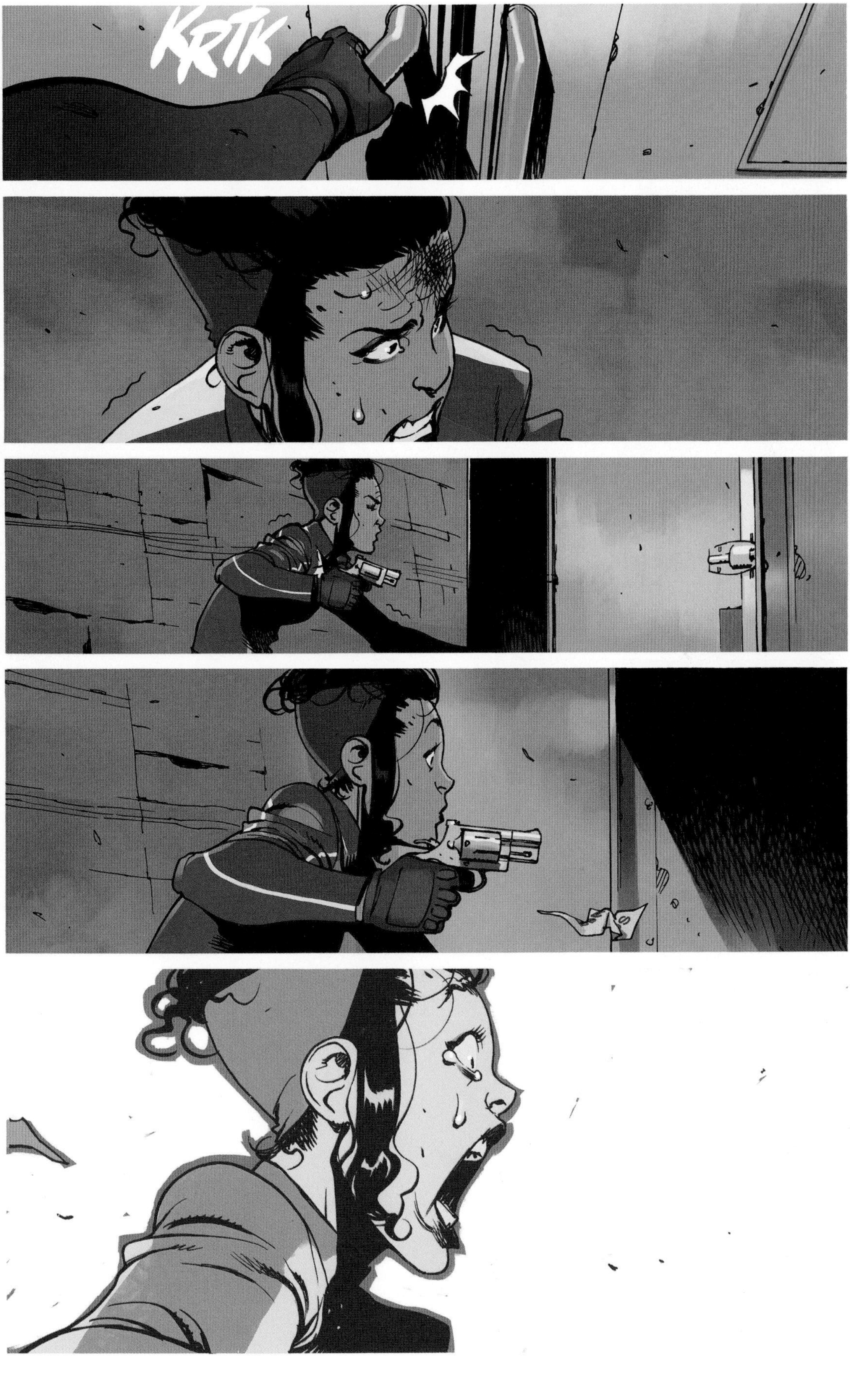
KRIK

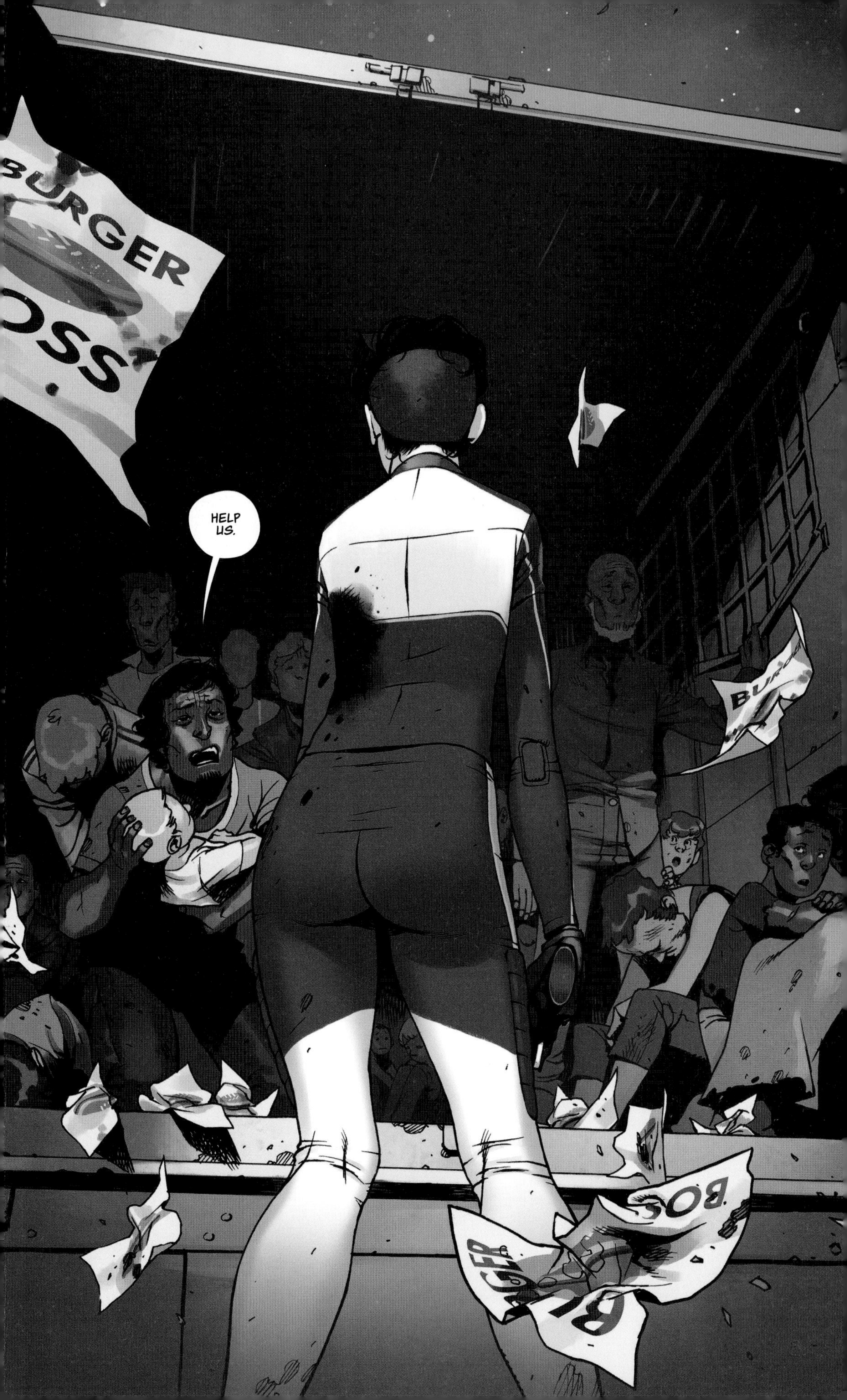
HELP US.
BURGER

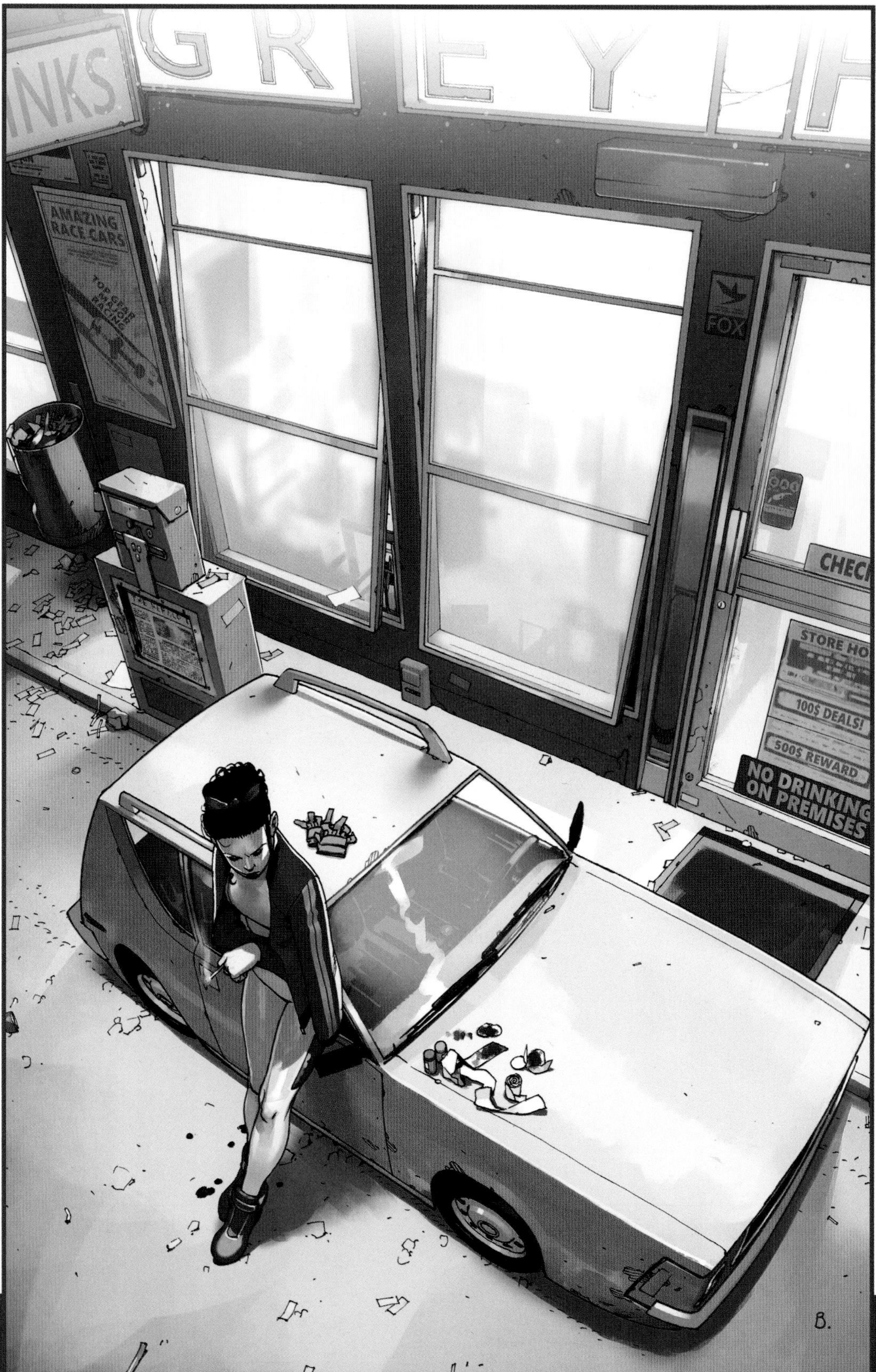
AMAZING RACE CARS
TOP GEAR MAJOR RACING
FOX
100$ DEALS!
500$ REWARD
NO DRINKING ON PREMISES
B.

TWO

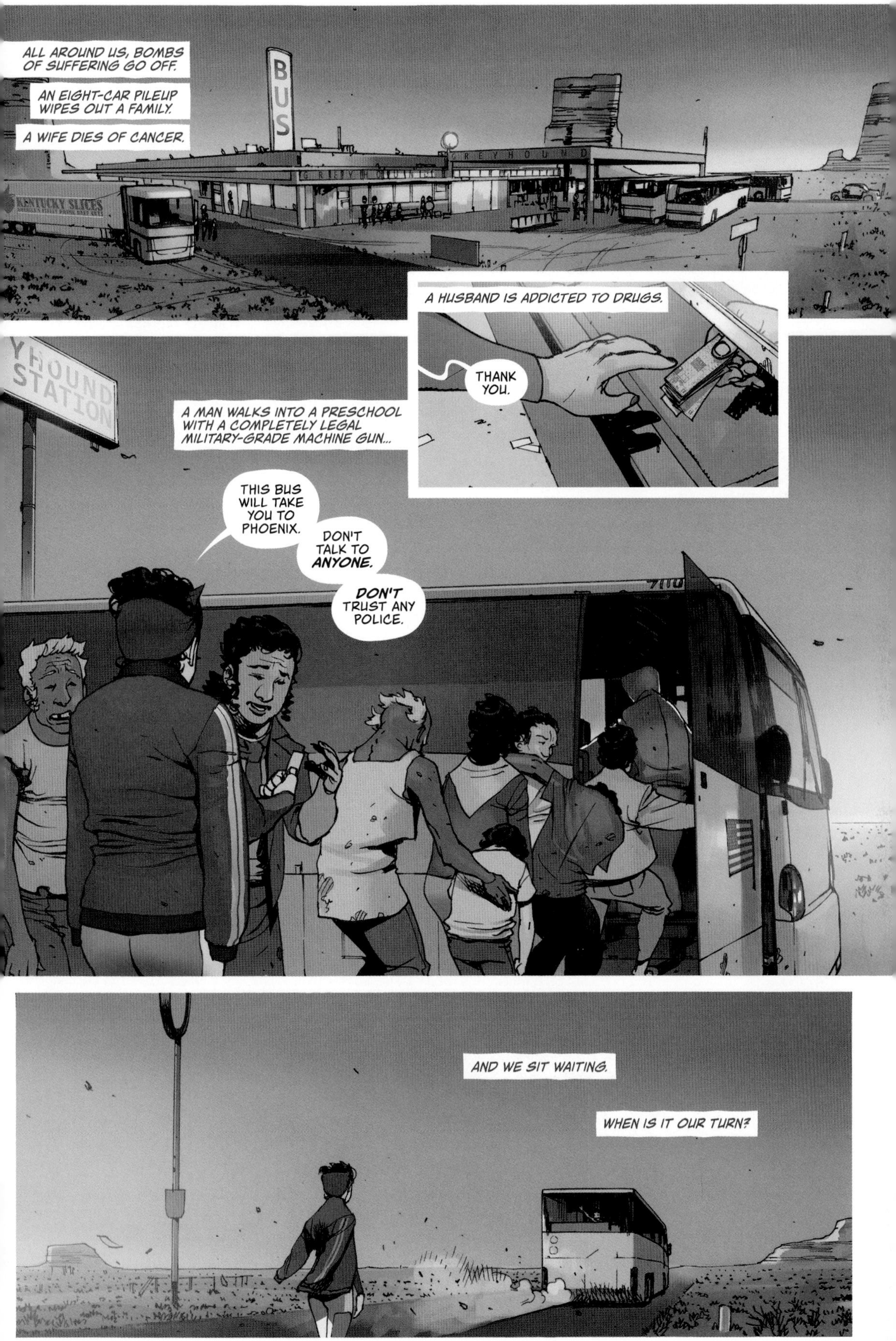
ALL AROUND US, BOMBS OF SUFFERING GO OFF.
AN EIGHT-CAR PILEUP WIPES OUT A FAMILY.
A WIFE DIES OF CANCER.
BUS
GREYHOUND
KENTUCKY SLICES
A HUSBAND IS ADDICTED TO DRUGS.
THANK YOU.
A MAN WALKS INTO A PRESCHOOL WITH A COMPLETELY LEGAL MILITARY-GRADE MACHINE GUN...
THIS BUS WILL TAKE YOU TO PHOENIX.
DON'T TALK TO ANYONE.
DON'T TRUST ANY POLICE.
AND WE SIT WAITING.
WHEN IS IT OUR TURN?

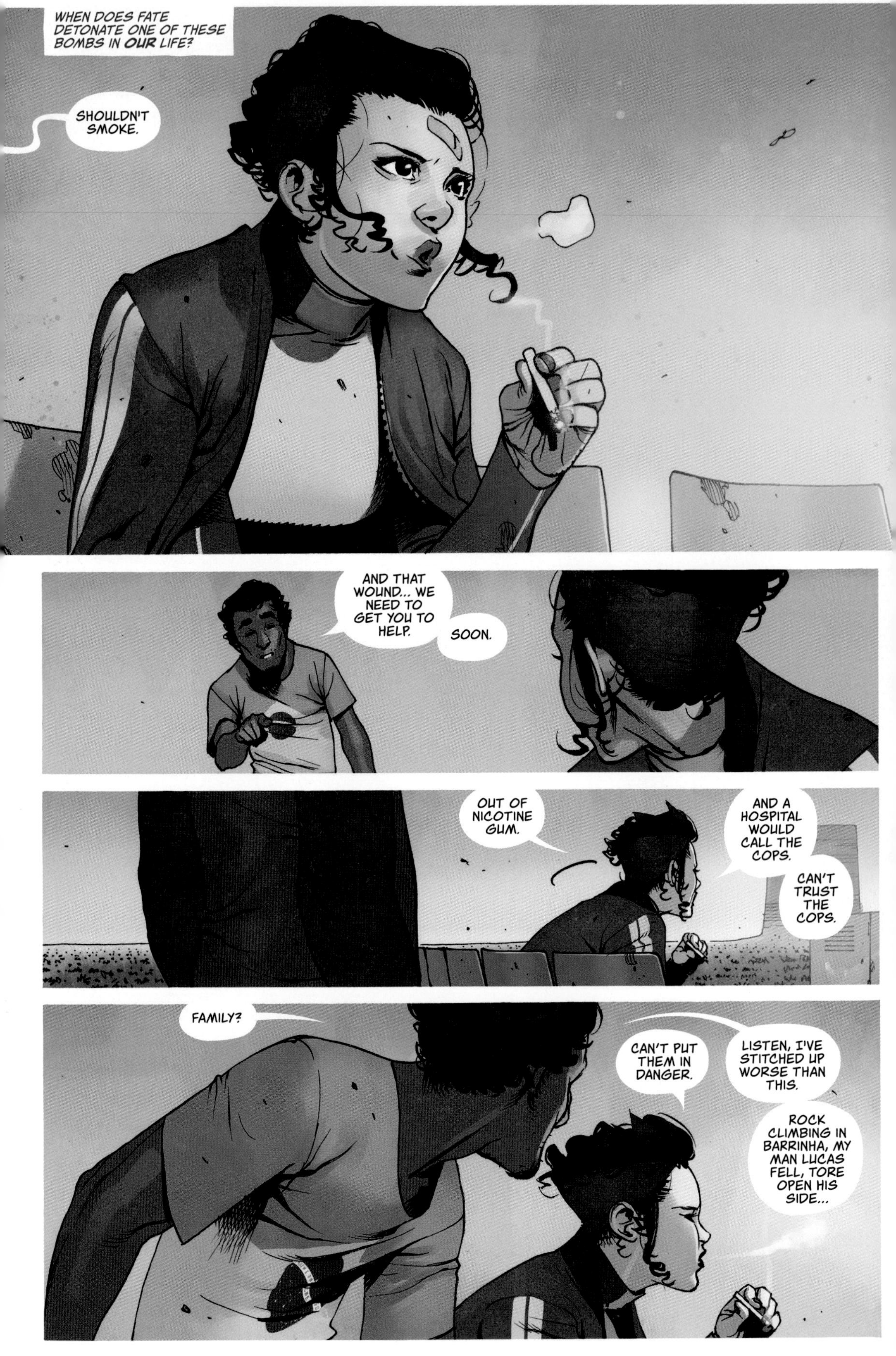
WHEN DOES FATE DETONATE ONE OF THESE BOMBS IN OUR LIFE?
SHOULDN'T SMOKE.
AND THAT WOUND... WE NEED TO GET YOU TO HELP.
SOON.
OUT OF NICOTINE GUM.
AND A HOSPITAL WOULD CALL THE COPS.
CAN'T TRUST THE COPS.
FAMILY?
CAN'T PUT THEM IN DANGER.
LISTEN, I'VE STITCHED UP WORSE THAN THIS.
ROCK CLIMBING IN BARRINHA, MY MAN LUCAS FELL, TORE OPEN HIS SIDE...

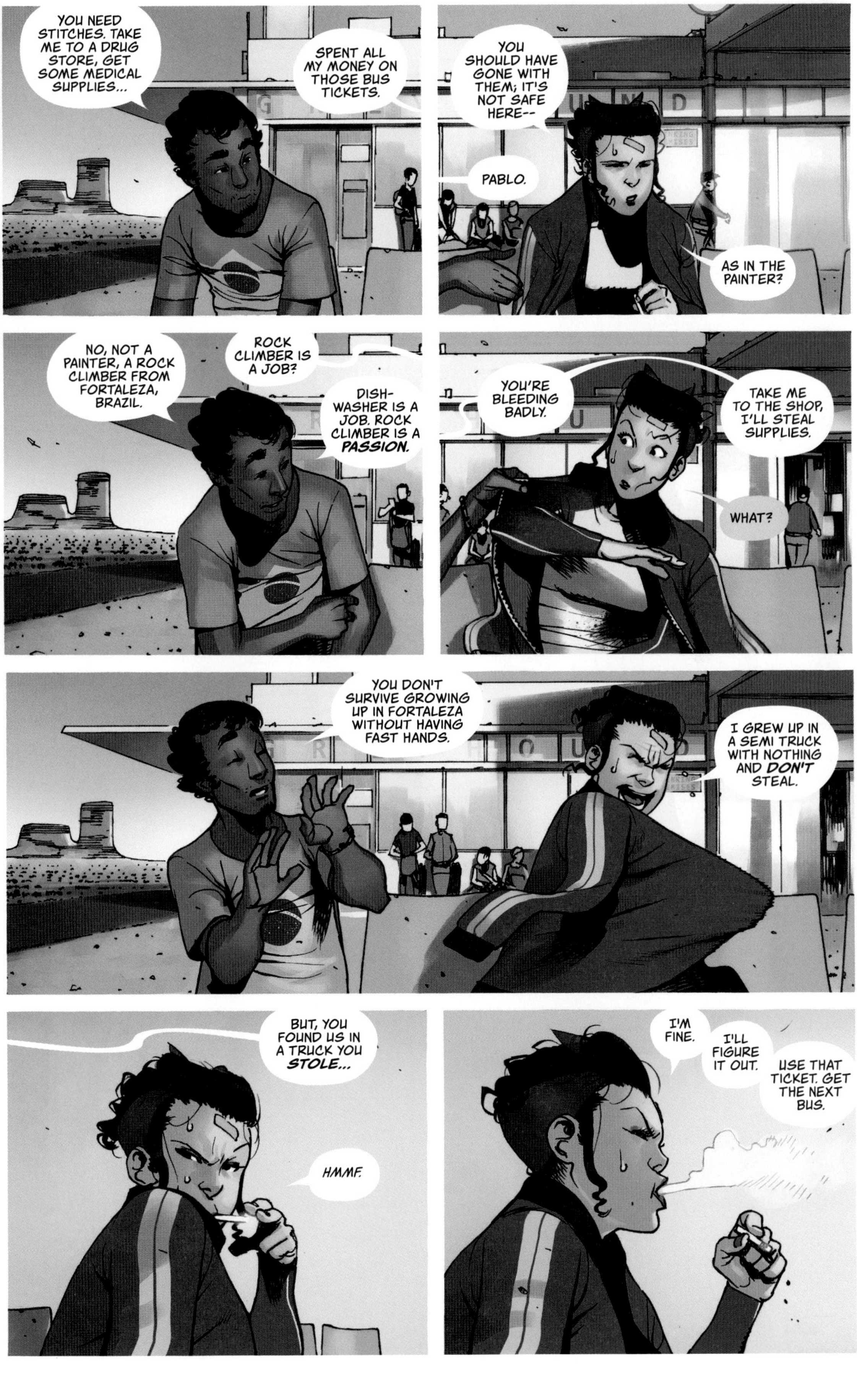
YOU NEED STITCHES. TAKE ME TO A DRUG STORE, GET SOME MEDICAL SUPPLIES...
SPENT ALL MY MONEY ON THOSE BUS TICKETS.
YOU SHOULD HAVE GONE WITH THEM; IT'S NOT SAFE HERE--
PABLO.
AS IN THE PAINTER?
NO, NOT A PAINTER, A ROCK CLIMBER FROM FORTALEZA, BRAZIL.
ROCK CLIMBER IS A JOB?
DISH-WASHER IS A JOB. ROCK CLIMBER IS A PASSION.
YOU'RE BLEEDING BADLY.
TAKE ME TO THE SHOP, I'LL STEAL SUPPLIES.
WHAT?
YOU DON'T SURVIVE GROWING UP IN FORTALEZA WITHOUT HAVING FAST HANDS.
I GREW UP IN A SEMI TRUCK WITH NOTHING AND DON'T STEAL.
BUT, YOU FOUND US IN A TRUCK YOU STOLE...
HMMF.
I'M FINE.
I'LL FIGURE IT OUT.
USE THAT TICKET. GET THE NEXT BUS.

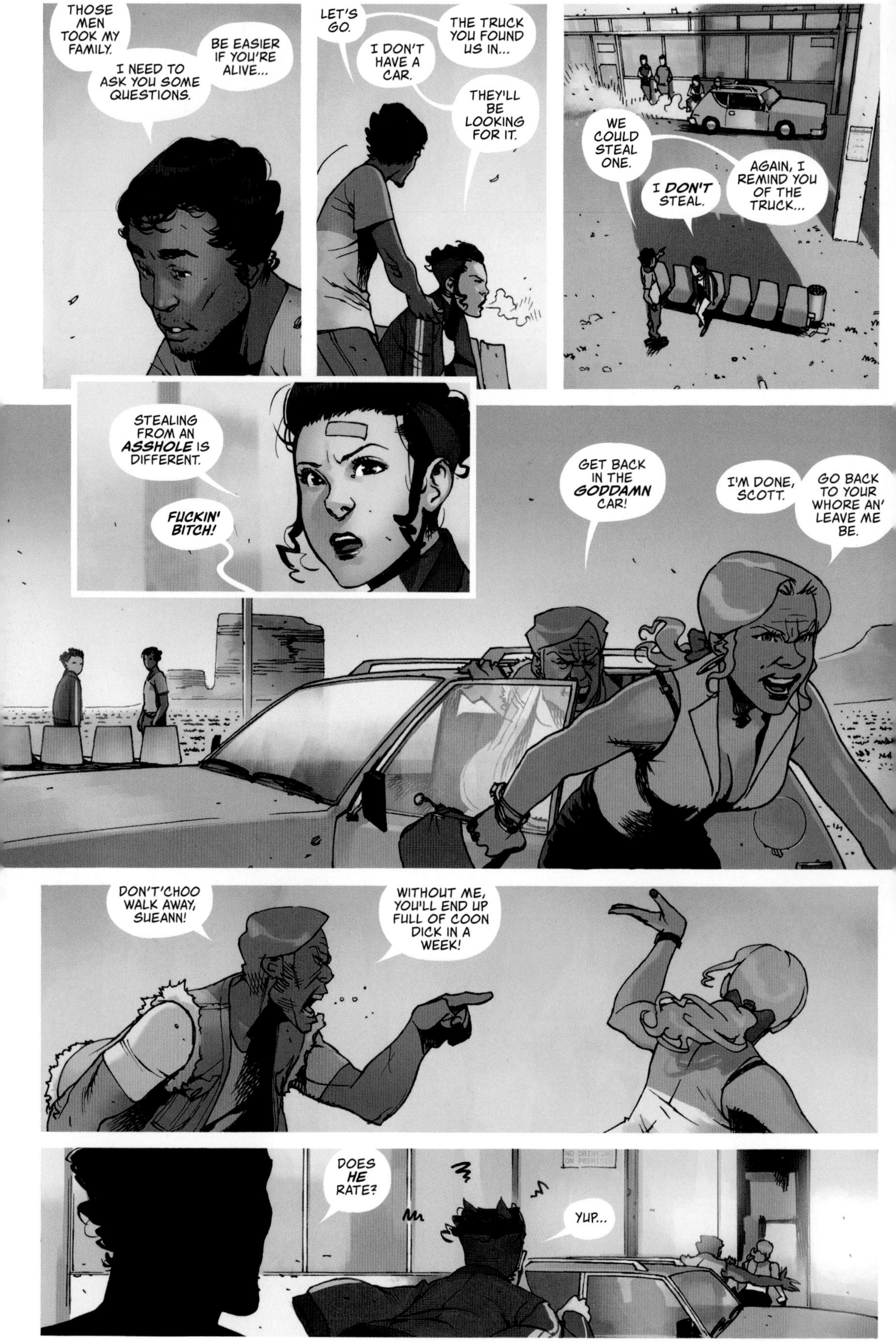

THOSE MEN TOOK MY FAMILY.
BE EASIER IF YOU'RE ALIVE...
I NEED TO ASK YOU SOME QUESTIONS.
LET'S GO.
THE TRUCK YOU FOUND US IN...
I DON'T HAVE A CAR.
THEY'LL BE LOOKING FOR IT.
WE COULD STEAL ONE.
AGAIN, I REMIND YOU OF THE TRUCK...
I DON'T STEAL.
STEALING FROM AN ASSHOLE IS DIFFERENT.
FUCKIN' BITCH!
GET BACK IN THE GODDAMN CAR!
I'M DONE, SCOTT.
GO BACK TO YOUR WHORE AN' LEAVE ME BE.
DON'T'CHOO WALK AWAY, SUEANN!
WITHOUT ME, YOU'LL END UP FULL OF COON DICK IN A WEEK!
NO DRINKING ON PREMISES
DOES HE RATE?
YUP...

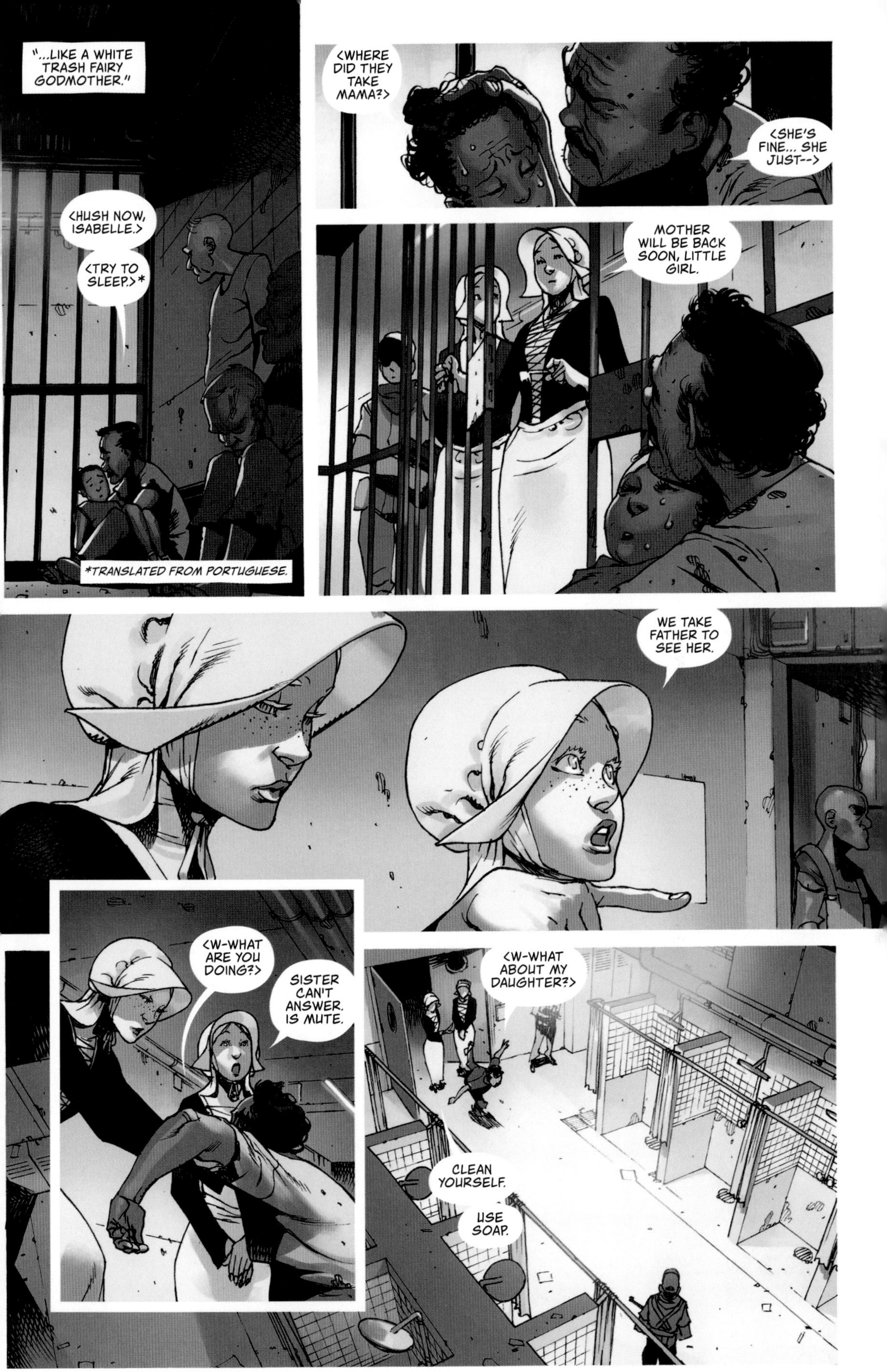
"...LIKE A WHITE TRASH FAIRY GODMOTHER."
<HUSH NOW, ISABELLE.>
<TRY TO SLEEP.>*
*TRANSLATED FROM PORTUGUESE.
<WHERE DID THEY TAKE MAMA?>
<SHE'S FINE... SHE JUST-->
MOTHER WILL BE BACK SOON, LITTLE GIRL.
WE TAKE FATHER TO SEE HER.
<W-WHAT ARE YOU DOING?>
SISTER CAN'T ANSWER. IS MUTE.
<W-WHAT ABOUT MY DAUGHTER?>
CLEAN YOURSELF.
USE SOAP.

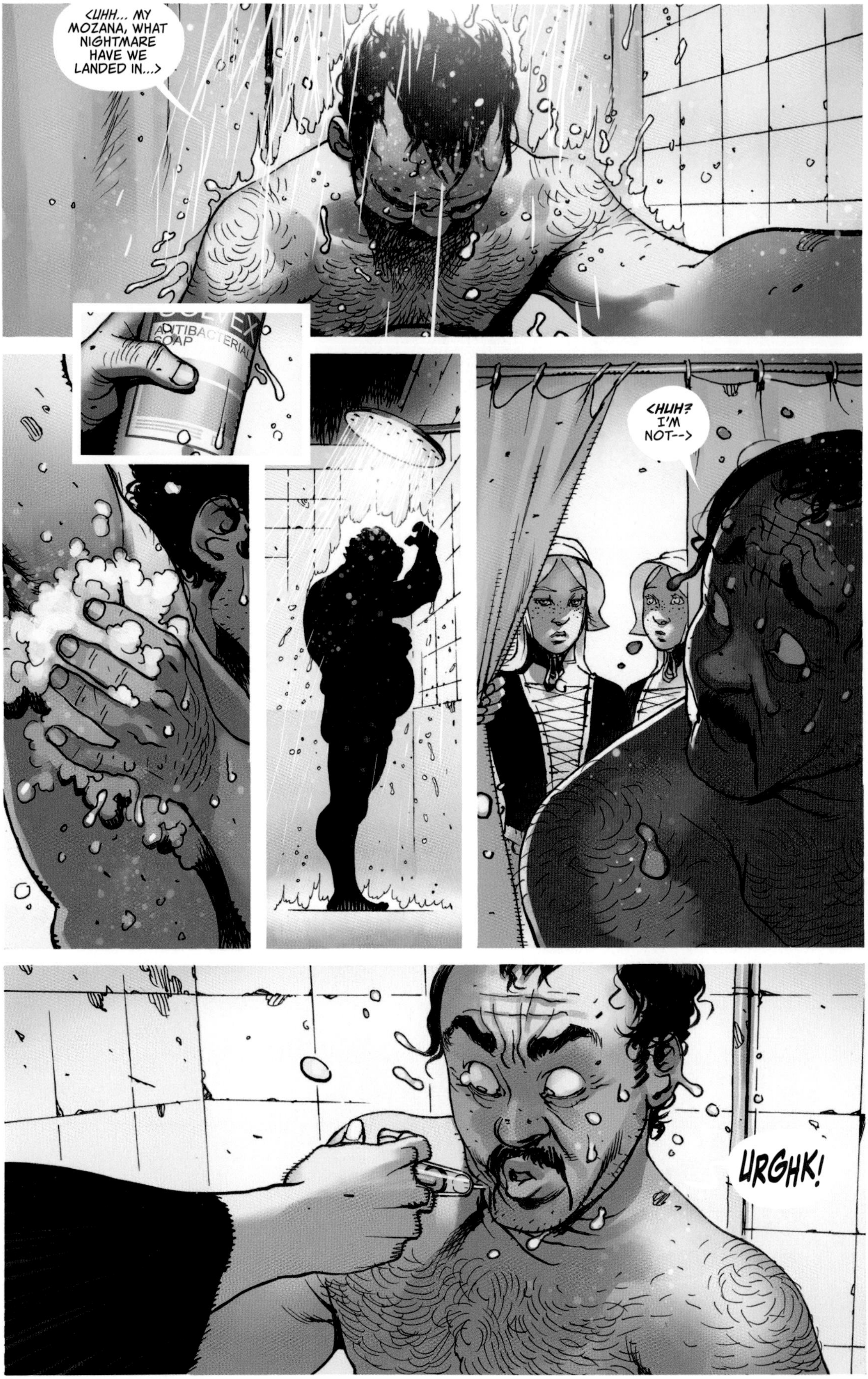

<UHH... MY MOZANA, WHAT NIGHTMARE HAVE WE LANDED IN...>
ANTIBACTERIAL SOAP
<HUH? I'M NOT-->
URGHK!

PLOOSH

THOUGH BLIND...

I SMELL.

WAA...?

CLEAN NOW. VERY GOOD.

WHA... WHAT RRE...

MURGRGLE...

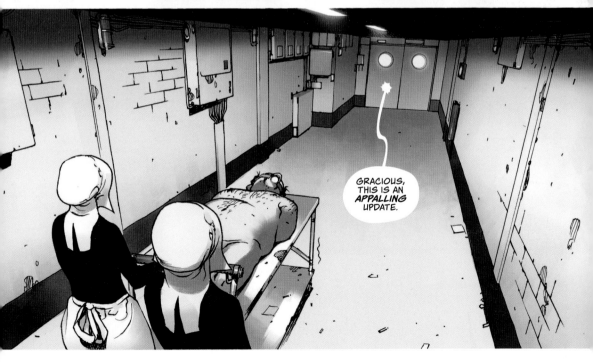

GRACIOUS, THIS IS AN *APPALLING* UPDATE.

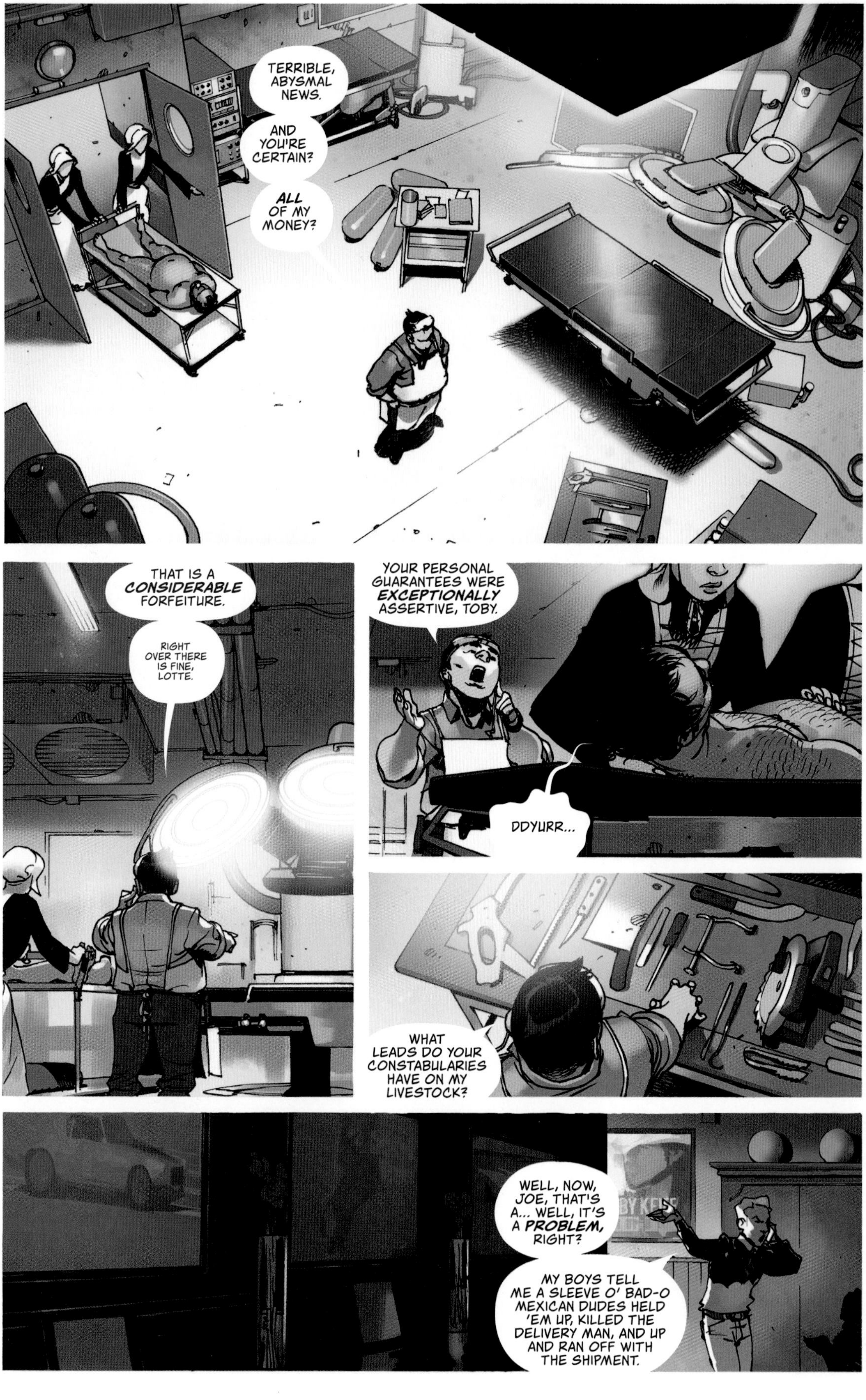
TERRIBLE, ABYSMAL NEWS.
AND YOU'RE CERTAIN?
ALL OF MY MONEY?
THAT IS A CONSIDERABLE FORFEITURE.
RIGHT OVER THERE IS FINE, LOTTE.
YOUR PERSONAL GUARANTEES WERE EXCEPTIONALLY ASSERTIVE, TOBY.
DDYURR...
WHAT LEADS DO YOUR CONSTABULARIES HAVE ON MY LIVESTOCK?
WELL, NOW, JOE, THAT'S A... WELL, IT'S A PROBLEM, RIGHT?
MY BOYS TELL ME A SLEEVE O' BAD-O MEXICAN DUDES HELD 'EM UP, KILLED THE DELIVERY MAN, AND UP AND RAN OFF WITH THE SHIPMENT.

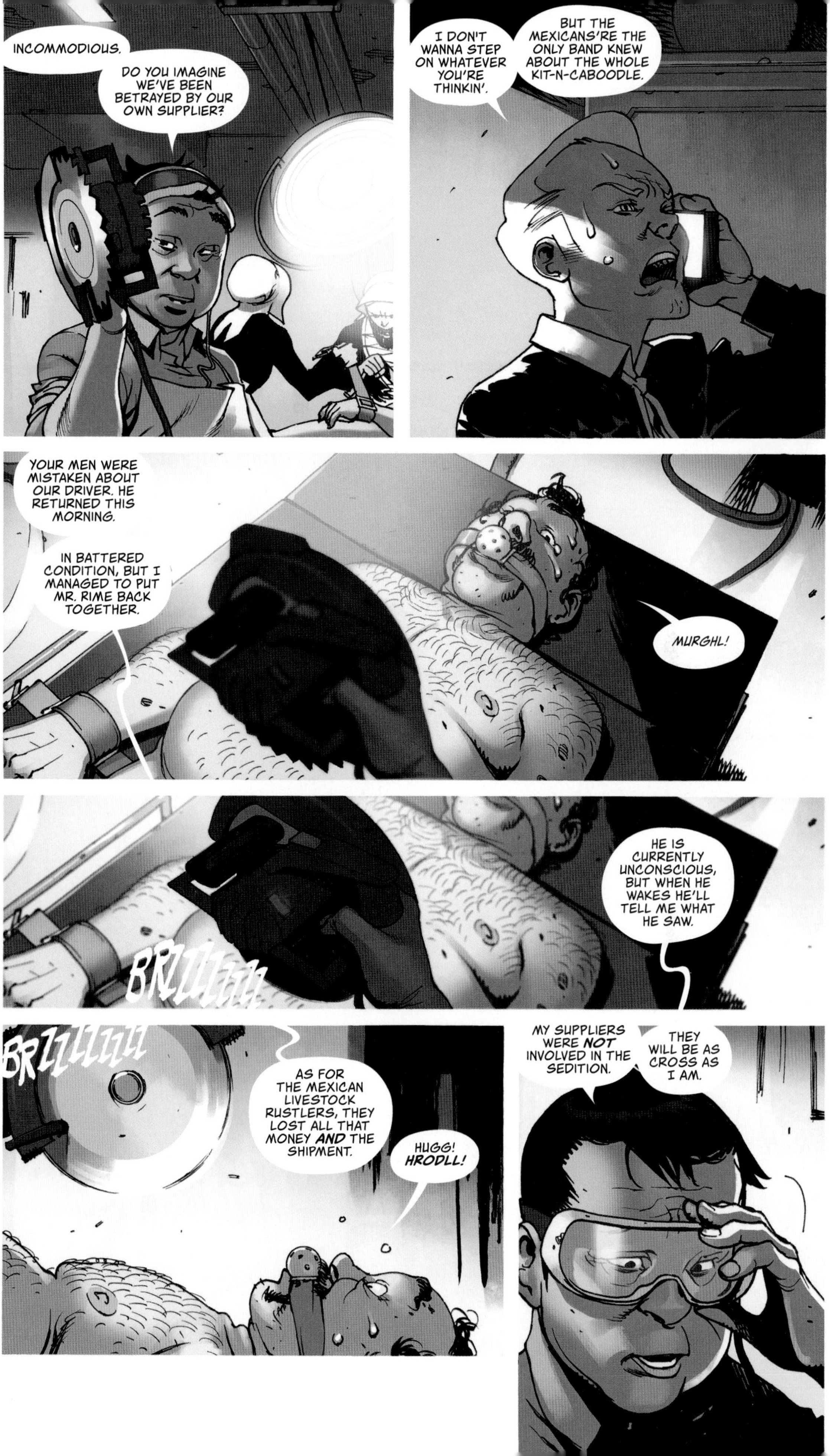
INCOMMODIOUS.
DO YOU IMAGINE WE'VE BEEN BETRAYED BY OUR OWN SUPPLIER?
I DON'T WANNA STEP ON WHATEVER YOU'RE THINKIN'.
BUT THE MEXICANS'RE THE ONLY BAND KNEW ABOUT THE WHOLE KIT-N-CABOODLE.
YOUR MEN WERE MISTAKEN ABOUT OUR DRIVER. HE RETURNED THIS MORNING.
IN BATTERED CONDITION, BUT I MANAGED TO PUT MR. RIME BACK TOGETHER.
MURGHL!
HE IS CURRENTLY UNCONSCIOUS, BUT WHEN HE WAKES HE'LL TELL ME WHAT HE SAW.
BRZZZZZZ
BRZZZZZZZ
AS FOR THE MEXICAN LIVESTOCK RUSTLERS, THEY LOST ALL THAT MONEY AND THE SHIPMENT.
HUGG! HRODLL!
MY SUPPLIERS WERE NOT INVOLVED IN THE SEDITION.
THEY WILL BE AS CROSS AS I AM.

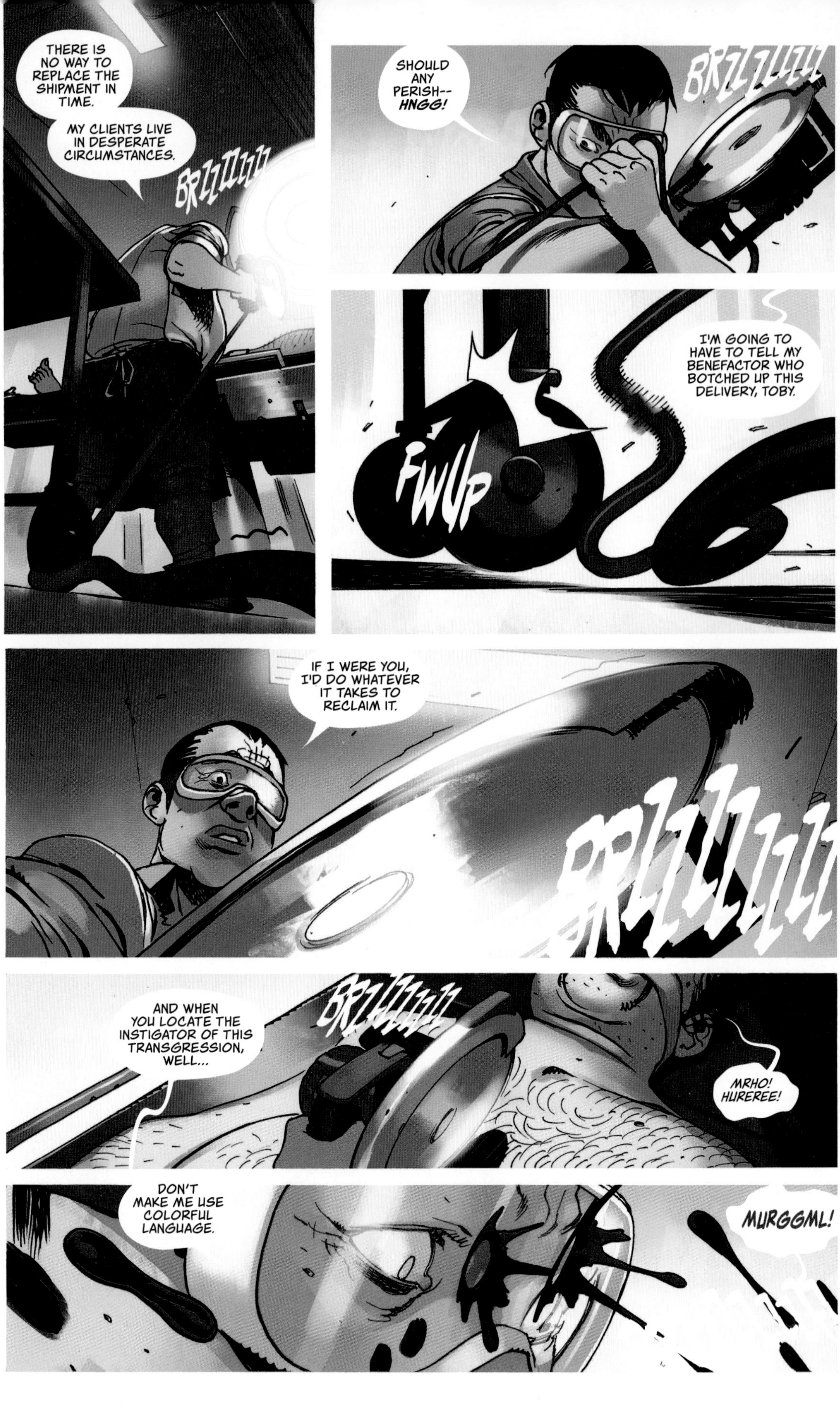
THERE IS NO WAY TO REPLACE THE SHIPMENT IN TIME.
MY CLIENTS LIVE IN DESPERATE CIRCUMSTANCES.
BRZZZZZZZ
SHOULD ANY PERISH-- HNGG!
BRZZZZZZZ
FWUP
I'M GOING TO HAVE TO TELL MY BENEFACTOR WHO BOTCHED UP THIS DELIVERY, TOBY.
IF I WERE YOU, I'D DO WHATEVER IT TAKES TO RECLAIM IT.
BRZZZZZZZ
AND WHEN YOU LOCATE THE INSTIGATOR OF THIS TRANSGRESSION, WELL...
BRZZZZZZZ
MRHO! HUREREE!
DON'T MAKE ME USE COLORFUL LANGUAGE.
MURGGML!

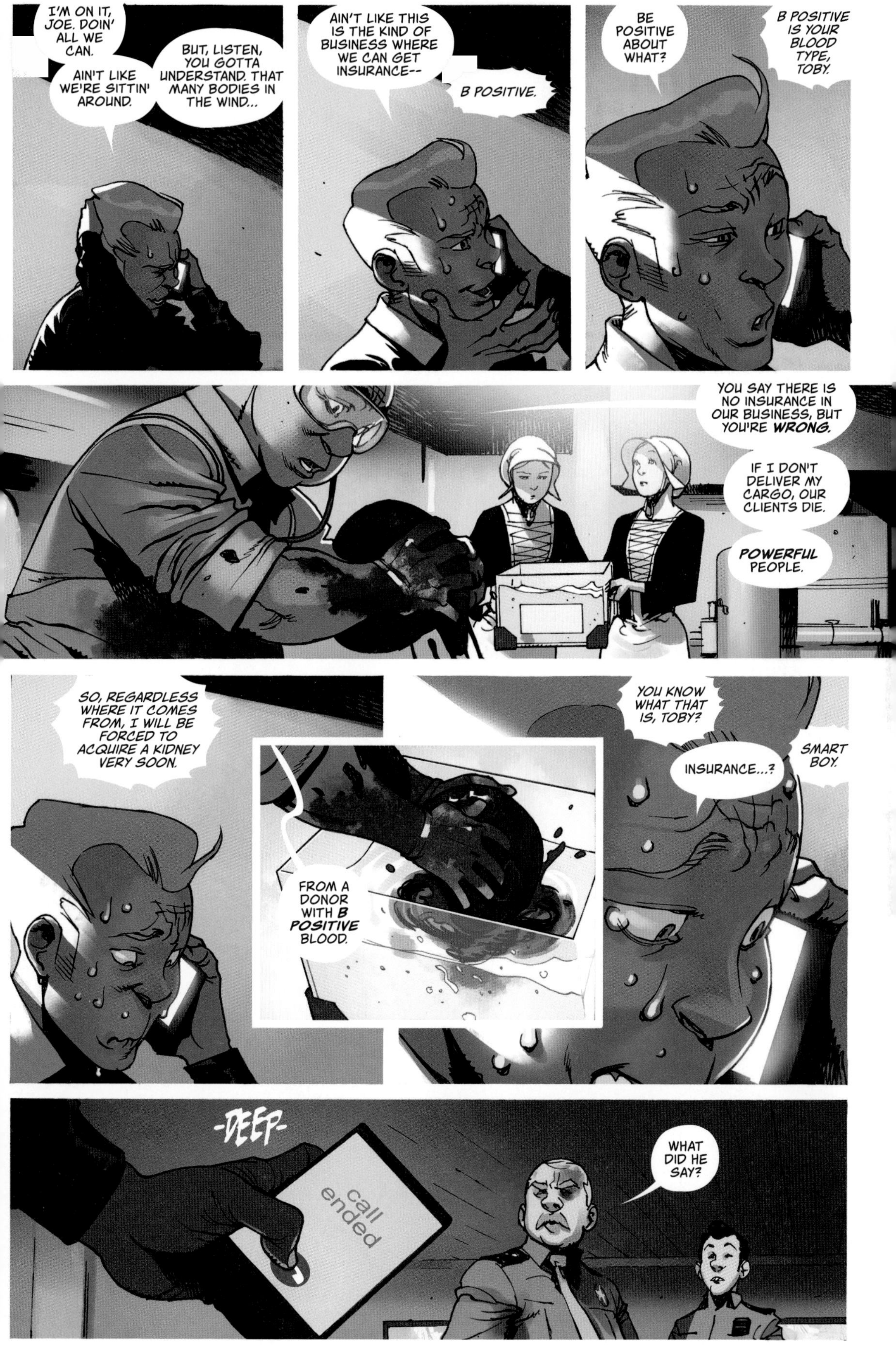
I'M ON IT, JOE. DOIN' ALL WE CAN.
AIN'T LIKE WE'RE SITTIN' AROUND.
BUT, LISTEN, YOU GOTTA UNDERSTAND. THAT MANY BODIES IN THE WIND...
AIN'T LIKE THIS IS THE KIND OF BUSINESS WHERE WE CAN GET INSURANCE--
B POSITIVE.
BE POSITIVE ABOUT WHAT?
B POSITIVE IS YOUR BLOOD TYPE, TOBY.
YOU SAY THERE IS NO INSURANCE IN OUR BUSINESS, BUT YOU'RE WRONG.
IF I DON'T DELIVER MY CARGO, OUR CLIENTS DIE.
POWERFUL PEOPLE.
SO, REGARDLESS WHERE IT COMES FROM, I WILL BE FORCED TO ACQUIRE A KIDNEY VERY SOON.
FROM A DONOR WITH B POSITIVE BLOOD.
YOU KNOW WHAT THAT IS, TOBY?
INSURANCE...?
SMART BOY.
-DEEP-
call ended
WHAT DID HE SAY?

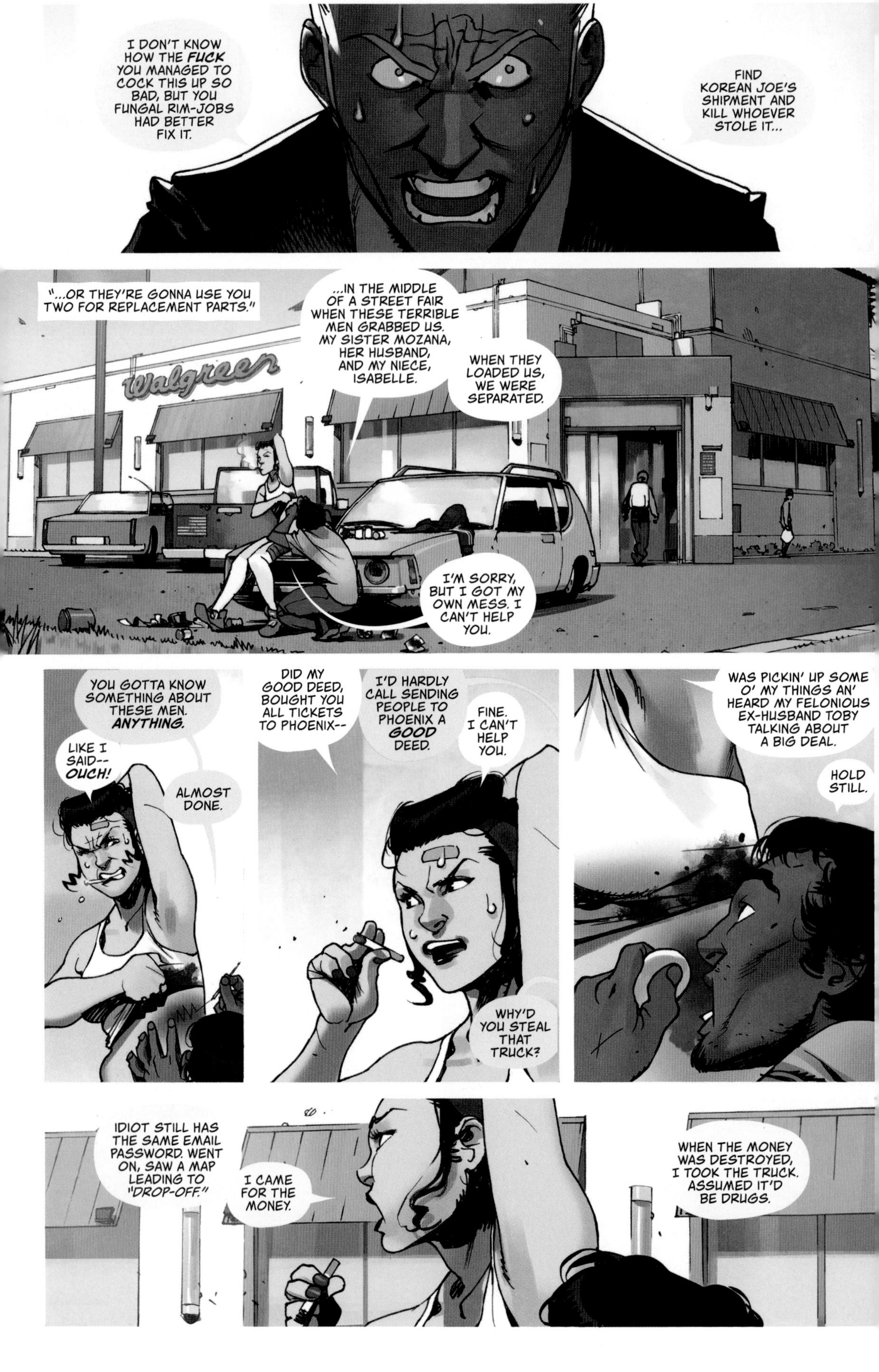
I DON'T KNOW HOW THE FUCK YOU MANAGED TO COCK THIS UP SO BAD, BUT YOU FUNGAL RIM-JOBS HAD BETTER FIX IT.
FIND KOREAN JOE'S SHIPMENT AND KILL WHOEVER STOLE IT...
"...OR THEY'RE GONNA USE YOU TWO FOR REPLACEMENT PARTS."
...IN THE MIDDLE OF A STREET FAIR WHEN THESE TERRIBLE MEN GRABBED US. MY SISTER MOZANA, HER HUSBAND, AND MY NIECE, ISABELLE.
WHEN THEY LOADED US, WE WERE SEPARATED.
I'M SORRY, BUT I GOT MY OWN MESS. I CAN'T HELP YOU.
YOU GOTTA KNOW SOMETHING ABOUT THESE MEN. ANYTHING.
LIKE I SAID-- OUCH!
ALMOST DONE.
DID MY GOOD DEED, BOUGHT YOU ALL TICKETS TO PHOENIX--
I'D HARDLY CALL SENDING PEOPLE TO PHOENIX A GOOD DEED.
FINE. I CAN'T HELP YOU.
WHY'D YOU STEAL THAT TRUCK?
WAS PICKIN' UP SOME O' MY THINGS AN' HEARD MY FELONIOUS EX-HUSBAND TOBY TALKING ABOUT A BIG DEAL.
HOLD STILL.
IDIOT STILL HAS THE SAME EMAIL PASSWORD. WENT ON, SAW A MAP LEADING TO "DROP-OFF."
I CAME FOR THE MONEY.
WHEN THE MONEY WAS DESTROYED, I TOOK THE TRUCK. ASSUMED IT'D BE DRUGS.

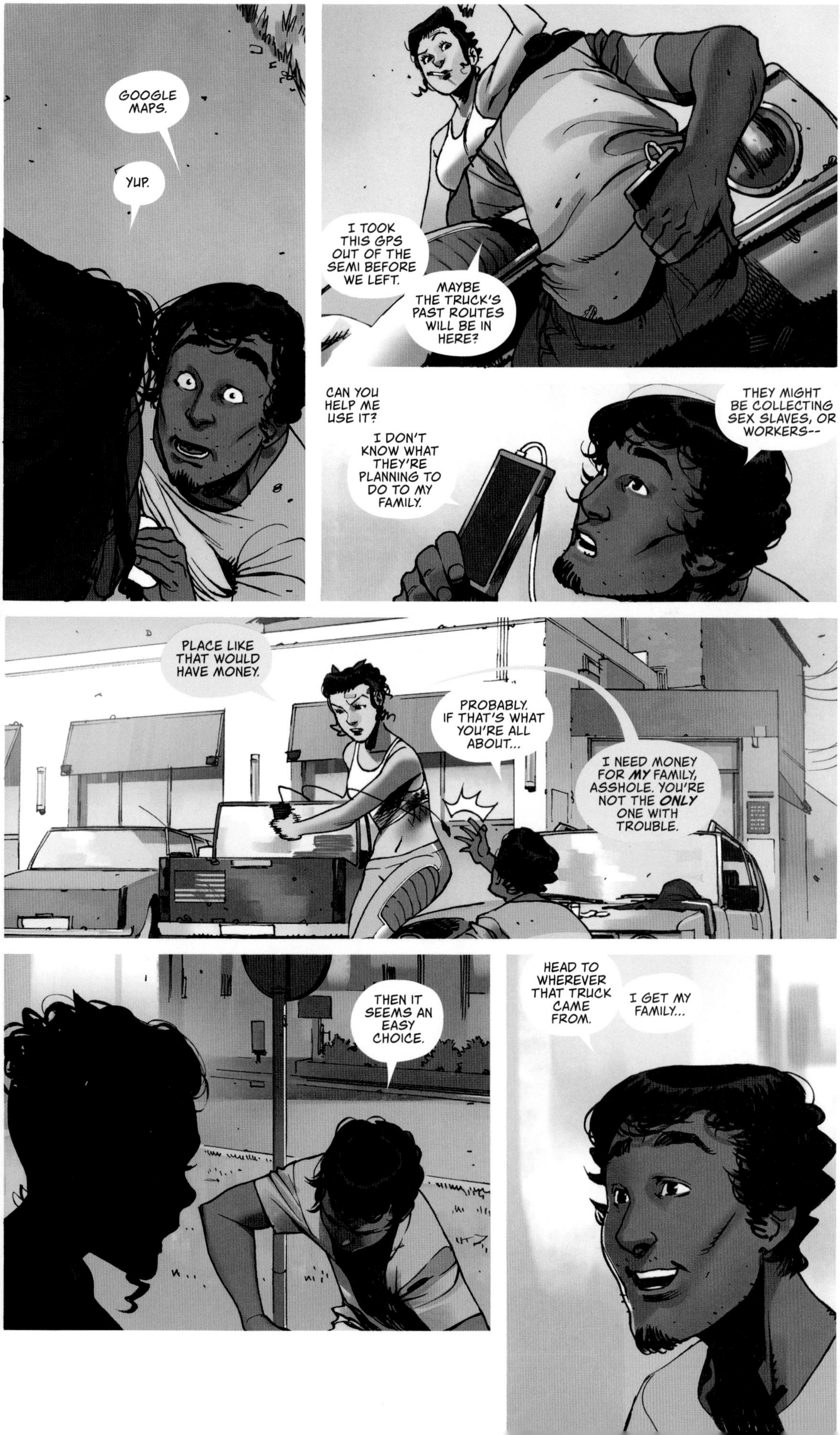
GOOGLE MAPS.
YUP.
I TOOK THIS GPS OUT OF THE SEMI BEFORE WE LEFT.
MAYBE THE TRUCK'S PAST ROUTES WILL BE IN HERE?
CAN YOU HELP ME USE IT?
I DON'T KNOW WHAT THEY'RE PLANNING TO DO TO MY FAMILY.
THEY MIGHT BE COLLECTING SEX SLAVES, OR WORKERS--
PLACE LIKE THAT WOULD HAVE MONEY.
PROBABLY. IF THAT'S WHAT YOU'RE ALL ABOUT...
I NEED MONEY FOR *MY* FAMILY, ASSHOLE. YOU'RE NOT THE *ONLY* ONE WITH TROUBLE.
THEN IT SEEMS AN EASY CHOICE.
HEAD TO WHEREVER THAT TRUCK CAME FROM.
I GET MY FAMILY...

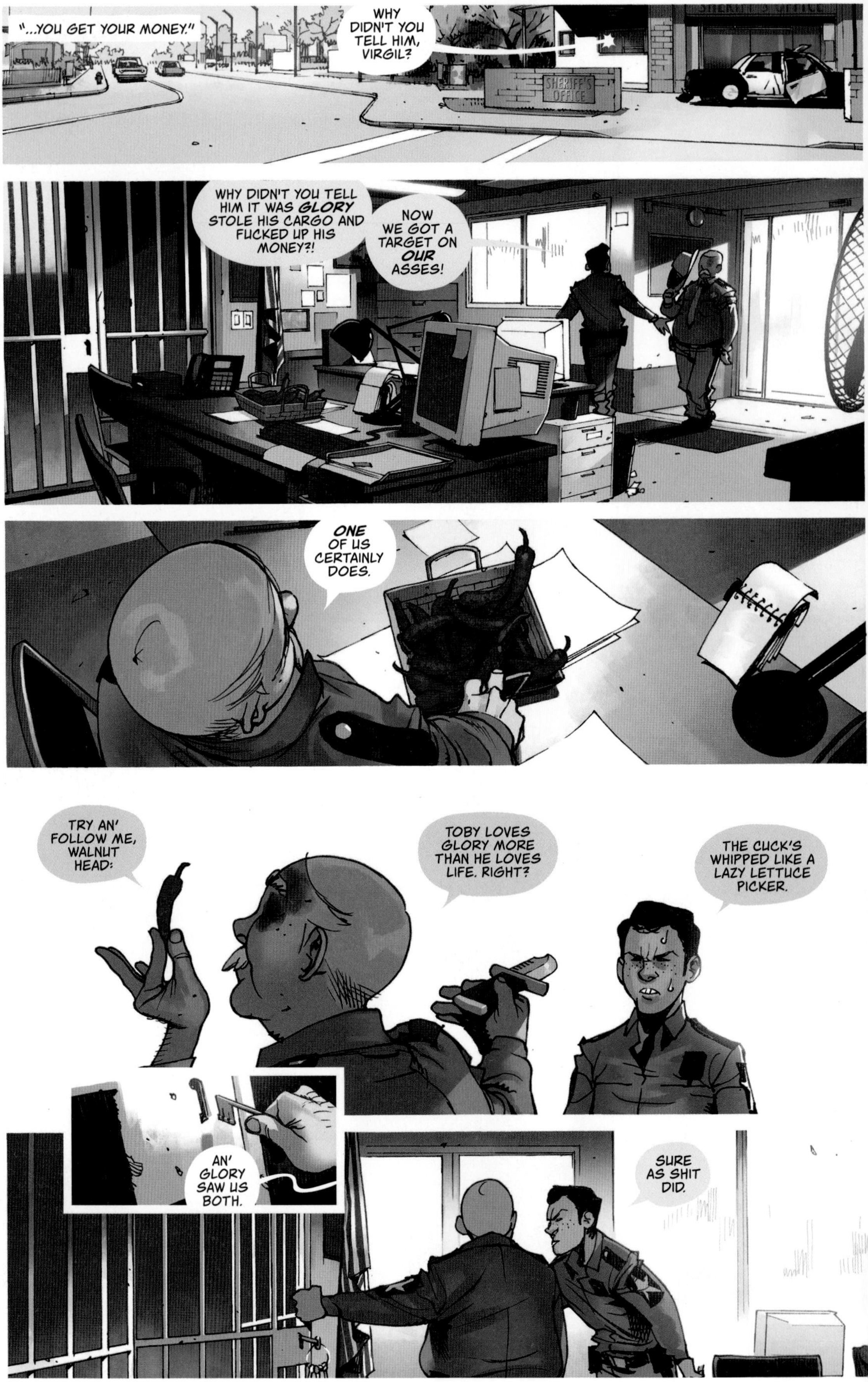
"...YOU GET YOUR MONEY."
WHY DIDN'T YOU TELL HIM, VIRGIL?
SHERIFF'S OFFICE
WHY DIDN'T YOU TELL HIM IT WAS GLORY STOLE HIS CARGO AND FUCKED UP HIS MONEY?!
NOW WE GOT A TARGET ON OUR ASSES!
ONE OF US CERTAINLY DOES.
TRY AN' FOLLOW ME, WALNUT HEAD:
TOBY LOVES GLORY MORE THAN HE LOVES LIFE. RIGHT?
THE CUCK'S WHIPPED LIKE A LAZY LETTUCE PICKER.
AN' GLORY SAW US BOTH.
SURE AS SHIT DID.

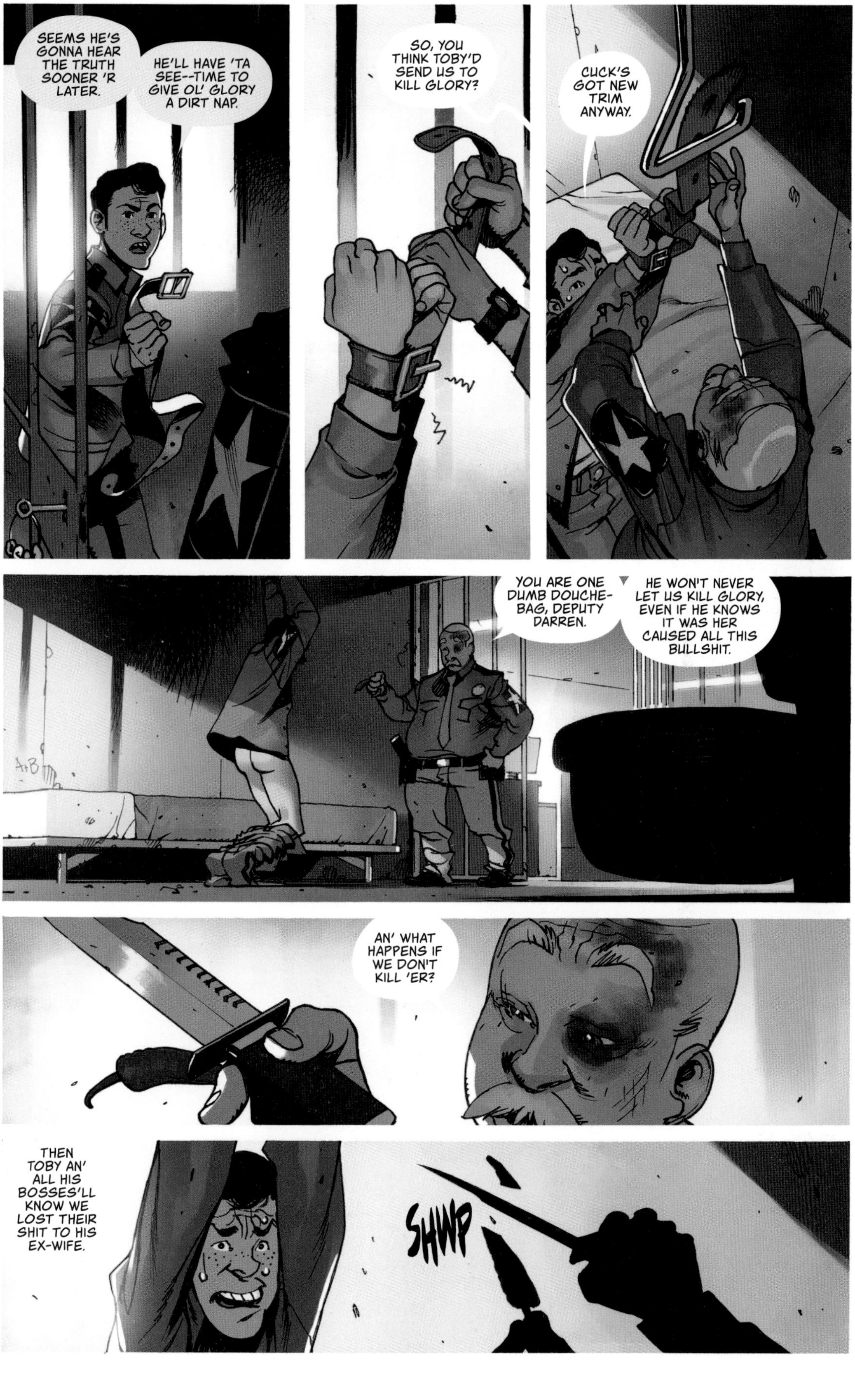
SEEMS HE'S GONNA HEAR THE TRUTH SOONER 'R LATER.
HE'LL HAVE 'TA SEE--TIME TO GIVE OL' GLORY A DIRT NAP.
SO, YOU THINK TOBY'D SEND US TO KILL GLORY?
CUCK'S GOT NEW TRIM ANYWAY.
YOU ARE ONE DUMB DOUCHE-BAG, DEPUTY DARREN.
HE WON'T NEVER LET US KILL GLORY, EVEN IF HE KNOWS IT WAS HER CAUSED ALL THIS BULLSHIT.
AN' WHAT HAPPENS IF WE DON'T KILL 'ER?
THEN TOBY AN' ALL HIS BOSSES'LL KNOW WE LOST THEIR SHIT TO HIS EX-WIFE.
SHWP

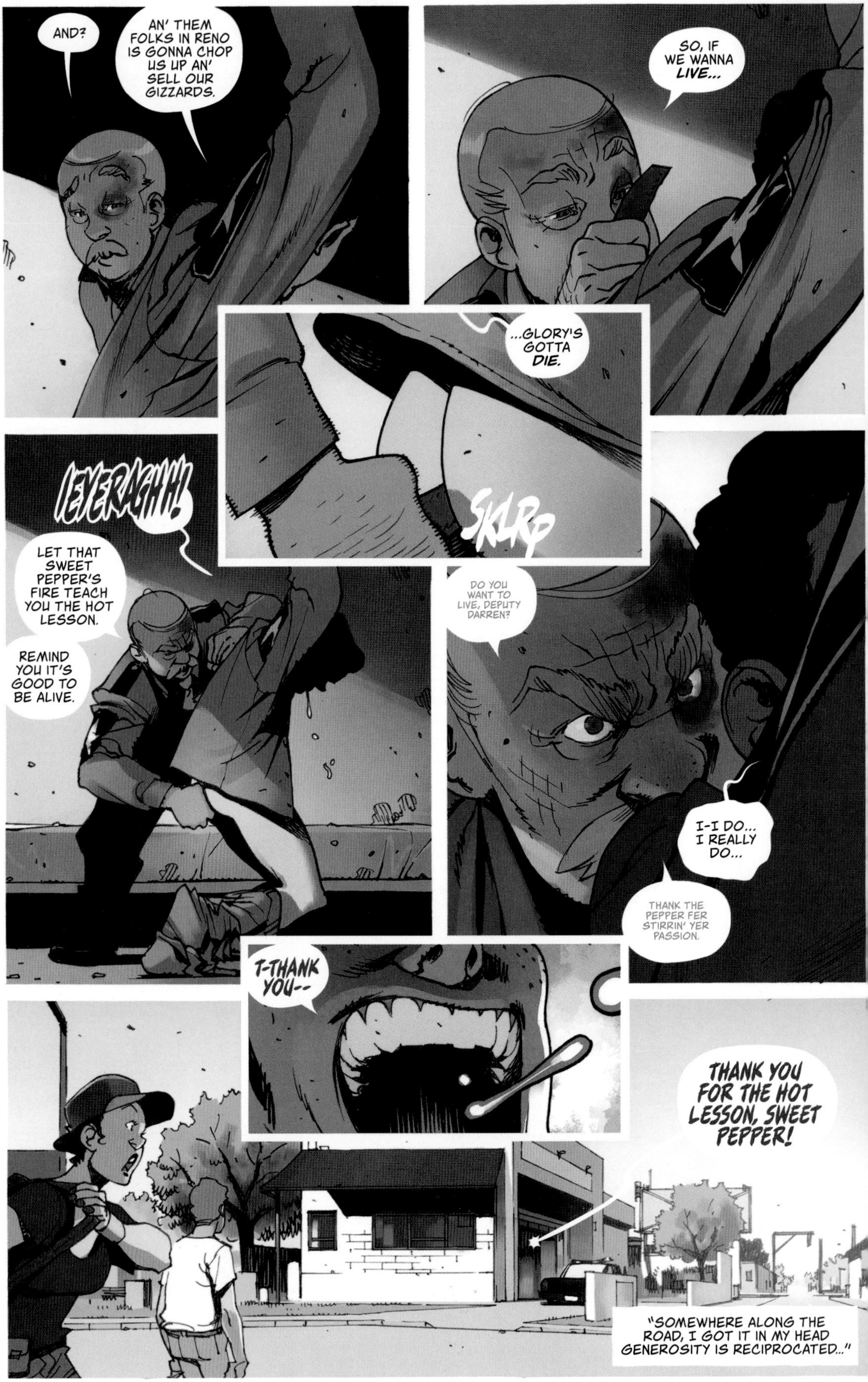
AND?
AN' THEM FOLKS IN RENO IS GONNA CHOP US UP AN' SELL OUR GIZZARDS.
SO, IF WE WANNA LIVE...
...GLORY'S GOTTA DIE.
SKLRP
IEYERAGHH!
LET THAT SWEET PEPPER'S FIRE TEACH YOU THE HOT LESSON.
REMIND YOU IT'S GOOD TO BE ALIVE.
DO YOU WANT TO LIVE, DEPUTY DARREN?
I-I DO... I REALLY DO...
THANK THE PEPPER FER STIRRIN' YER PASSION.
T-THANK YOU--
THANK YOU FOR THE HOT LESSON, SWEET PEPPER!
"SOMEWHERE ALONG THE ROAD, I GOT IT IN MY HEAD GENEROSITY IS RECIPROCATED..."

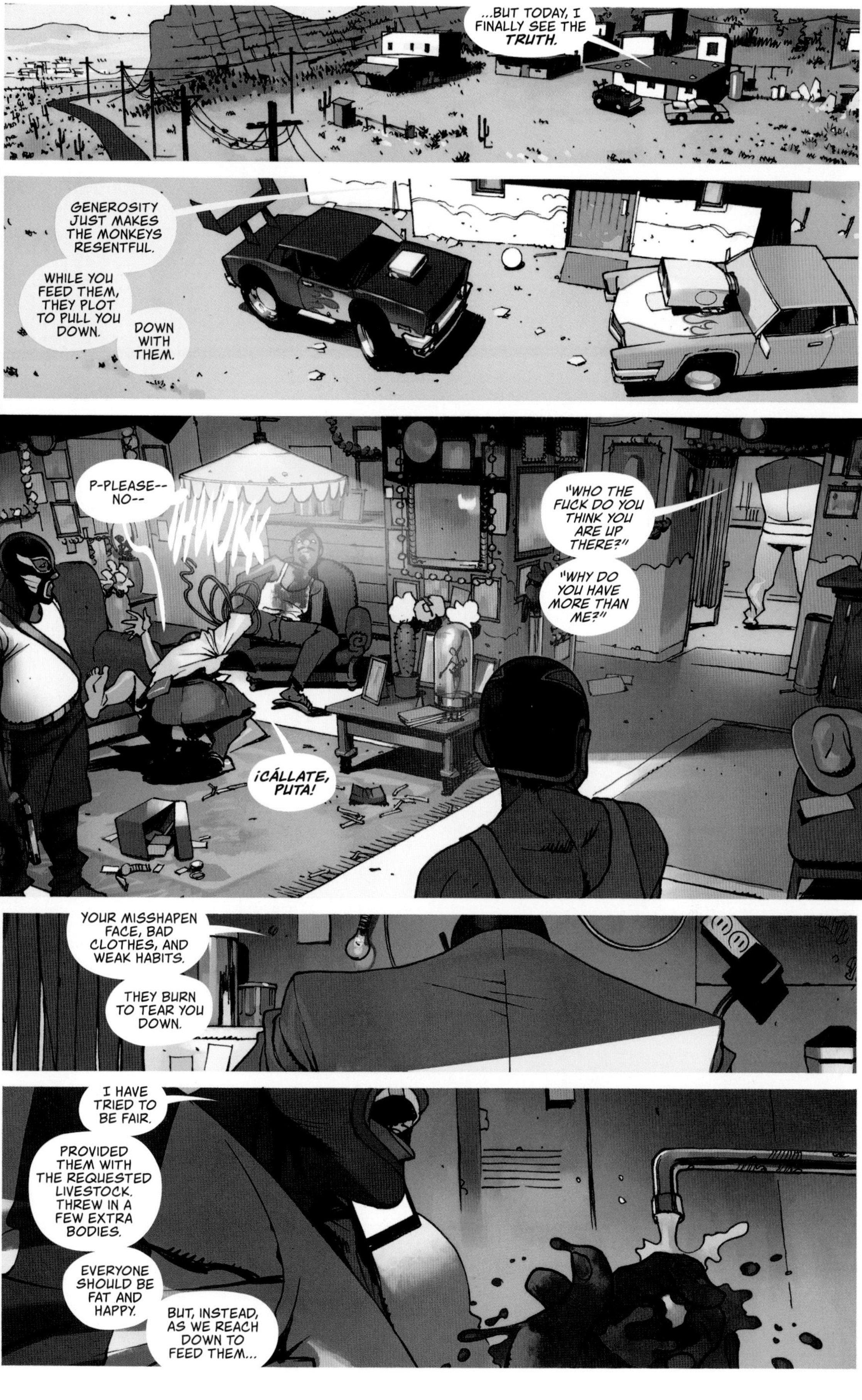
...BUT TODAY, I FINALLY SEE THE TRUTH.
GENEROSITY JUST MAKES THE MONKEYS RESENTFUL.
WHILE YOU FEED THEM, THEY PLOT TO PULL YOU DOWN.
DOWN WITH THEM.
P-PLEASE-- NO--
THWOKK
"WHO THE FUCK DO YOU THINK YOU ARE UP THERE?"
"WHY DO YOU HAVE MORE THAN ME?"
¡CÁLLATE, PUTA!
YOUR MISSHAPEN FACE, BAD CLOTHES, AND WEAK HABITS.
THEY BURN TO TEAR YOU DOWN.
I HAVE TRIED TO BE FAIR.
PROVIDED THEM WITH THE REQUESTED LIVESTOCK. THREW IN A FEW EXTRA BODIES.
EVERYONE SHOULD BE FAT AND HAPPY.
BUT, INSTEAD, AS WE REACH DOWN TO FEED THEM...

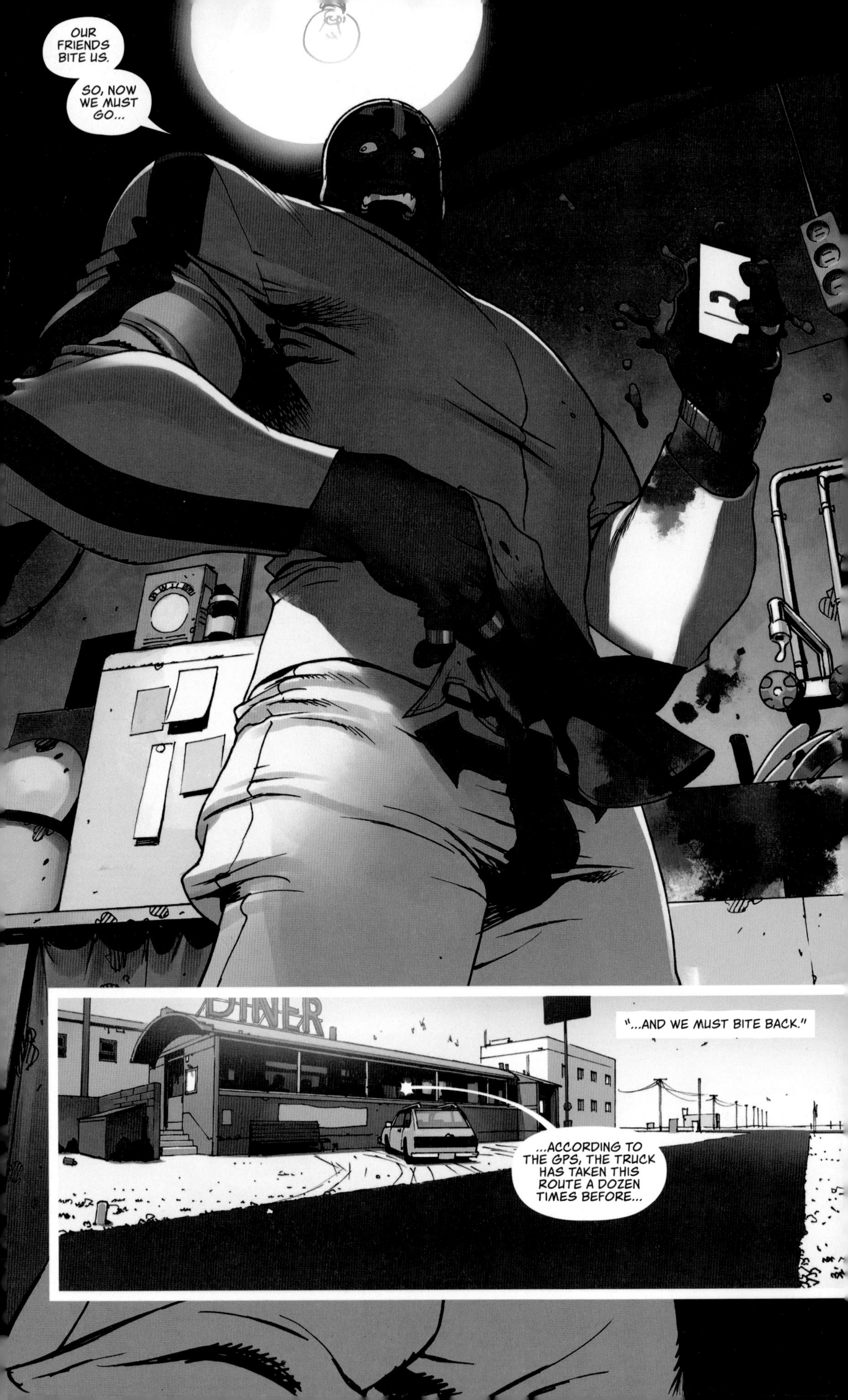
OUR FRIENDS BITE US.
SO, NOW WE MUST GO...
"...AND WE MUST BITE BACK."
...ACCORDING TO THE GPS, THE TRUCK HAS TAKEN THIS ROUTE A DOZEN TIMES BEFORE...

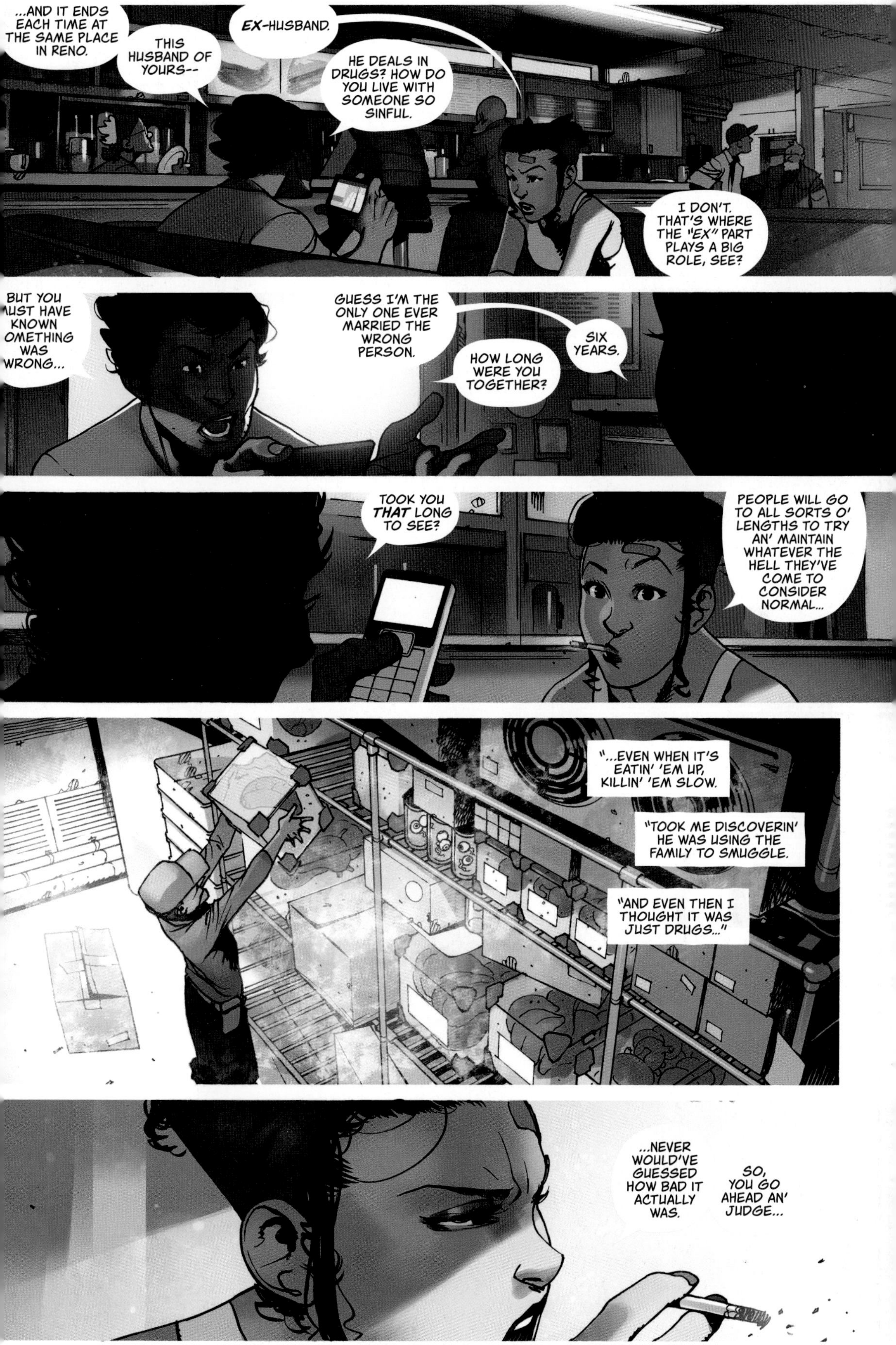
...AND IT ENDS EACH TIME AT THE SAME PLACE IN RENO.
THIS HUSBAND OF YOURS--
EX-HUSBAND.
HE DEALS IN DRUGS? HOW DO YOU LIVE WITH SOMEONE SO SINFUL.
I DON'T. THAT'S WHERE THE "EX" PART PLAYS A BIG ROLE, SEE?
BUT YOU MUST HAVE KNOWN SOMETHING WAS WRONG...
GUESS I'M THE ONLY ONE EVER MARRIED THE WRONG PERSON.
HOW LONG WERE YOU TOGETHER?
SIX YEARS.
TOOK YOU THAT LONG TO SEE?
PEOPLE WILL GO TO ALL SORTS O' LENGTHS TO TRY AN' MAINTAIN WHATEVER THE HELL THEY'VE COME TO CONSIDER NORMAL...
"...EVEN WHEN IT'S EATIN' 'EM UP, KILLIN' 'EM SLOW.
"TOOK ME DISCOVERIN' HE WAS USING THE FAMILY TO SMUGGLE.
"AND EVEN THEN I THOUGHT IT WAS JUST DRUGS..."
...NEVER WOULD'VE GUESSED HOW BAD IT ACTUALLY WAS.
SO, YOU GO AHEAD AN' JUDGE...

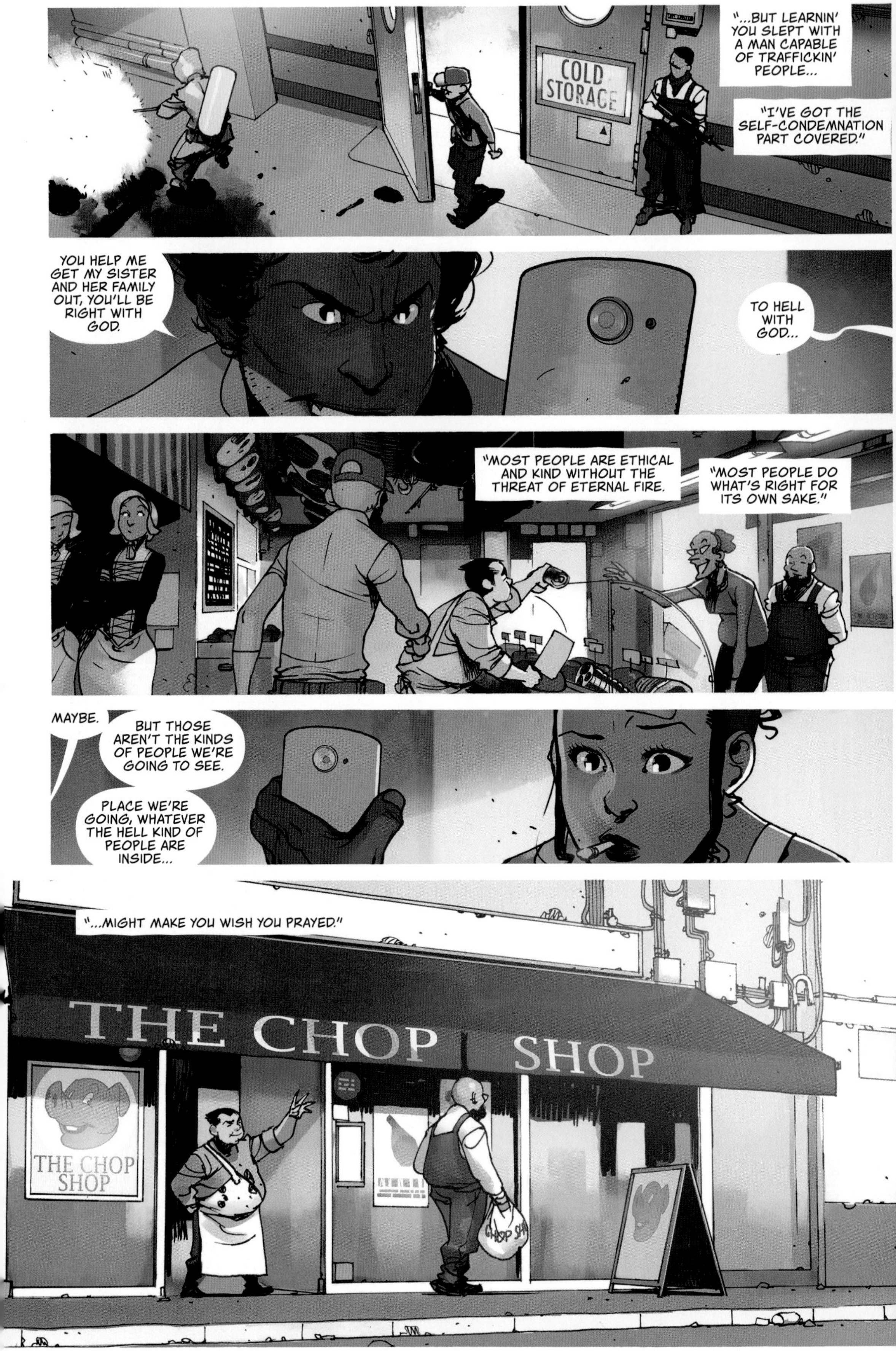
"...BUT LEARNIN' YOU SLEPT WITH A MAN CAPABLE OF TRAFFICKIN' PEOPLE...
"I'VE GOT THE SELF-CONDEMNATION PART COVERED."
COLD STORAGE
YOU HELP ME GET MY SISTER AND HER FAMILY OUT, YOU'LL BE RIGHT WITH GOD.
TO HELL WITH GOD...
"MOST PEOPLE ARE ETHICAL AND KIND WITHOUT THE THREAT OF ETERNAL FIRE.
"MOST PEOPLE DO WHAT'S RIGHT FOR ITS OWN SAKE."
MAYBE.
BUT THOSE AREN'T THE KINDS OF PEOPLE WE'RE GOING TO SEE.
PLACE WE'RE GOING, WHATEVER THE HELL KIND OF PEOPLE ARE INSIDE...
"...MIGHT MAKE YOU WISH YOU PRAYED."
THE CHOP SHOP
THE CHOP SHOP
CHOP SHO

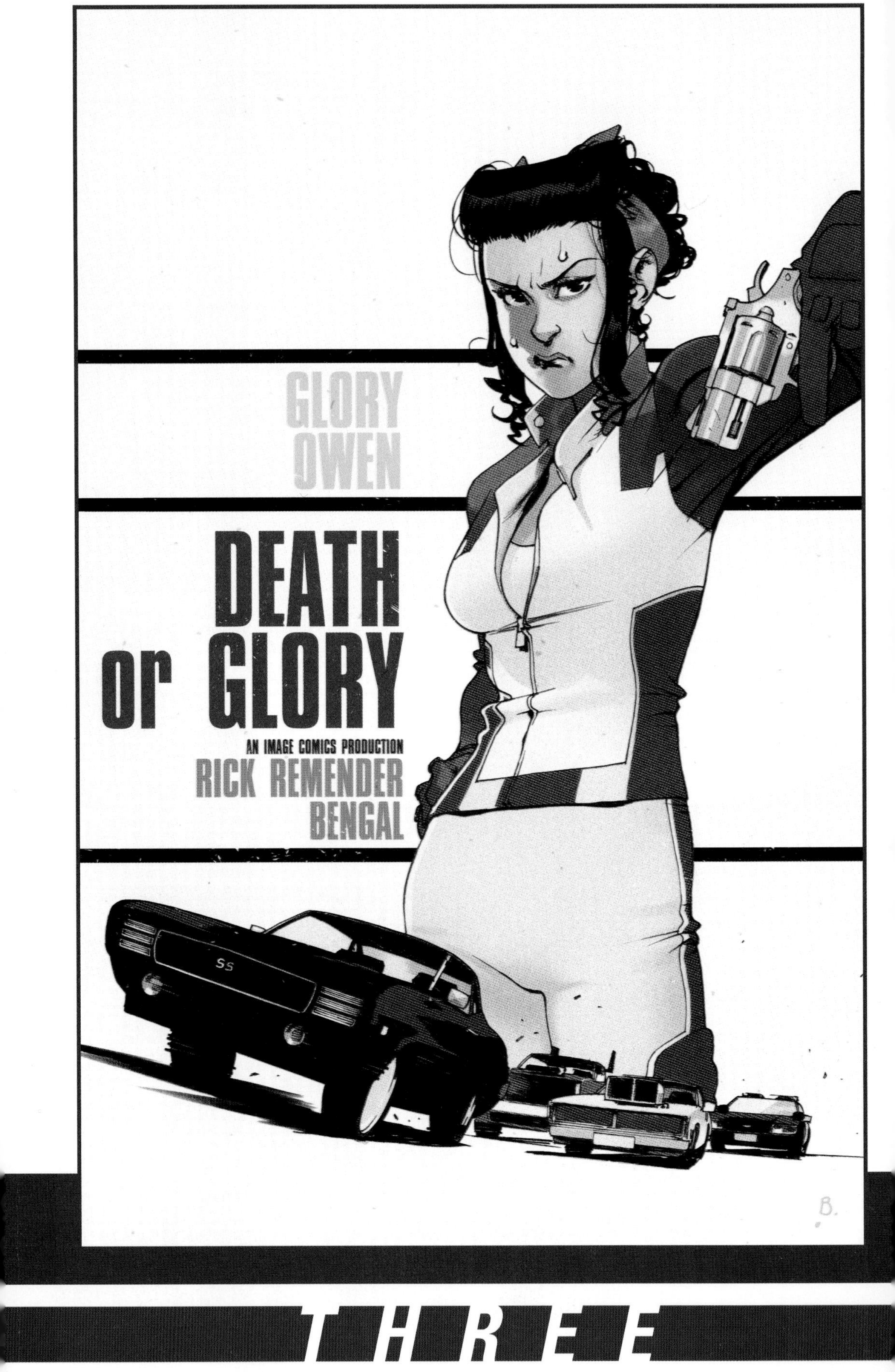
GLORY
OWEN
DEATH
or GLORY
AN IMAGE COMICS PRODUCTION
RICK REMENDER
BENGAL
SS
B.

THREE

WE'VE ALL BEEN STUCK IN SOMETHING WE COULDN'T GET OUT OF.

RIDDLED WITH ANXIETY AND DREAMS OF PACKIN' IT ALL UP, UNPLUGGING FROM THE GAME, AND HEADIN' OFF INTO THE UNKNOWN HORIZON.

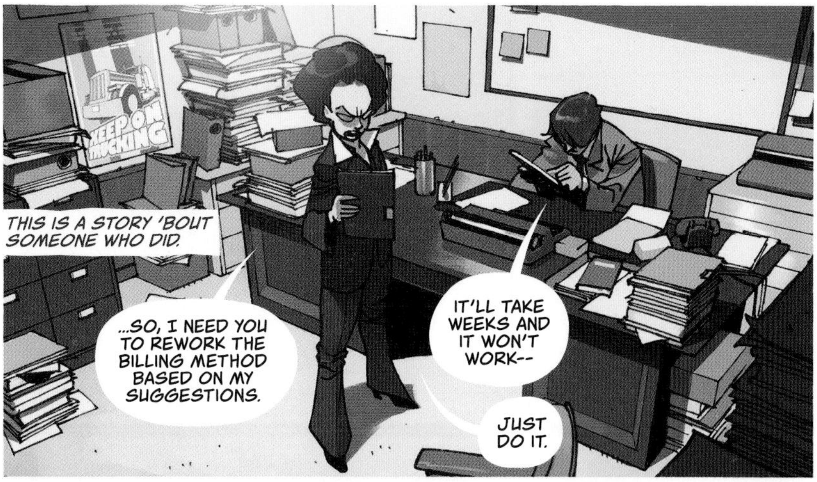
KEEP ON TRUCKING
THIS IS A STORY 'BOUT SOMEONE WHO DID.
...SO, I NEED YOU TO REWORK THE BILLING METHOD BASED ON MY SUGGESTIONS.
IT'LL TAKE WEEKS AND IT WON'T WORK--
JUST DO IT.

NOW, ALL MY LIFE, I'VE ONLY EVER KNOWN RED TO BE ENTIRELY FREE OF SHACKLES...

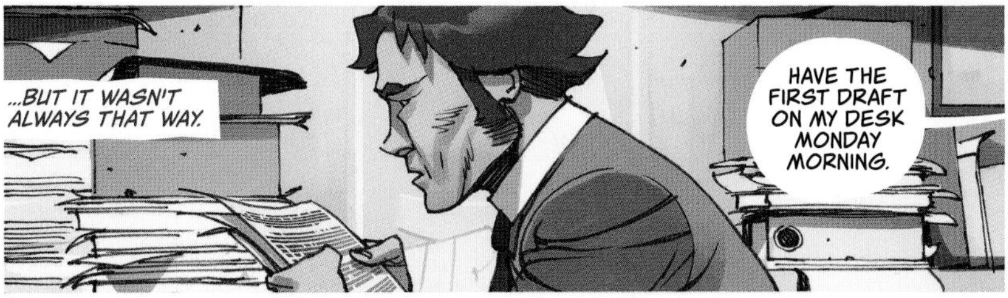
...BUT IT WASN'T ALWAYS THAT WAY.
HAVE THE FIRST DRAFT ON MY DESK MONDAY MORNING.

NO MATTER HOW HARD MOM AND RED WORKED, THEY COULDN'T GET AHEAD.

AN' THEY NEVER HAD TIME FOR EACH OTHER.

WHEN YOUR MARRIAGE BECOMES ALL ABOUT HOLDING THINGS TOGETHER WITH NO TIME FOR LOVE AND JOY...

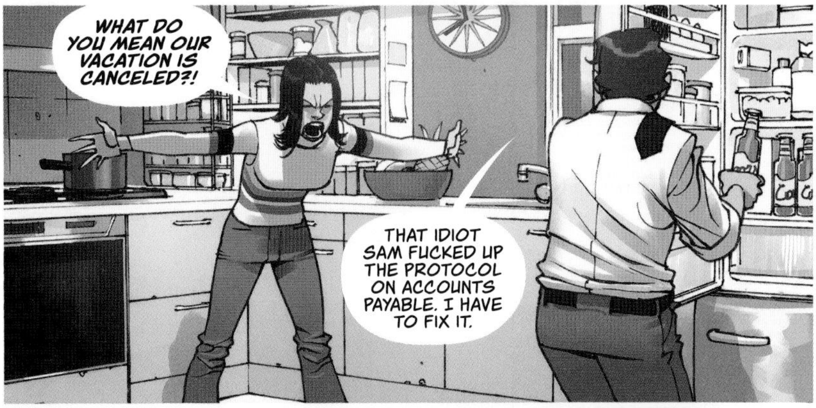
WHAT DO YOU MEAN OUR VACATION IS CANCELED?!
THAT IDIOT SAM FUCKED UP THE PROTOCOL ON ACCOUNTS PAYABLE. I HAVE TO FIX IT.

MOM WAS DONE. RED HAD FORGOTTEN WHY HE WAS EVEN WAKING UP IN THE MORNING.

EVERY DAY WAS A WASH, ONE BLURRING INTO THE NEXT.

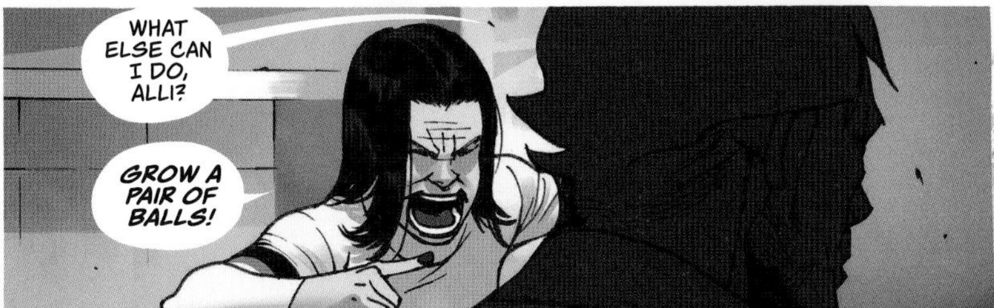
WHAT ELSE CAN I DO, ALLI?
GROW A PAIR OF BALLS!

THEY FOUGHT ALL NIGHT.

VOMITING UP YEARS OF FRUSTRATION.

THEY TORE INTO EACH OTHER AS DEEP AS THEY COULD.

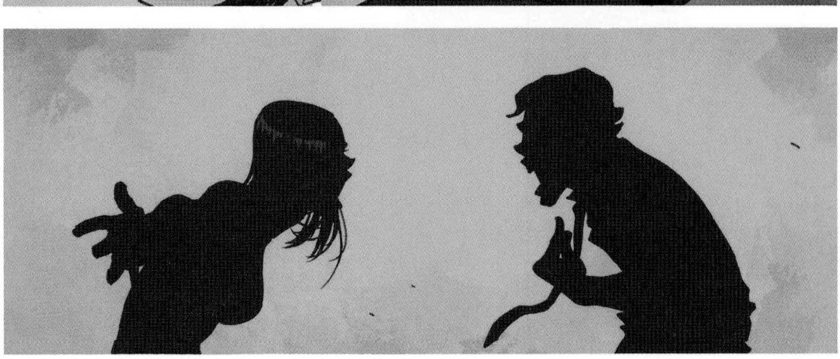

BY THE TIME RED LEFT FOR WORK THE NEXT MORNING, THEY'D DECIDED THE ONLY WAY FORWARD WAS DIVORCE.

IT WAS A SATURDAY.

IT WAS ALSO RED'S THIRTY-FIFTH BIRTHDAY.

HE WAS BROKENHEARTED OVER HIS FAILING MARRIAGE BUT HAD NO IDEA HOW TO FIX IT.

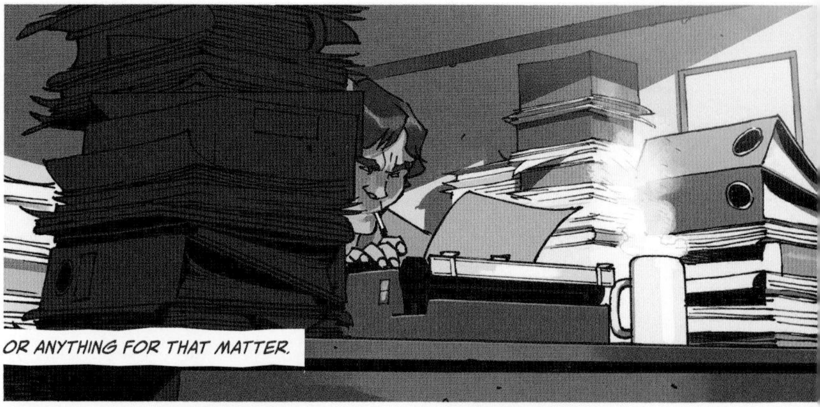
OR ANYTHING FOR THAT MATTER.

HE'D TAKEN THAT JOB WHEN HE WAS JUST A YOUNG MAN. EVERYONE AROUND HIM TOLD HIM HOW LUCKY HE WAS TO HAVE IT.

THEY TOLD HIM NOT TO RUFFLE HIS SUPERIOR'S FEATHERS, OUTPERFORM HIS CONTEMPORARIES, STAY THE COURSE AND CLIMB ONE RUNG AT A TIME.

BUT ALL THESE YEARS LATER...

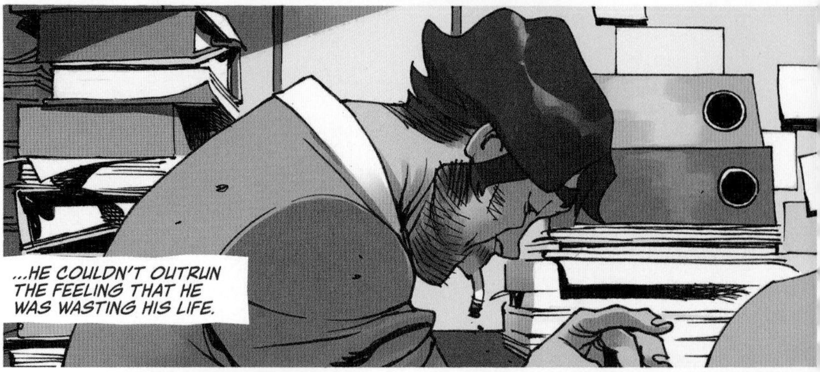
...HE COULDN'T OUTRUN THE FEELING THAT HE WAS WASTING HIS LIFE.

HE NEVER TOLD ME EXACTLY WHAT INSPIRED IT, MAYBE HE'D BEEN THINKING ABOUT IT FOR YEARS, I DON'T KNOW.

BUT THAT SATURDAY MORNING SOMETHING WOKE HIM UP.

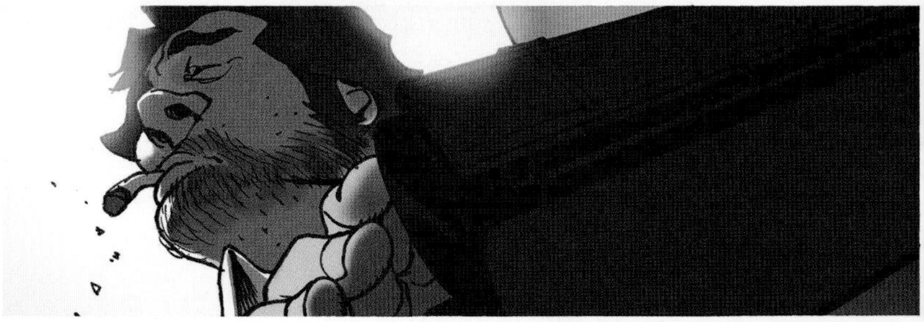

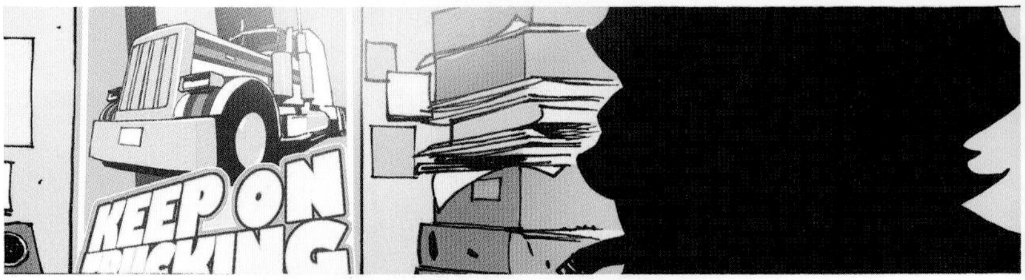
KEEP ON

HE TOOK A PIECE OF PAPER AND WROTE HIS RESIGNATION.

WHAT HE WROTE STANDS AS ONE OF MY FAVORITE THINGS IN THE WHOLE WORLD...

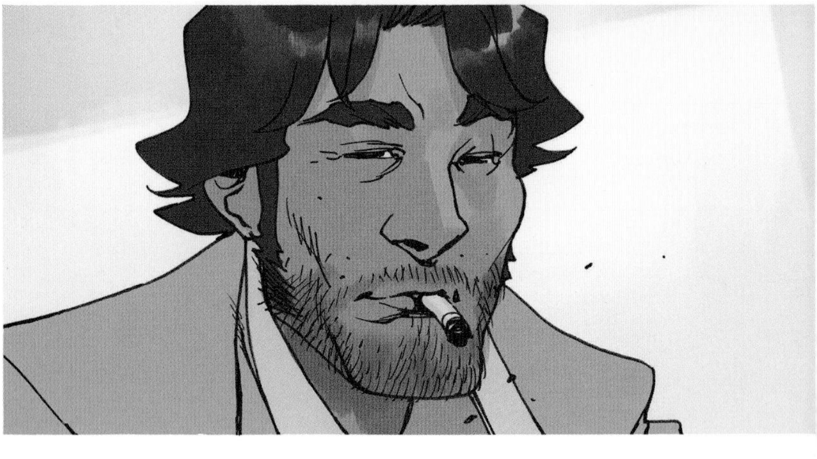

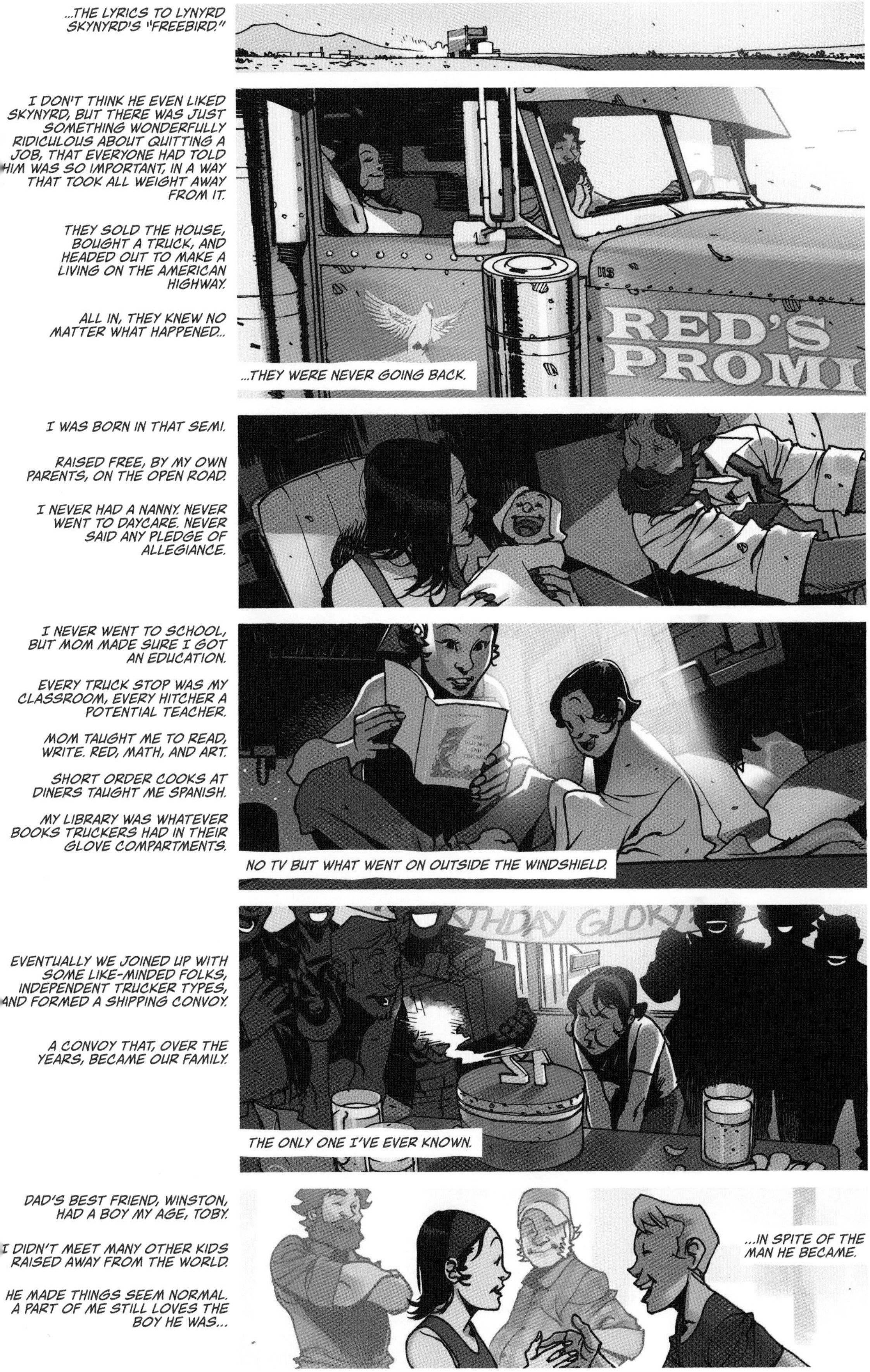
...THE LYRICS TO LYNYRD SKYNYRD'S "FREEBIRD."
I DON'T THINK HE EVEN LIKED SKYNYRD, BUT THERE WAS JUST SOMETHING WONDERFULLY RIDICULOUS ABOUT QUITTING A JOB, THAT EVERYONE HAD TOLD HIM WAS SO IMPORTANT, IN A WAY THAT TOOK ALL WEIGHT AWAY FROM IT.
THEY SOLD THE HOUSE, BOUGHT A TRUCK, AND HEADED OUT TO MAKE A LIVING ON THE AMERICAN HIGHWAY.
ALL IN, THEY KNEW NO MATTER WHAT HAPPENED...
...THEY WERE NEVER GOING BACK.
RED'S PROMI
I WAS BORN IN THAT SEMI.
RAISED FREE, BY MY OWN PARENTS, ON THE OPEN ROAD.
I NEVER HAD A NANNY. NEVER WENT TO DAYCARE. NEVER SAID ANY PLEDGE OF ALLEGIANCE.
I NEVER WENT TO SCHOOL, BUT MOM MADE SURE I GOT AN EDUCATION.
EVERY TRUCK STOP WAS MY CLASSROOM, EVERY HITCHER A POTENTIAL TEACHER.
MOM TAUGHT ME TO READ, WRITE. RED, MATH, AND ART.
SHORT ORDER COOKS AT DINERS TAUGHT ME SPANISH.
MY LIBRARY WAS WHATEVER BOOKS TRUCKERS HAD IN THEIR GLOVE COMPARTMENTS.
NO TV BUT WHAT WENT ON OUTSIDE THE WINDSHIELD.
EVENTUALLY WE JOINED UP WITH SOME LIKE-MINDED FOLKS, INDEPENDENT TRUCKER TYPES, AND FORMED A SHIPPING CONVOY.
A CONVOY THAT, OVER THE YEARS, BECAME OUR FAMILY.
THE ONLY ONE I'VE EVER KNOWN.
DAD'S BEST FRIEND, WINSTON, HAD A BOY MY AGE, TOBY.
I DIDN'T MEET MANY OTHER KIDS RAISED AWAY FROM THE WORLD.
HE MADE THINGS SEEM NORMAL. A PART OF ME STILL LOVES THE BOY HE WAS...
...IN SPITE OF THE MAN HE BECAME.

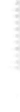

AND THAT'S HOW LIFE WAS FOR A LONG TIME.

UNTIL THE SUMMER OF MY TWELFTH BIRTHDAY. WE WERE ON OUR WAY TO YOSEMITE FOR A BIG CAMPING TRIP. ALL THE WAY UP I WAS COMPLAINING ABOUT THE FOOD CHOICES, DETERMINED TO GET MY MOM'S FRIED CHICKEN.

WHEN YOU'RE A KID YOU GET YOUR HEAD STUCK ON THINGS LIKE THAT.

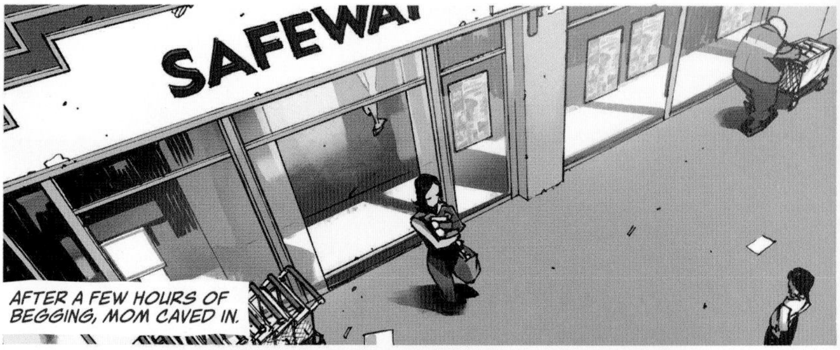
SAFEWA
AFTER A FEW HOURS OF BEGGING, MOM CAVED IN.

RED DROPPED HER OFF TO PICK UP THE INGREDIENTS TO MAKE HER MAGIC FRIED CHICKEN FOR ME.

ON HER WAY TO MEET US, SHE RAN INTO A MAN WHO'D SHOT HIS WIFE WHO WAS LEAVING HIM.

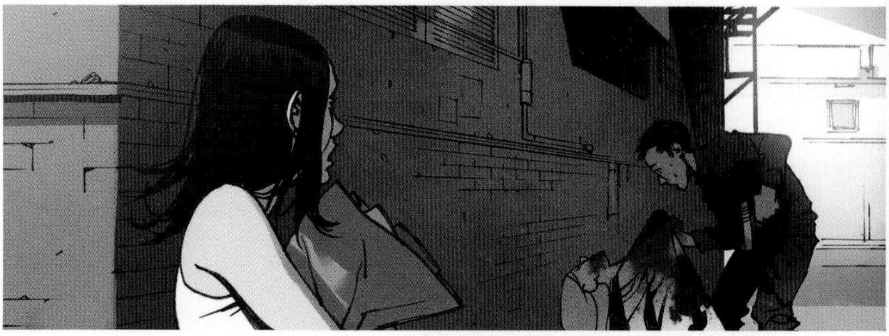

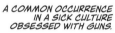

BAD STRANGE LUCK.

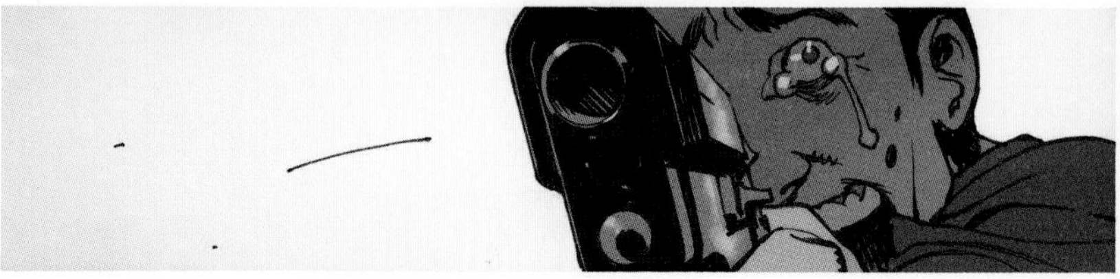

A COMMON OCCURRENCE IN A SICK CULTURE OBSESSED WITH GUNS.

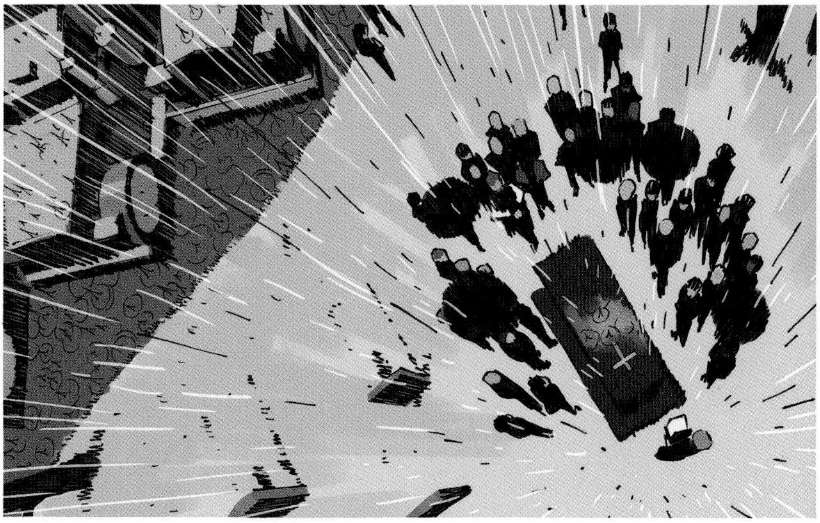

THE GRAND CANYON WAS MOM'S FAVORITE PLACE IN THE WORLD.

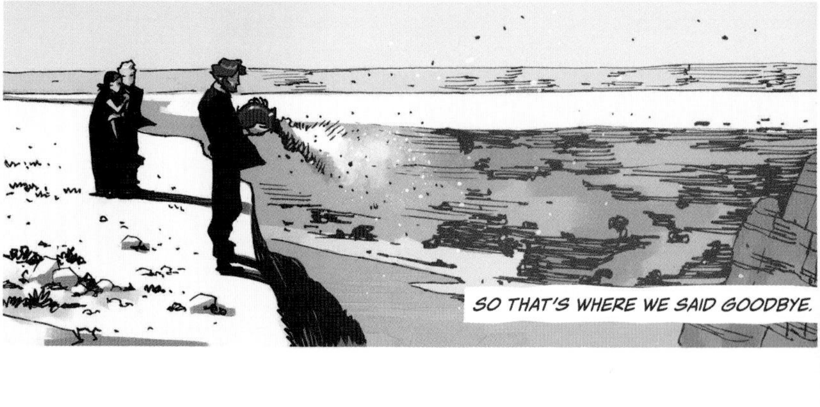
SO THAT'S WHERE WE SAID GOODBYE.

WE DID OUR BEST TO MOVE ON.

RED AND MOM HAD PROMISED EACH OTHER THAT IF ANYTHING EVER HAPPENED TO ONE, THE OTHER WOULD STAY THE COURSE.

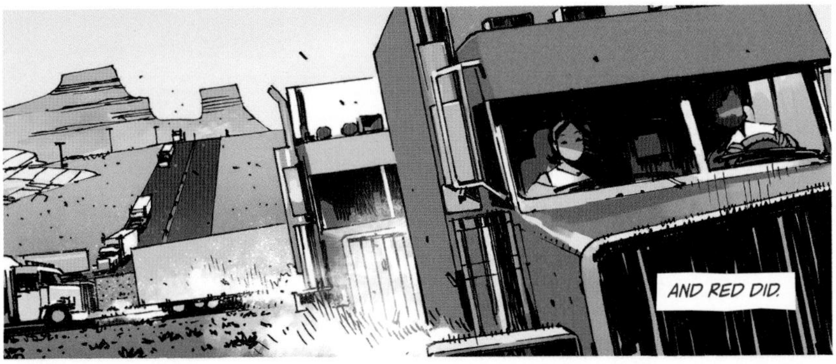
AND RED DID.

BUT LOSING MOM ONLY SOLIDIFIED RED'S IDEALS. THE WORLD HAD GONE MAD. BETTER TO STAY AWAY FROM IT. IT MADE HIM SUSPICIOUS OF EVERYONE.

WE PULLED EVEN FURTHER AWAY FROM "NORMAL" SOCIETY. IF SOMEONE WASN'T A MEMBER OF OUR CONVOY...

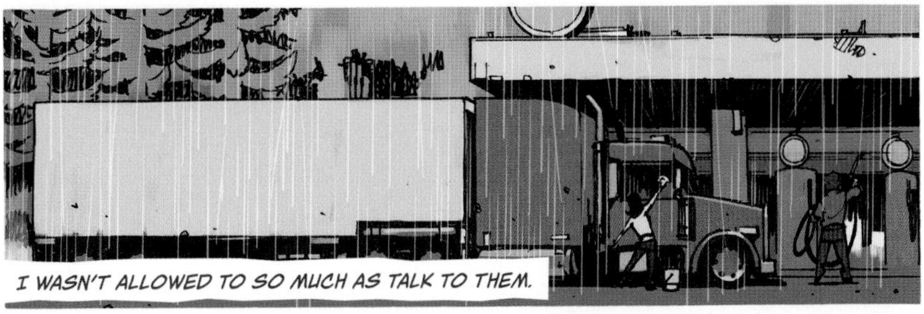
I WASN'T ALLOWED TO SO MUCH AS TALK TO THEM.

RED PICKED UP MY SCHOOLING, BUT HIS HEART WASN'T IN IT.

HE DIDN'T WANT TO WASTE TIME TEACHING ME THINGS I'D NEVER USE IN LIFE.

AND TO BE HONEST...

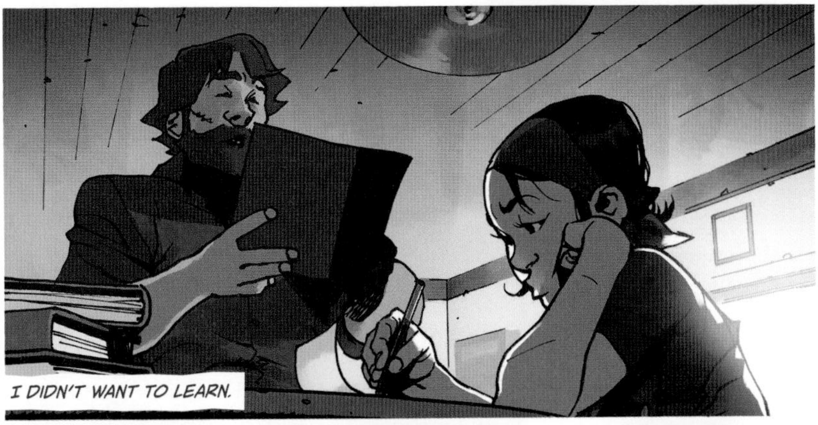
I DIDN'T WANT TO LEARN.

RED ALWAYS SAID THAT THE WORLD WILL LET YOU KNOW WHERE IT WANTS YOU.

THE GARAGE WAS WHERE MY HEART WAS, SO BY THE TIME I WAS THIRTEEN THAT WAS ALL HE BOTHERED TEACHING ME.

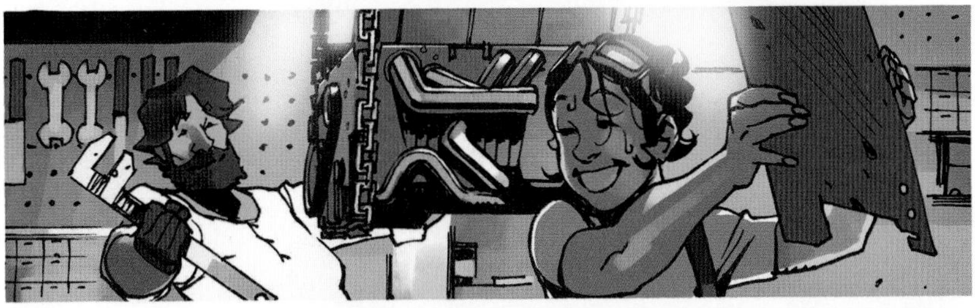

MONEY WAS ALWAYS TIGHT.

ONCE THE BIG COMPANY HAULERS BECAME THE NORM, INDEPENDENT TRUCKERS LIKE US WOULD GO LONG STRETCHES OF TIME WHERE NO WORK CAME AT ALL.

THE PRICE OF FREEDOM WAS OFTEN STARK POVERTY.

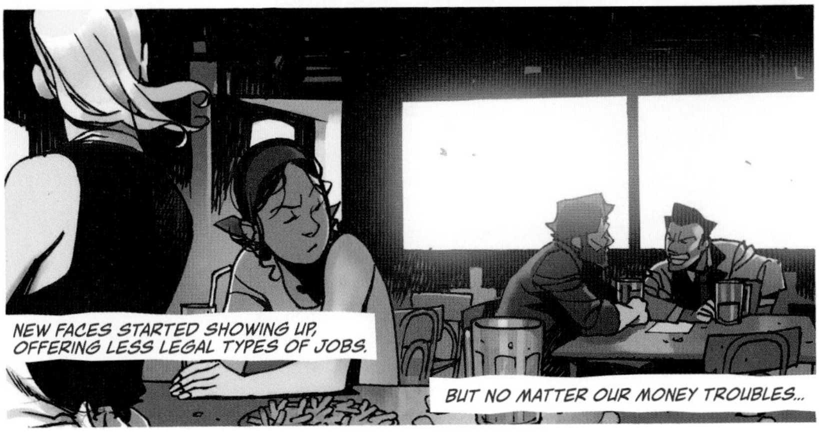
NEW FACES STARTED SHOWING UP, OFFERING LESS LEGAL TYPES OF JOBS.
BUT NO MATTER OUR MONEY TROUBLES...

RED WOULDN'T BECOME A BANDIT.

HE HAD A CODE.

HE MIGHT NOT PAY TAXES OR PARTICIPATE IN ALL THE BULLSHIT, BUT HE WOULDN'T SPREAD SUFFERING.

HE SAW IT ALL AS A TEST, AND KNEW IF WE HELD ON A BIT LONGER...

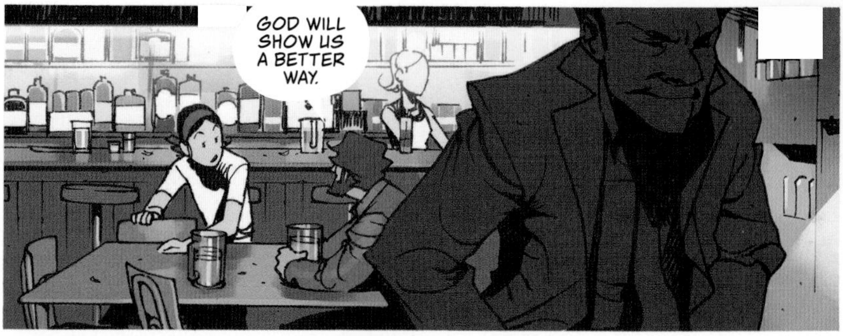
GOD WILL SHOW US A BETTER WAY.

AND IN THE END, HE WAS RIGHT. IT ALL WORKED OUT. THE NEXT FEW YEARS WERE GREAT.

WE FOUND REGULAR WORK WITH A MANUFACTURER THAT MADE RACECAR PARTS. USING SPARES AND JUNK, WE BUILT SOME DAMN FAST CARS...

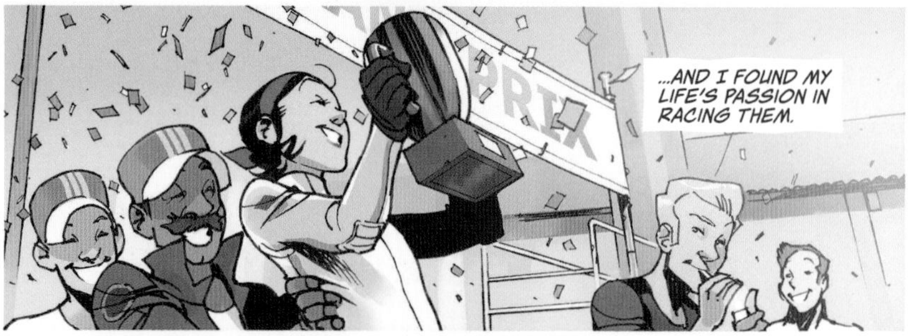
...AND I FOUND MY LIFE'S PASSION IN RACING THEM.

THAT AND TOBY'S DEVILISH SMILE.

HE WAS SO COOL.

BY THEN HE'D HAD A FEW RUN-INS WITH THE LAW AND RED DIDN'T WANT ME SPENDING TIME WITH HIM.

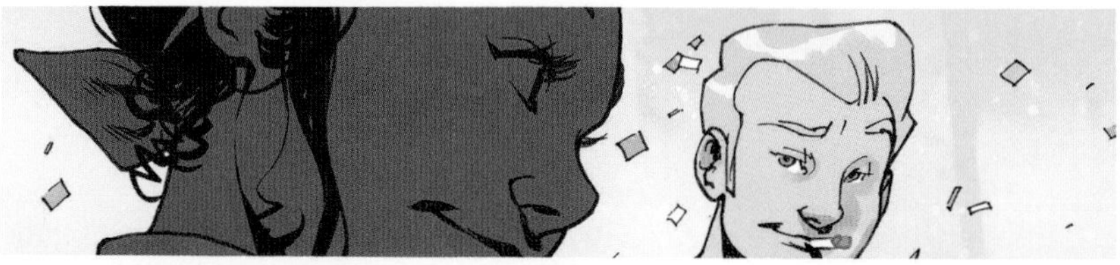

WHICH MADE HIM ALL THE MORE ALLURING.

I DID WHAT SO MANY YOUNG GIRLS DO...

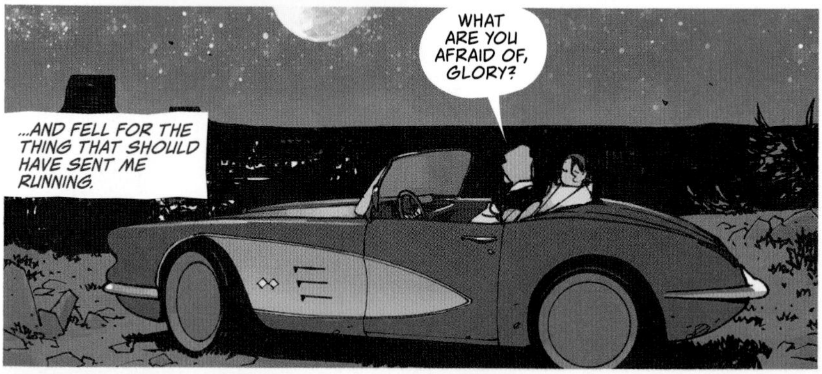
WHAT ARE YOU AFRAID OF, GLORY?
...AND FELL FOR THE THING THAT SHOULD HAVE SENT ME RUNNING.

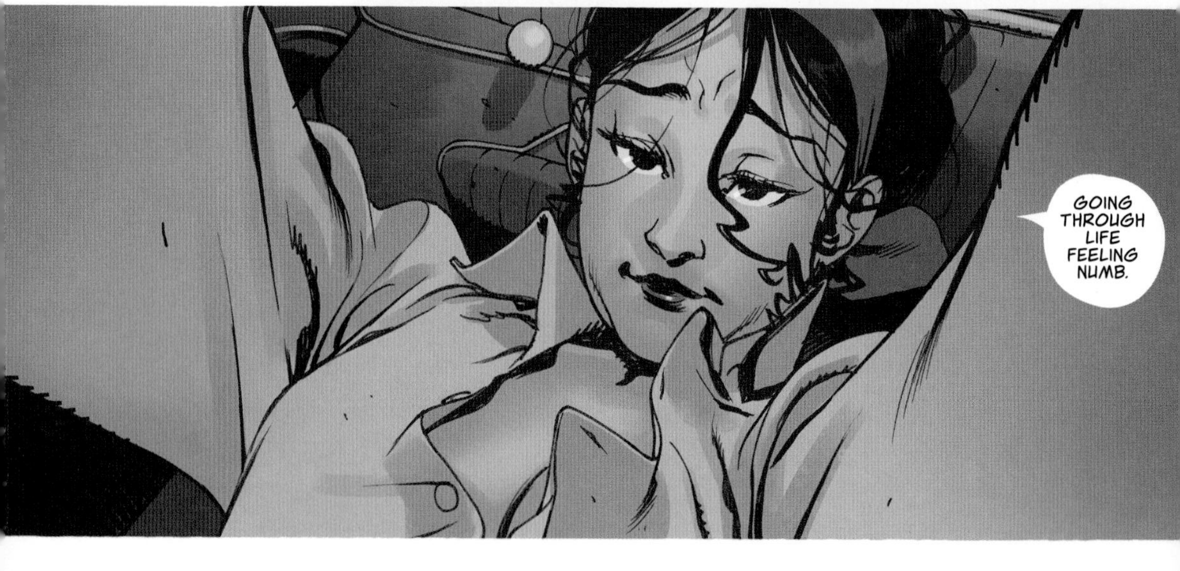
GOING THROUGH LIFE FEELING NUMB.

WE WERE MARRIED JUST AFTER MY TWENTY-FIRST BIRTHDAY. AGAINST RED'S WISHES.

HE'D TAKEN A CROSS-COUNTRY JOB...

I'D NEVER BEEN SO MAD AT ANYONE. NEVER FELT SO ABANDONED...

...AND WE WOULDN'T SPEAK FOR YEARS AFTER.

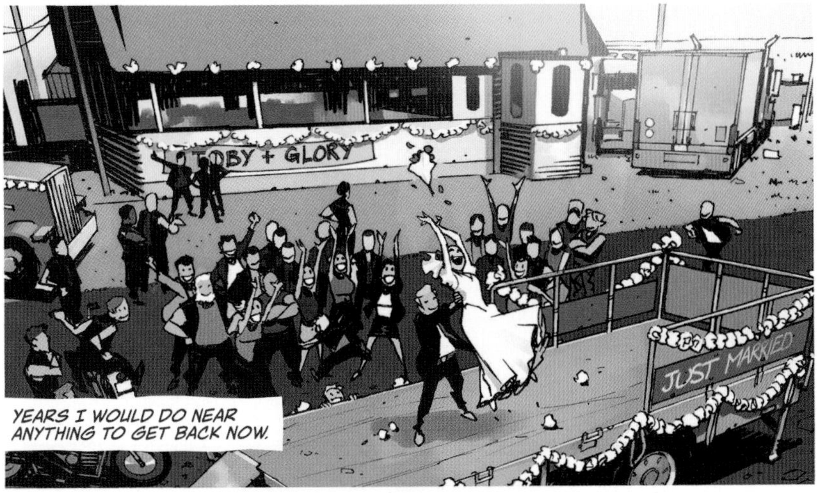
TOBY + GLORY
JUST MARRIED
YEARS I WOULD DO NEAR ANYTHING TO GET BACK NOW.

BUT BACK THEN I WAS DRUNK IN LOVE, LIFE WAS MOVING SO QUICKLY, A JET STREAM PULLING ME INTO TOBY'S WORLD.

A WORLD OF BIG HOUSES AND EXPENSIVE THINGS.

THE MATERIAL COMFORTS THAT RED HAD MADE SO TABOO.

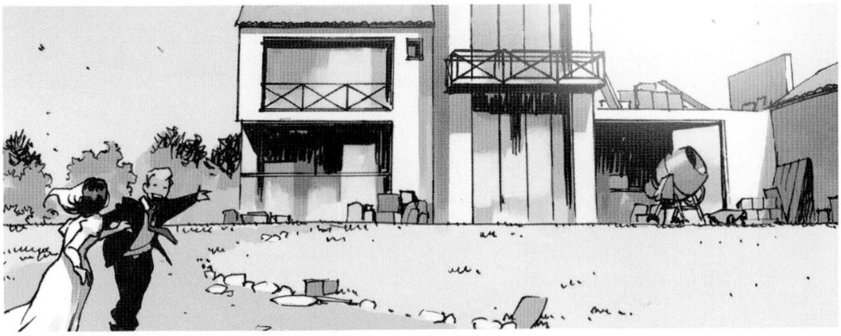

BUT IT WASN'T LONG BEFORE I COULD SEE RED WAS RIGHT: IT WAS ALL AN ANCHOR. NONE OF THAT MATTERED.

I MISSED THE OPEN ROAD WHILE TOBY JUST WANTED MORE AND MORE.

EVENTUALLY HIS MYSTERIOUS WEALTH AND SHADY FRIENDS, WELL...

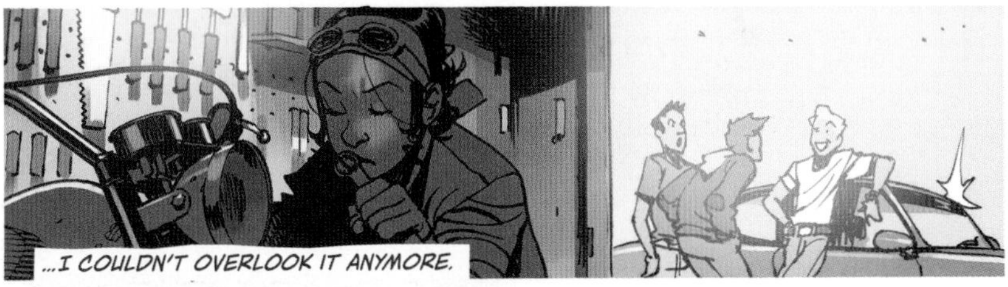
...I COULDN'T OVERLOOK IT ANYMORE.

I FOLLOWED HIM TO A MEETING WHERE I SAW HIM WITH A FAMILIAR FACE.

THE SAME MAN RED HAD TURNED AWAY WHEN WE WERE AT ROCK BOTTOM.

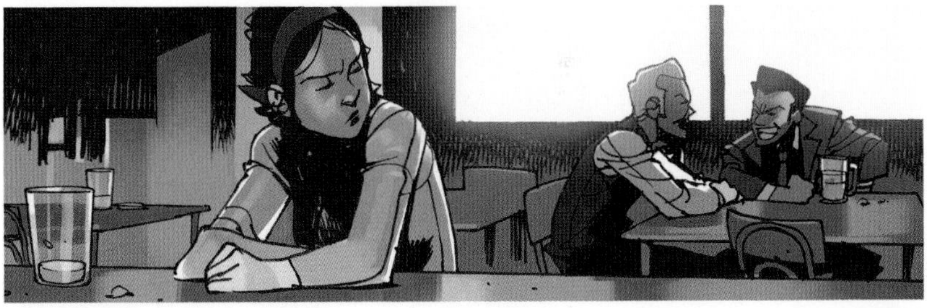

I TOLD TOBY I KNEW HE WAS USING THE FAMILY CONVOY TO DEAL DRUGS, AND THAT I WOULDN'T HAVE IT.

HE WENT CRAZY.

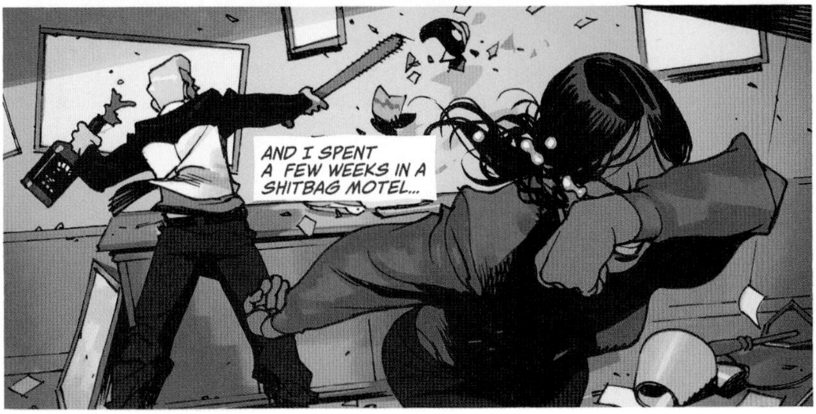
AND I SPENT A FEW WEEKS IN A SHITBAG MOTEL...

...LONG ENOUGH TO LET THE BLACK EYE HEAL BEFORE I WENT BACK HOME TO RED.

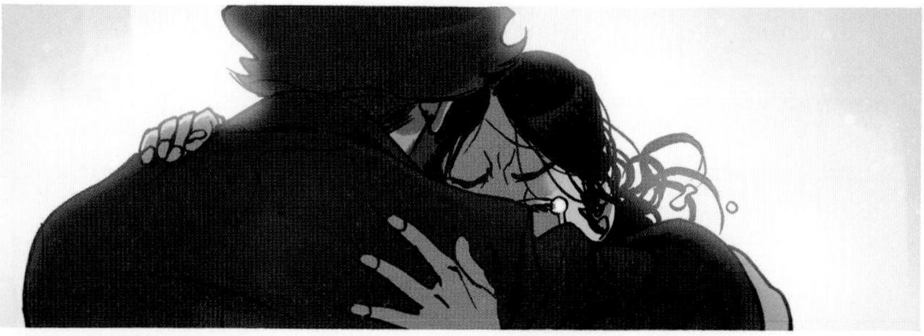

BUT IN THE TIME WE'D BEEN ESTRANGED, RED HAD GOTTEN SICK.

AND IN CLASSIC RED FASHION, FIGURING HE HAD NO MONEY TO PAY FOR ANYTHING ANYWAY...

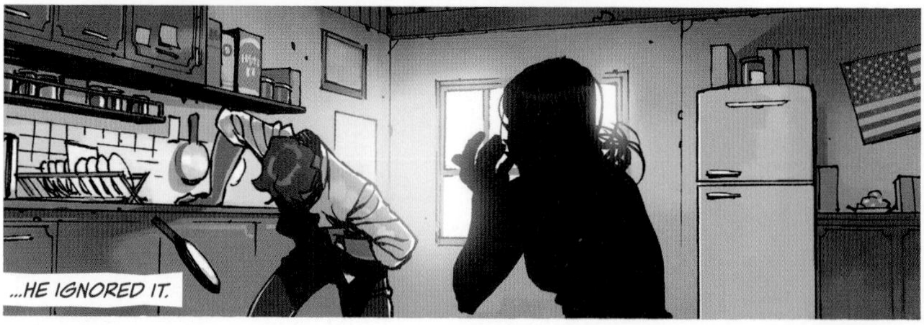

...HE IGNORED IT.

LIVER CANCER.

HE'D NEED A REPLACEMENT, A COSTLY PROCEDURE, AND VERY SOON.

NO SOCIAL SECURITY NUMBER, NO INSURANCE, NO TAX RETURNS...

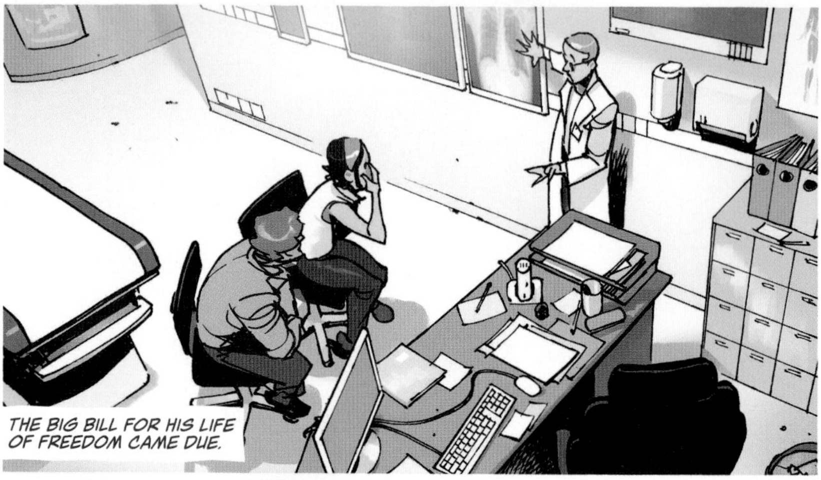

THE BIG BILL FOR HIS LIFE OF FREEDOM CAME DUE.

WE NEEDED AROUND $300,000 CASH.

EVEN THEN THE WAIT FOR THE LIVER IS LONG...

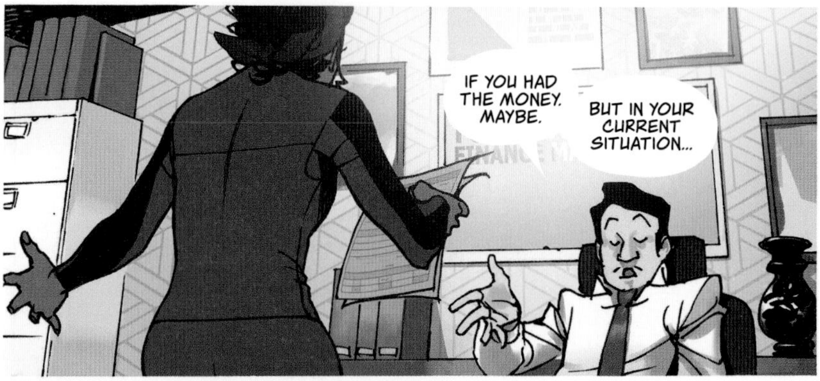

IF YOU HAD THE MONEY. MAYBE.
BUT IN YOUR CURRENT SITUATION...

I APPLIED FOR A DOZEN LOANS.

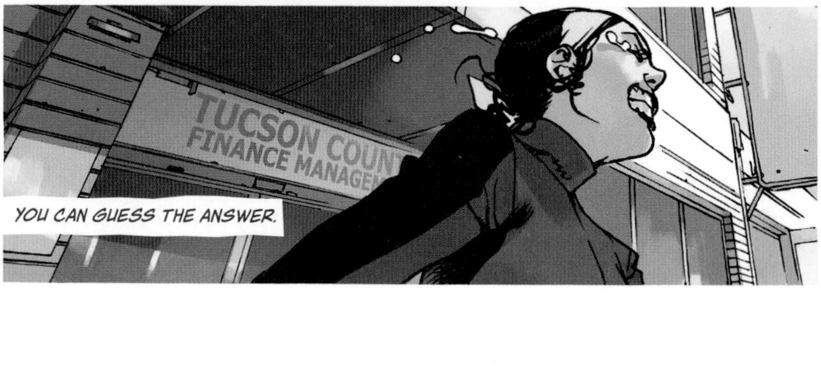

TUCSON COUN
FINANCE MANAGE
YOU CAN GUESS THE ANSWER.

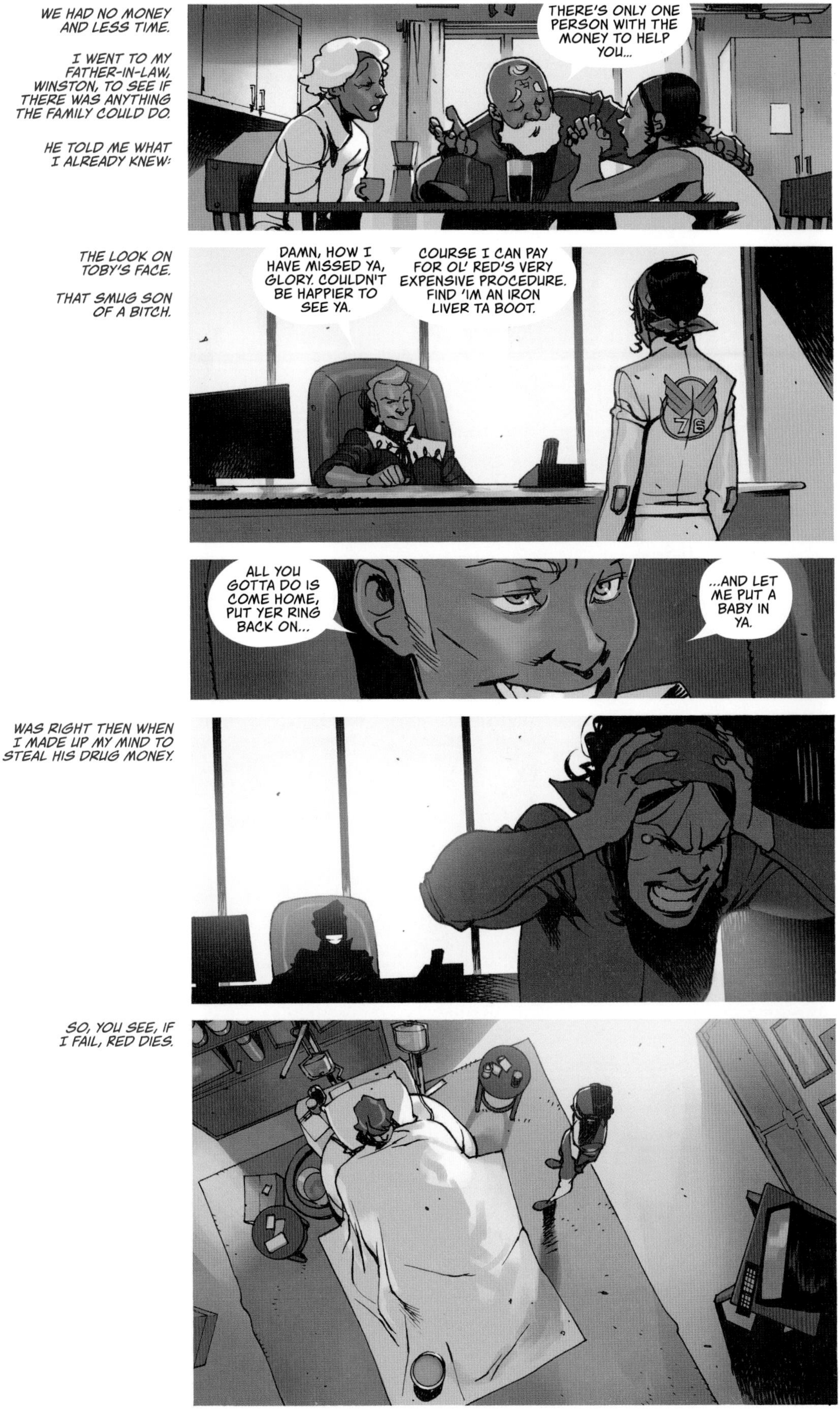
WE HAD NO MONEY AND LESS TIME.
I WENT TO MY FATHER-IN-LAW, WINSTON, TO SEE IF THERE WAS ANYTHING THE FAMILY COULD DO.
HE TOLD ME WHAT I ALREADY KNEW:
THERE'S ONLY ONE PERSON WITH THE MONEY TO HELP YOU...
THE LOOK ON TOBY'S FACE.
THAT SMUG SON OF A BITCH.
DAMN, HOW I HAVE MISSED YA, GLORY. COULDN'T BE HAPPIER TO SEE YA.
COURSE I CAN PAY FOR OL' RED'S VERY EXPENSIVE PROCEDURE. FIND 'IM AN IRON LIVER TA BOOT.
76
ALL YOU GOTTA DO IS COME HOME, PUT YER RING BACK ON...
...AND LET ME PUT A BABY IN YA.
WAS RIGHT THEN WHEN I MADE UP MY MIND TO STEAL HIS DRUG MONEY.
SO, YOU SEE, IF I FAIL, RED DIES.

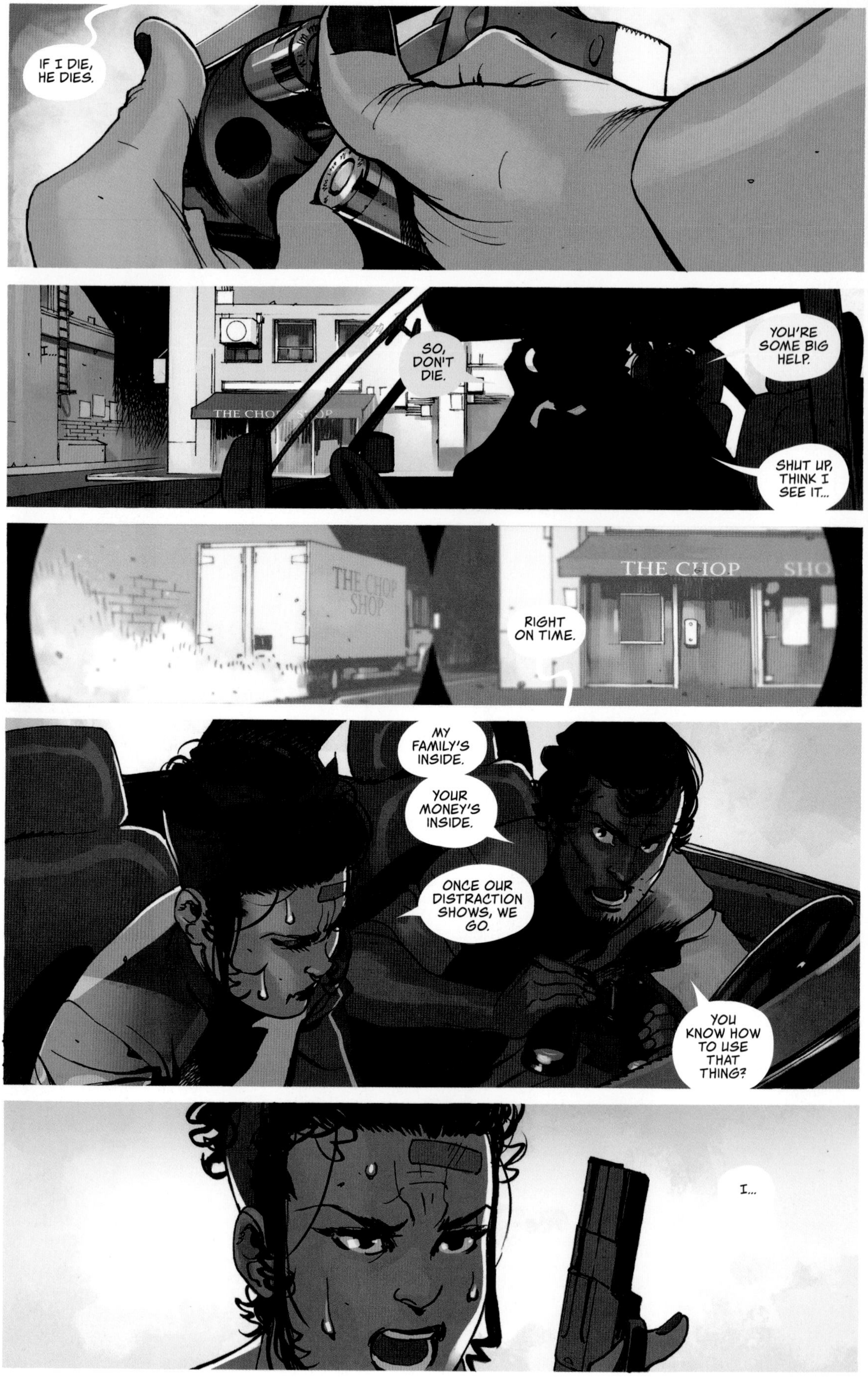
IF I DIE, HE DIES.
I...
SO, DON'T DIE.
YOU'RE SOME BIG HELP.
SHUT UP, THINK I SEE IT...
THE CHOP SHOP
THE CHOP SHOP
THE CHOP
RIGHT ON TIME.
MY FAMILY'S INSIDE.
YOUR MONEY'S INSIDE.
ONCE OUR DISTRACTION SHOWS, WE GO.
YOU KNOW HOW TO USE THAT THING?
I...

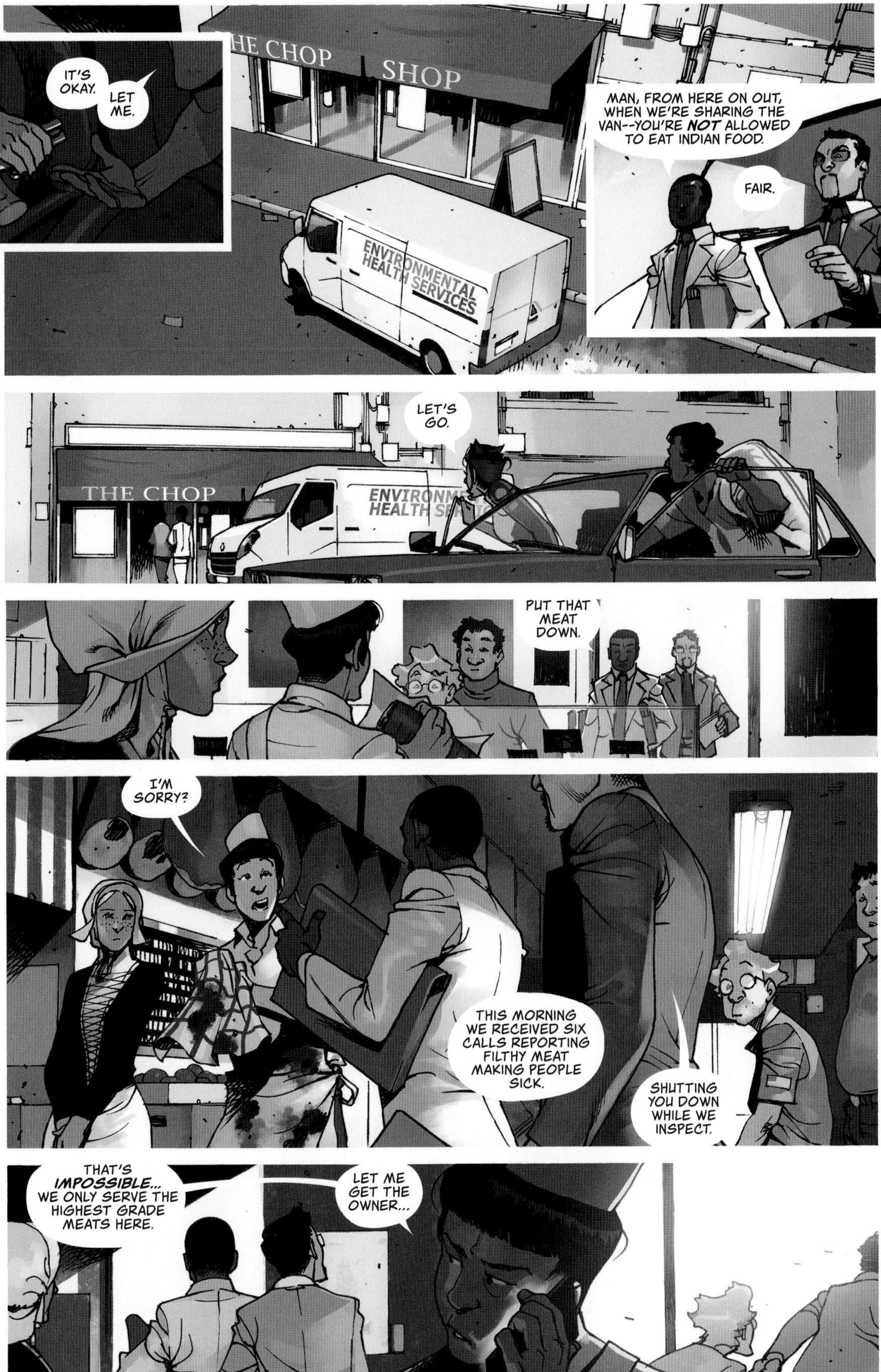
IT'S OKAY.
LET ME.
THE CHOP SHOP
ENVIRONMENTAL HEALTH SERVICES
MAN, FROM HERE ON OUT, WHEN WE'RE SHARING THE VAN--YOU'RE **NOT** ALLOWED TO EAT INDIAN FOOD.
FAIR.
LET'S GO.
THE CHOP
PUT THAT MEAT DOWN.
I'M SORRY?
THIS MORNING WE RECEIVED SIX CALLS REPORTING FILTHY MEAT MAKING PEOPLE SICK.
SHUTTING YOU DOWN WHILE WE INSPECT.
THAT'S ***IMPOSSIBLE...*** WE ONLY SERVE THE HIGHEST GRADE MEATS HERE.
LET ME GET THE OWNER...

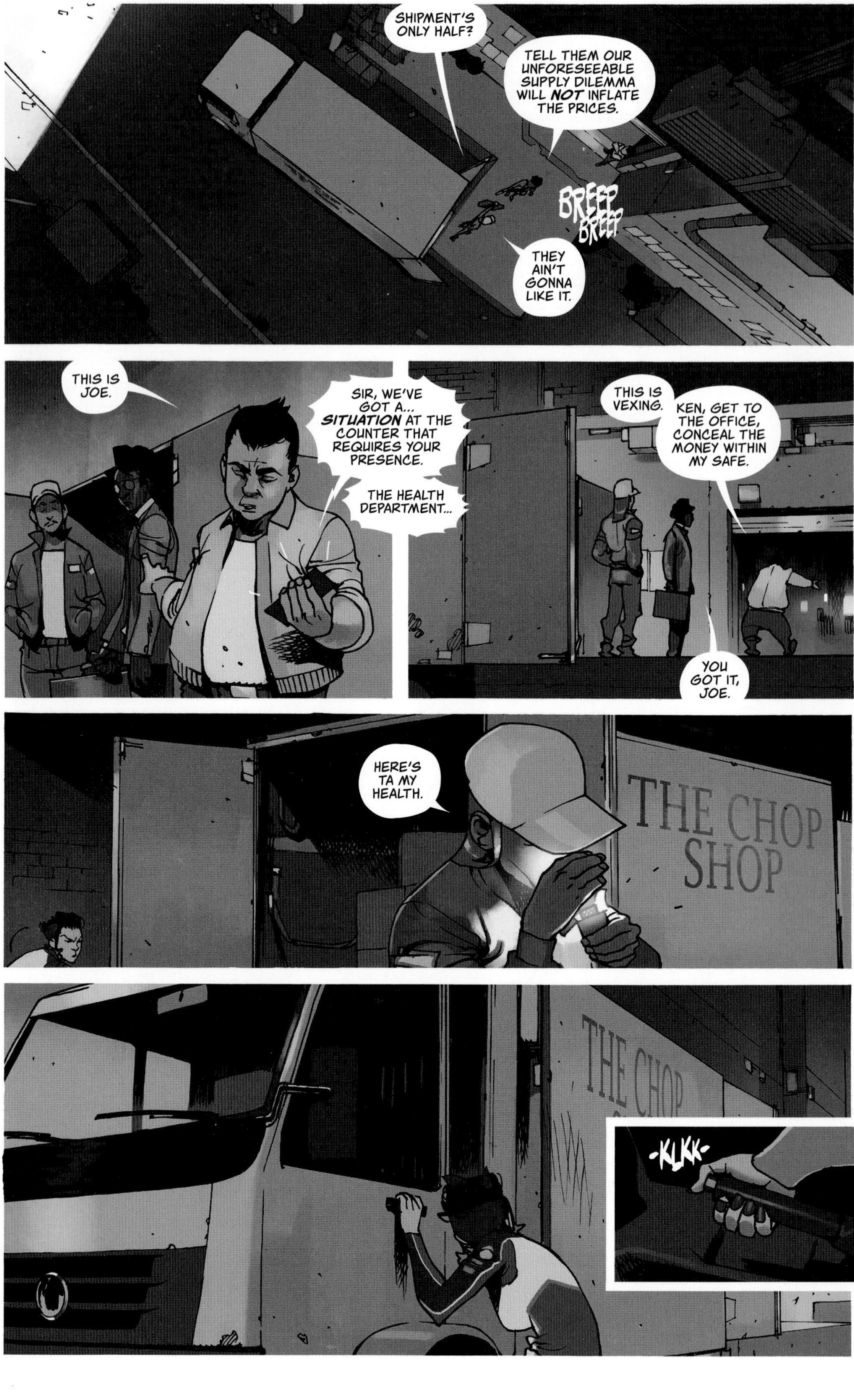
SHIPMENT'S ONLY HALF?
TELL THEM OUR UNFORESEEABLE SUPPLY DILEMMA WILL NOT INFLATE THE PRICES.
BREEP BREEP
THEY AIN'T GONNA LIKE IT.
THIS IS JOE.
SIR, WE'VE GOT A... SITUATION AT THE COUNTER THAT REQUIRES YOUR PRESENCE.
THE HEALTH DEPARTMENT...
THIS IS VEXING.
KEN, GET TO THE OFFICE, CONCEAL THE MONEY WITHIN MY SAFE.
YOU GOT IT, JOE.
HERE'S TA MY HEALTH.
THE CHOP SHOP
THE CHOP
KLIKK

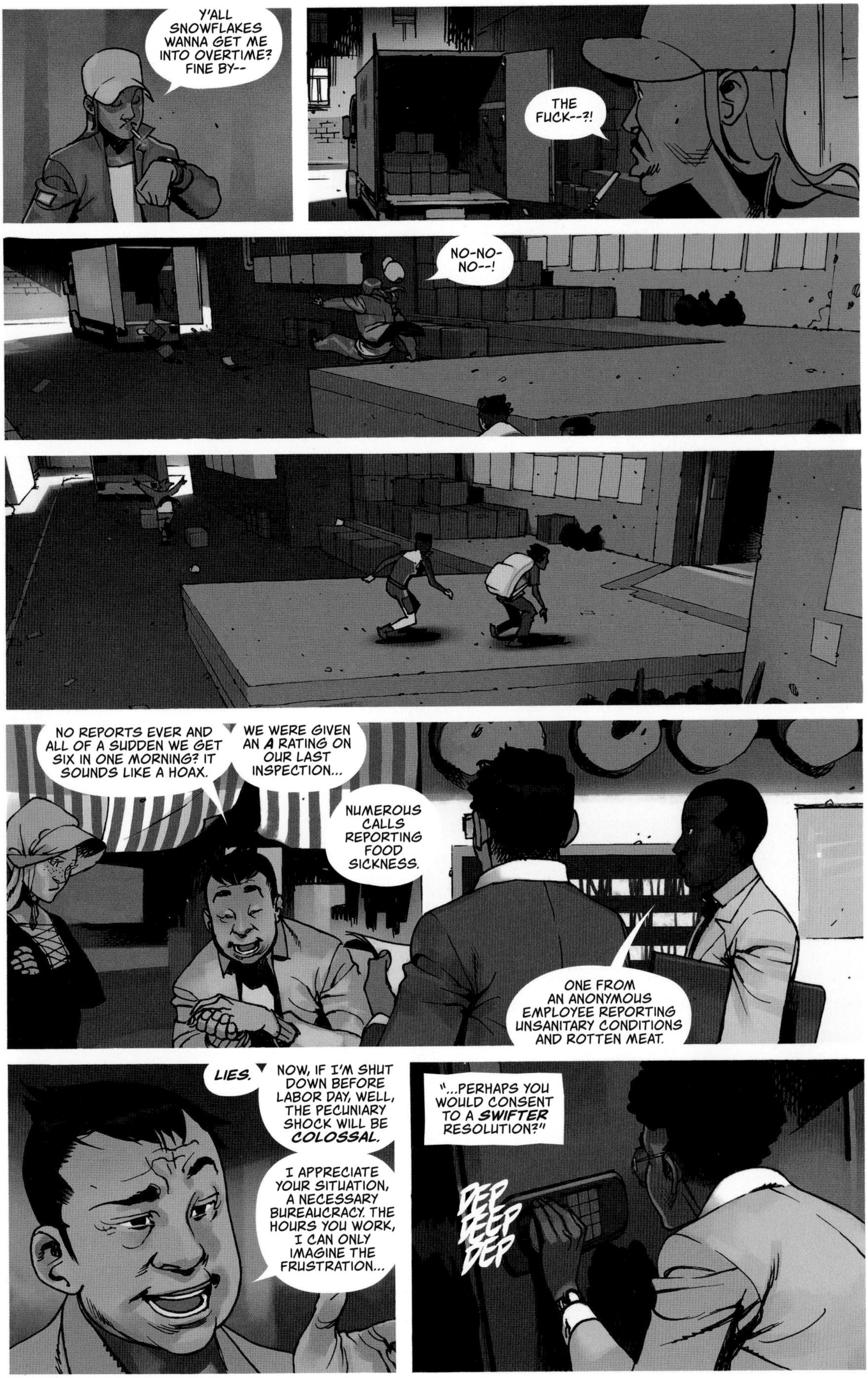
Y'ALL SNOWFLAKES WANNA GET ME INTO OVERTIME? FINE BY--
THE FUCK--?!
NO-NO-NO--!
NO REPORTS EVER AND ALL OF A SUDDEN WE GET SIX IN ONE MORNING? IT SOUNDS LIKE A HOAX.
WE WERE GIVEN AN A RATING ON OUR LAST INSPECTION...
NUMEROUS CALLS REPORTING FOOD SICKNESS.
ONE FROM AN ANONYMOUS EMPLOYEE REPORTING UNSANITARY CONDITIONS AND ROTTEN MEAT.
LIES.
NOW, IF I'M SHUT DOWN BEFORE LABOR DAY, WELL, THE PECUNIARY SHOCK WILL BE COLOSSAL.
I APPRECIATE YOUR SITUATION, A NECESSARY BUREAUCRACY. THE HOURS YOU WORK, I CAN ONLY IMAGINE THE FRUSTRATION...
"...PERHAPS YOU WOULD CONSENT TO A SWIFTER RESOLUTION?"
DEP DEEP DEP DEP

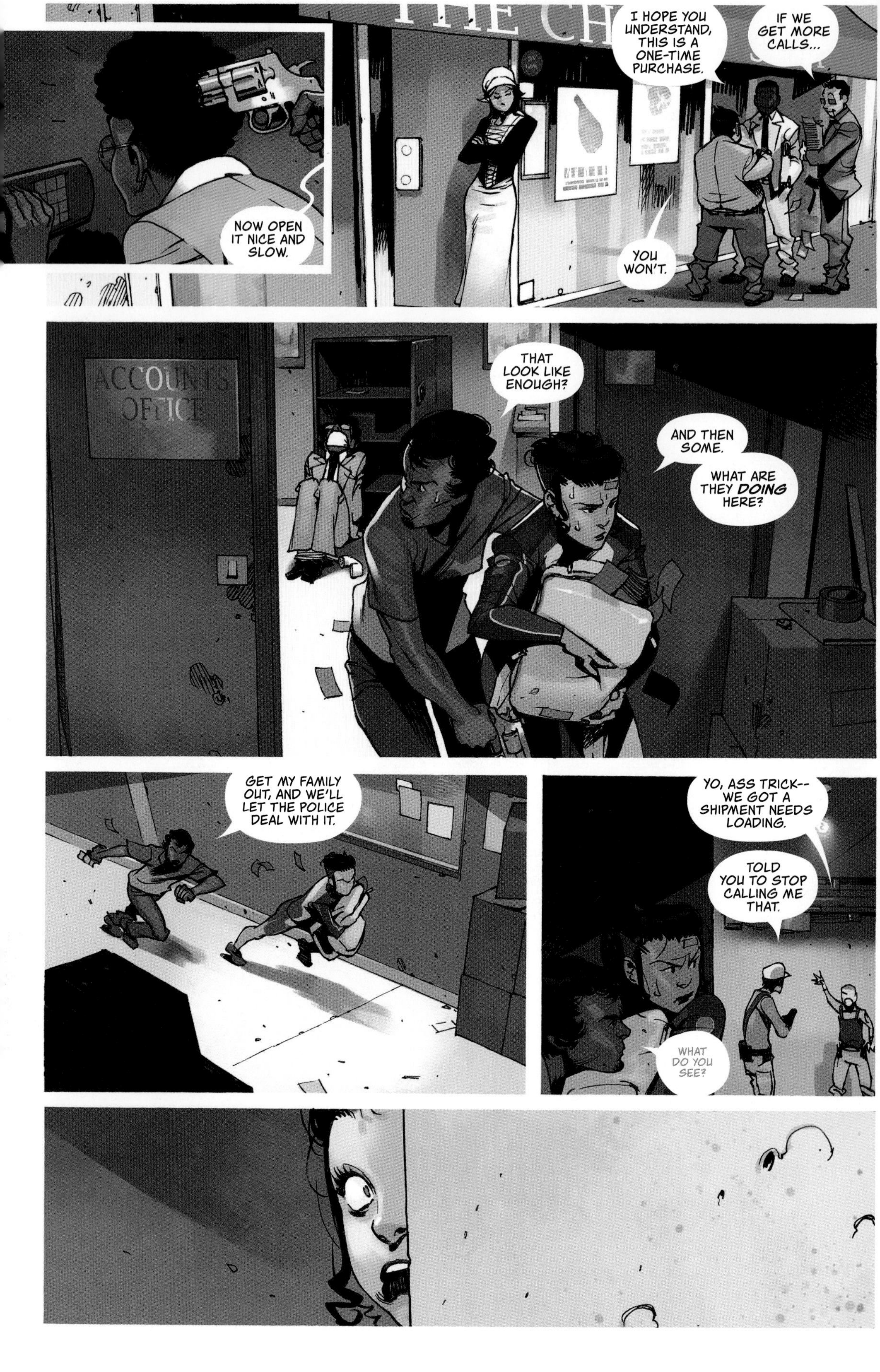
NOW OPEN IT NICE AND SLOW.
I HOPE YOU UNDERSTAND, THIS IS A ONE-TIME PURCHASE.
IF WE GET MORE CALLS...
YOU WON'T.
ACCOUNTS OFFICE
THAT LOOK LIKE ENOUGH?
AND THEN SOME.
WHAT ARE THEY DOING HERE?
GET MY FAMILY OUT, AND WE'LL LET THE POLICE DEAL WITH IT.
YO, ASS TRICK-- WE GOT A SHIPMENT NEEDS LOADING.
TOLD YOU TO STOP CALLING ME THAT.
WHAT DO YOU SEE?

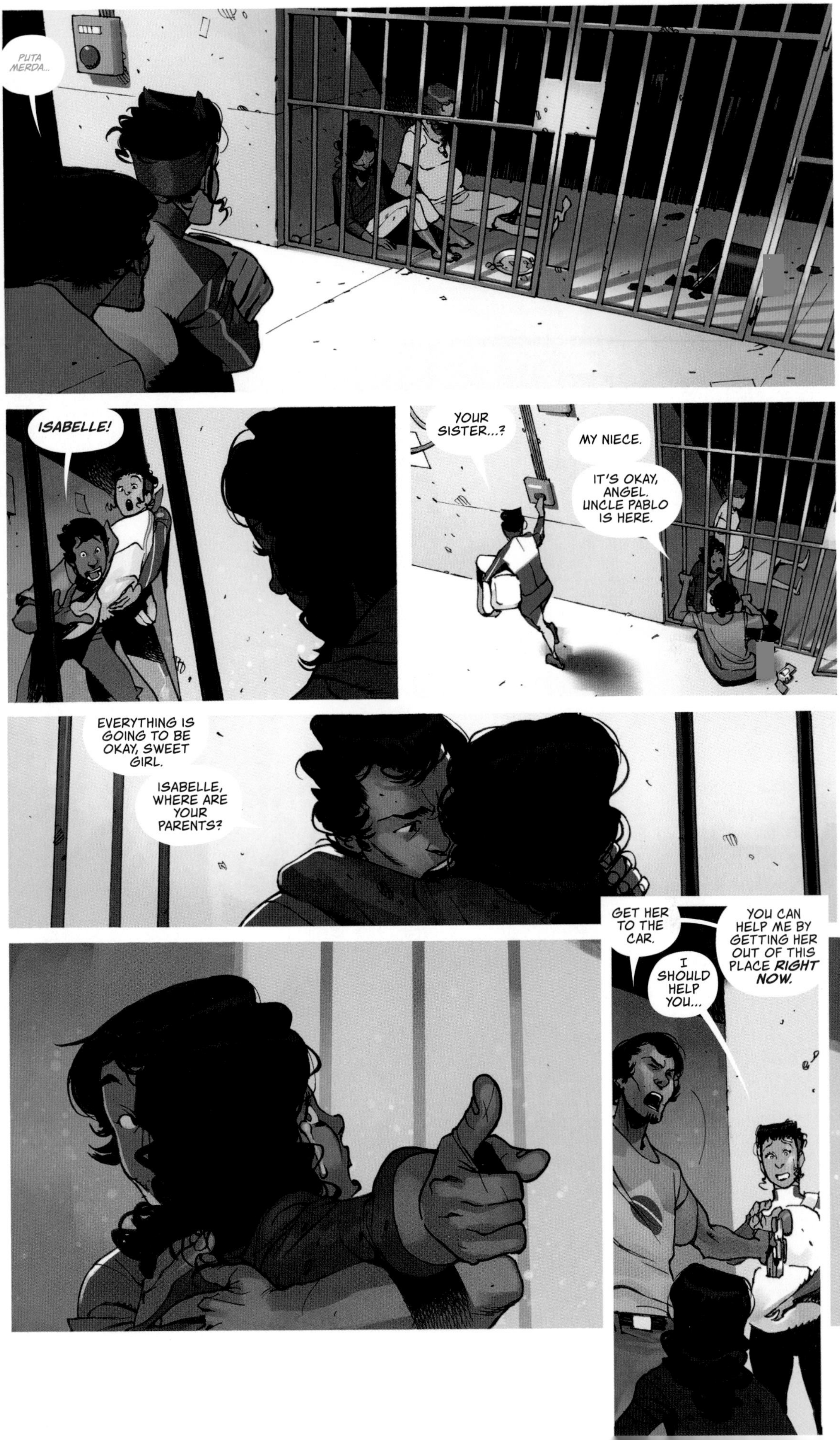
PUTA MERDA...
ISABELLE!
YOUR SISTER...?
MY NIECE.
IT'S OKAY, ANGEL. UNCLE PABLO IS HERE.
EVERYTHING IS GOING TO BE OKAY, SWEET GIRL.
ISABELLE, WHERE ARE YOUR PARENTS?
GET HER TO THE CAR.
I SHOULD HELP YOU...
YOU CAN HELP ME BY GETTING HER OUT OF THIS PLACE RIGHT NOW.

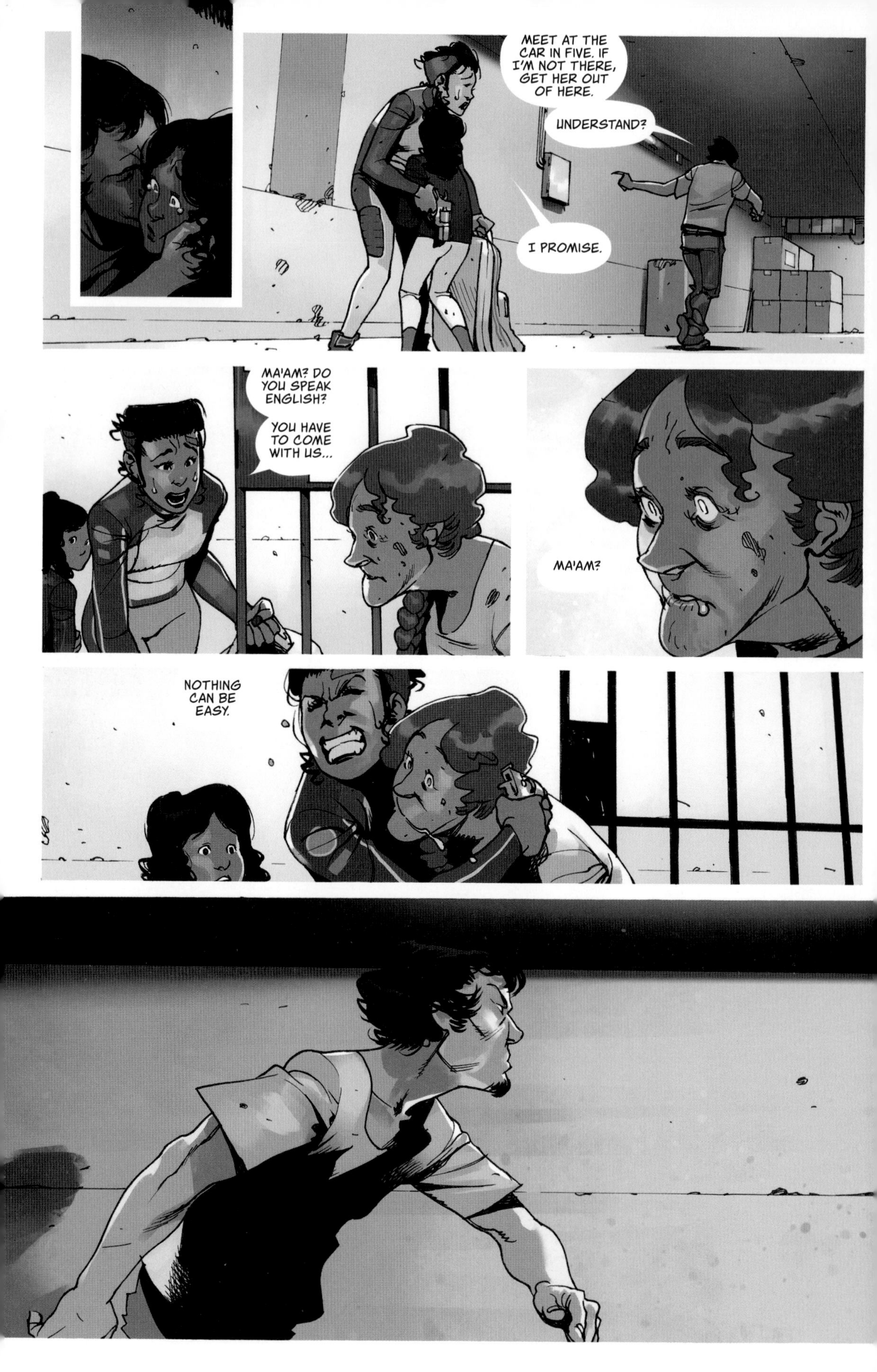
MEET AT THE CAR IN FIVE. IF I'M NOT THERE, GET HER OUT OF HERE.
UNDERSTAND?
I PROMISE.
MA'AM? DO YOU SPEAK ENGLISH?
YOU HAVE TO COME WITH US...
MA'AM?
NOTHING CAN BE EASY.

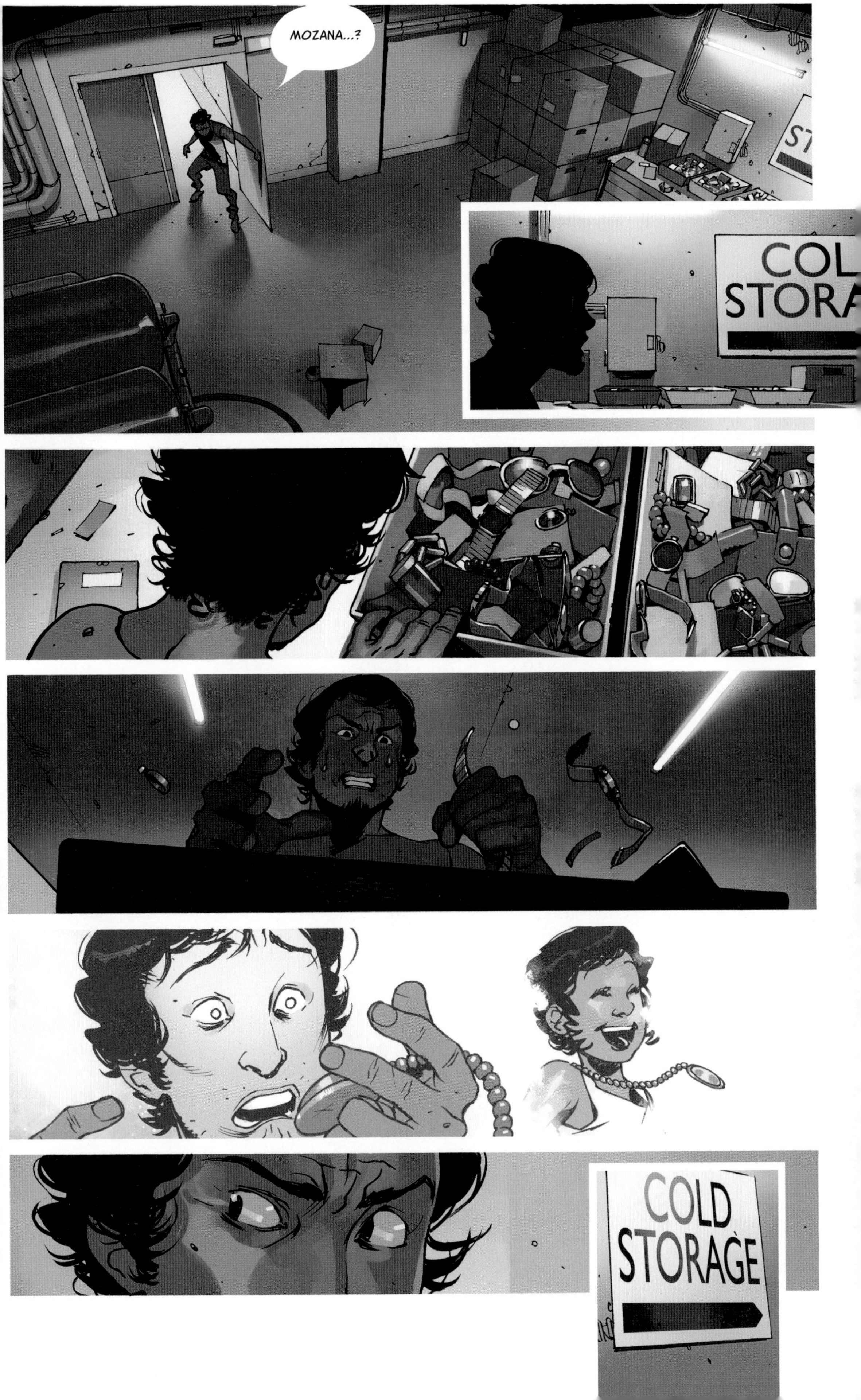
MOZANA...?
COLD
STORAGE

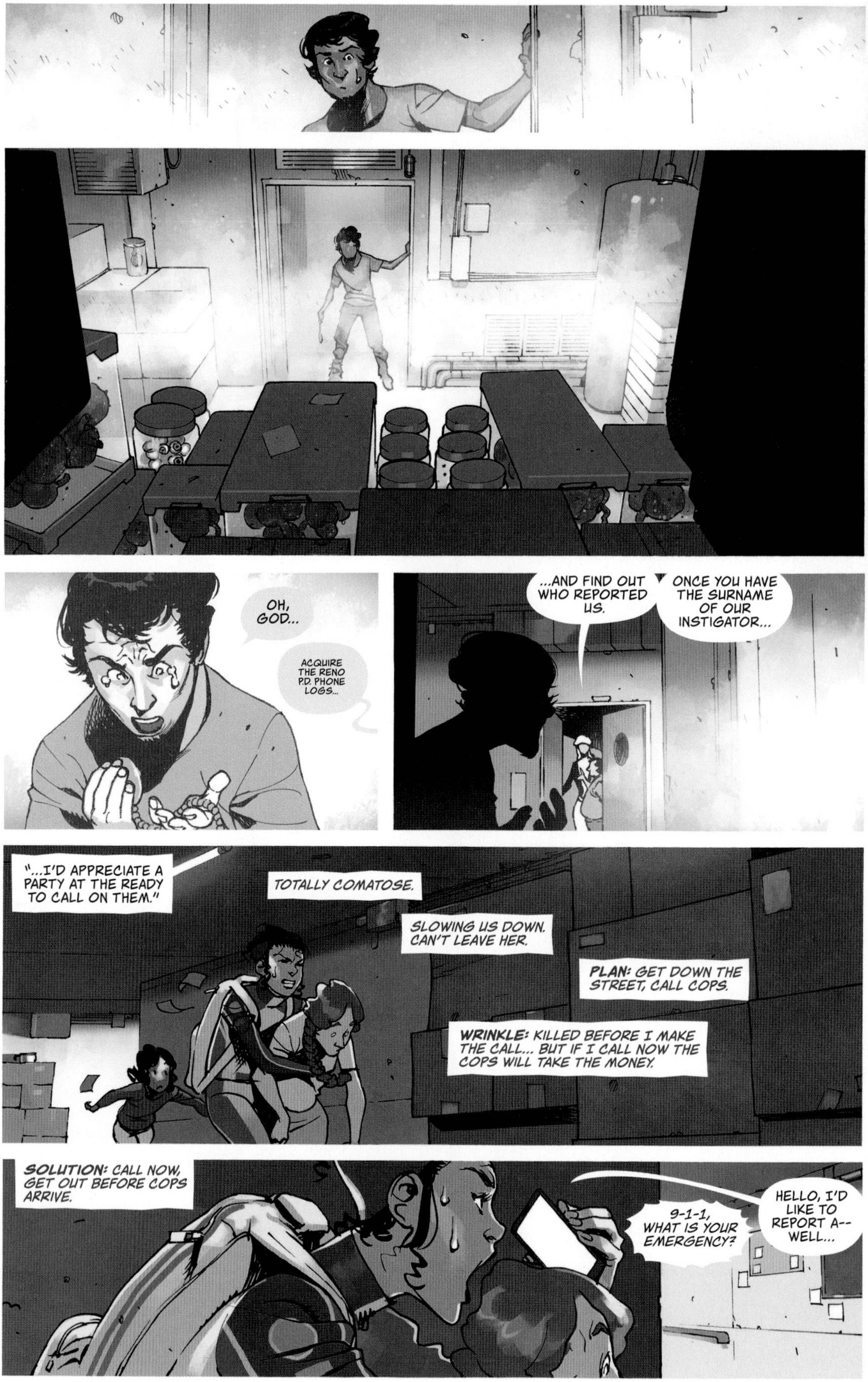
OH, GOD...
ACQUIRE THE RENO P.D. PHONE LOGS...
...AND FIND OUT WHO REPORTED US.
ONCE YOU HAVE THE SURNAME OF OUR INSTIGATOR...
"...I'D APPRECIATE A PARTY AT THE READY TO CALL ON THEM."
TOTALLY COMATOSE.
SLOWING US DOWN. CAN'T LEAVE HER.
PLAN: GET DOWN THE STREET, CALL COPS.
WRINKLE: KILLED BEFORE I MAKE THE CALL... BUT IF I CALL NOW THE COPS WILL TAKE THE MONEY.
SOLUTION: CALL NOW, GET OUT BEFORE COPS ARRIVE.
9-1-1, WHAT IS YOUR EMERGENCY?
HELLO, I'D LIKE TO REPORT A-- WELL...

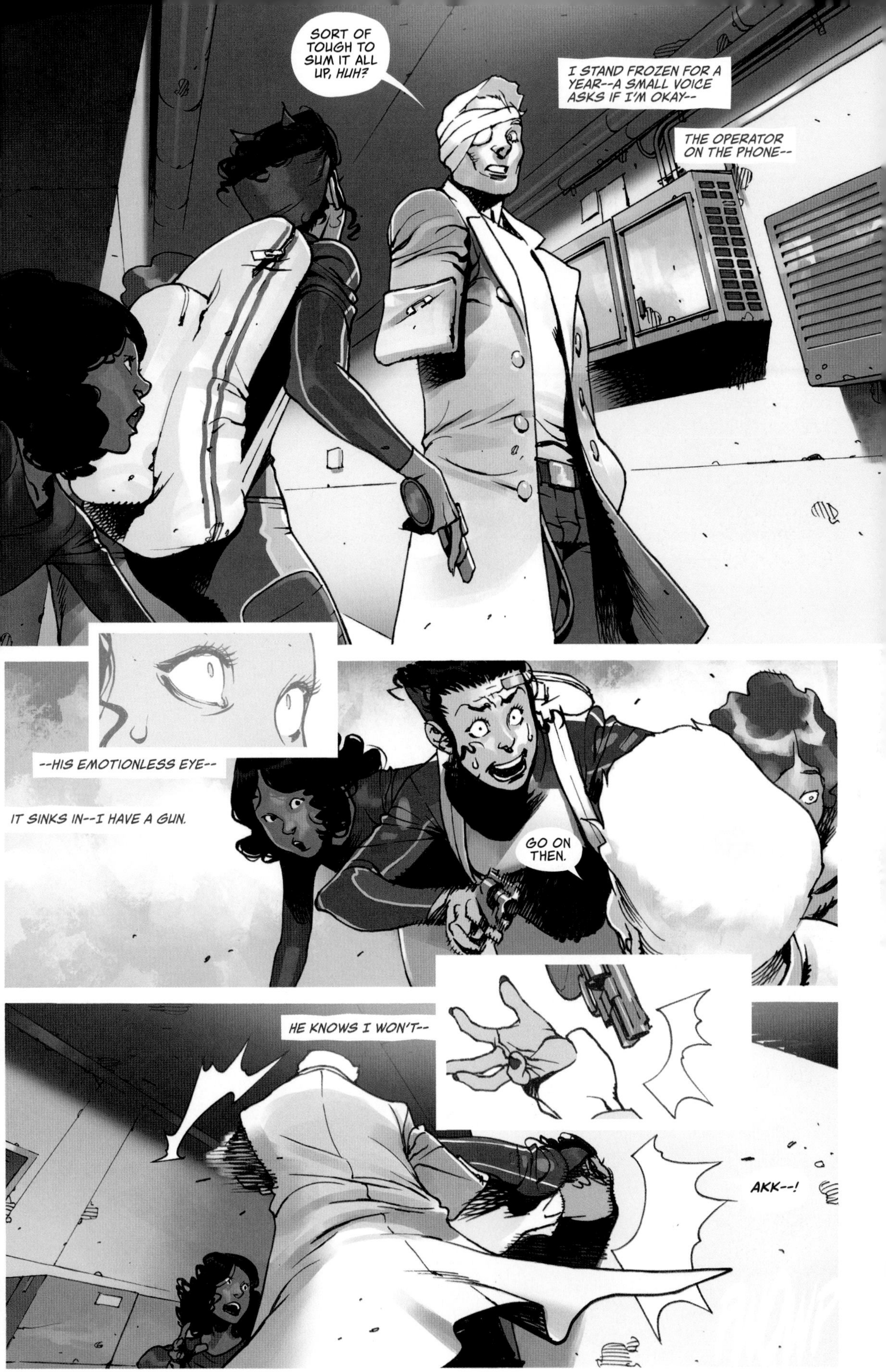
SORT OF TOUGH TO SUM IT ALL UP, HUH?
I STAND FROZEN FOR A YEAR--A SMALL VOICE ASKS IF I'M OKAY--
THE OPERATOR ON THE PHONE--
--HIS EMOTIONLESS EYE--
IT SINKS IN--I HAVE A GUN.
GO ON THEN.
HE KNOWS I WON'T--
AKK--!

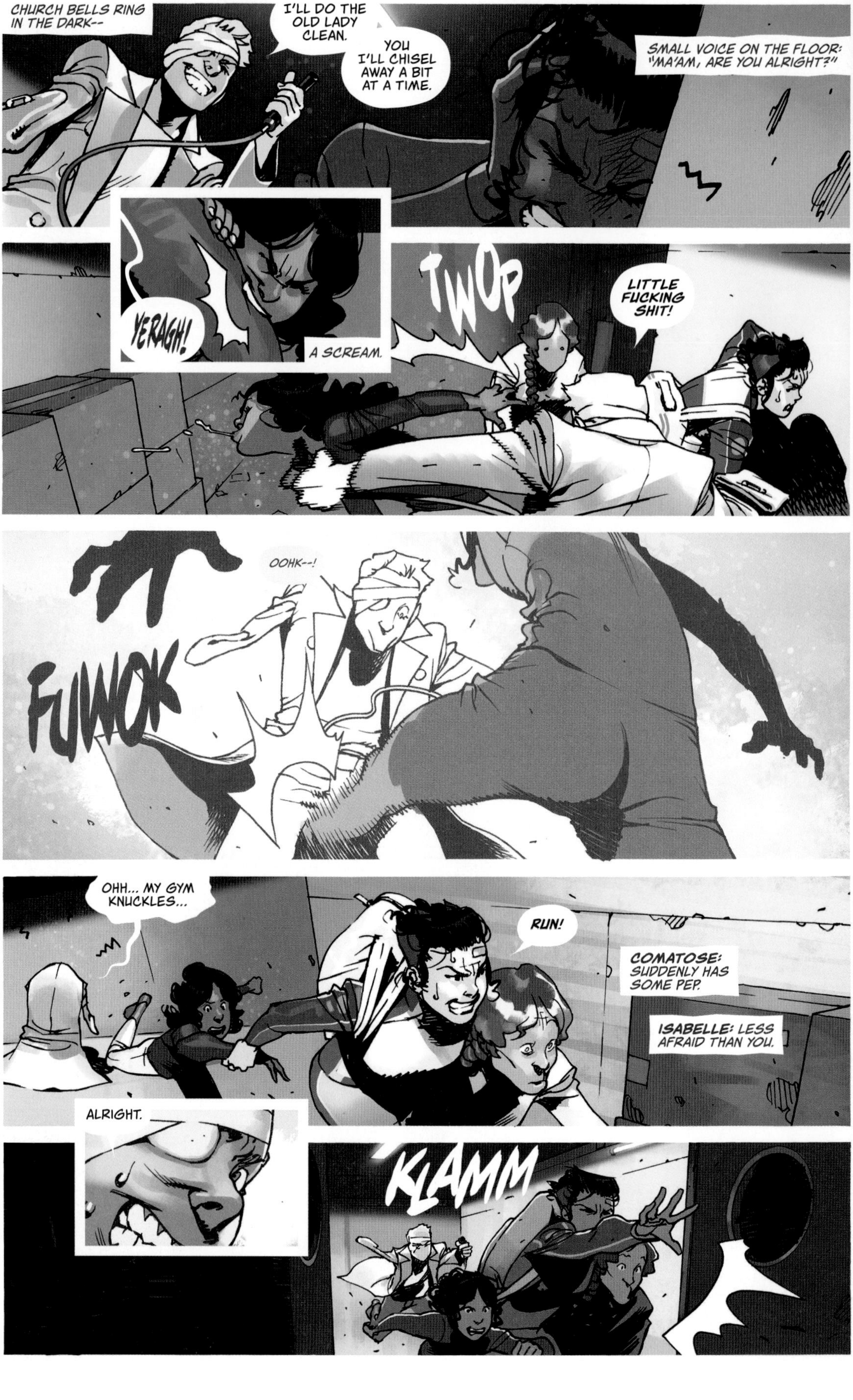
CHURCH BELLS RING IN THE DARK--
I'LL DO THE OLD LADY CLEAN.
YOU I'LL CHISEL AWAY A BIT AT A TIME.
SMALL VOICE ON THE FLOOR: "MA'AM, ARE YOU ALRIGHT?"
YERAGH!
A SCREAM.
TWOP
LITTLE FUCKING SHIT!
OOHK--!
FUWOK
OHH... MY GYM KNUCKLES...
RUN!
COMATOSE: SUDDENLY HAS SOME PEP.
ISABELLE: LESS AFRAID THAN YOU.
ALRIGHT.
KLAMM

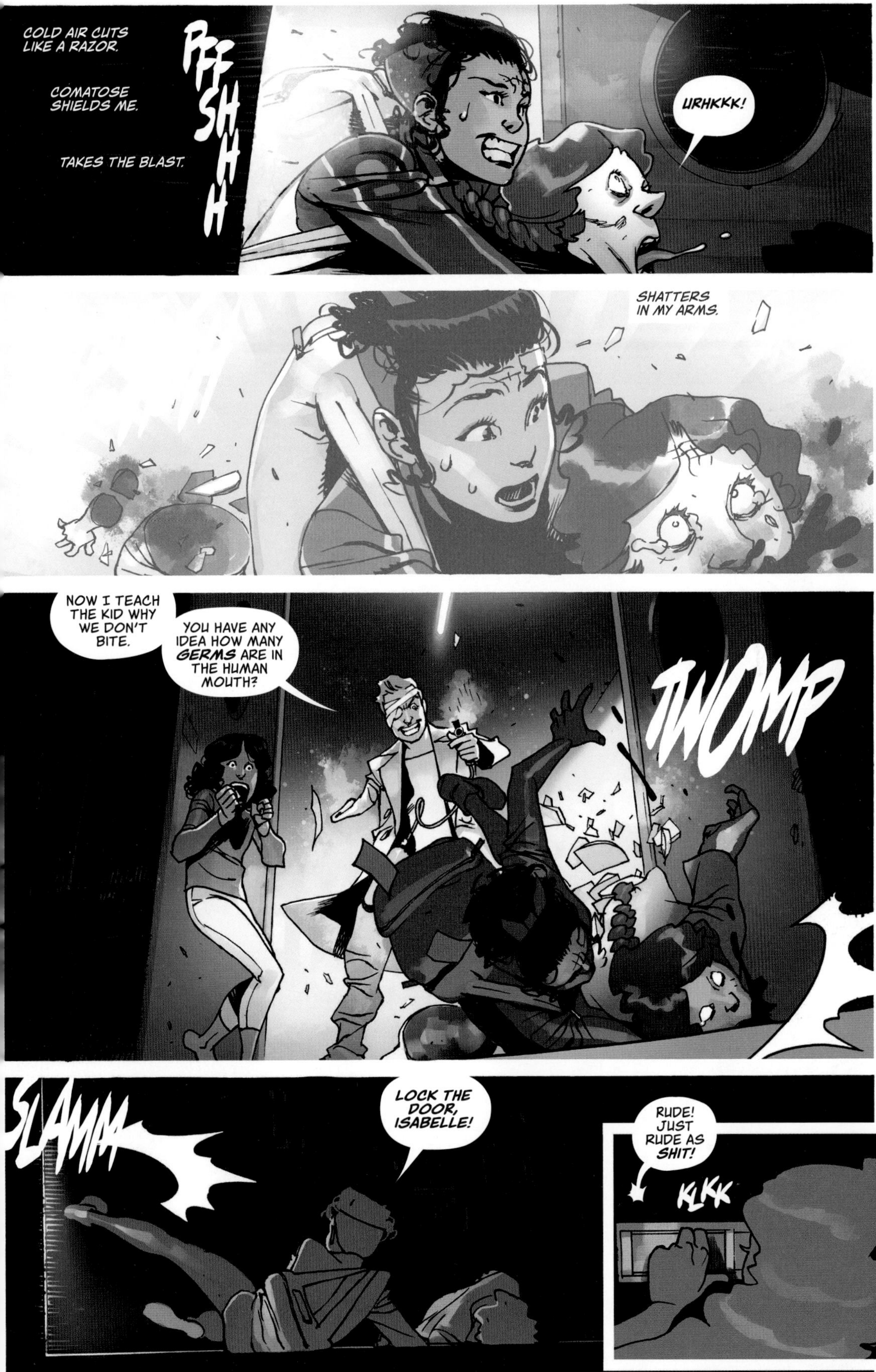
COLD AIR CUTS LIKE A RAZOR.
PFFSHHHH
COMATOSE SHIELDS ME.
TAKES THE BLAST.
URHKKK!
SHATTERS IN MY ARMS.
NOW I TEACH THE KID WHY WE DON'T BITE.
YOU HAVE ANY IDEA HOW MANY GERMS ARE IN THE HUMAN MOUTH?
TWOMP
SLAMM
LOCK THE DOOR, ISABELLE!
RUDE! JUST RUDE AS SHIT!
KLKK

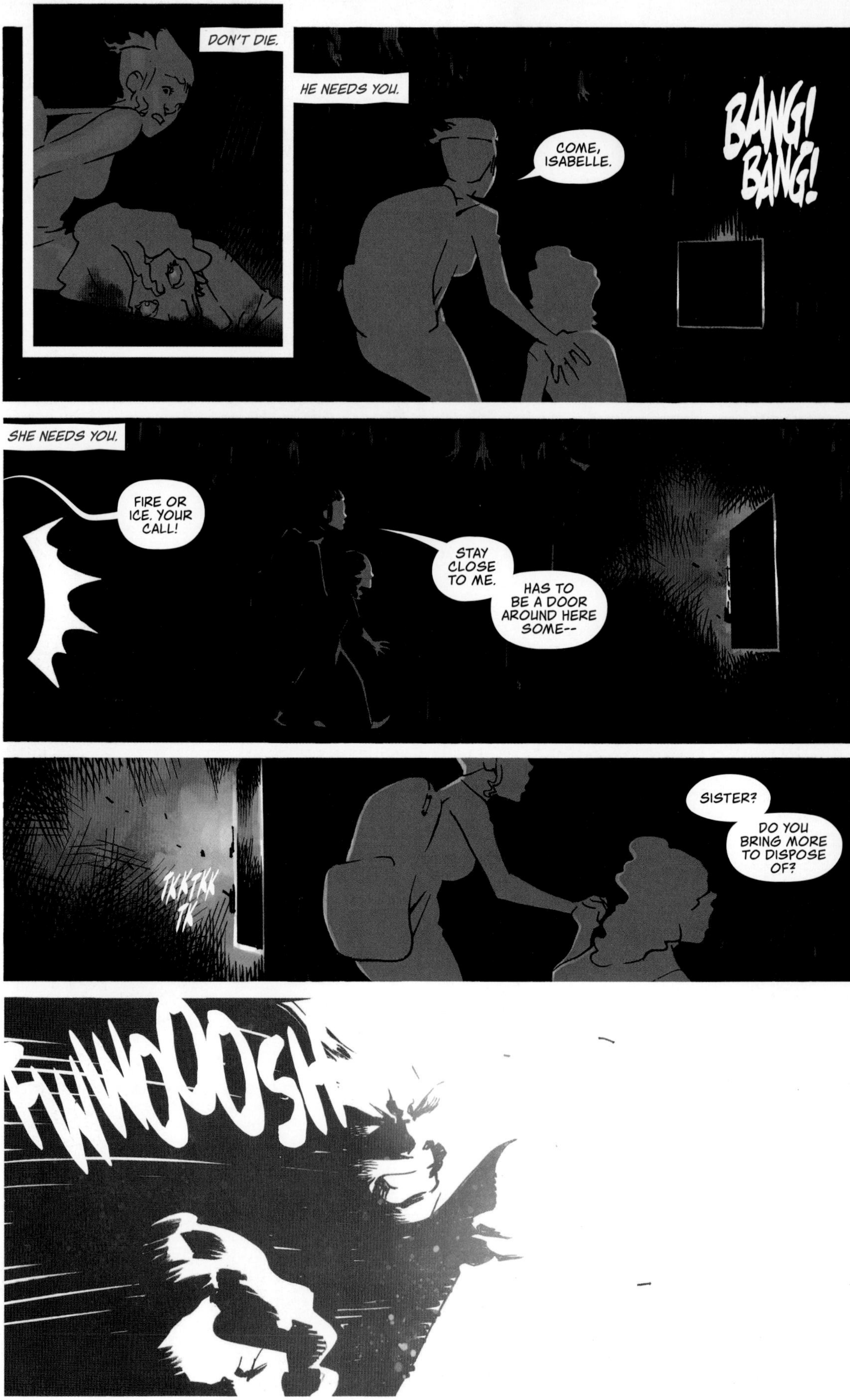
DON'T DIE.
HE NEEDS YOU.
COME, ISABELLE.
BANG! BANG!
SHE NEEDS YOU.
FIRE OR ICE. YOUR CALL!
STAY CLOSE TO ME.
HAS TO BE A DOOR AROUND HERE SOME--
TKKTKK TK
SISTER?
DO YOU BRING MORE TO DISPOSE OF?
FWWOOOSH

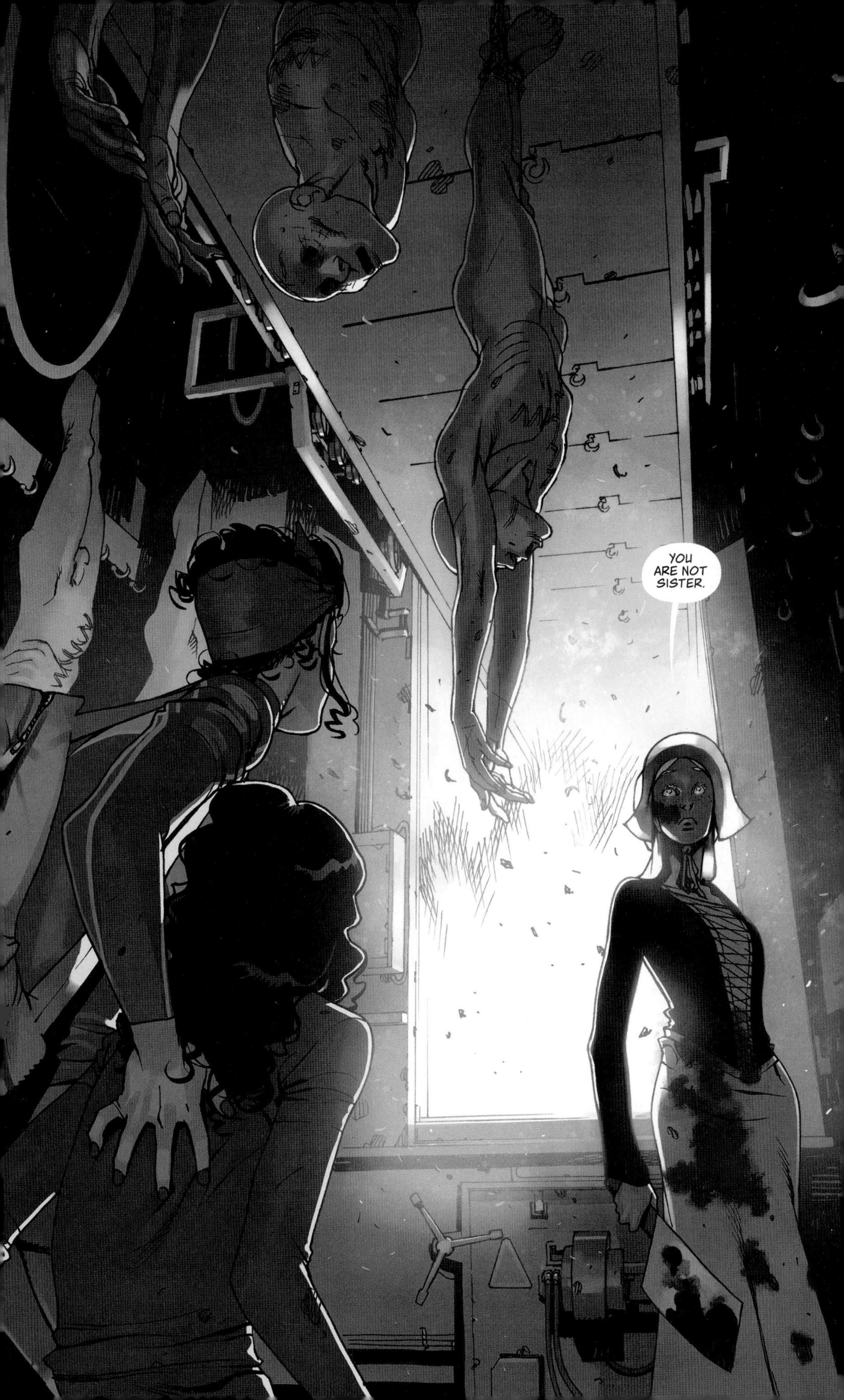
YOU ARE NOT SISTER.

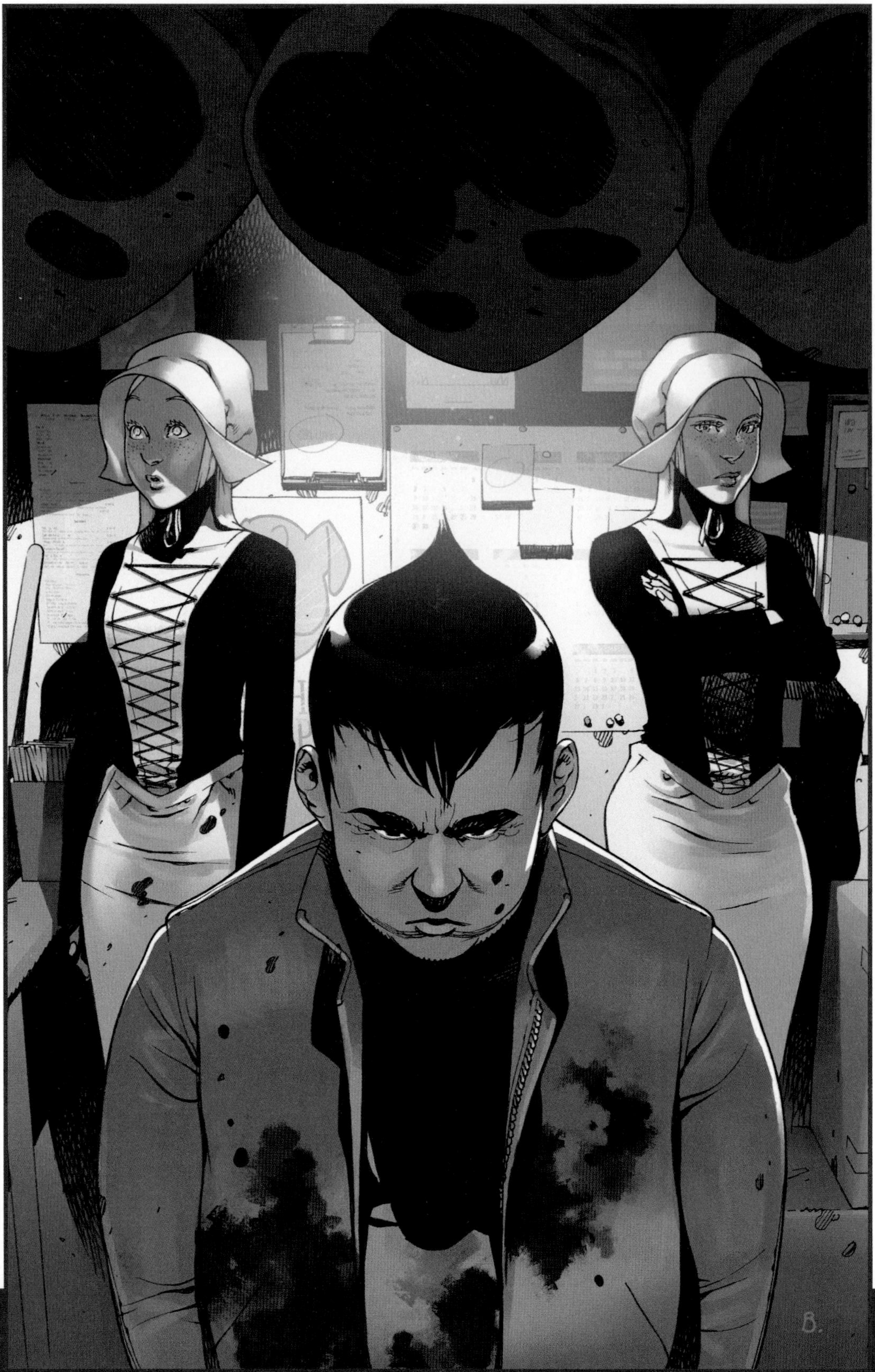

F O U R

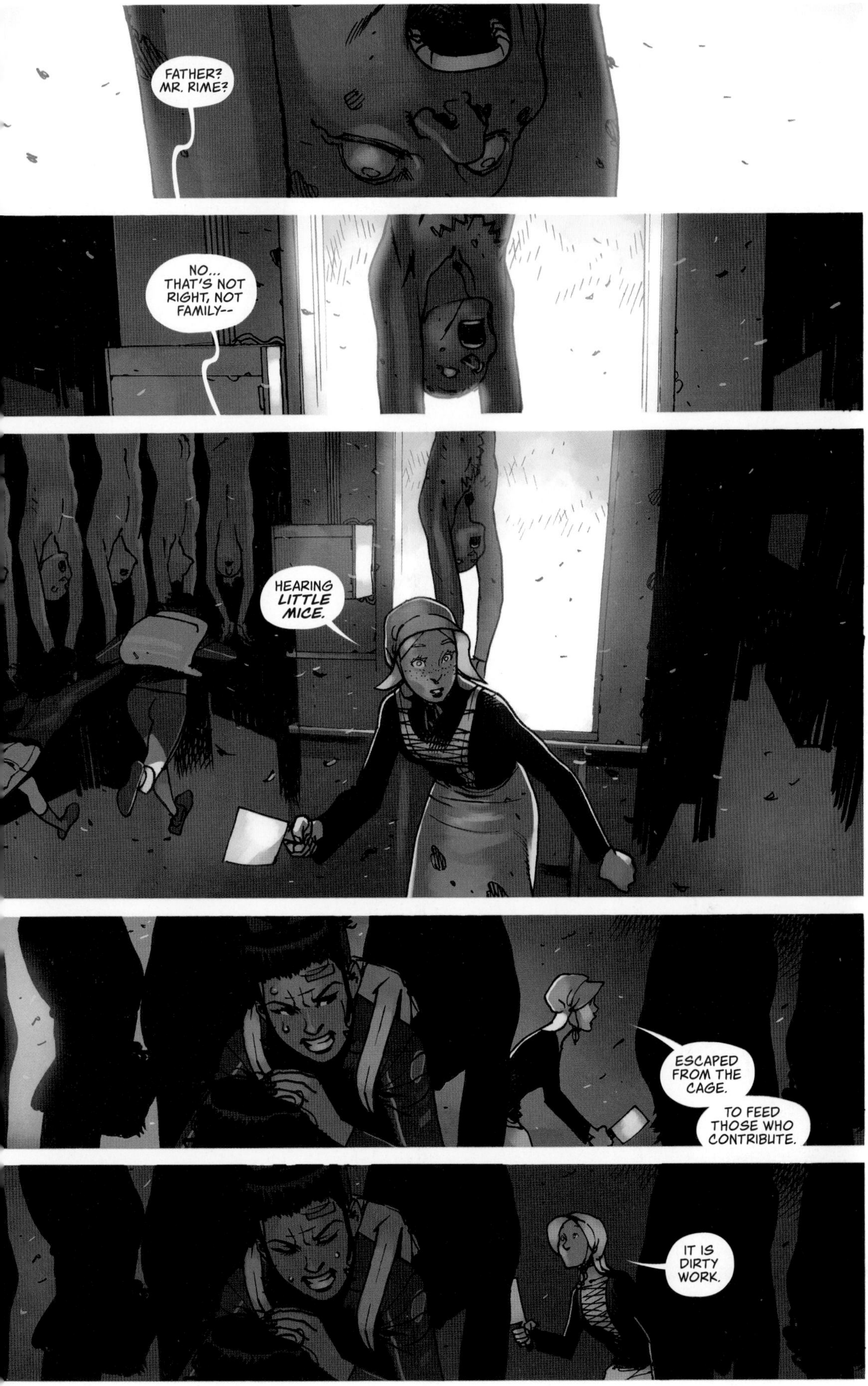
FATHER? MR. RIME?
NO... THAT'S NOT RIGHT, NOT FAMILY--
HEARING *LITTLE MICE.*
ESCAPED FROM THE CAGE.
TO FEED THOSE WHO CONTRIBUTE.
IT IS DIRTY WORK.

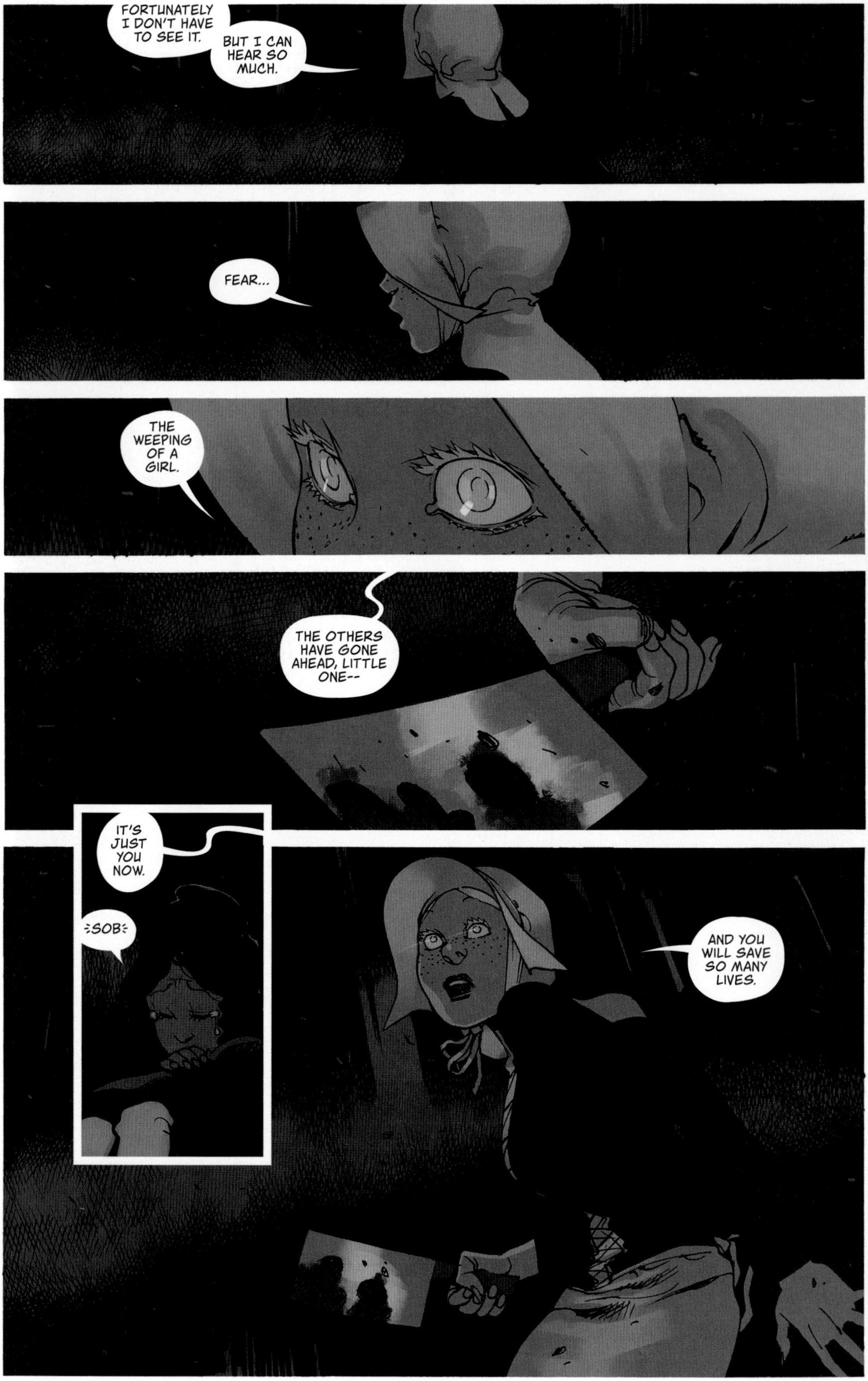
FORTUNATELY I DON'T HAVE TO SEE IT.
BUT I CAN HEAR SO MUCH.
FEAR...
THE WEEPING OF A GIRL.
THE OTHERS HAVE GONE AHEAD, LITTLE ONE--
IT'S JUST YOU NOW.
SOB
AND YOU WILL SAVE SO MANY LIVES.

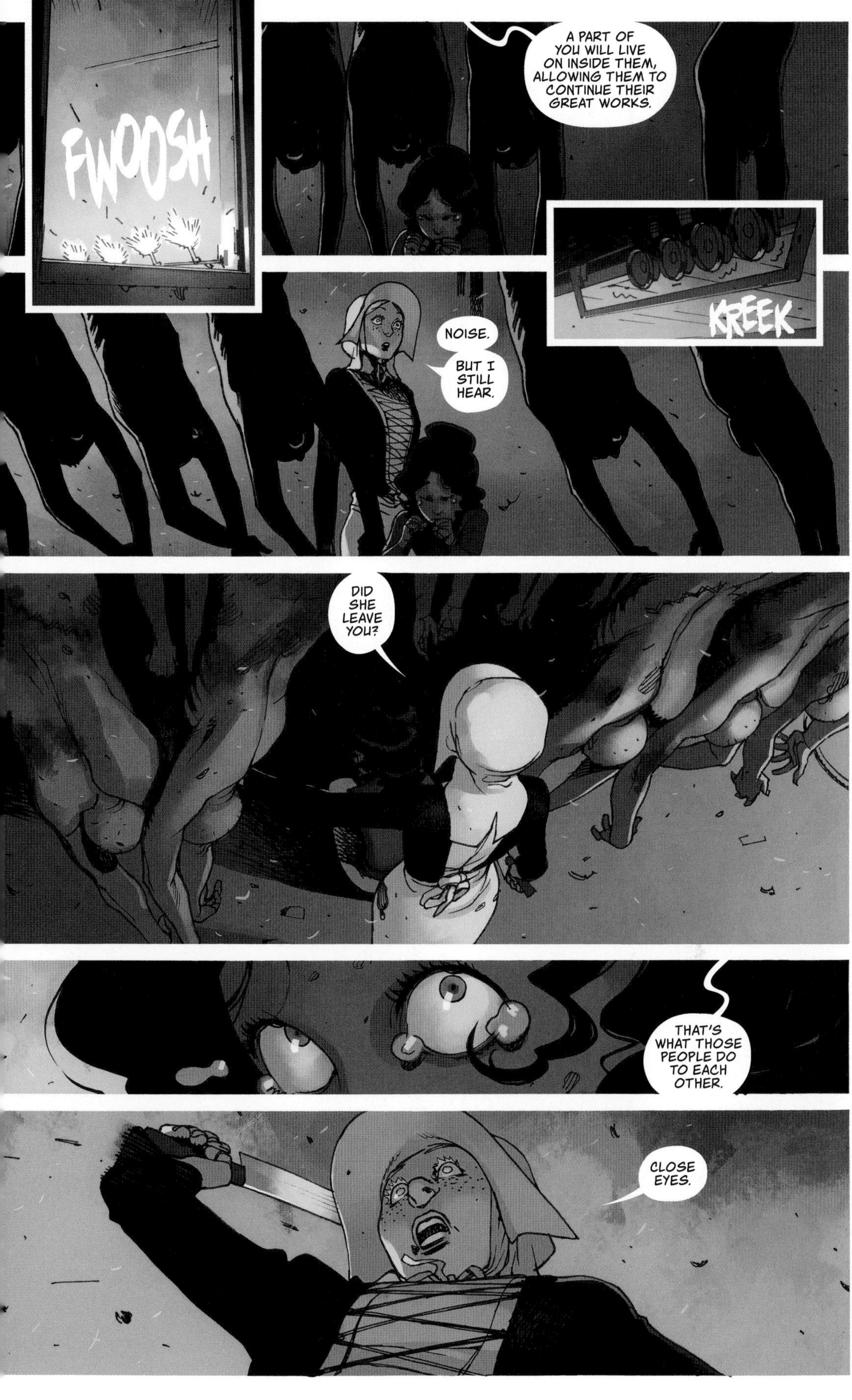
FWOOSH
A PART OF YOU WILL LIVE ON INSIDE THEM, ALLOWING THEM TO CONTINUE THEIR GREAT WORKS.
KREEK
NOISE.
BUT I STILL HEAR.
DID SHE LEAVE YOU?
THAT'S WHAT THOSE PEOPLE DO TO EACH OTHER.
CLOSE EYES.

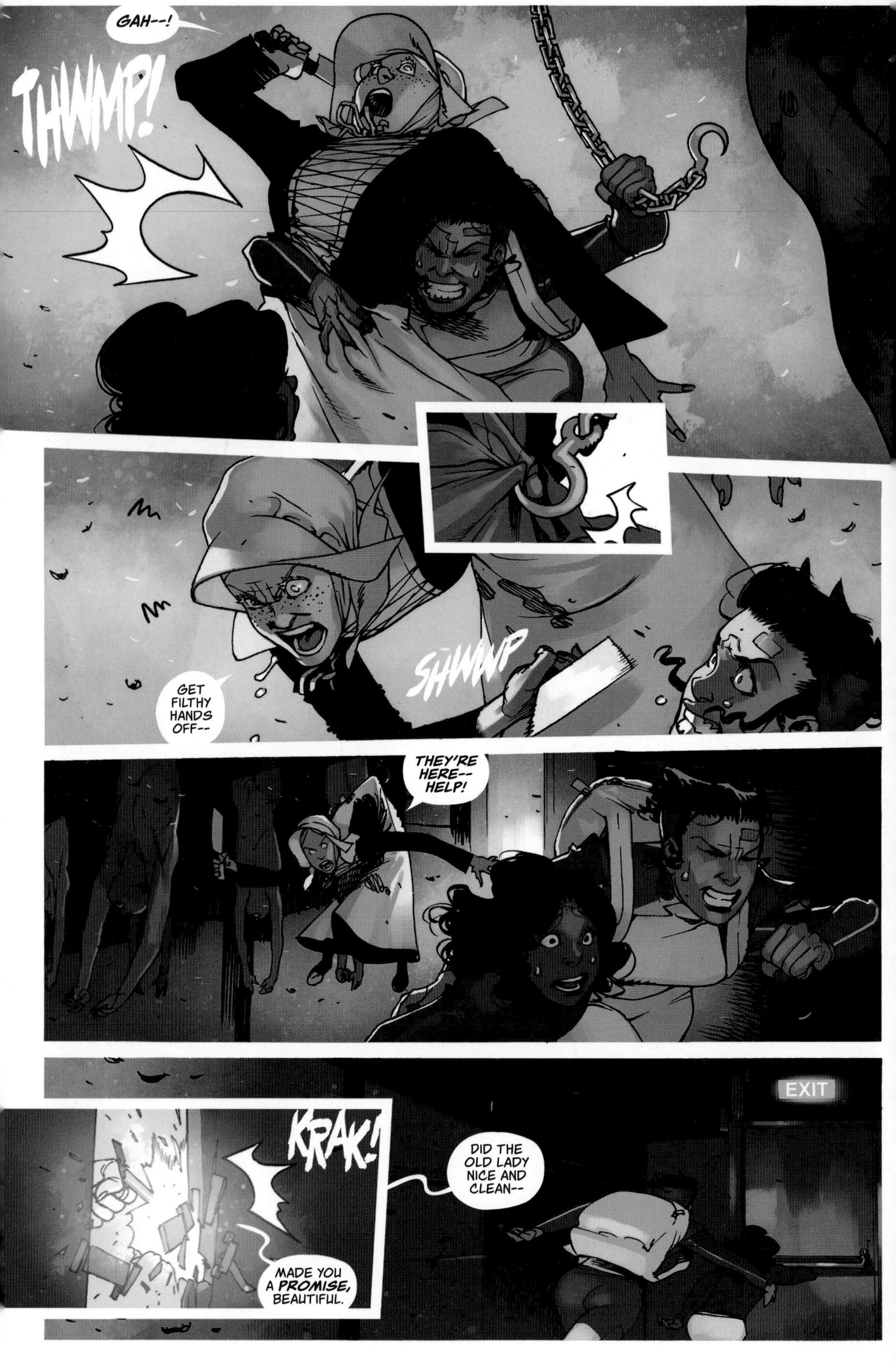
GAH--!
THWMP!
GET FILTHY HANDS OFF--
SHWMP
THEY'RE HERE-- HELP!
EXIT
KRAK!
DID THE OLD LADY NICE AND CLEAN--
MADE YOU A PROMISE, BEAUTIFUL.

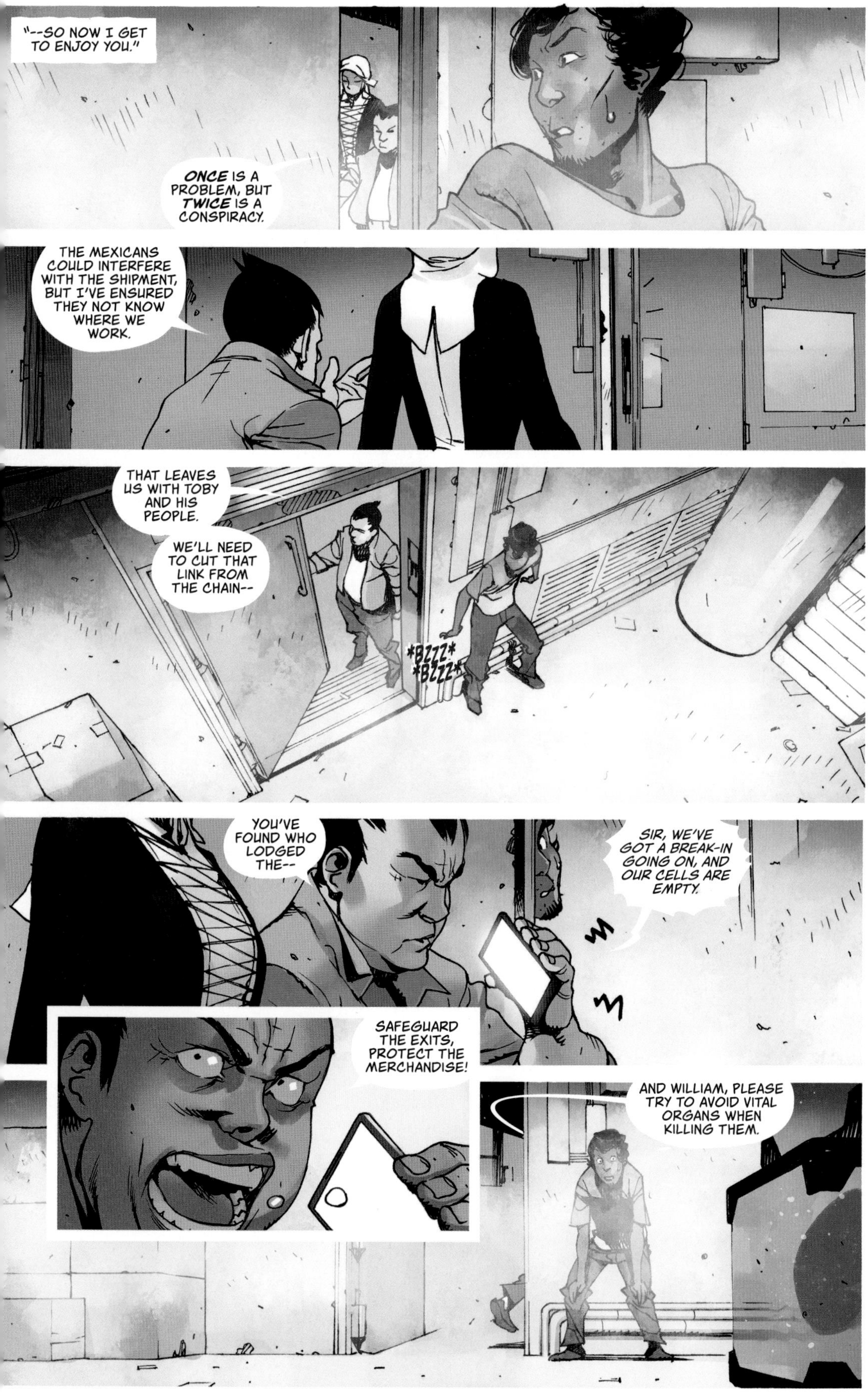
"--SO NOW I GET TO ENJOY YOU."
ONCE IS A PROBLEM, BUT TWICE IS A CONSPIRACY.
THE MEXICANS COULD INTERFERE WITH THE SHIPMENT, BUT I'VE ENSURED THEY NOT KNOW WHERE WE WORK.
THAT LEAVES US WITH TOBY AND HIS PEOPLE.
WE'LL NEED TO CUT THAT LINK FROM THE CHAIN--
BZZZ *BZZZ*
YOU'VE FOUND WHO LODGED THE--
SIR, WE'VE GOT A BREAK-IN GOING ON, AND OUR CELLS ARE EMPTY.
SAFEGUARD THE EXITS, PROTECT THE MERCHANDISE!
AND WILLIAM, PLEASE TRY TO AVOID VITAL ORGANS WHEN KILLING THEM.

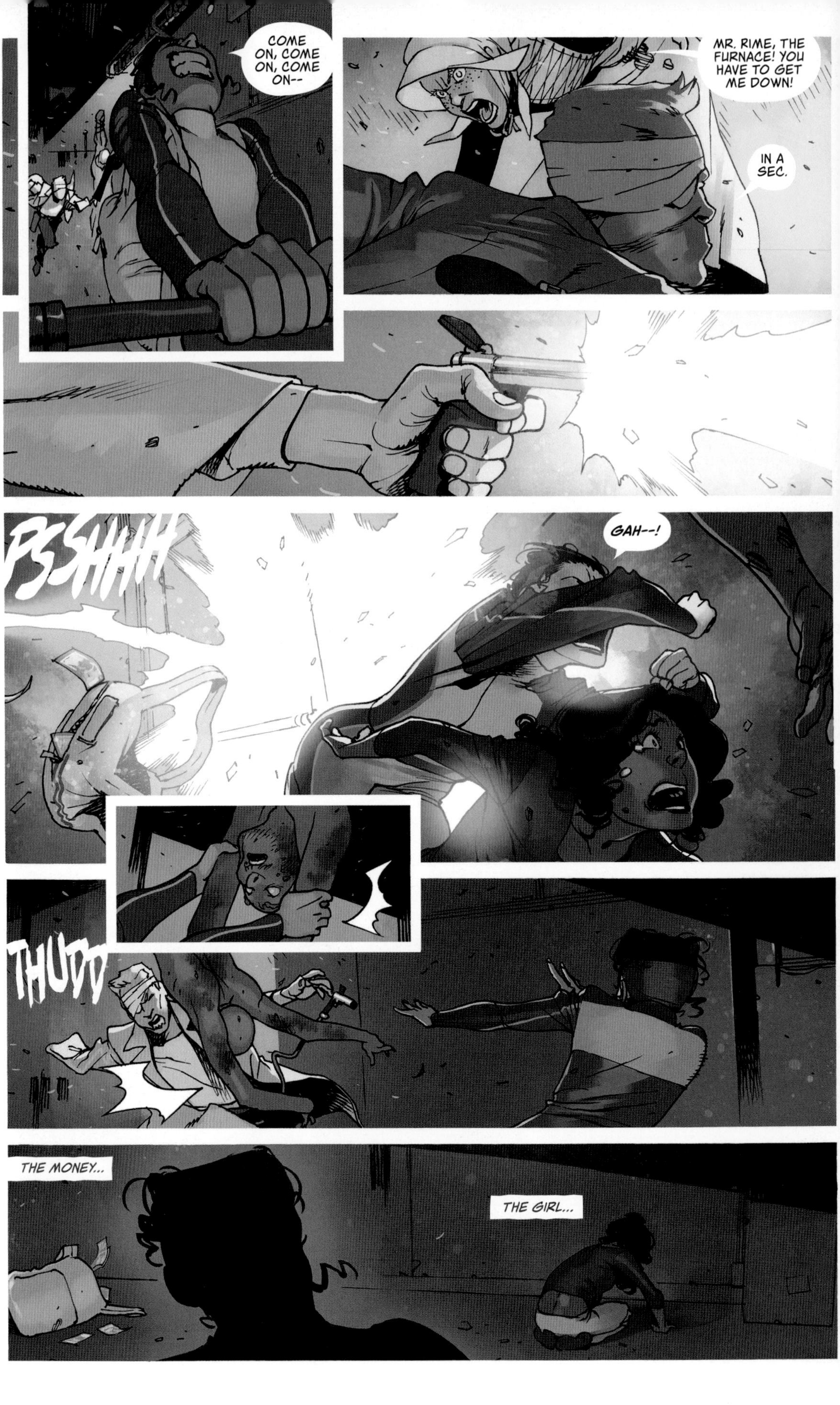
COME ON, COME ON, COME ON--
MR. RIME, THE FURNACE! YOU HAVE TO GET ME DOWN!
IN A SEC.
PSSHHH
GAH--!
THUDD
THE MONEY...
THE GIRL...

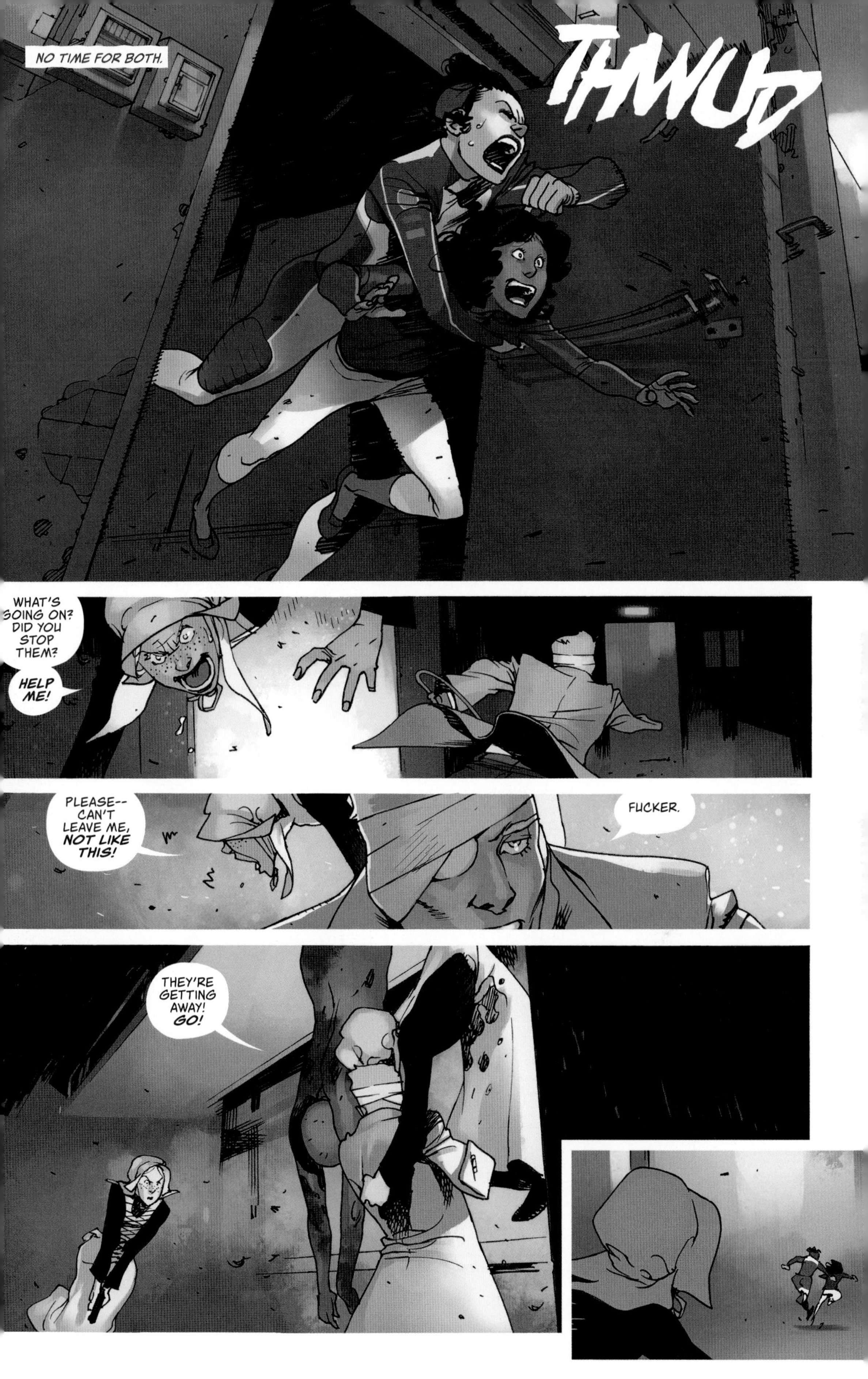
NO TIME FOR BOTH.
THWUD
WHAT'S GOING ON? DID YOU STOP THEM?
HELP ME!
PLEASE-- CAN'T LEAVE ME, NOT LIKE THIS!
FUCKER.
THEY'RE GETTING AWAY! GO!

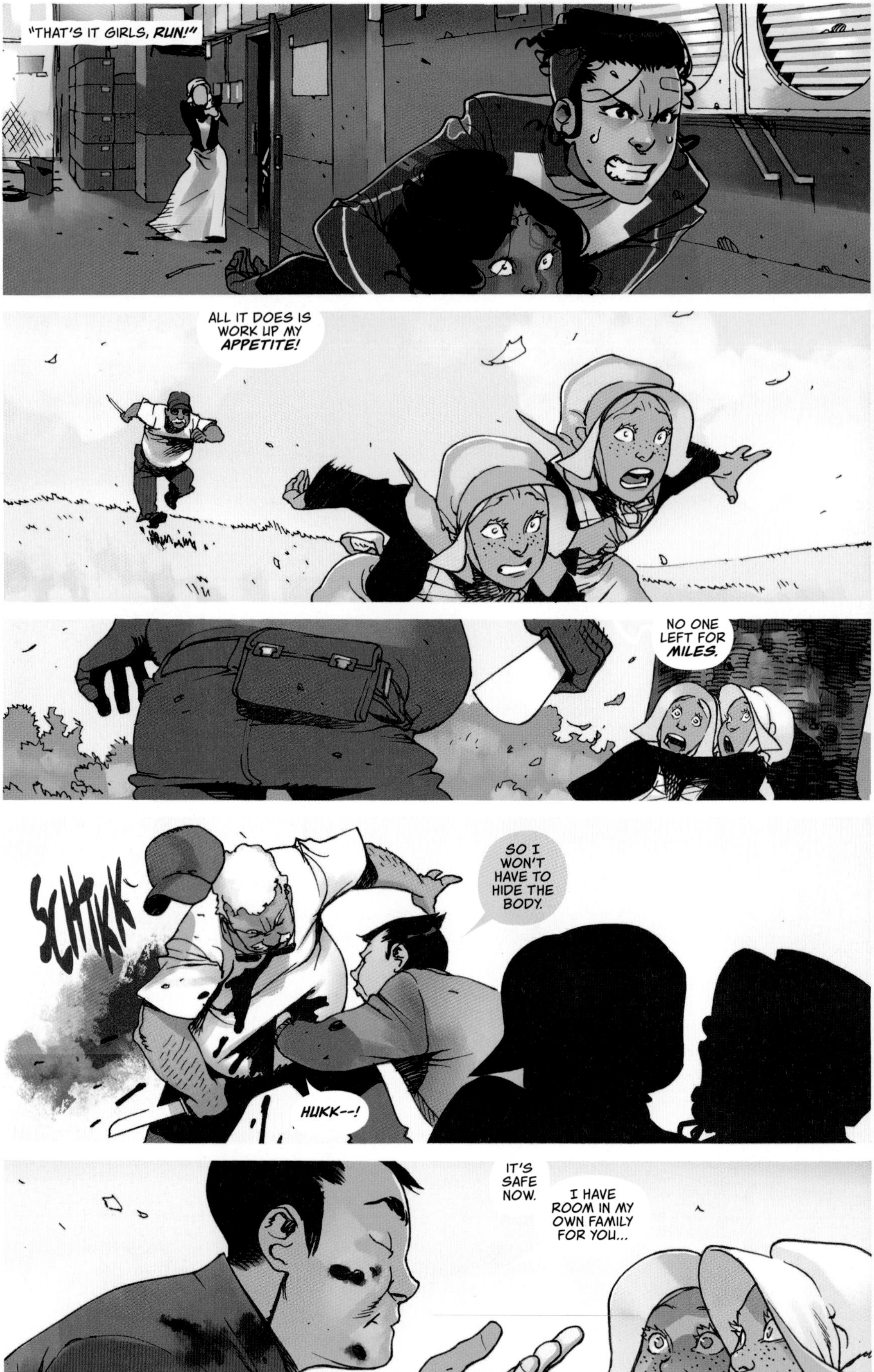
"THAT'S IT GIRLS, RUN!"
ALL IT DOES IS WORK UP MY APPETITE!
NO ONE LEFT FOR MILES.
SCHTIKK
SO I WON'T HAVE TO HIDE THE BODY.
HUKK--!
IT'S SAFE NOW.
I HAVE ROOM IN MY OWN FAMILY FOR YOU...

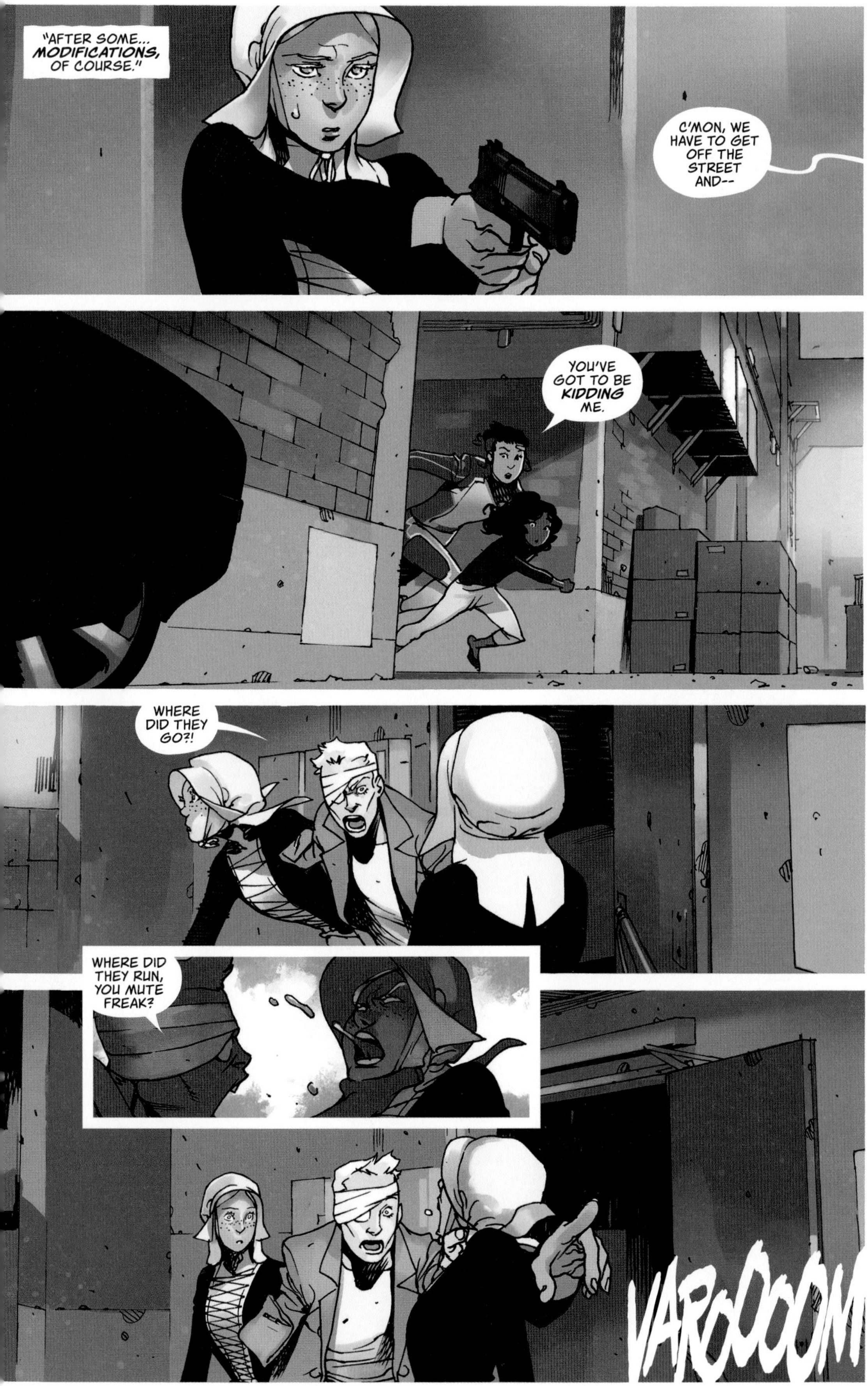
"AFTER SOME... MODIFICATIONS, OF COURSE."
C'MON, WE HAVE TO GET OFF THE STREET AND--
YOU'VE GOT TO BE KIDDING ME.
WHERE DID THEY GO?!
WHERE DID THEY RUN, YOU MUTE FREAK?
VAROOOOM

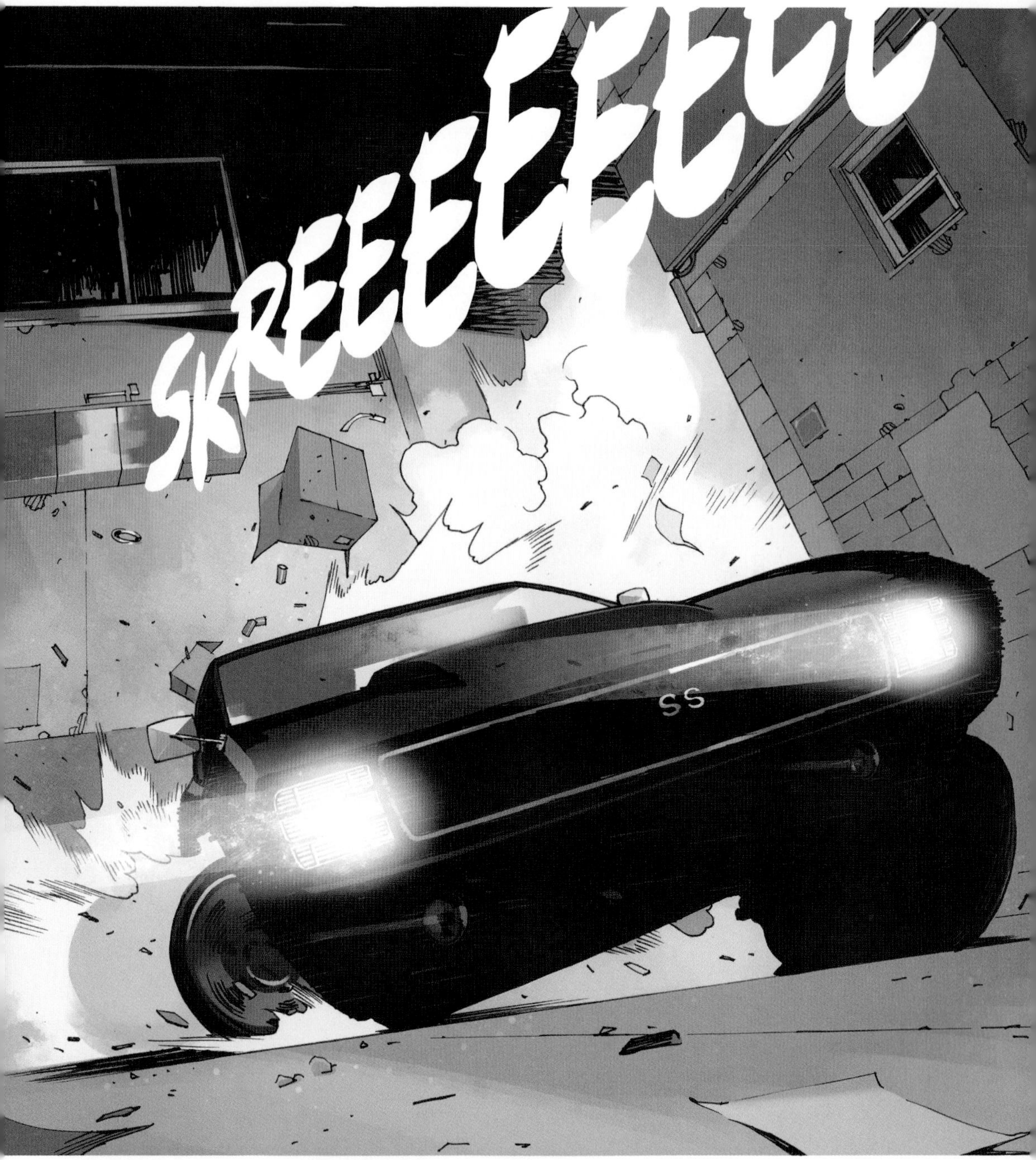
SKREEEEEEEEEEEE

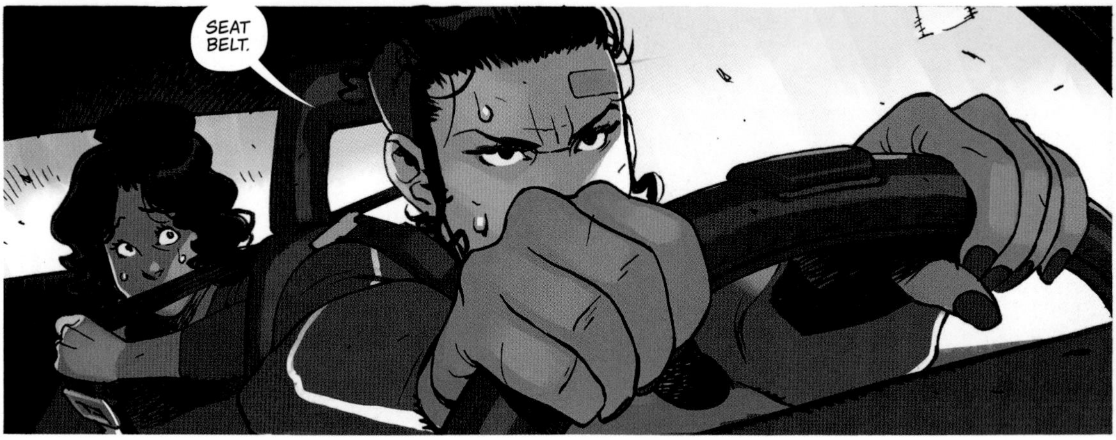
SEAT BELT.

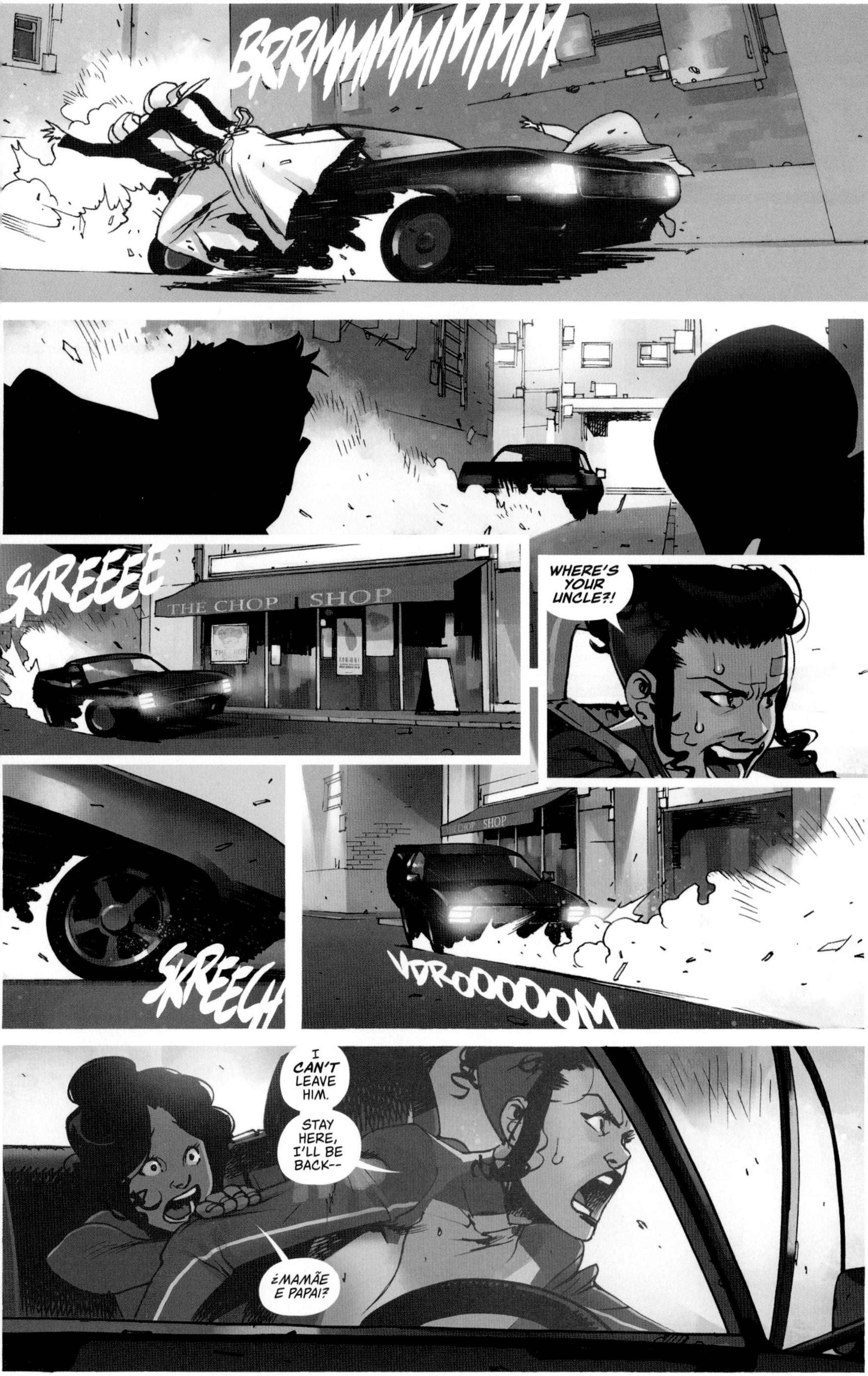
BRRMMMMMMMM
SKREEEEE
THE CHOP SHOP
WHERE'S YOUR UNCLE?!
SKREECH
CHOP SHOP
VDROOOOOOM
I CAN'T LEAVE HIM.
STAY HERE, I'LL BE BACK--
¿MAMÃE E PAPAI?

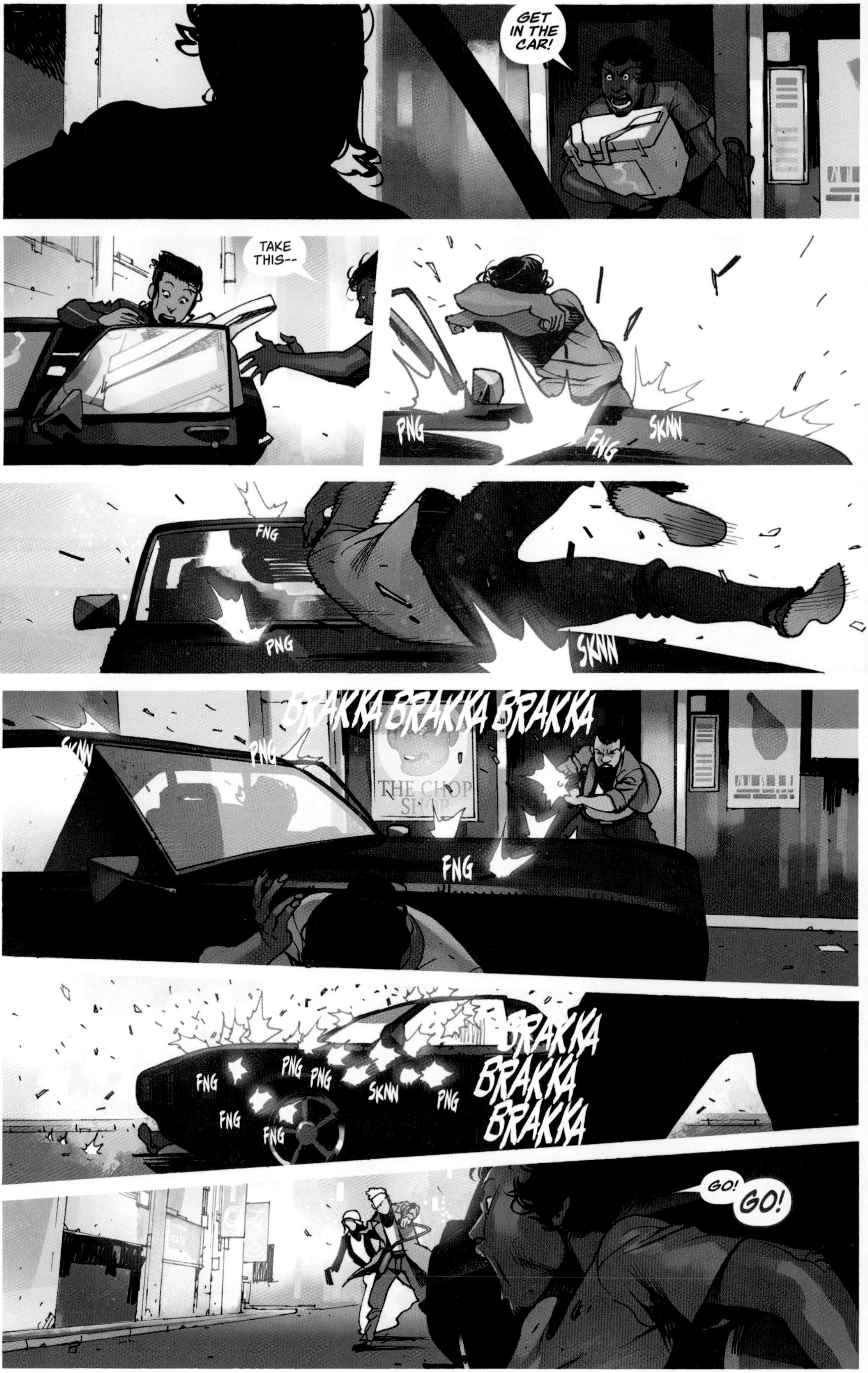
GET IN THE CAR!
TAKE THIS--
PNG
FNG
SKNN
FNG
PNG
SKNN
BRAKKA BRAKKA BRAKKA
SKNN
PNG
THE CHOP SHOP
FNG
BRAKKA BRAKKA BRAKKA
FNG
PNG
PNG
SKNN
PNG
FNG
FNG
GO!
GO!

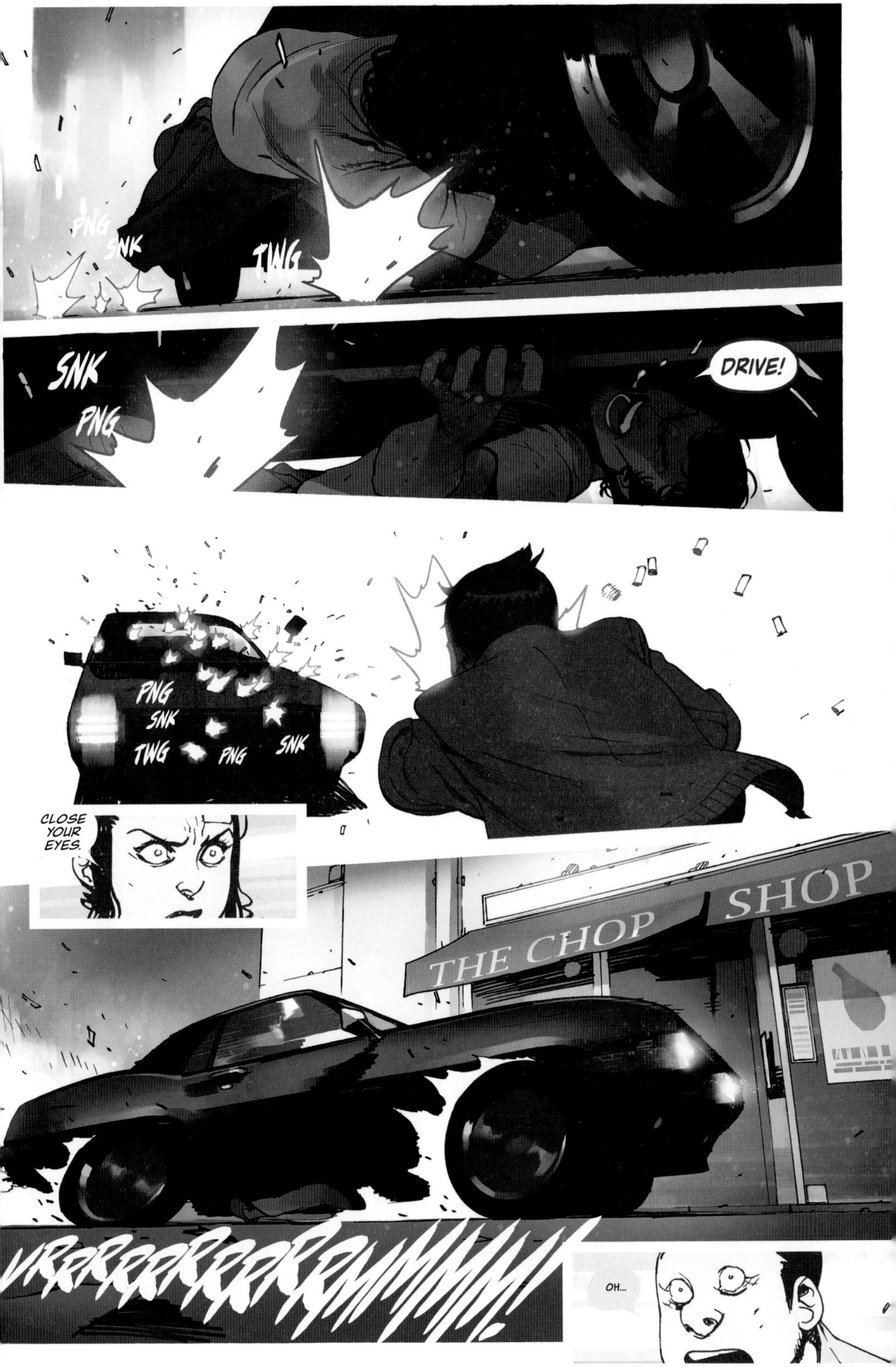
PNG
SNK
TWG
SNK
PNG
DRIVE!
PNG
SNK
TWG
PNG
SNK
CLOSE YOUR EYES.
THE CHOP SHOP
VRRRRRRRRRRRMMMMM!
OH...

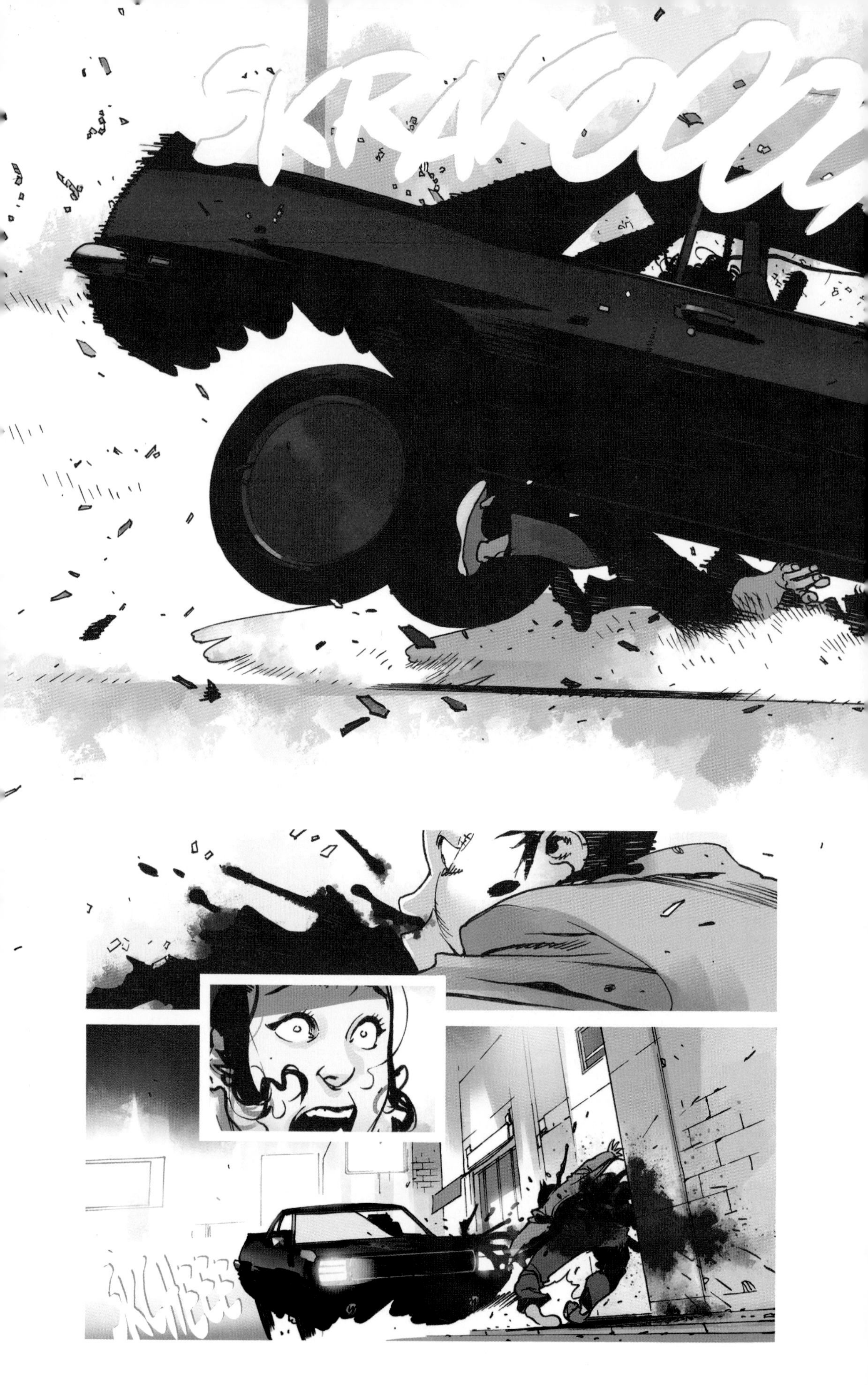
SKRAKOOO
SKLHEEE

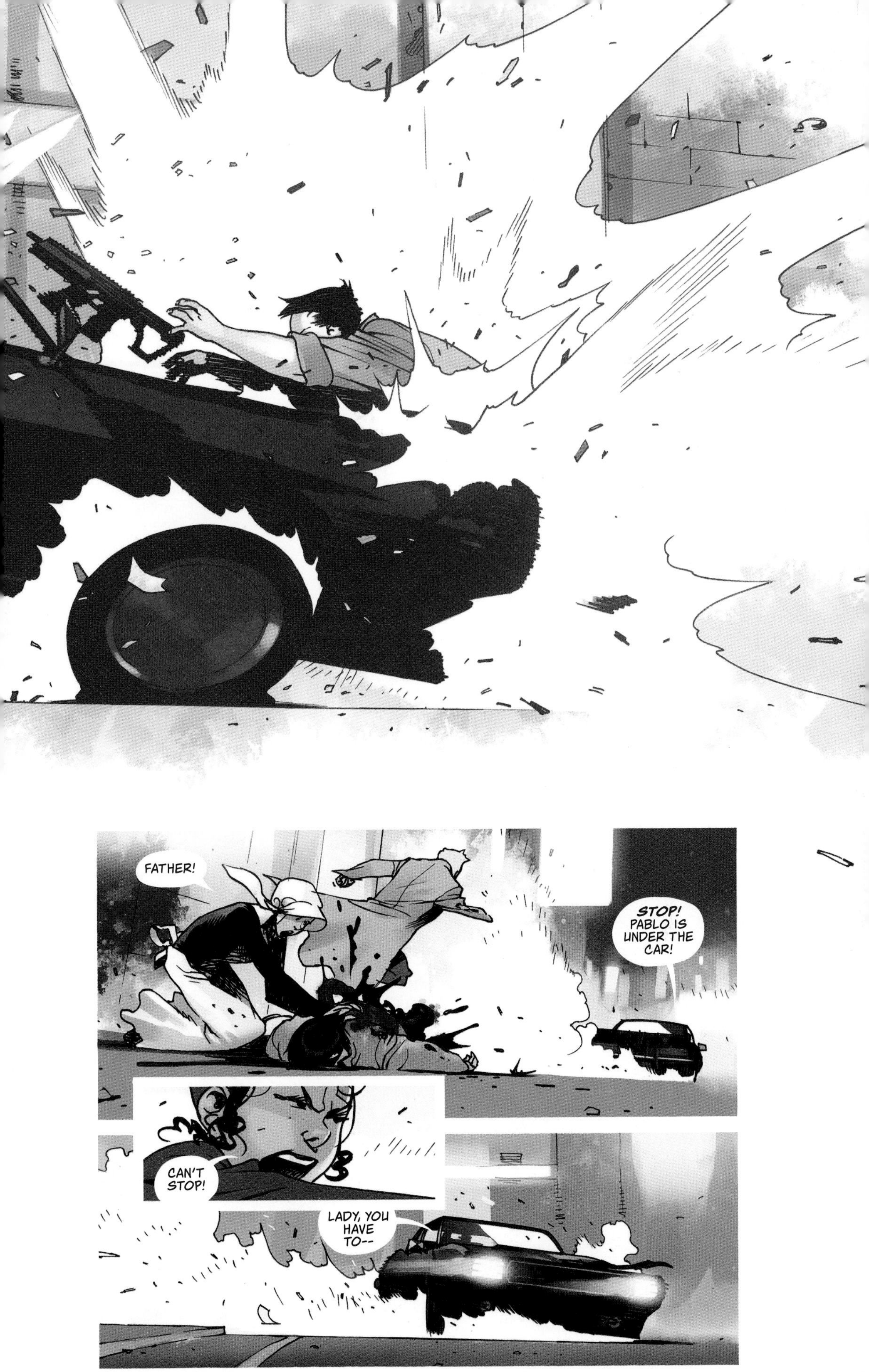
FATHER!
STOP! PABLO IS UNDER THE CAR!
CAN'T STOP!
LADY, YOU HAVE TO--

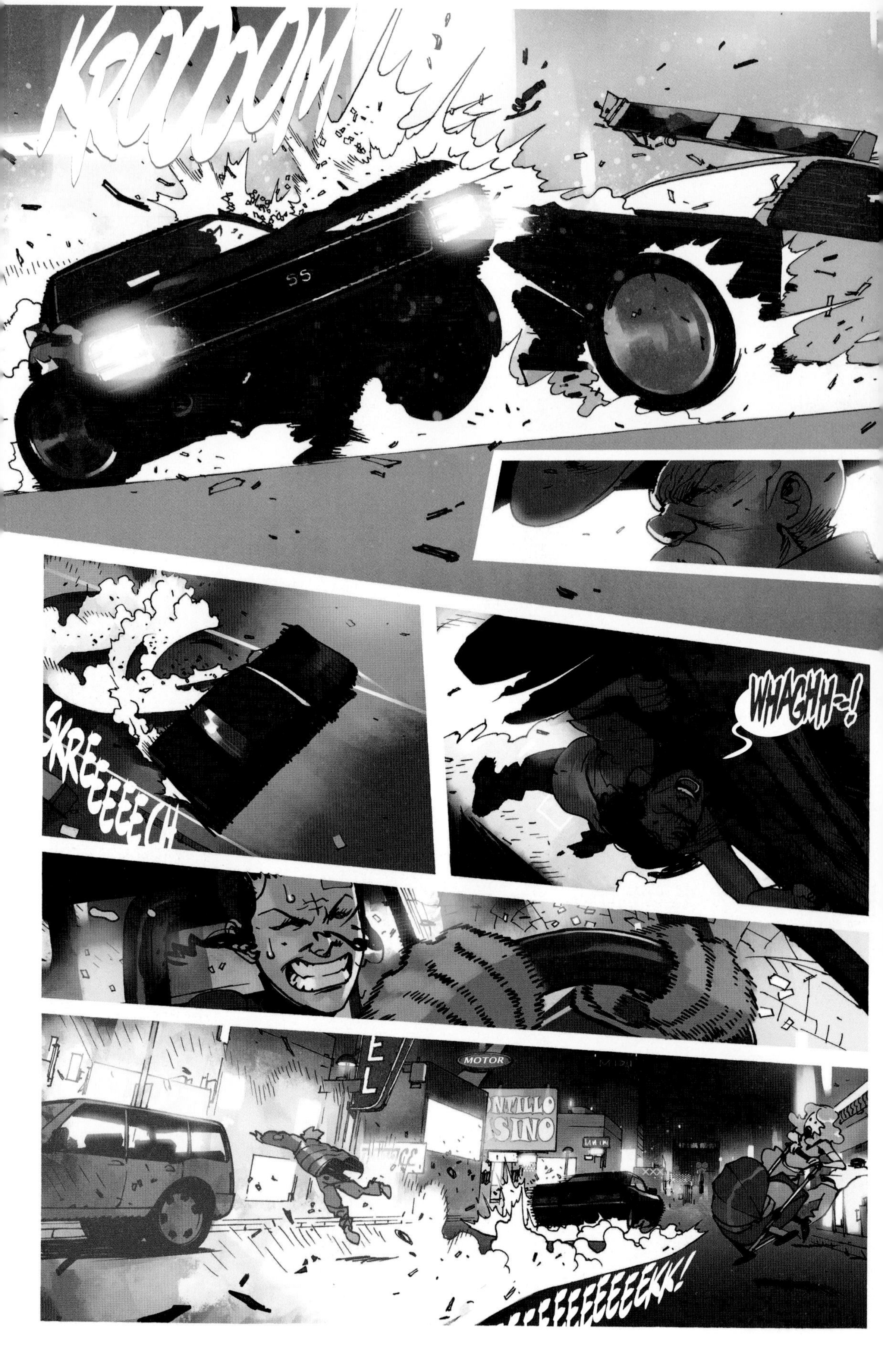
KROOOM
SKREEEEEECH
WHAGHH-!
MOTOR
SINO

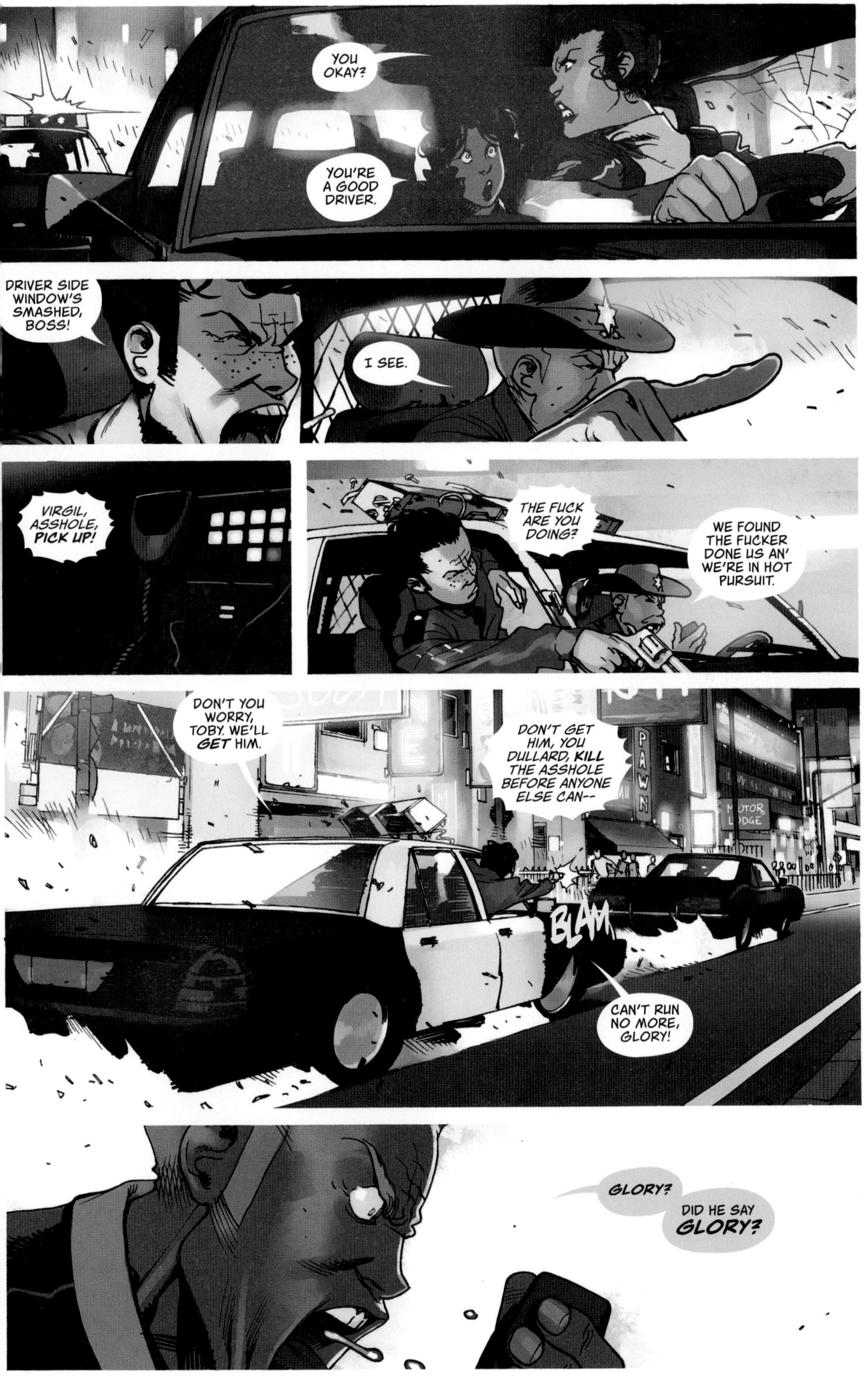
YOU OKAY?
YOU'RE A GOOD DRIVER.
DRIVER SIDE WINDOW'S SMASHED, BOSS!
I SEE.
VIRGIL, ASSHOLE, PICK UP!
THE FUCK ARE YOU DOING?
WE FOUND THE FUCKER DONE US AN' WE'RE IN HOT PURSUIT.
DON'T YOU WORRY, TOBY. WE'LL GET HIM.
DON'T GET HIM, YOU DULLARD, KILL THE ASSHOLE BEFORE ANYONE ELSE CAN--
PAWN
MOTOR LODGE
BLAM
CAN'T RUN NO MORE, GLORY!
GLORY?
DID HE SAY GLORY?

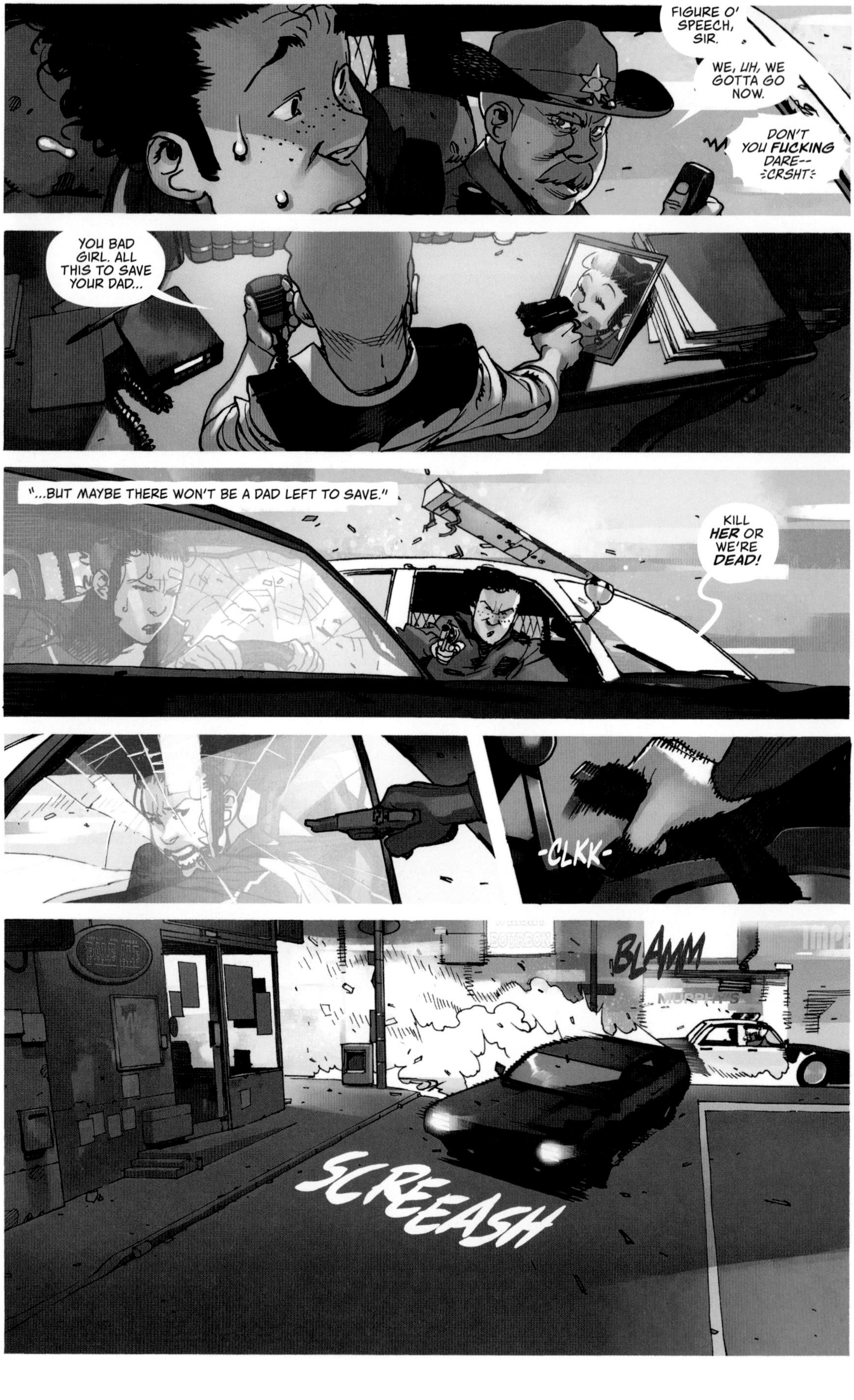
FIGURE O' SPEECH, SIR.
WE, UH, WE GOTTA GO NOW.
DON'T YOU FUCKING DARE-- =CRSHT=
YOU BAD GIRL. ALL THIS TO SAVE YOUR DAD...
"...BUT MAYBE THERE WON'T BE A DAD LEFT TO SAVE."
KILL HER OR WE'RE DEAD!
-CLKK-
BOURBON
BLAMM
MURPHY'S
SCREEASH

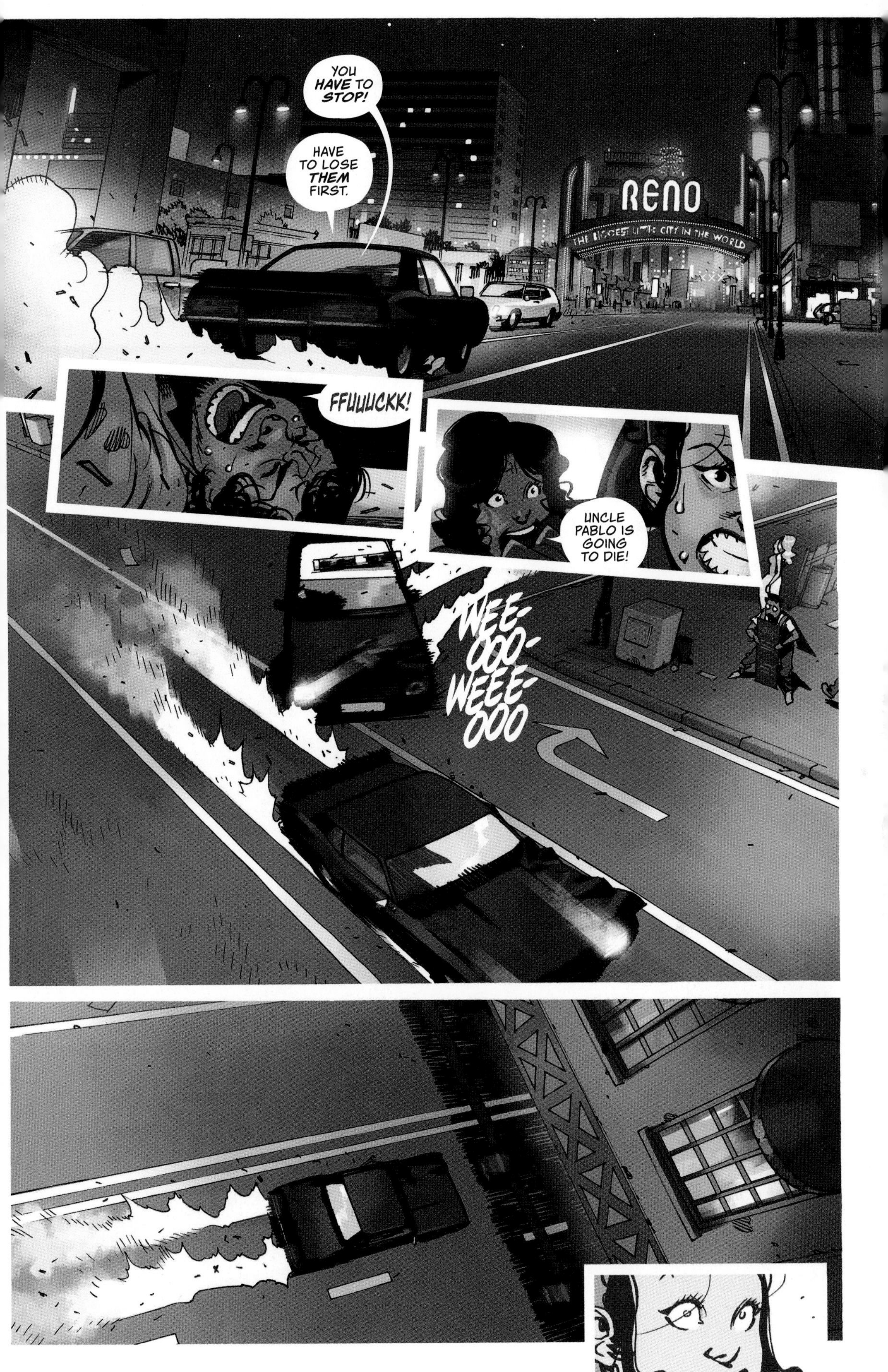
YOU HAVE TO STOP!
HAVE TO LOSE THEM FIRST.
RENO
FFUUUCKK!
UNCLE PABLO IS GOING TO DIE!
WEE-OOO-WEEE-OOO

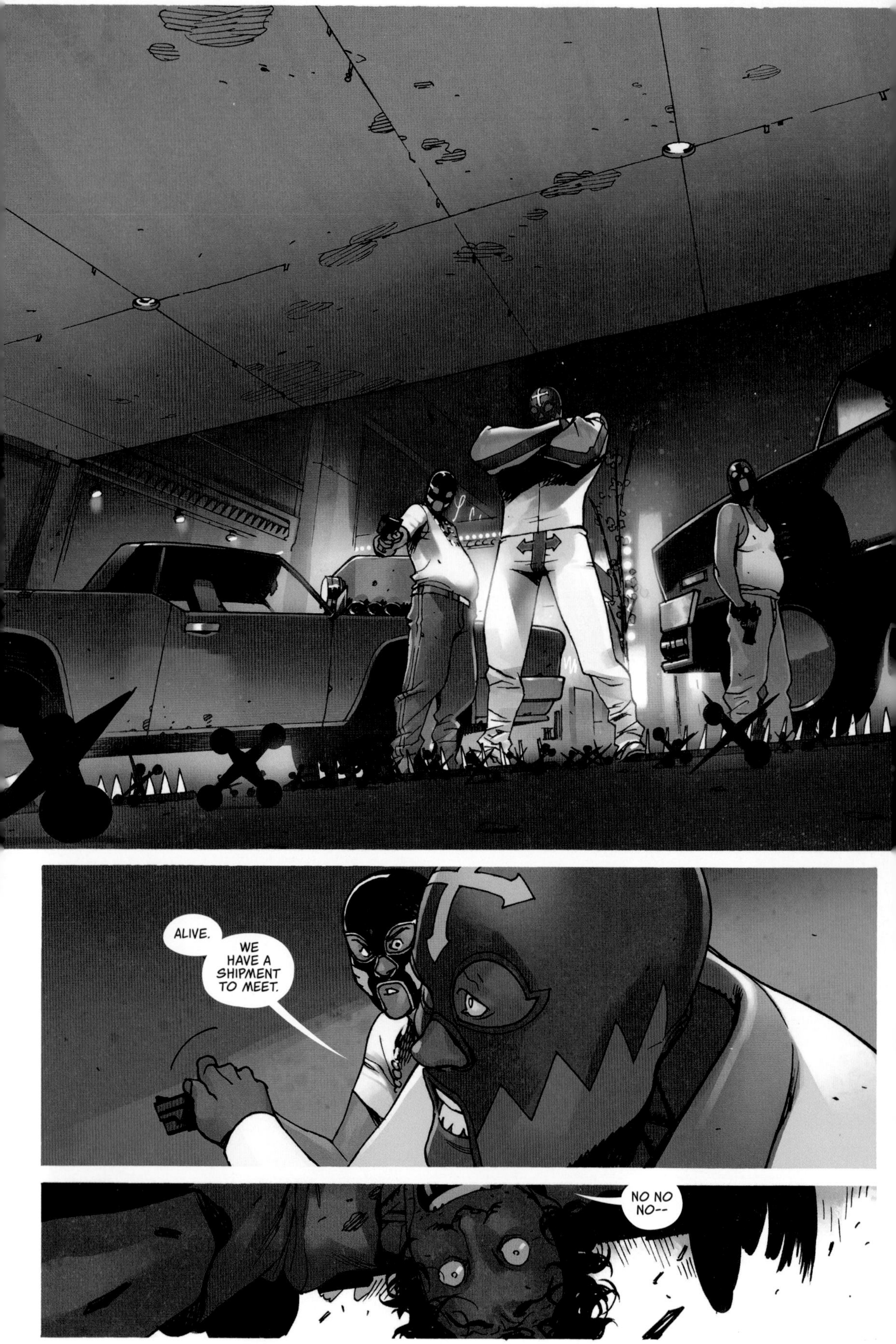
ALIVE.
WE HAVE A SHIPMENT TO MEET.
NO NO NO--

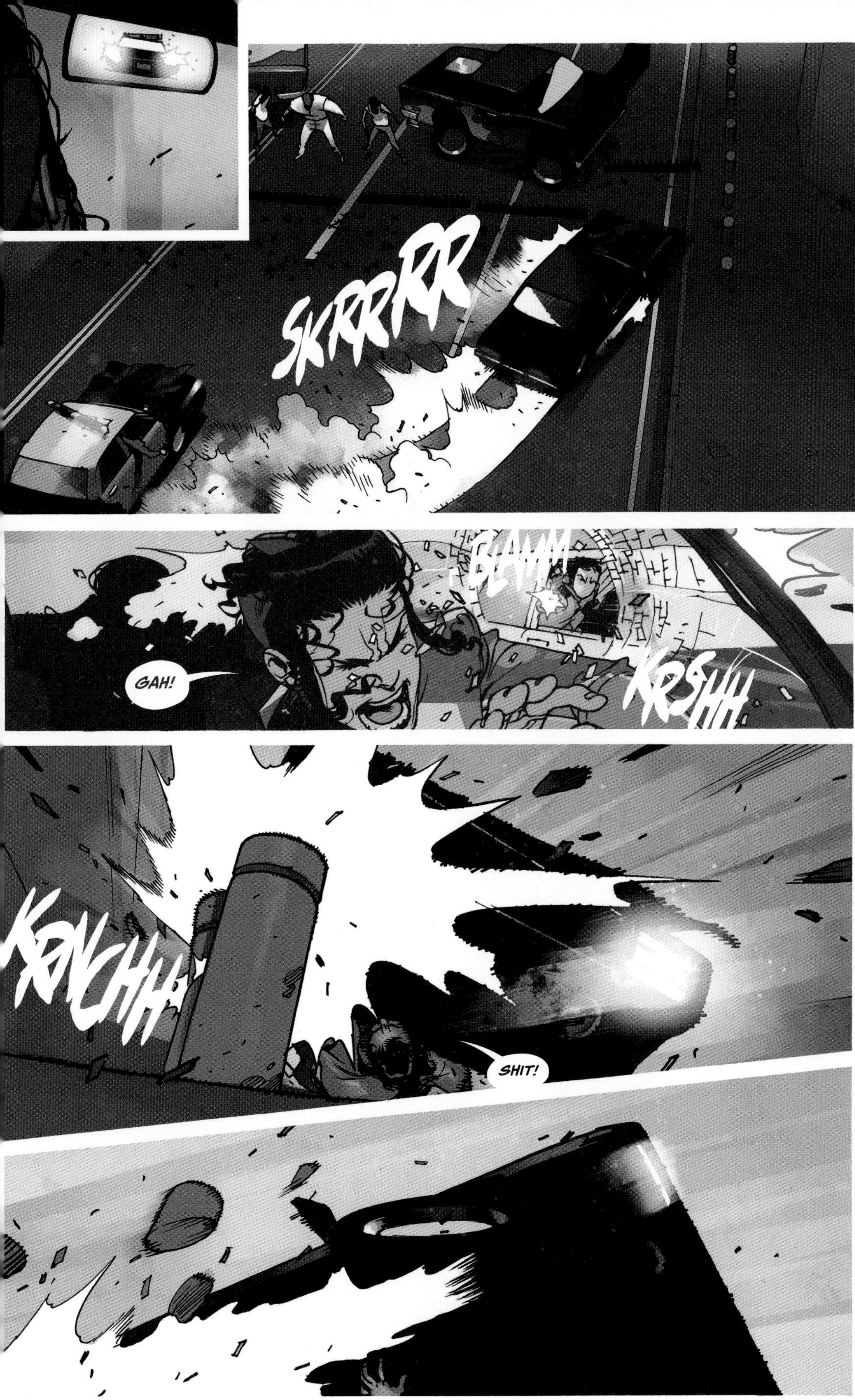
SKRRRRR
BLAMM
GAH!
KRSHH
KRNCHH
SHIT!

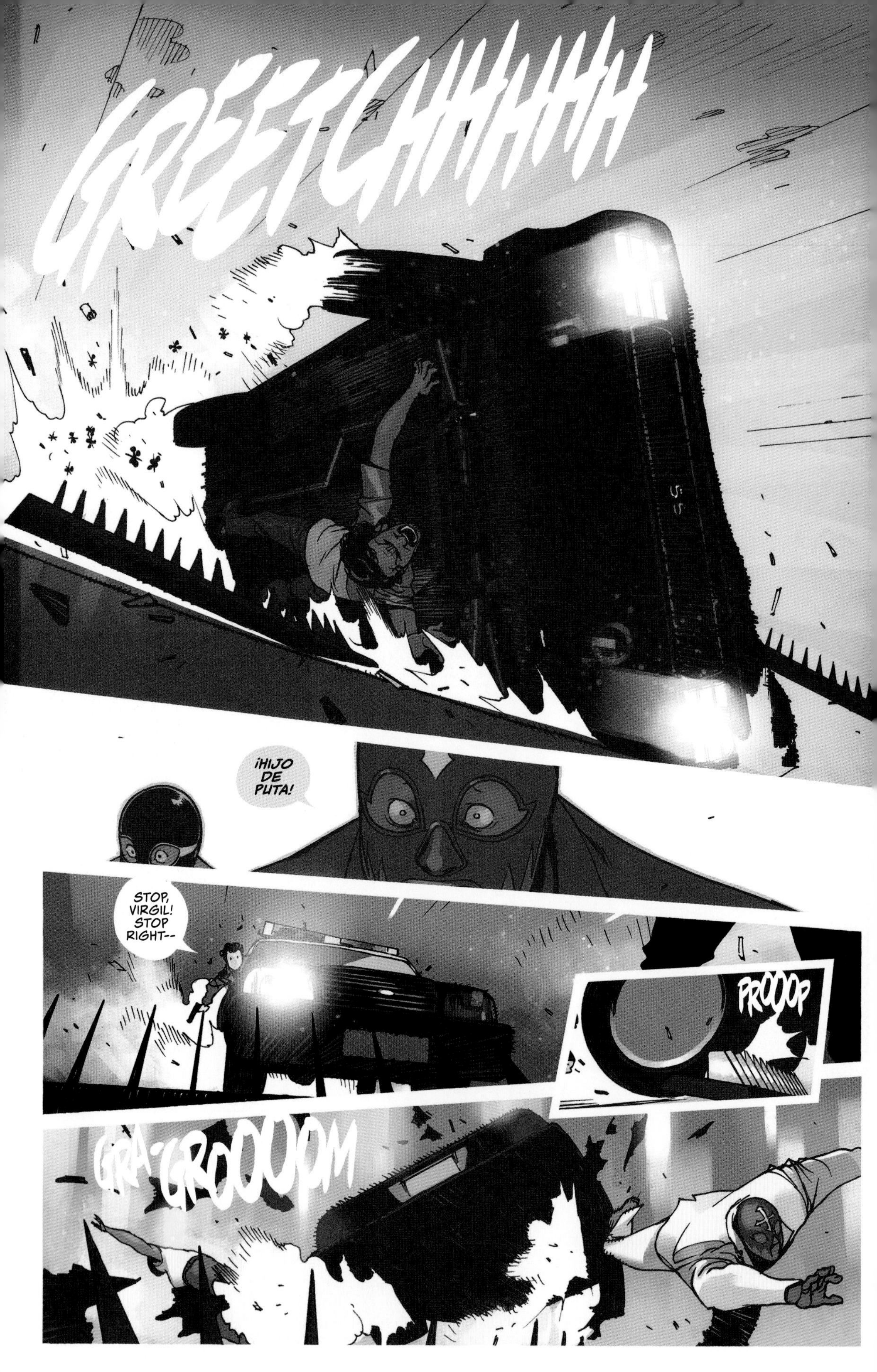
GREETCHHHHH
¡HIJO DE PUTA!
STOP, VIRGIL! STOP RIGHT--
PROOOP
GRA-GROOOOOM

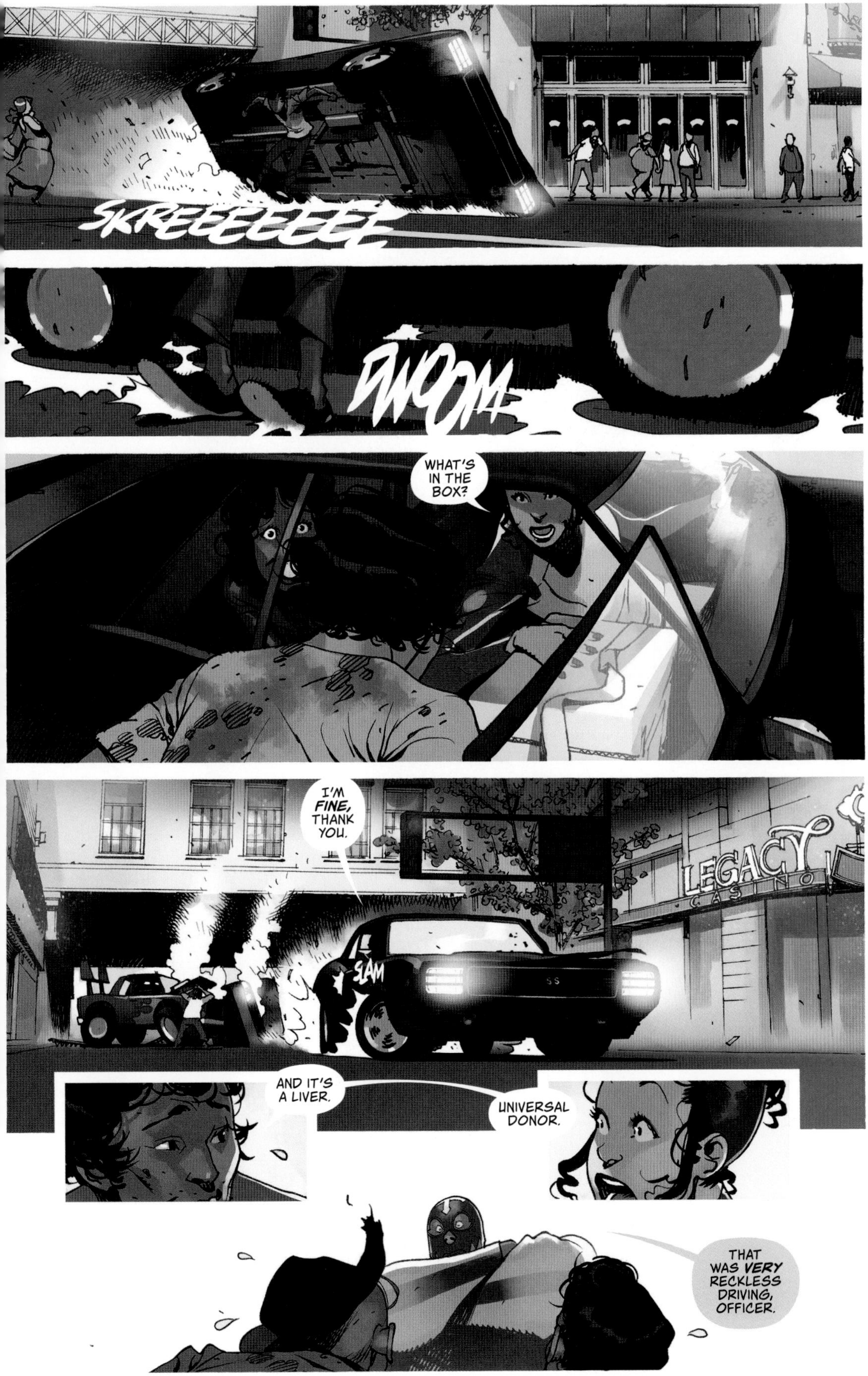
SKREEEEEEEE
DWOOM
WHAT'S IN THE BOX?
I'M FINE, THANK YOU.
SLAM
LEGACY CASINO
AND IT'S A LIVER.
UNIVERSAL DONOR.
THAT WAS VERY RECKLESS DRIVING, OFFICER.

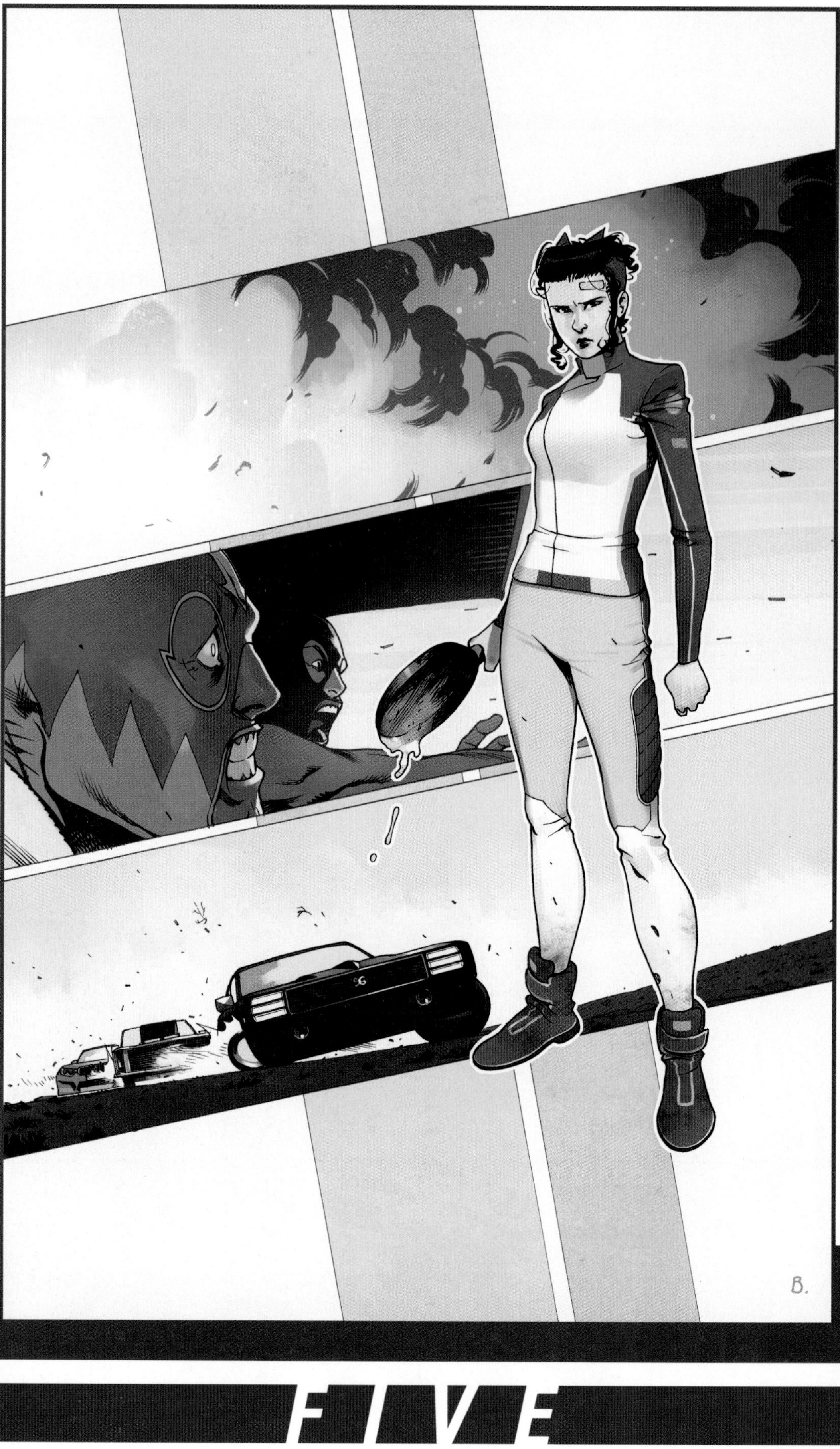
!

FIVE

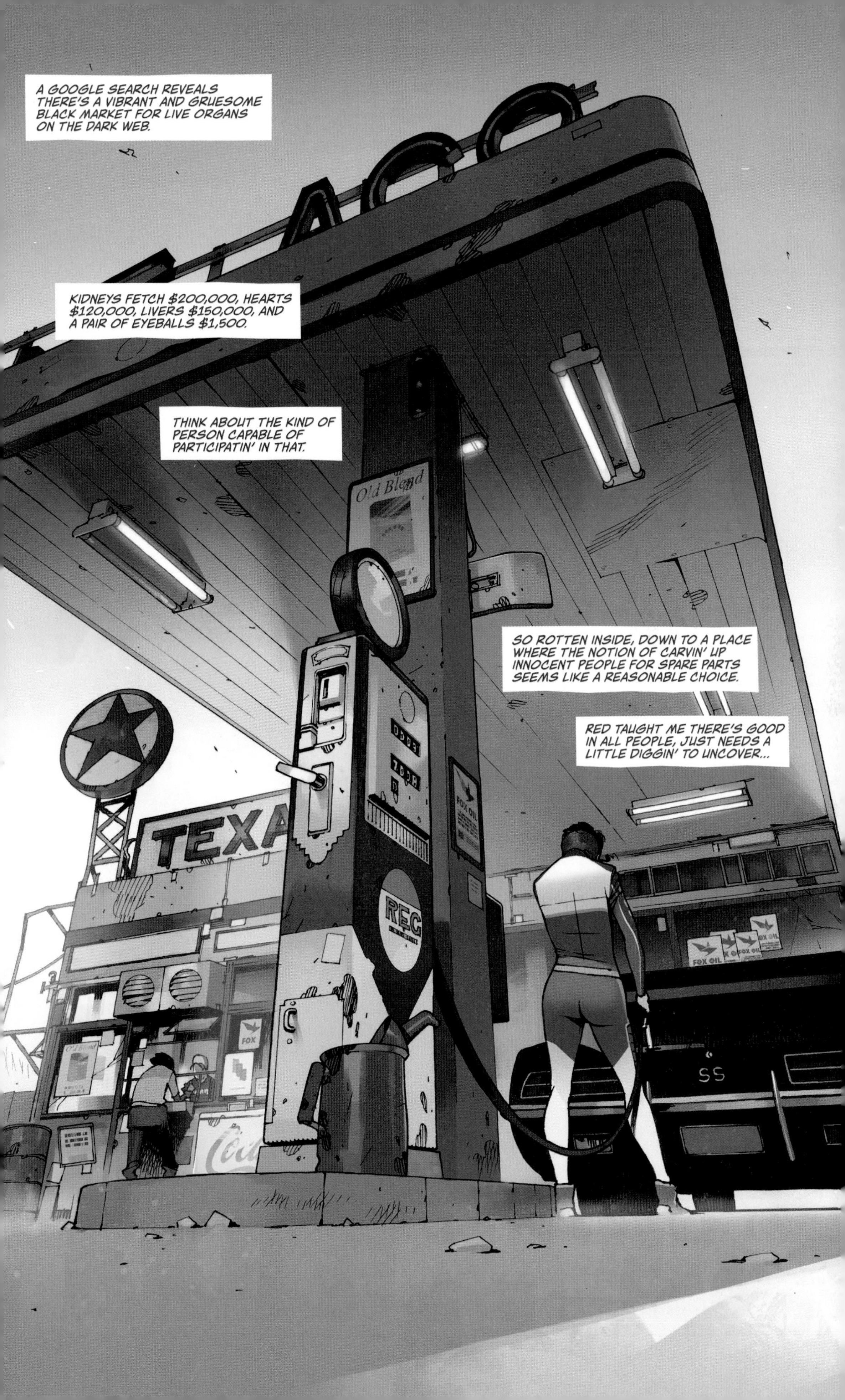
A GOOGLE SEARCH REVEALS THERE'S A VIBRANT AND GRUESOME BLACK MARKET FOR LIVE ORGANS ON THE DARK WEB.
KIDNEYS FETCH $200,000, HEARTS $120,000, LIVERS $150,000, AND A PAIR OF EYEBALLS $1,500.
THINK ABOUT THE KIND OF PERSON CAPABLE OF PARTICIPATIN' IN THAT.
SO ROTTEN INSIDE, DOWN TO A PLACE WHERE THE NOTION OF CARVIN' UP INNOCENT PEOPLE FOR SPARE PARTS SEEMS LIKE A REASONABLE CHOICE.
RED TAUGHT ME THERE'S GOOD IN ALL PEOPLE, JUST NEEDS A LITTLE DIGGIN' TO UNCOVER...
Old Blend
TEXA
FOX OIL
SS

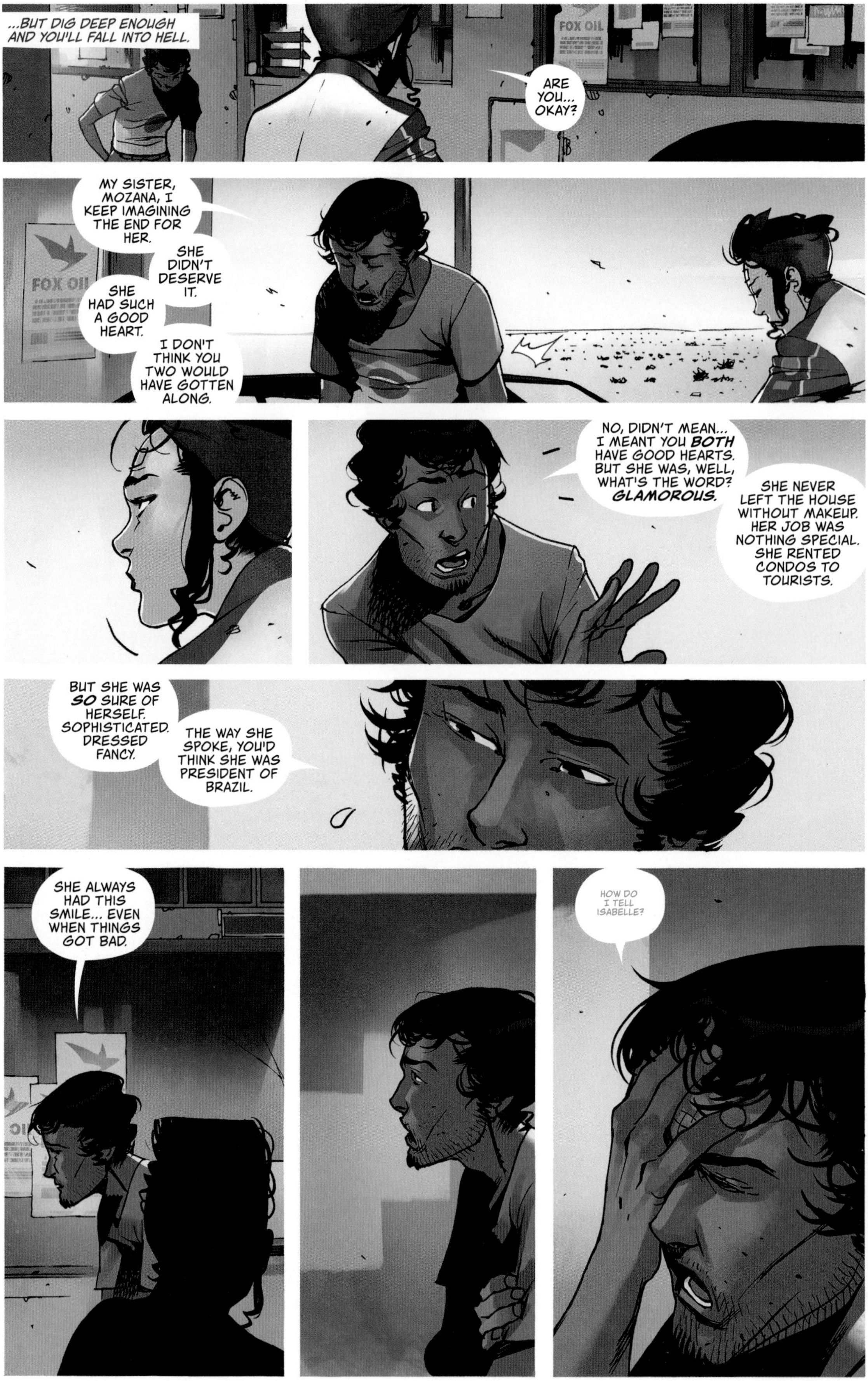

...BUT DIG DEEP ENOUGH AND YOU'LL FALL INTO HELL.
FOX OIL
ARE YOU... OKAY?
MY SISTER, MOZANA, I KEEP IMAGINING THE END FOR HER.
SHE DIDN'T DESERVE IT.
SHE HAD SUCH A GOOD HEART.
I DON'T THINK YOU TWO WOULD HAVE GOTTEN ALONG.
FOX OIL
NO, DIDN'T MEAN... I MEANT YOU BOTH HAVE GOOD HEARTS. BUT SHE WAS, WELL, WHAT'S THE WORD? GLAMOROUS.
SHE NEVER LEFT THE HOUSE WITHOUT MAKEUP. HER JOB WAS NOTHING SPECIAL. SHE RENTED CONDOS TO TOURISTS.
BUT SHE WAS SO SURE OF HERSELF. SOPHISTICATED. DRESSED FANCY.
THE WAY SHE SPOKE, YOU'D THINK SHE WAS PRESIDENT OF BRAZIL.
SHE ALWAYS HAD THIS SMILE... EVEN WHEN THINGS GOT BAD.
HOW DO I TELL ISABELLE?

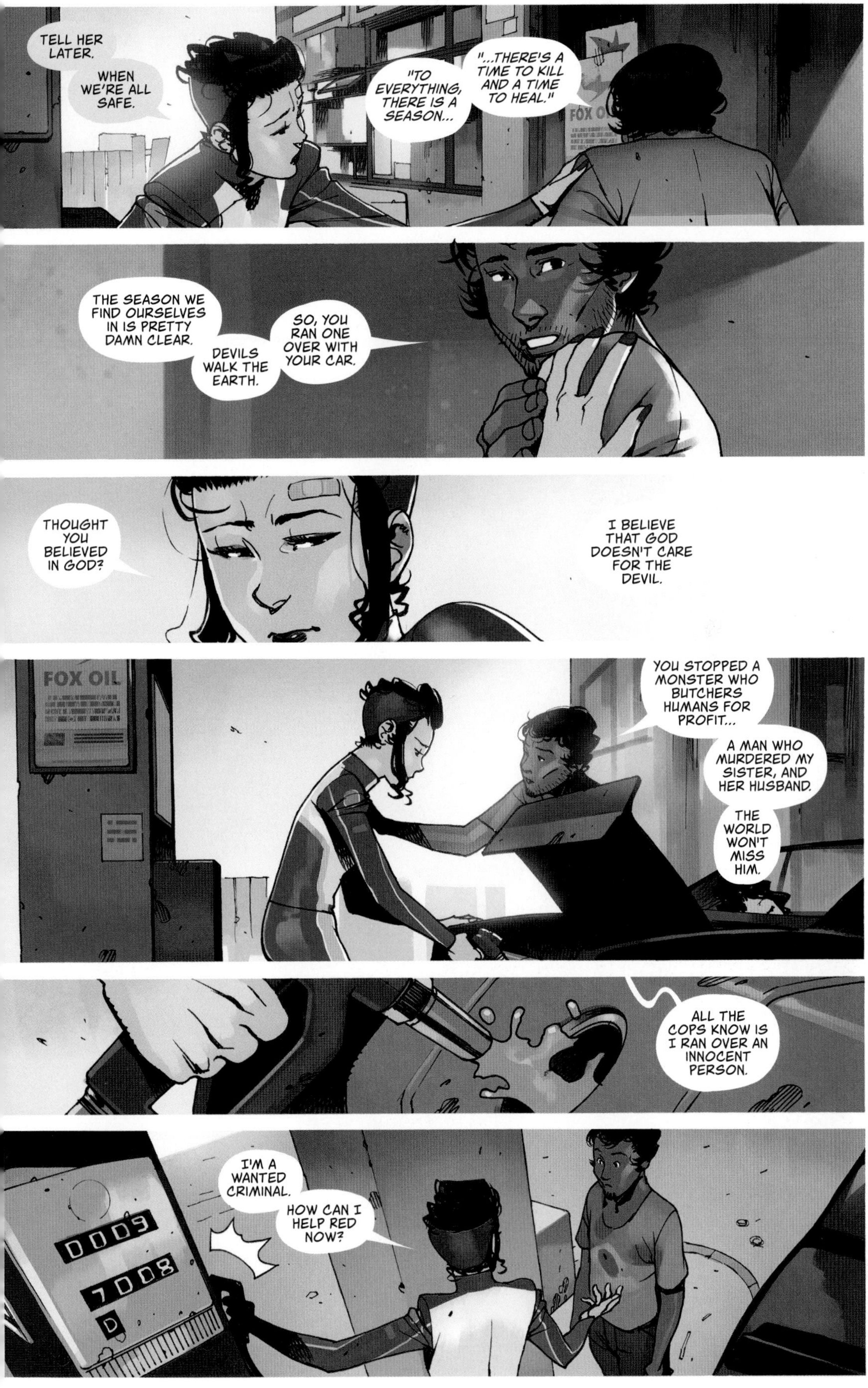
TELL HER LATER.
WHEN WE'RE ALL SAFE.
"TO EVERYTHING, THERE IS A SEASON...
"...THERE'S A TIME TO KILL AND A TIME TO HEAL."
FOX OIL
THE SEASON WE FIND OURSELVES IN IS PRETTY DAMN CLEAR.
DEVILS WALK THE EARTH.
SO, YOU RAN ONE OVER WITH YOUR CAR.
THOUGHT YOU BELIEVED IN GOD?
I BELIEVE THAT GOD DOESN'T CARE FOR THE DEVIL.
FOX OIL
YOU STOPPED A MONSTER WHO BUTCHERS HUMANS FOR PROFIT...
A MAN WHO MURDERED MY SISTER, AND HER HUSBAND.
THE WORLD WON'T MISS HIM.
ALL THE COPS KNOW IS I RAN OVER AN INNOCENT PERSON.
I'M A WANTED CRIMINAL.
HOW CAN I HELP RED NOW?
0009
7008
D

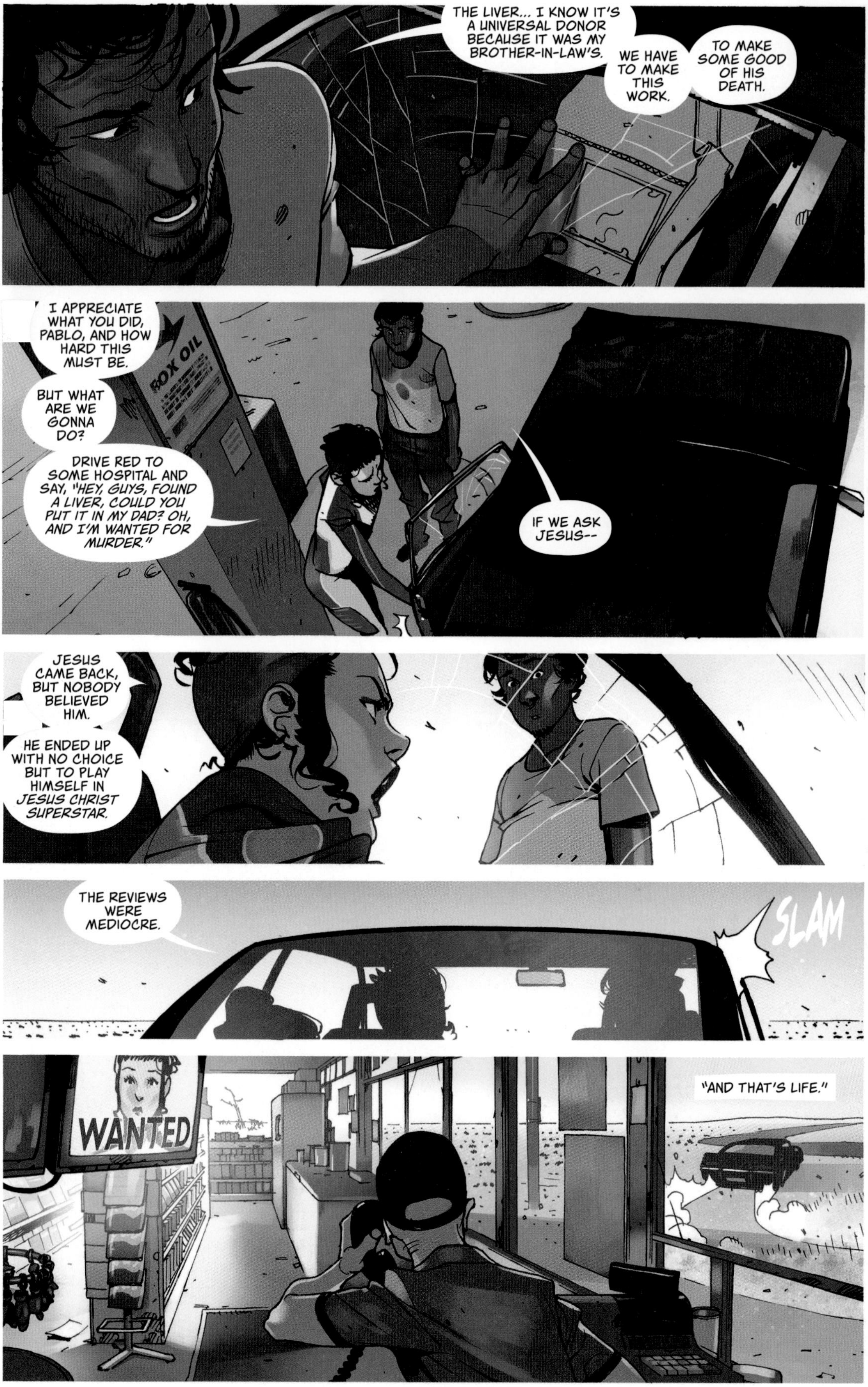
THE LIVER... I KNOW IT'S A UNIVERSAL DONOR BECAUSE IT WAS MY BROTHER-IN-LAW'S.
WE HAVE TO MAKE THIS WORK.
TO MAKE SOME GOOD OF HIS DEATH.
I APPRECIATE WHAT YOU DID, PABLO, AND HOW HARD THIS MUST BE.
BUT WHAT ARE WE GONNA DO?
DRIVE RED TO SOME HOSPITAL AND SAY, "HEY, GUYS, FOUND A LIVER, COULD YOU PUT IT IN MY DAD? OH, AND I'M WANTED FOR MURDER."
FOX OIL
IF WE ASK JESUS--
JESUS CAME BACK, BUT NOBODY BELIEVED HIM.
HE ENDED UP WITH NO CHOICE BUT TO PLAY HIMSELF IN *JESUS CHRIST SUPERSTAR*.
THE REVIEWS WERE MEDIOCRE.
SLAM
WANTED
"AND THAT'S LIFE."

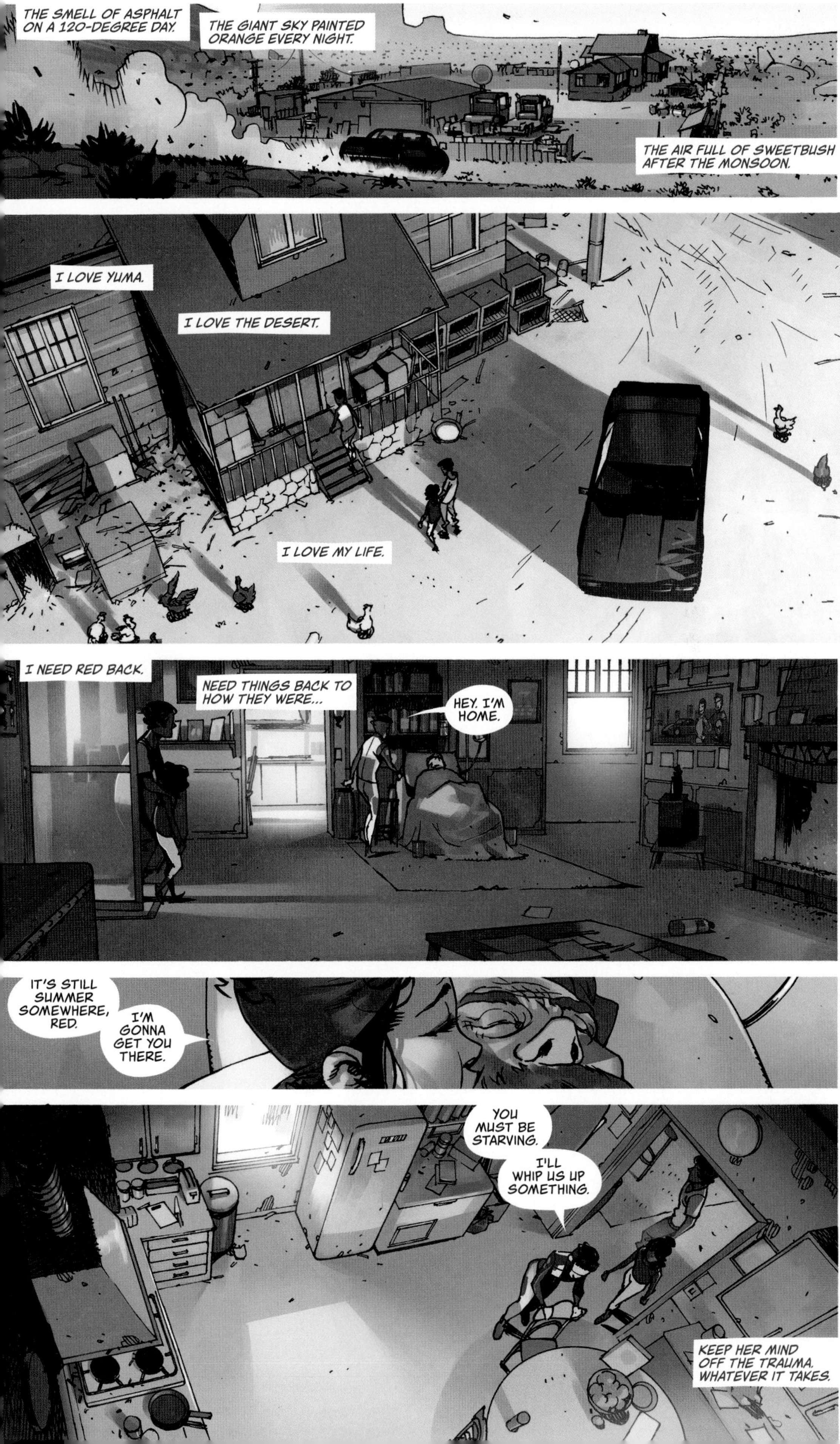
THE SMELL OF ASPHALT ON A 120-DEGREE DAY.
THE GIANT SKY PAINTED ORANGE EVERY NIGHT.
THE AIR FULL OF SWEETBUSH AFTER THE MONSOON.
I LOVE YUMA.
I LOVE THE DESERT.
I LOVE MY LIFE.
I NEED RED BACK.
NEED THINGS BACK TO HOW THEY WERE...
HEY. I'M HOME.
IT'S STILL SUMMER SOMEWHERE, RED.
I'M GONNA GET YOU THERE.
YOU MUST BE STARVING.
I'LL WHIP US UP SOMETHING.
KEEP HER MIND OFF THE TRAUMA. WHATEVER IT TAKES.

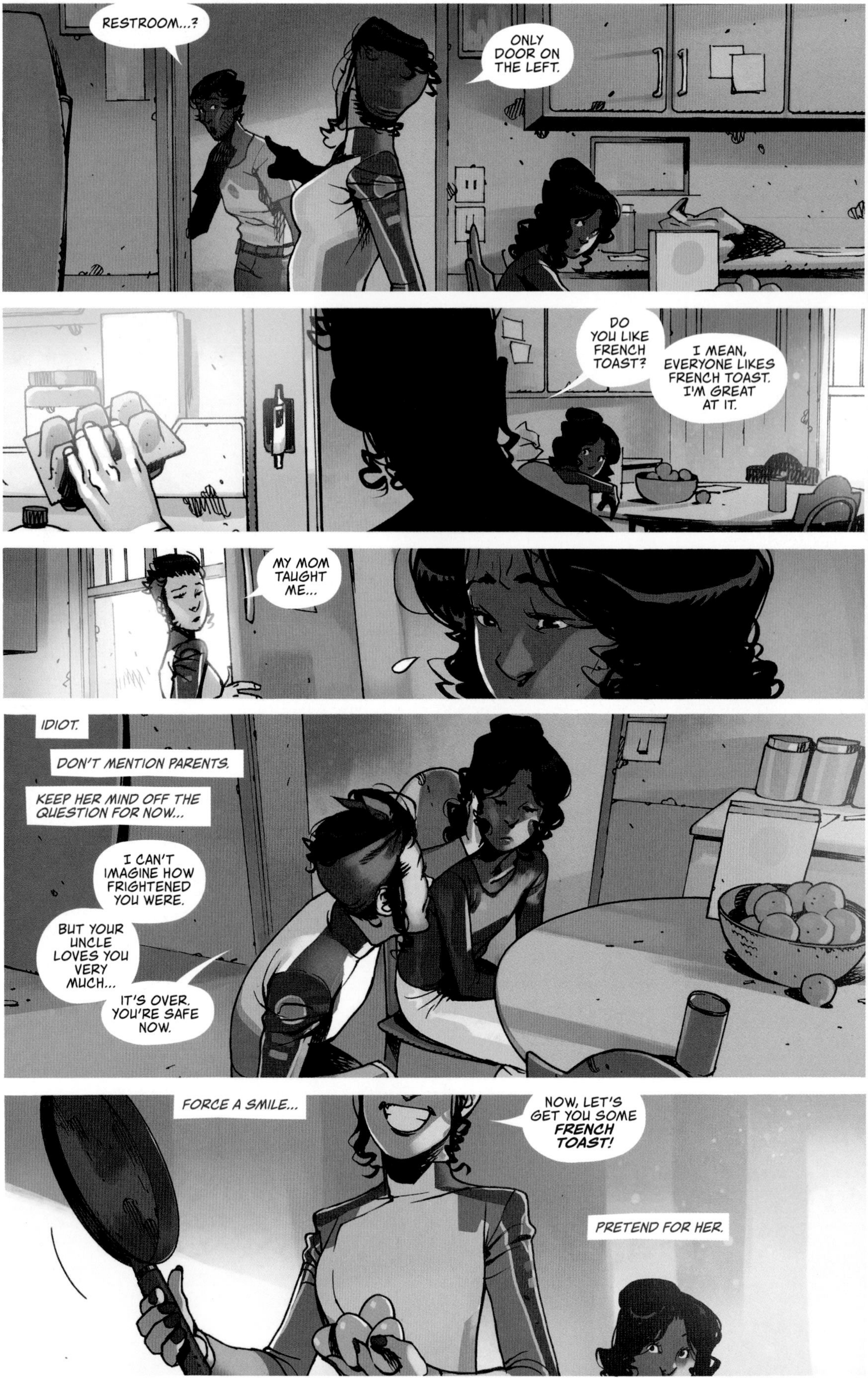
RESTROOM...?
ONLY DOOR ON THE LEFT.
DO YOU LIKE FRENCH TOAST?
I MEAN, EVERYONE LIKES FRENCH TOAST. I'M GREAT AT IT.
MY MOM TAUGHT ME...
IDIOT.
DON'T MENTION PARENTS.
KEEP HER MIND OFF THE QUESTION FOR NOW...
I CAN'T IMAGINE HOW FRIGHTENED YOU WERE.
BUT YOUR UNCLE LOVES YOU VERY MUCH...
IT'S OVER. YOU'RE SAFE NOW.
FORCE A SMILE...
NOW, LET'S GET YOU SOME FRENCH TOAST!
PRETEND FOR HER.

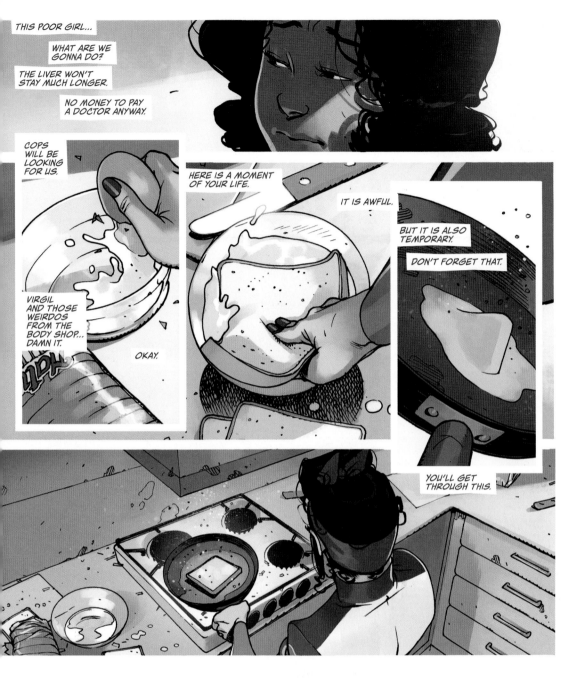

THIS POOR GIRL...

WHAT ARE WE GONNA DO?

THE LIVER WON'T STAY MUCH LONGER.

NO MONEY TO PAY A DOCTOR ANYWAY.

COPS WILL BE LOOKING FOR US.

HERE IS A MOMENT OF YOUR LIFE.

IT IS AWFUL.

BUT IT IS ALSO TEMPORARY.

DON'T FORGET THAT.

VIRGIL AND THOSE WEIRDOS FROM THE BODY SHOP... DAMN IT.

OKAY.

YOU'LL GET THROUGH THIS.

EVERYTHING WILL WORK OUT IN THE END--

AIIEEEEE--!

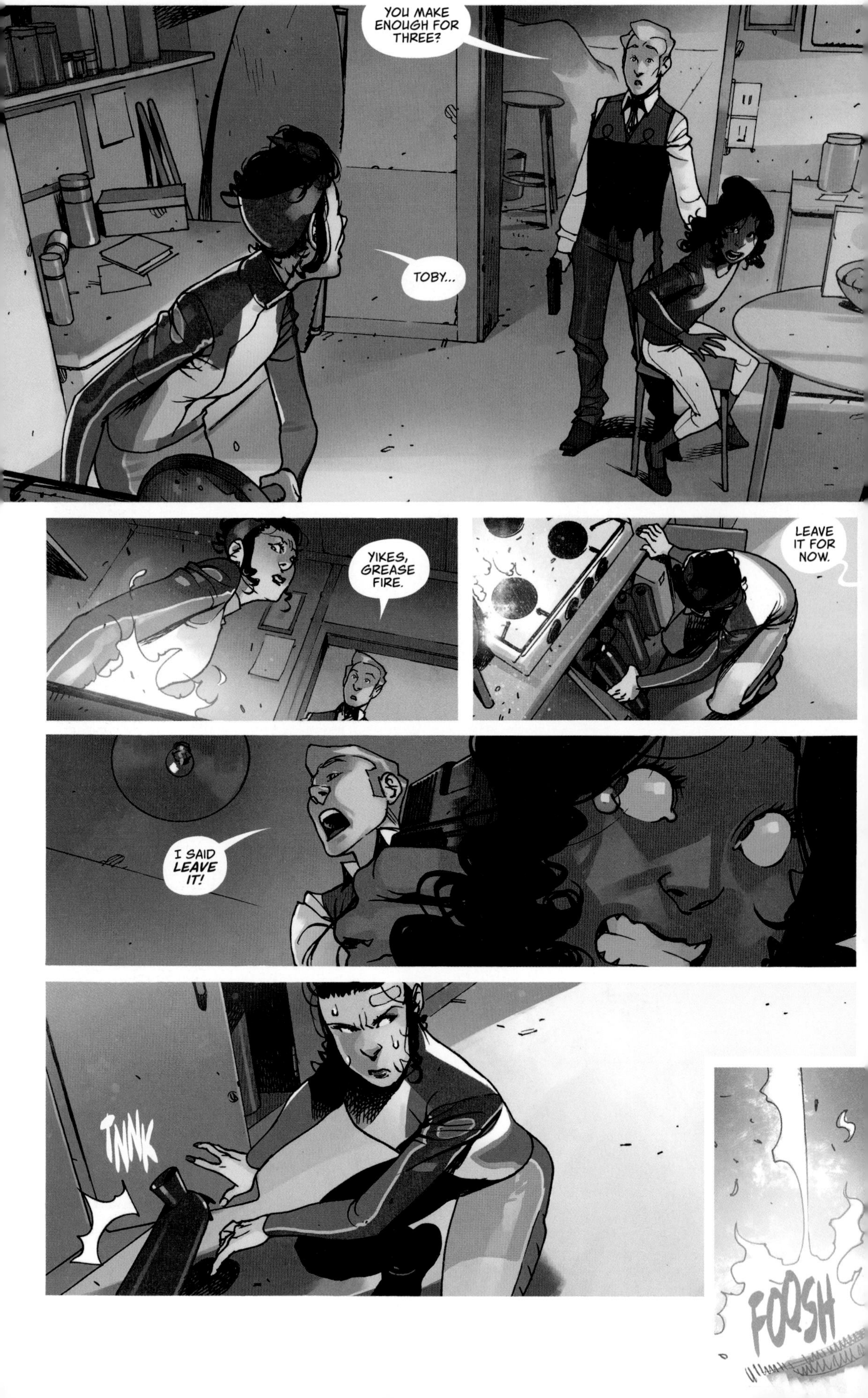
YOU MAKE ENOUGH FOR THREE?
TOBY...
YIKES, GREASE FIRE.
LEAVE IT FOR NOW.
I SAID *LEAVE* IT!
TNNK
FOOSH

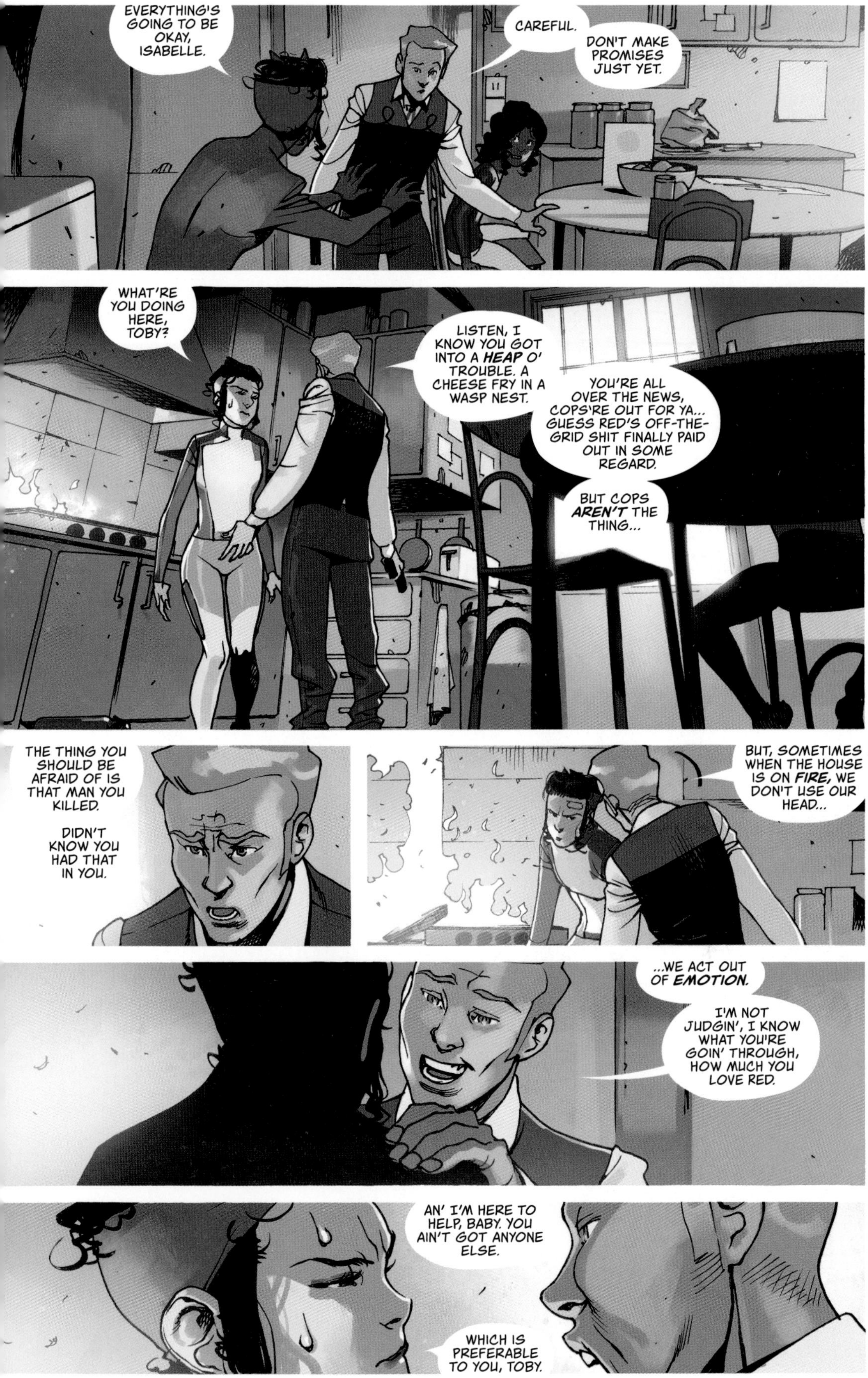
EVERYTHING'S GOING TO BE OKAY, ISABELLE.
CAREFUL.
DON'T MAKE PROMISES JUST YET.
WHAT'RE YOU DOING HERE, TOBY?
LISTEN, I KNOW YOU GOT INTO A *HEAP O'* TROUBLE. A CHEESE FRY IN A WASP NEST.
YOU'RE ALL OVER THE NEWS, COPS'RE OUT FOR YA... GUESS RED'S OFF-THE-GRID SHIT FINALLY PAID OUT IN SOME REGARD.
BUT COPS *AREN'T* THE THING...
THE THING YOU SHOULD BE AFRAID OF IS THAT MAN YOU KILLED.
DIDN'T KNOW YOU HAD THAT IN YOU.
BUT, SOMETIMES WHEN THE HOUSE IS ON *FIRE,* WE DON'T USE OUR HEAD...
...WE ACT OUT OF *EMOTION.*
I'M NOT JUDGIN', I KNOW WHAT YOU'RE GOIN' THROUGH, HOW MUCH YOU LOVE RED.
AN' I'M HERE TO HELP, BABY. YOU AIN'T GOT ANYONE ELSE.
WHICH IS PREFERABLE TO YOU, TOBY.

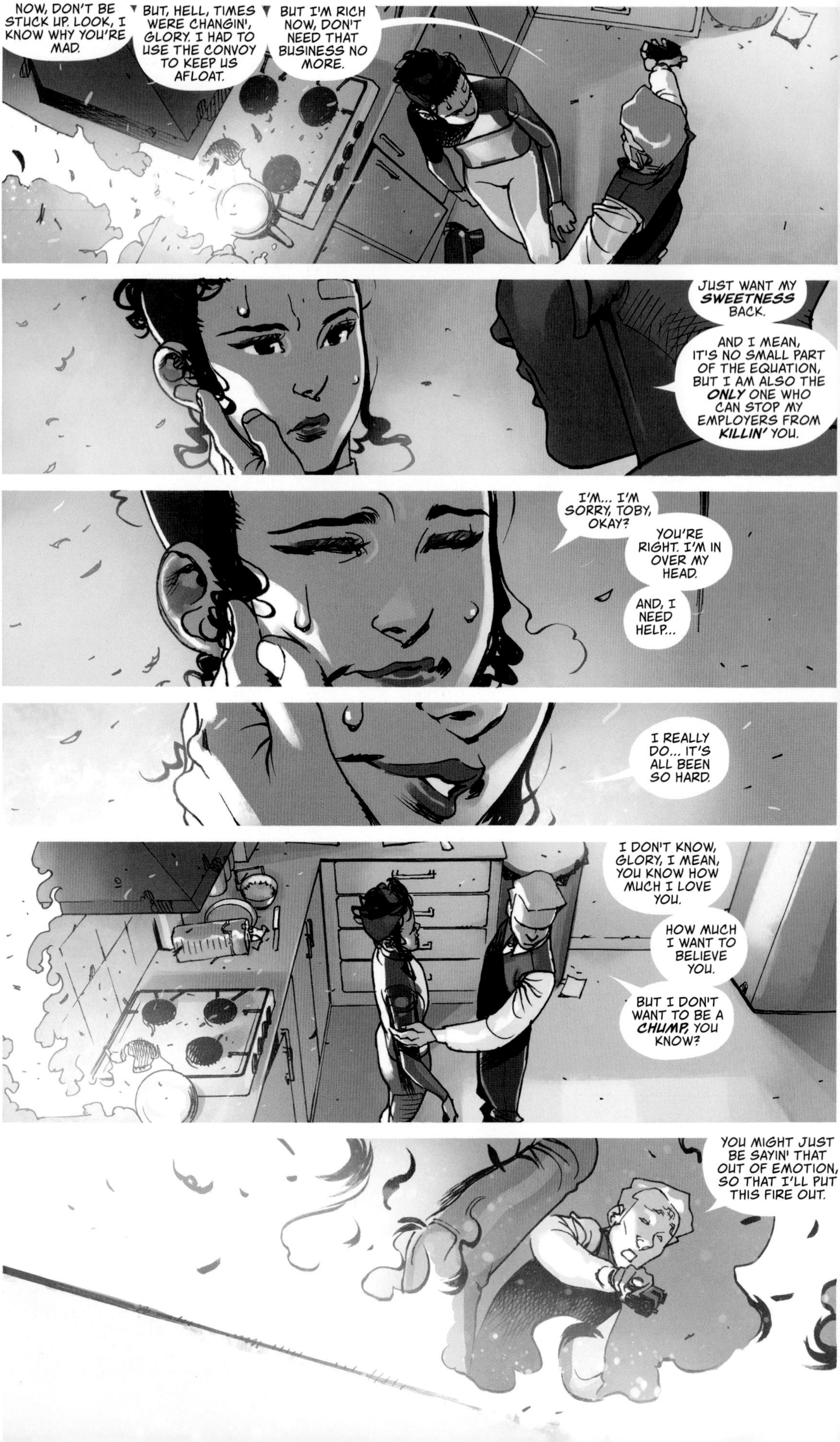
NOW, DON'T BE STUCK UP. LOOK, I KNOW WHY YOU'RE MAD.
BUT, HELL, TIMES WERE CHANGIN', GLORY. I HAD TO USE THE CONVOY TO KEEP US AFLOAT.
BUT I'M RICH NOW, DON'T NEED THAT BUSINESS NO MORE.
JUST WANT MY SWEETNESS BACK.
AND I MEAN, IT'S NO SMALL PART OF THE EQUATION, BUT I AM ALSO THE ONLY ONE WHO CAN STOP MY EMPLOYERS FROM KILLIN' YOU.
I'M... I'M SORRY, TOBY, OKAY?
YOU'RE RIGHT. I'M IN OVER MY HEAD.
AND, I NEED HELP...
I REALLY DO... IT'S ALL BEEN SO HARD.
I DON'T KNOW, GLORY, I MEAN, YOU KNOW HOW MUCH I LOVE YOU.
HOW MUCH I WANT TO BELIEVE YOU.
BUT I DON'T WANT TO BE A CHUMP, YOU KNOW?
YOU MIGHT JUST BE SAYIN' THAT OUT OF EMOTION, SO THAT I'LL PUT THIS FIRE OUT.

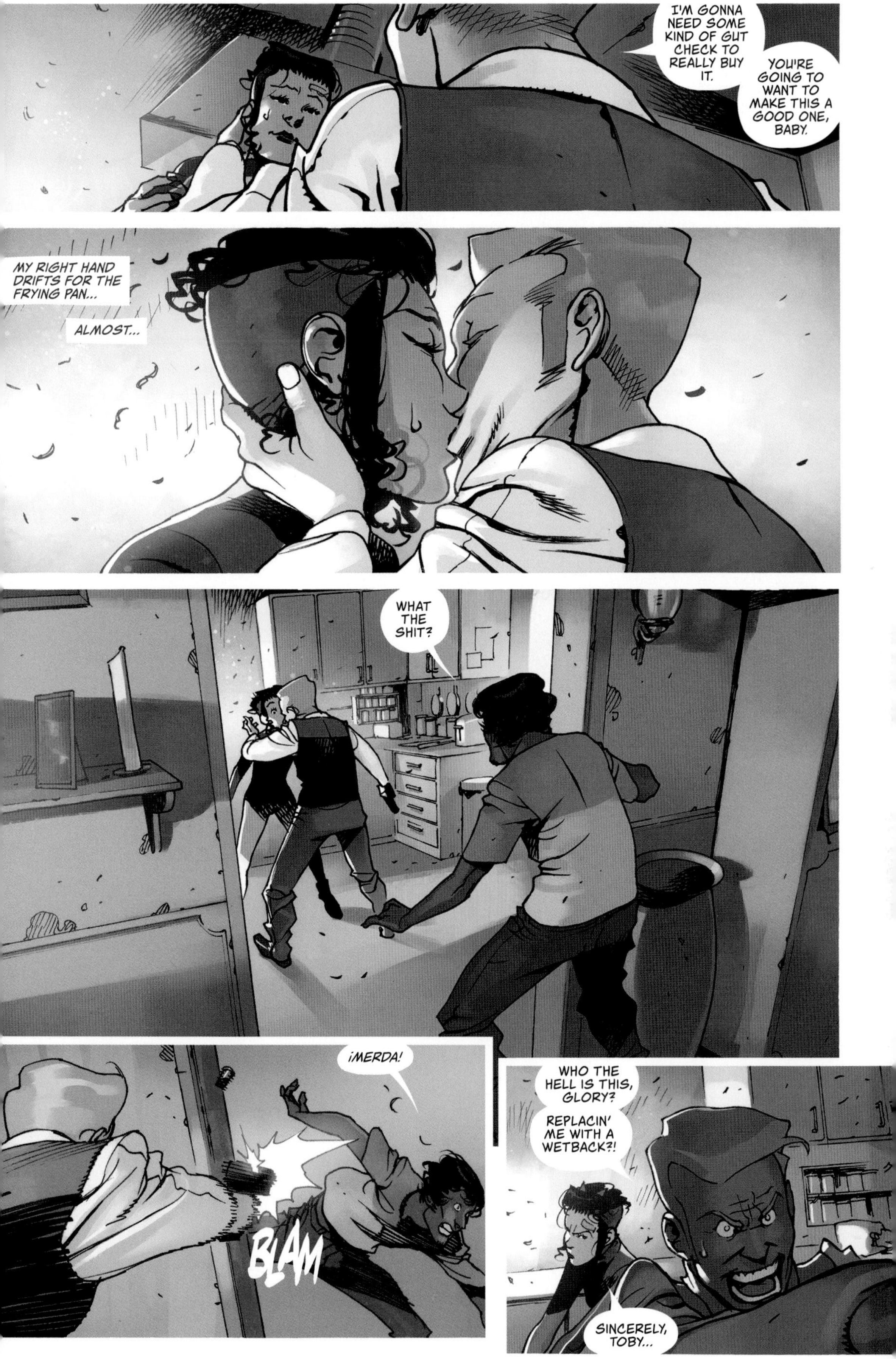
I'M GONNA NEED SOME KIND OF GUT CHECK TO REALLY BUY IT.
YOU'RE GOING TO WANT TO MAKE THIS A GOOD ONE, BABY.
MY RIGHT HAND DRIFTS FOR THE FRYING PAN...
ALMOST...
WHAT THE SHIT?
¡MERDA!
BLAM
WHO THE HELL IS THIS, GLORY?
REPLACIN' ME WITH A WETBACK?!
SINCERELY, TOBY...

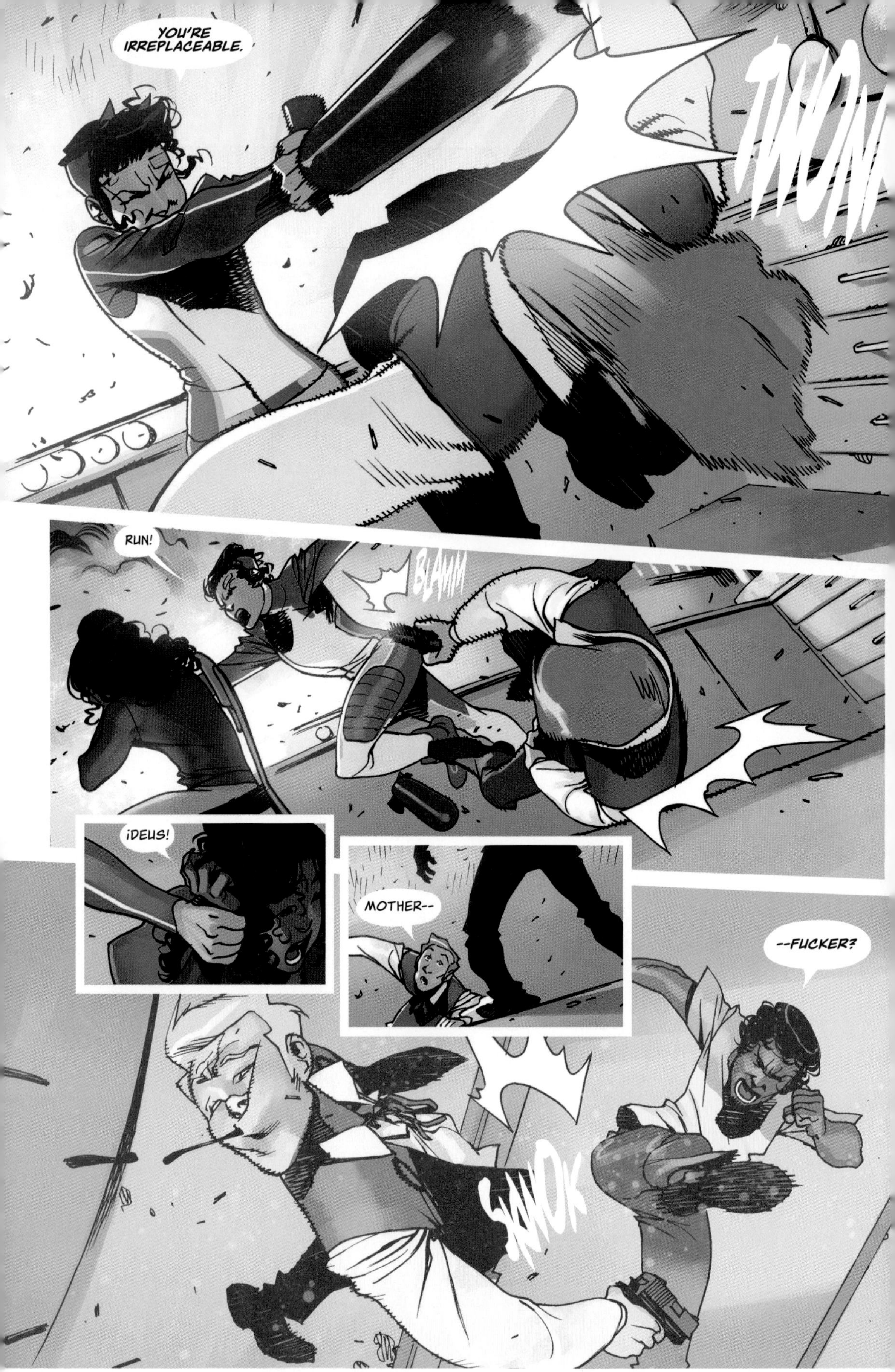
YOU'RE IRREPLACEABLE.
TWOM
RUN!
BLAMM
¡DEUS!
MOTHER--
--FUCKER?
SMOK

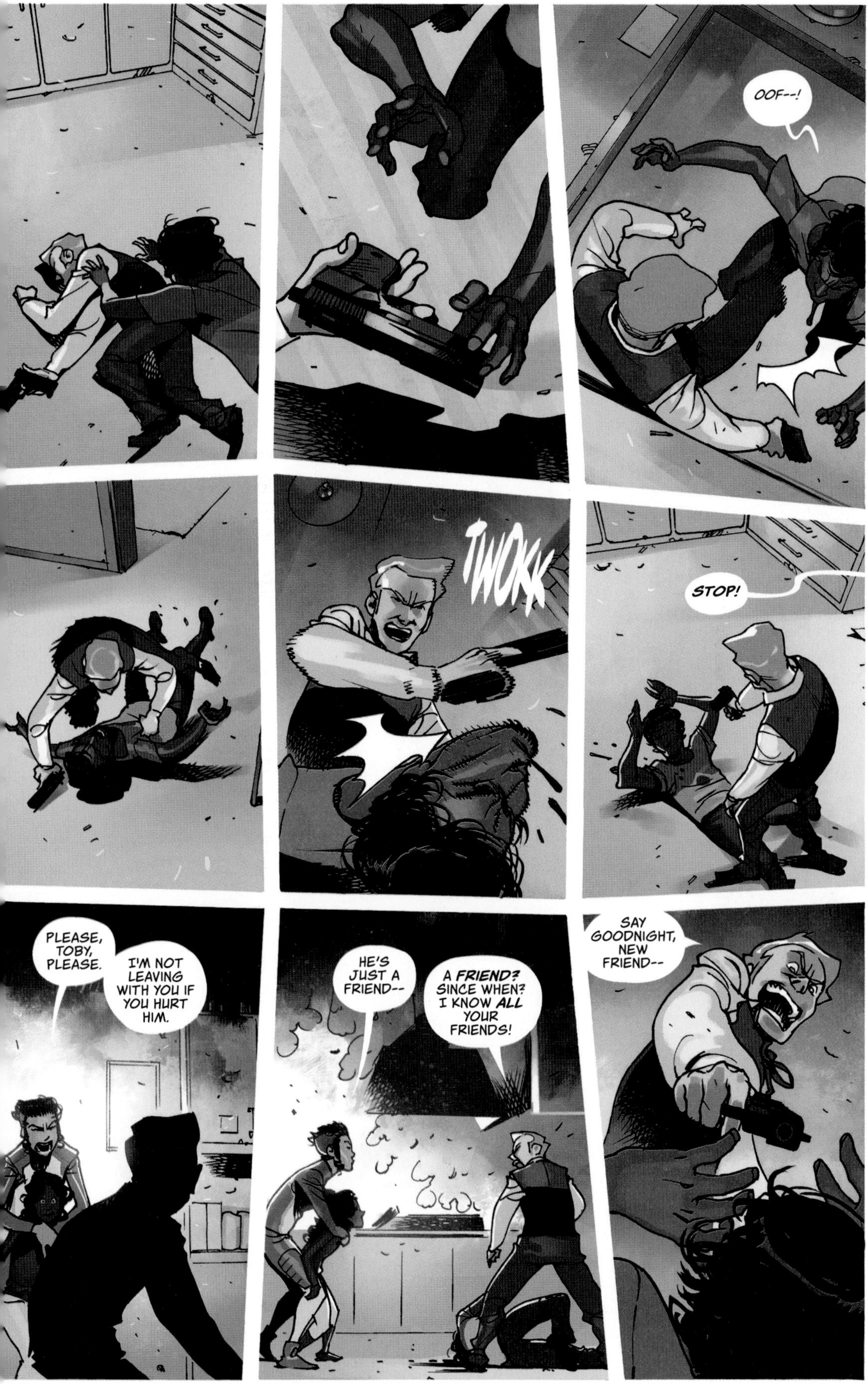
OOF--!
TWOKK
STOP!
PLEASE, TOBY, PLEASE.
I'M NOT LEAVING WITH YOU IF YOU HURT HIM.
HE'S JUST A FRIEND--
A FRIEND? SINCE WHEN? I KNOW ALL YOUR FRIENDS!
SAY GOODNIGHT, NEW FRIEND--

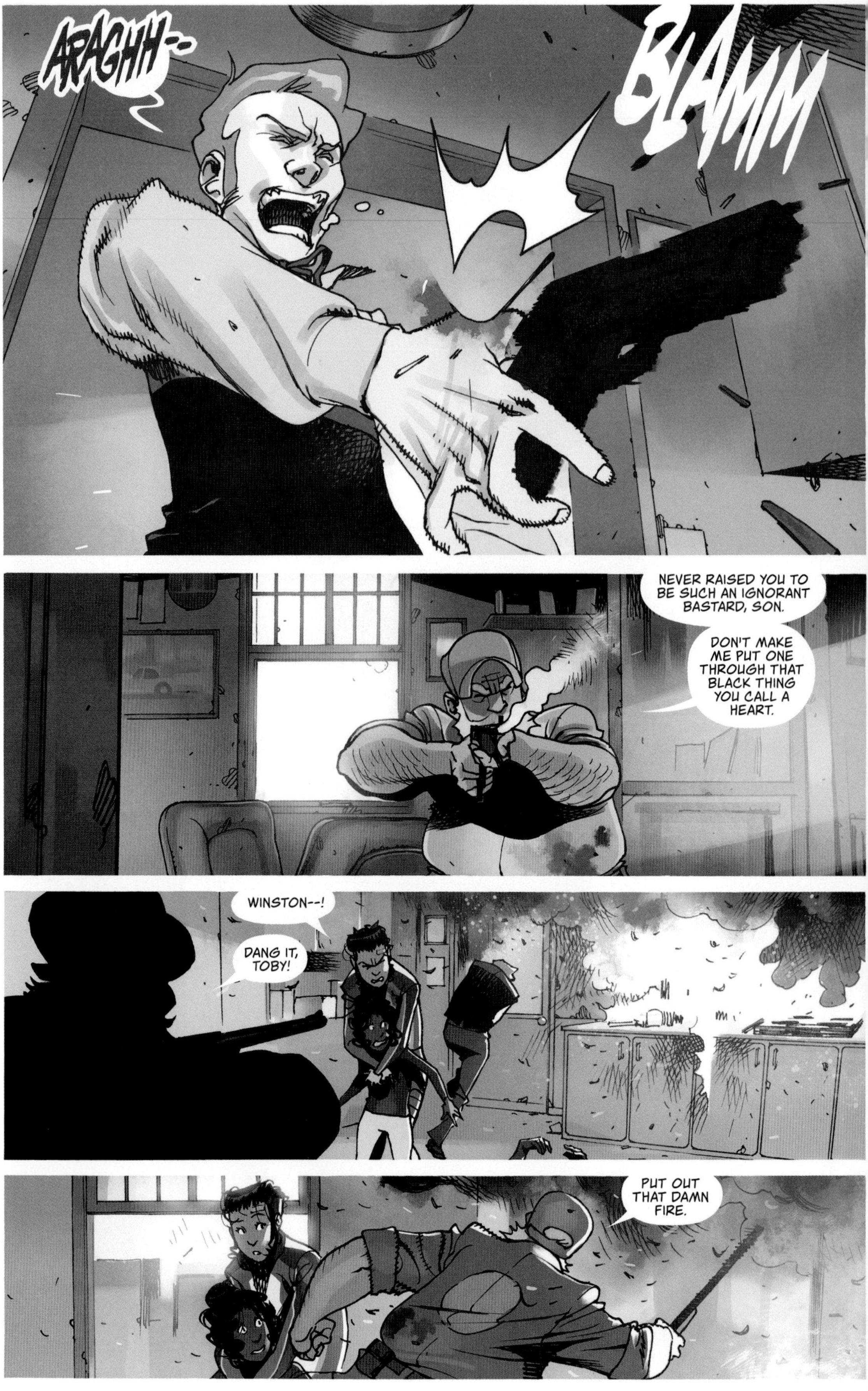
ARAGHH--
BLAMM
NEVER RAISED YOU TO BE SUCH AN IGNORANT BASTARD, SON.
DON'T MAKE ME PUT ONE THROUGH THAT BLACK THING YOU CALL A HEART.
WINSTON--!
DANG IT, TOBY!
PUT OUT THAT DAMN FIRE.

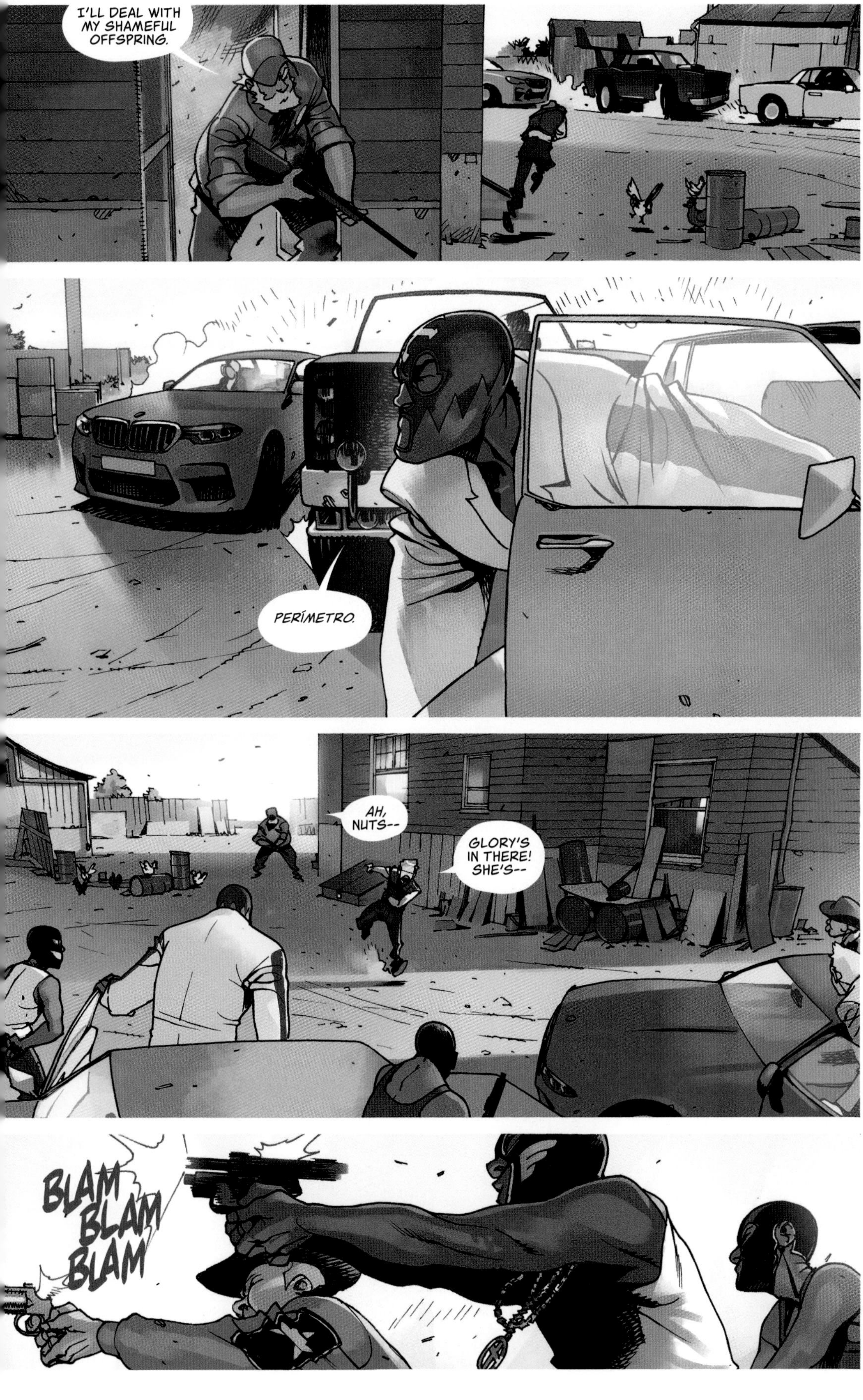
I'LL DEAL WITH MY SHAMEFUL OFFSPRING.
PERÍMETRO.
AH, NUTS--
GLORY'S IN THERE! SHE'S--
BLAM BLAM BLAM

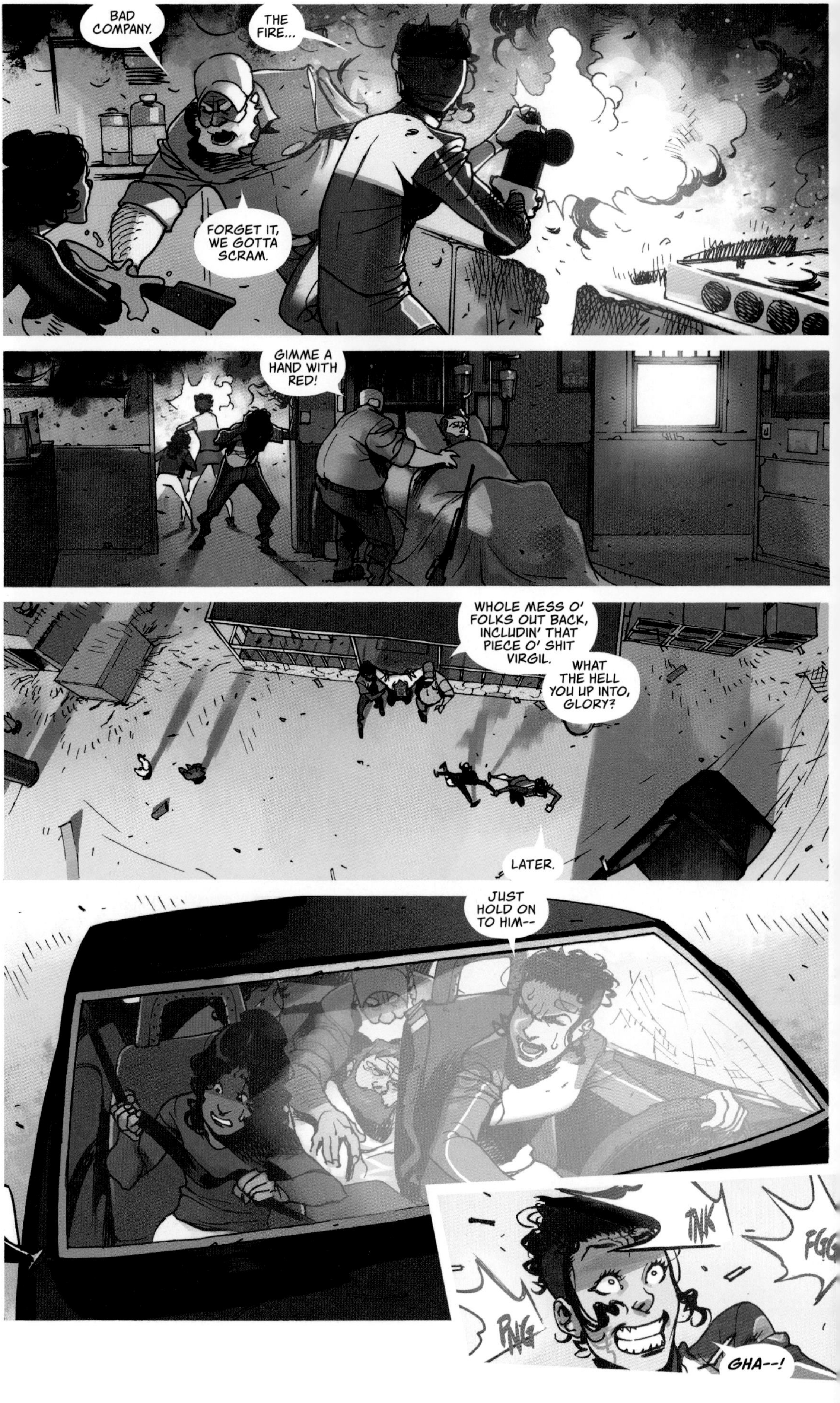

BAD COMPANY.
THE FIRE...
FORGET IT, WE GOTTA SCRAM.
GIMME A HAND WITH RED!
WHOLE MESS O' FOLKS OUT BACK, INCLUDIN' THAT PIECE O' SHIT VIRGIL.
WHAT THE HELL YOU UP INTO, GLORY?
LATER.
JUST HOLD ON TO HIM--
TNK
PNG
GHA--!

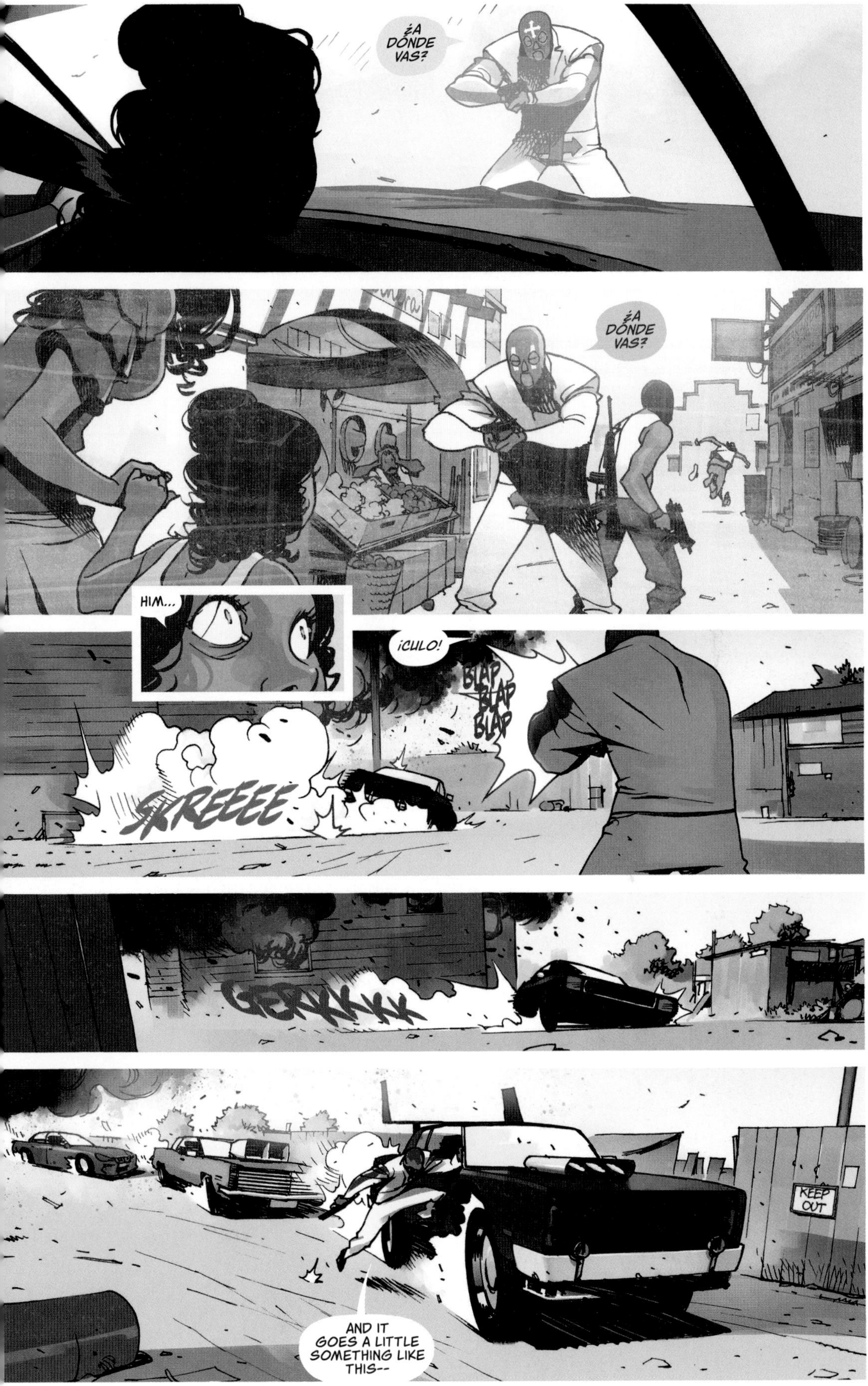
¿A DÓNDE VAS?
¿A DÓNDE VAS?
HIM...
¡CULO!
BLAP BLAP BLAP
SKREEEE
GERKKKK
KEEP OUT
AND IT GOES A LITTLE SOMETHING LIKE THIS--

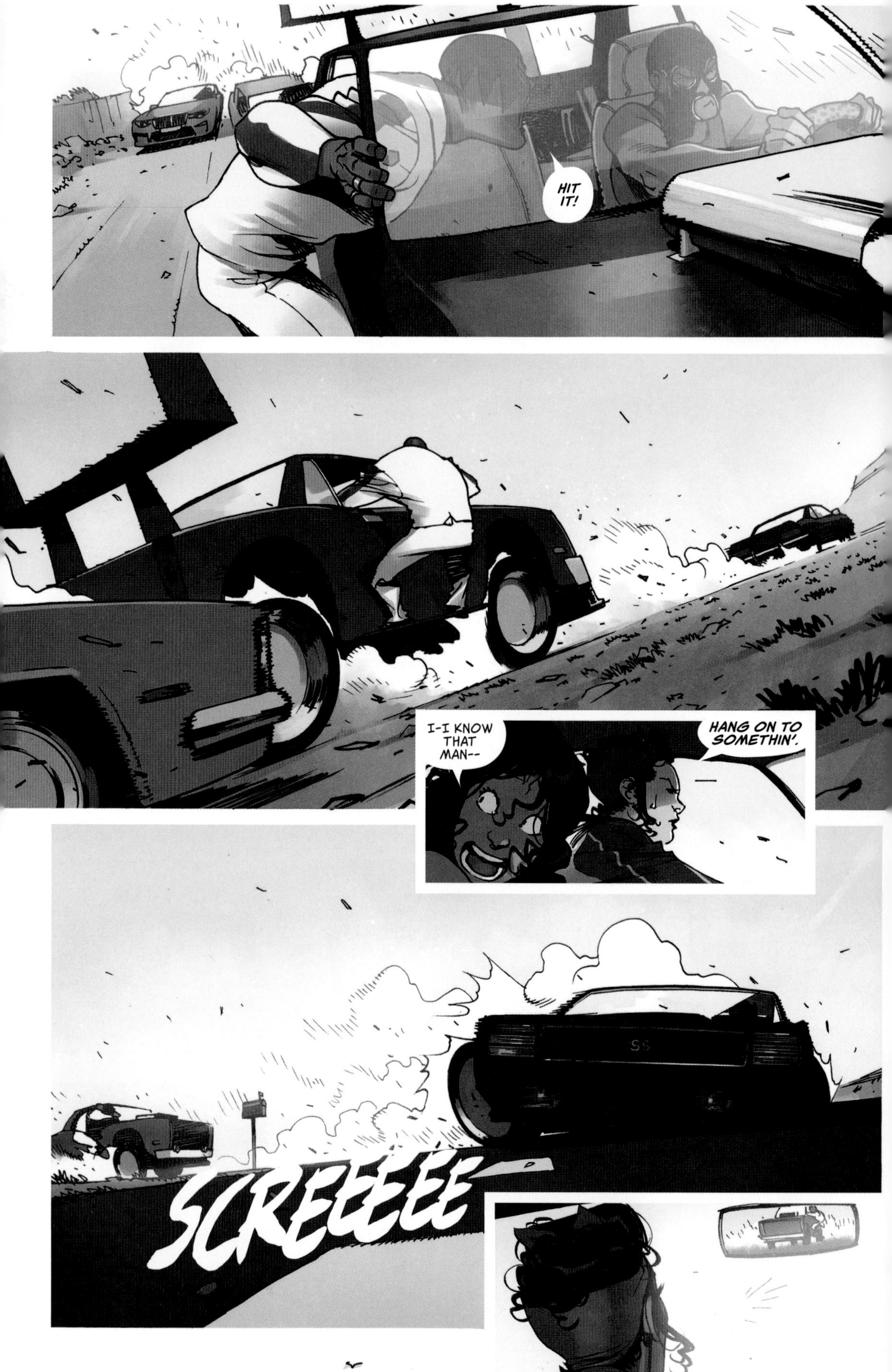
HIT IT!
I-I KNOW THAT MAN--
HANG ON TO SOMETHIN'.
SCREEEEE

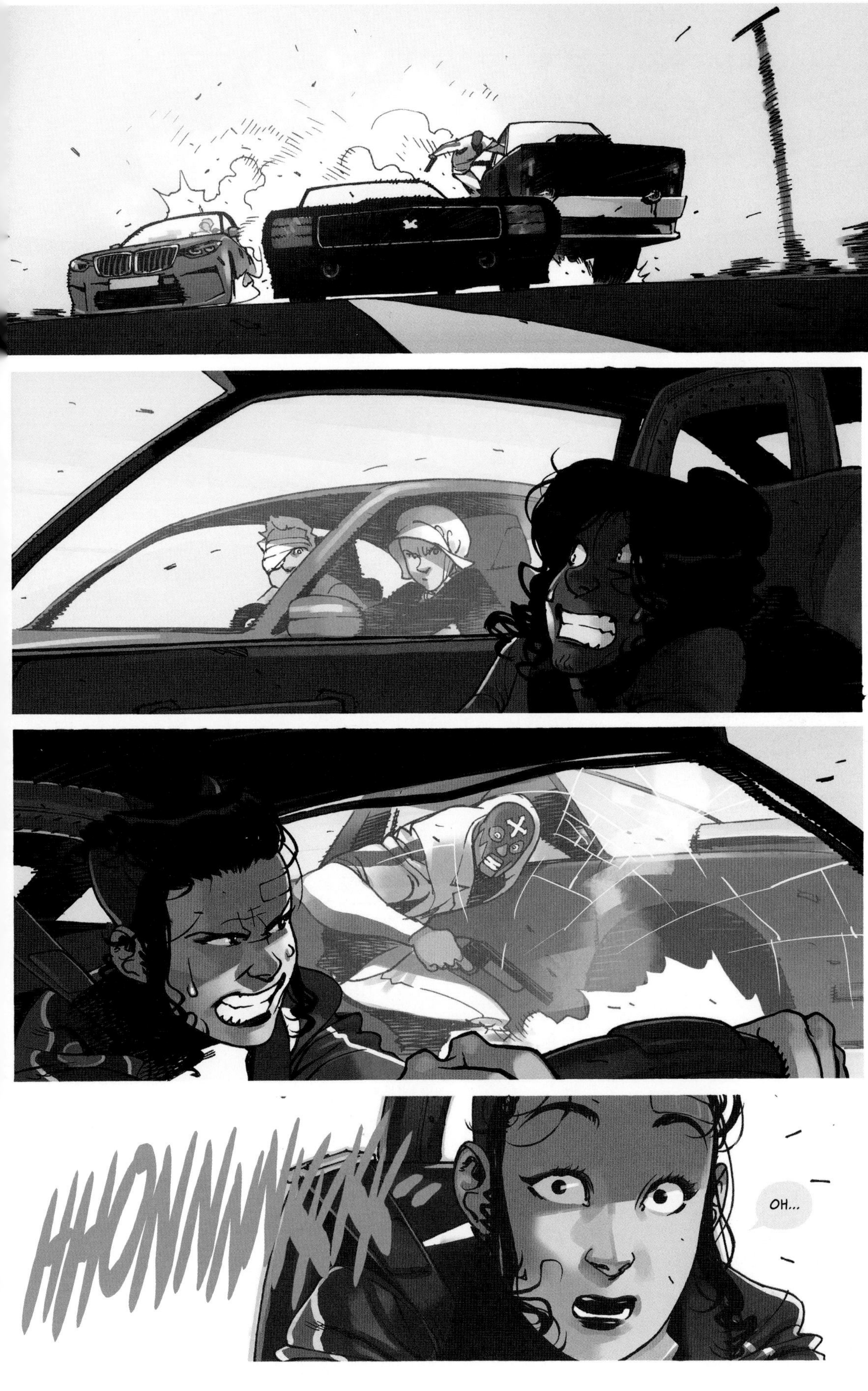
HHONNNKKK...
OH...

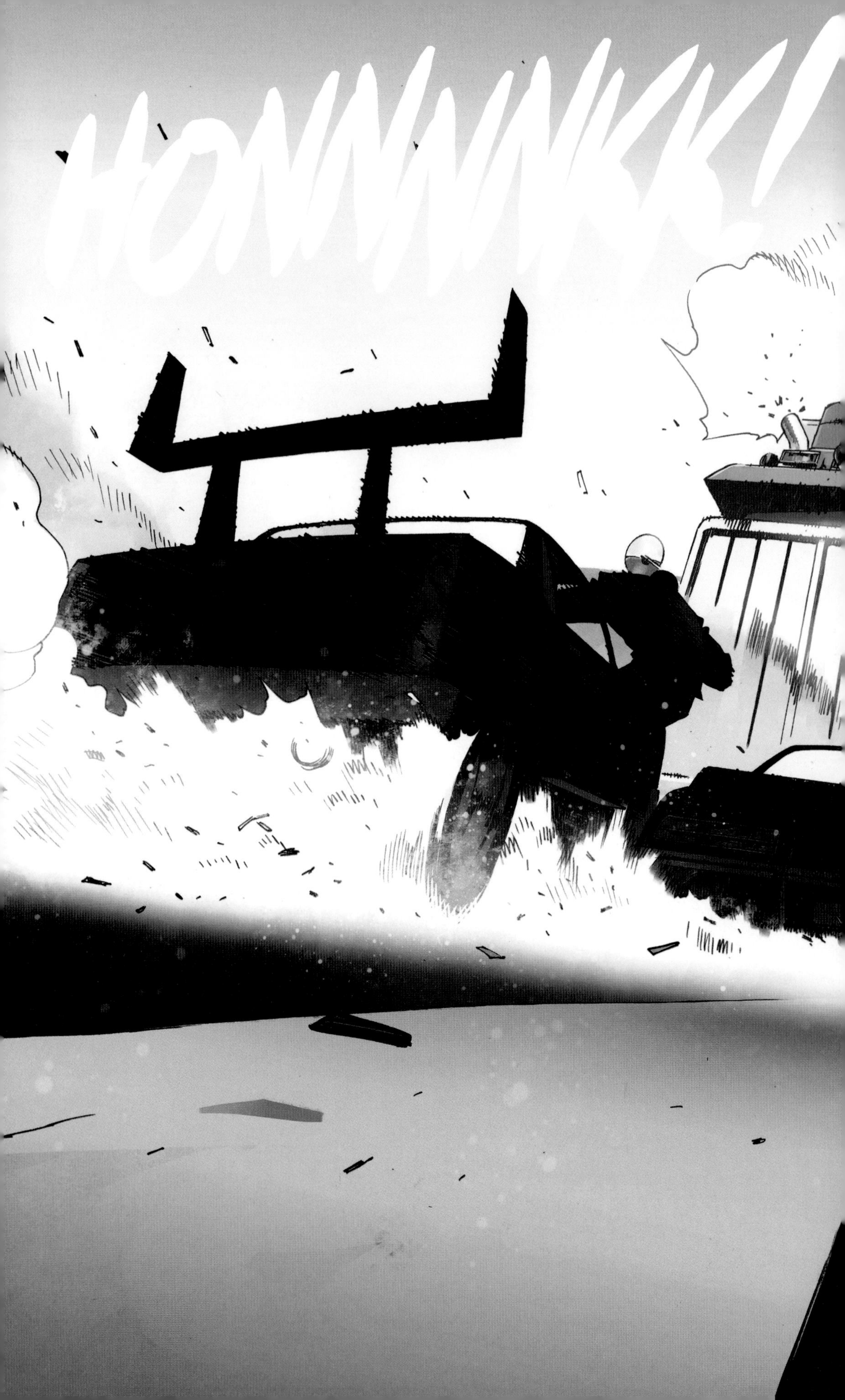
HONNNNKK!

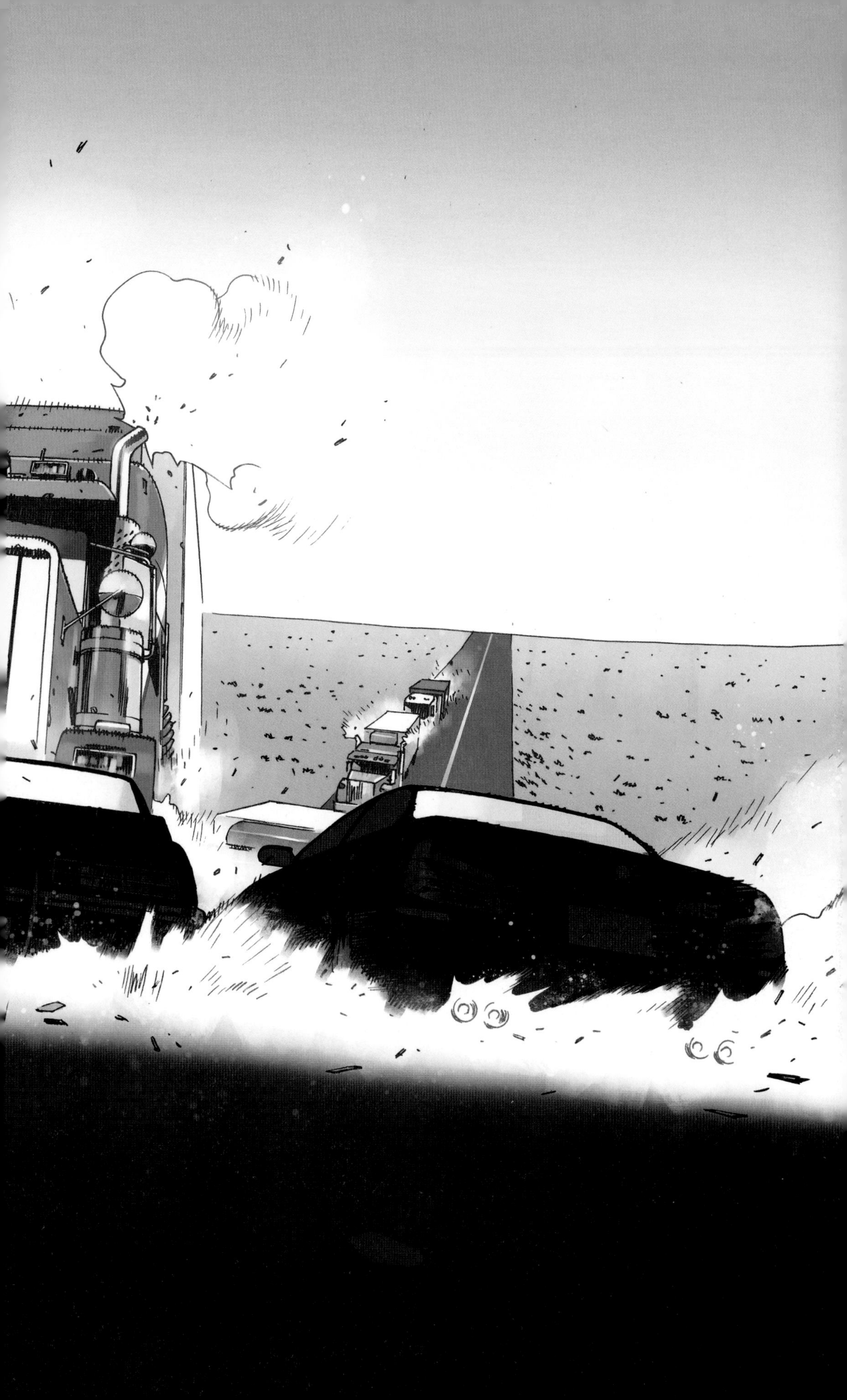

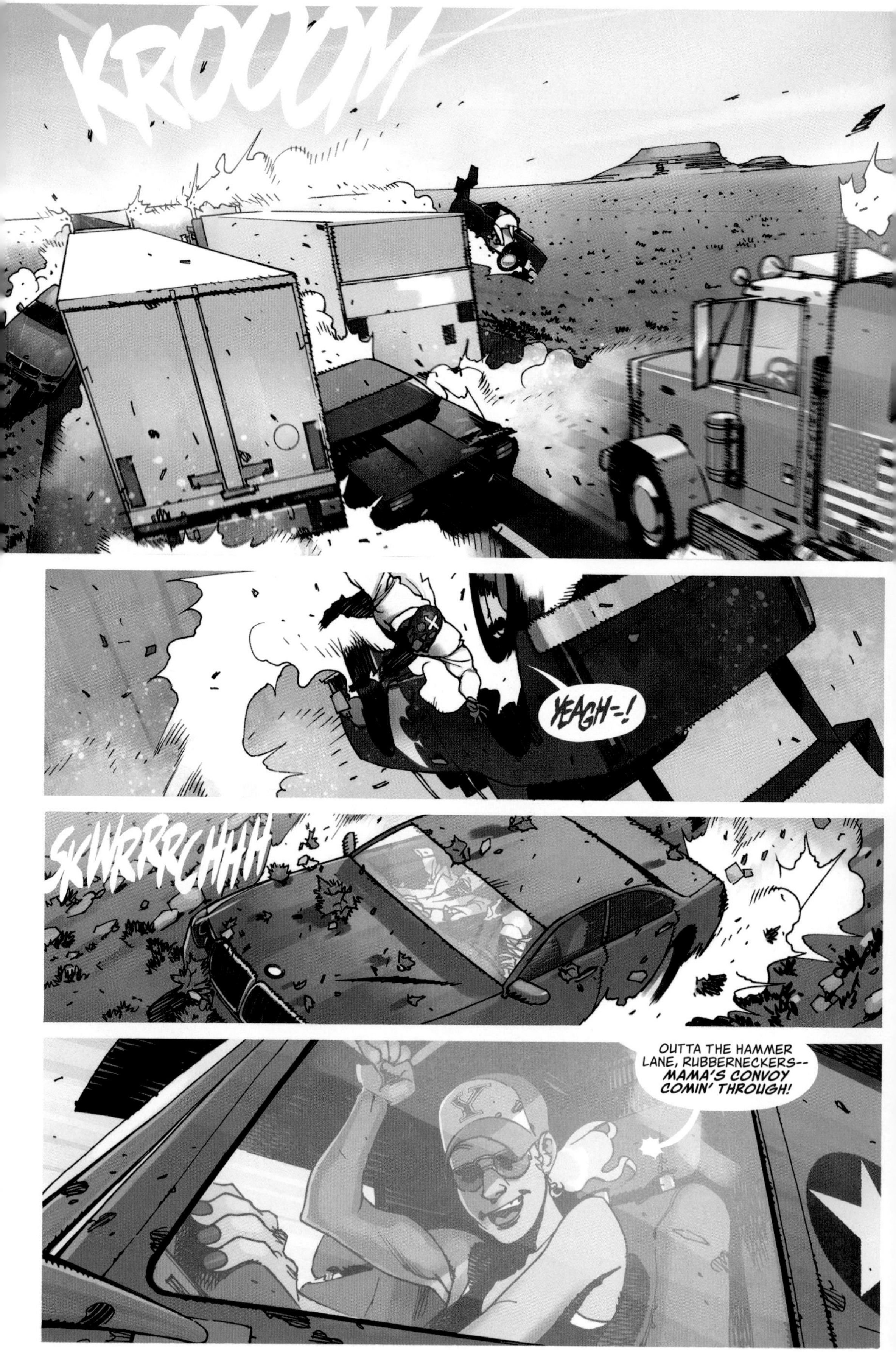
KROOOM
YEAGH--!
SKWRRRCHHH
OUTTA THE HAMMER LANE, RUBBERNECKERS-- *MAMA'S CONVOY COMIN' THROUGH!*

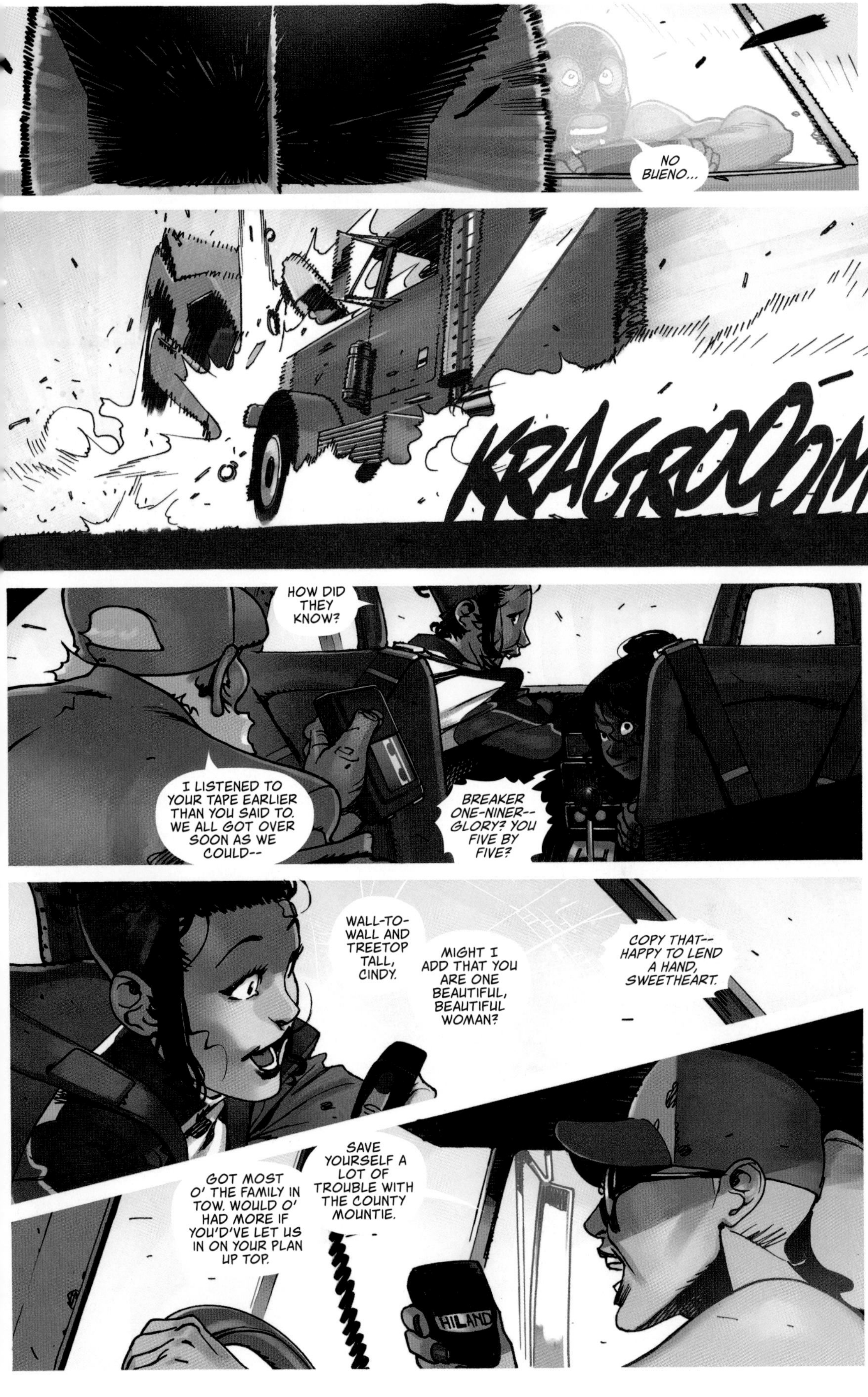
NO BUENO...
KRAGROOOM
HOW DID THEY KNOW?
I LISTENED TO YOUR TAPE EARLIER THAN YOU SAID TO. WE ALL GOT OVER SOON AS WE COULD--
BREAKER ONE-NINER-- GLORY? YOU FIVE BY FIVE?
WALL-TO-WALL AND TREETOP TALL, CINDY.
MIGHT I ADD THAT YOU ARE ONE BEAUTIFUL, BEAUTIFUL WOMAN?
COPY THAT-- HAPPY TO LEND A HAND, SWEETHEART.
GOT MOST O' THE FAMILY IN TOW. WOULD O' HAD MORE IF YOU'D'VE LET US IN ON YOUR PLAN UP TOP.
SAVE YOURSELF A LOT OF TROUBLE WITH THE COUNTY MOUNTIE.
HILAND

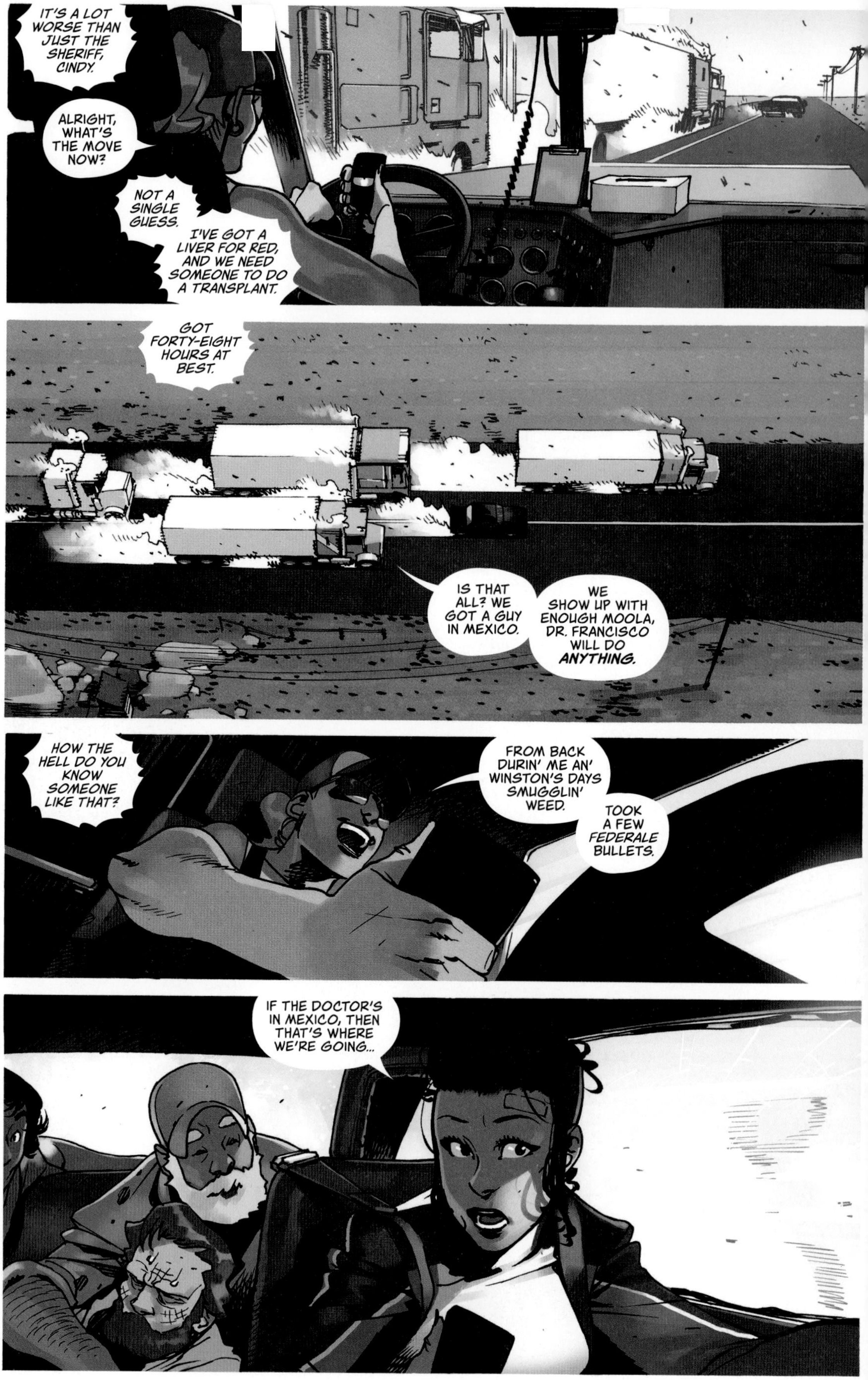

IT'S A LOT WORSE THAN JUST THE SHERIFF, CINDY.
ALRIGHT, WHAT'S THE MOVE NOW?
NOT A SINGLE GUESS.
I'VE GOT A LIVER FOR RED, AND WE NEED SOMEONE TO DO A TRANSPLANT.
GOT FORTY-EIGHT HOURS AT BEST.
IS THAT ALL? WE GOT A GUY IN MEXICO.
WE SHOW UP WITH ENOUGH MOOLA, DR. FRANCISCO WILL DO ANYTHING.
HOW THE HELL DO YOU KNOW SOMEONE LIKE THAT?
FROM BACK DURIN' ME AN' WINSTON'S DAYS SMUGGLIN' WEED.
TOOK A FEW FEDERALE BULLETS.
IF THE DOCTOR'S IN MEXICO, THEN THAT'S WHERE WE'RE GOING...

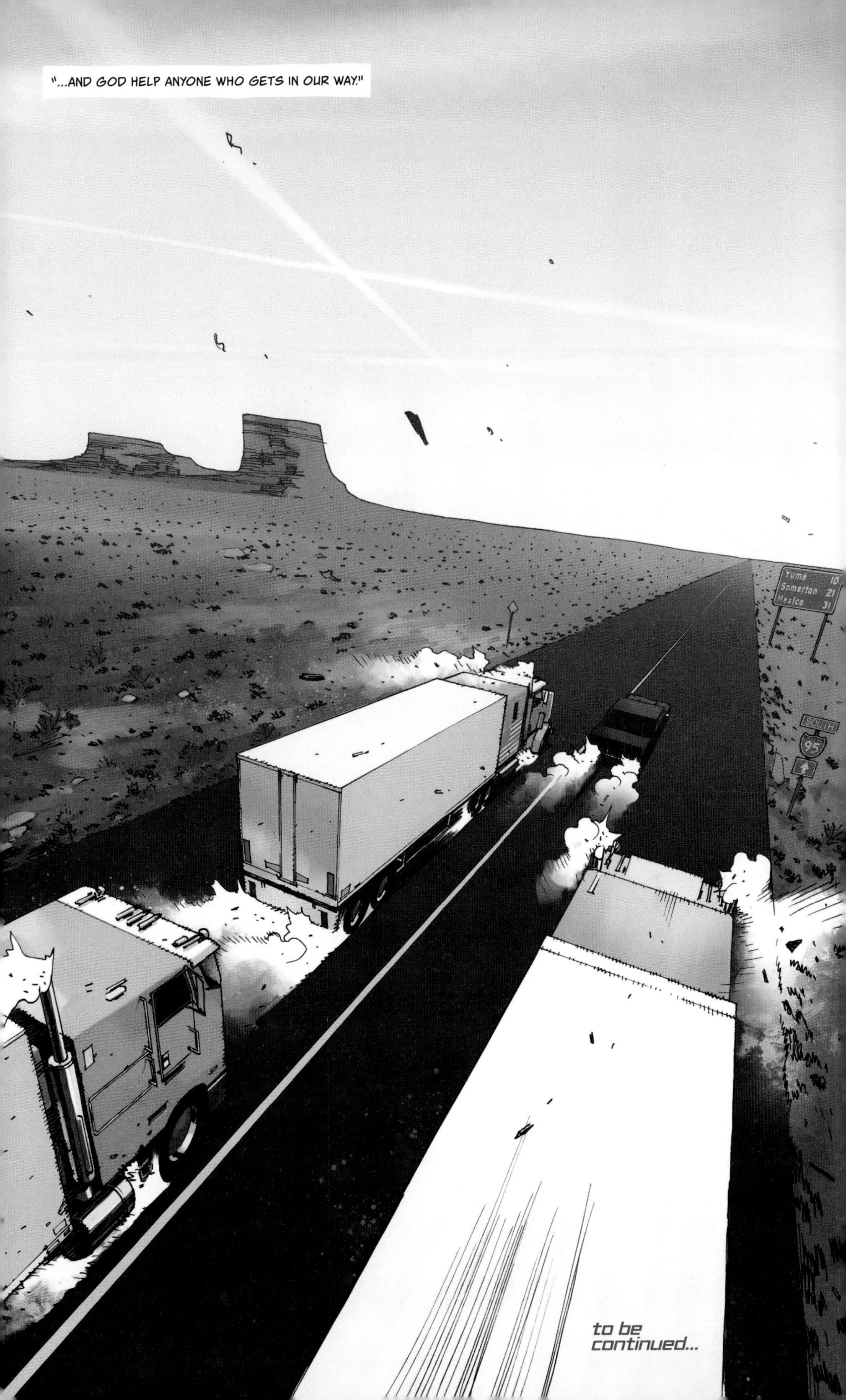
"...AND GOD HELP ANYONE WHO GETS IN OUR WAY."
Yuma 10
Somerton 21
Mexico 31
SOUTH
95
to be continued...

COVER GALLERY

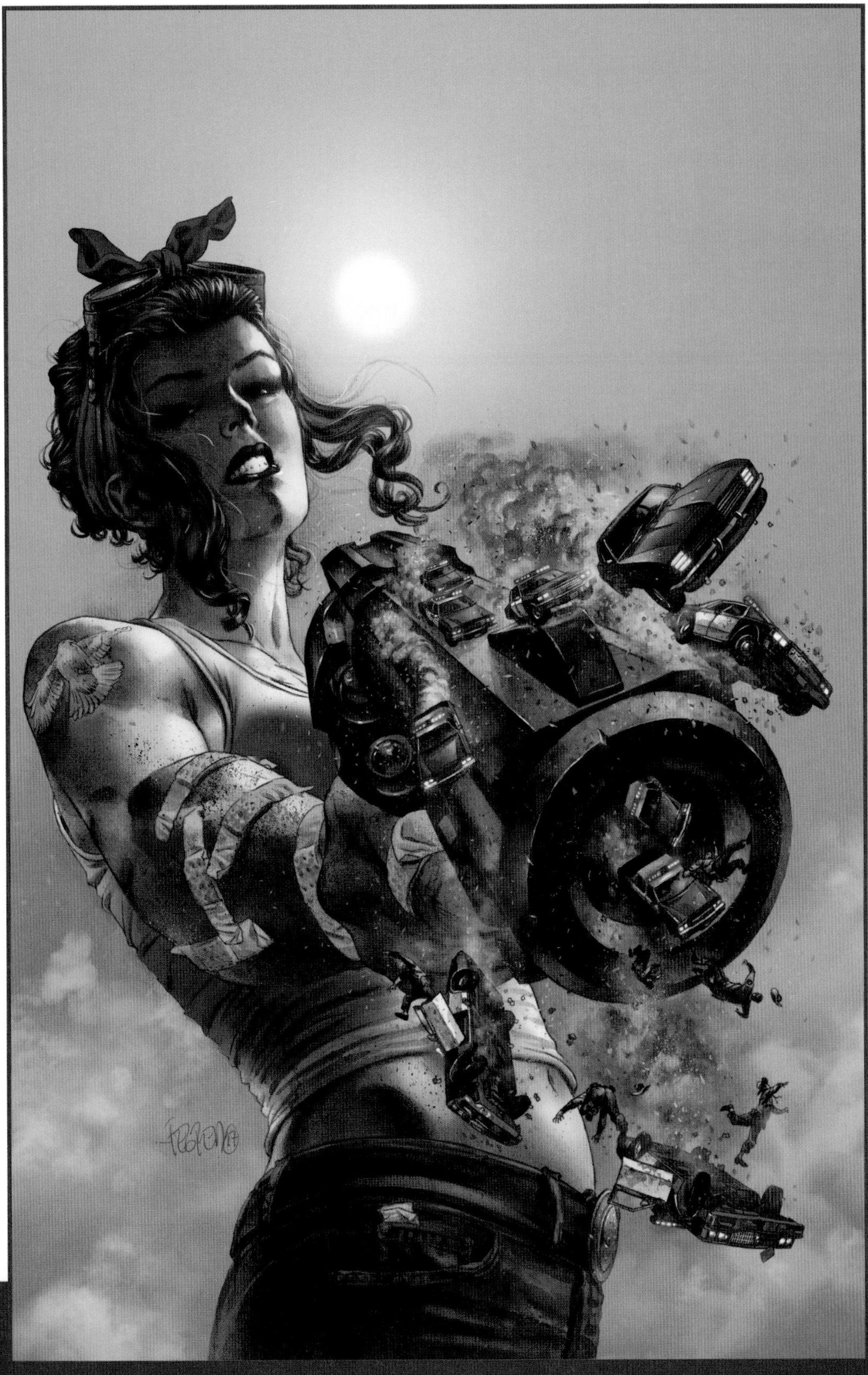

#1 VARIANT BY **DUNCAN FEGREDO**

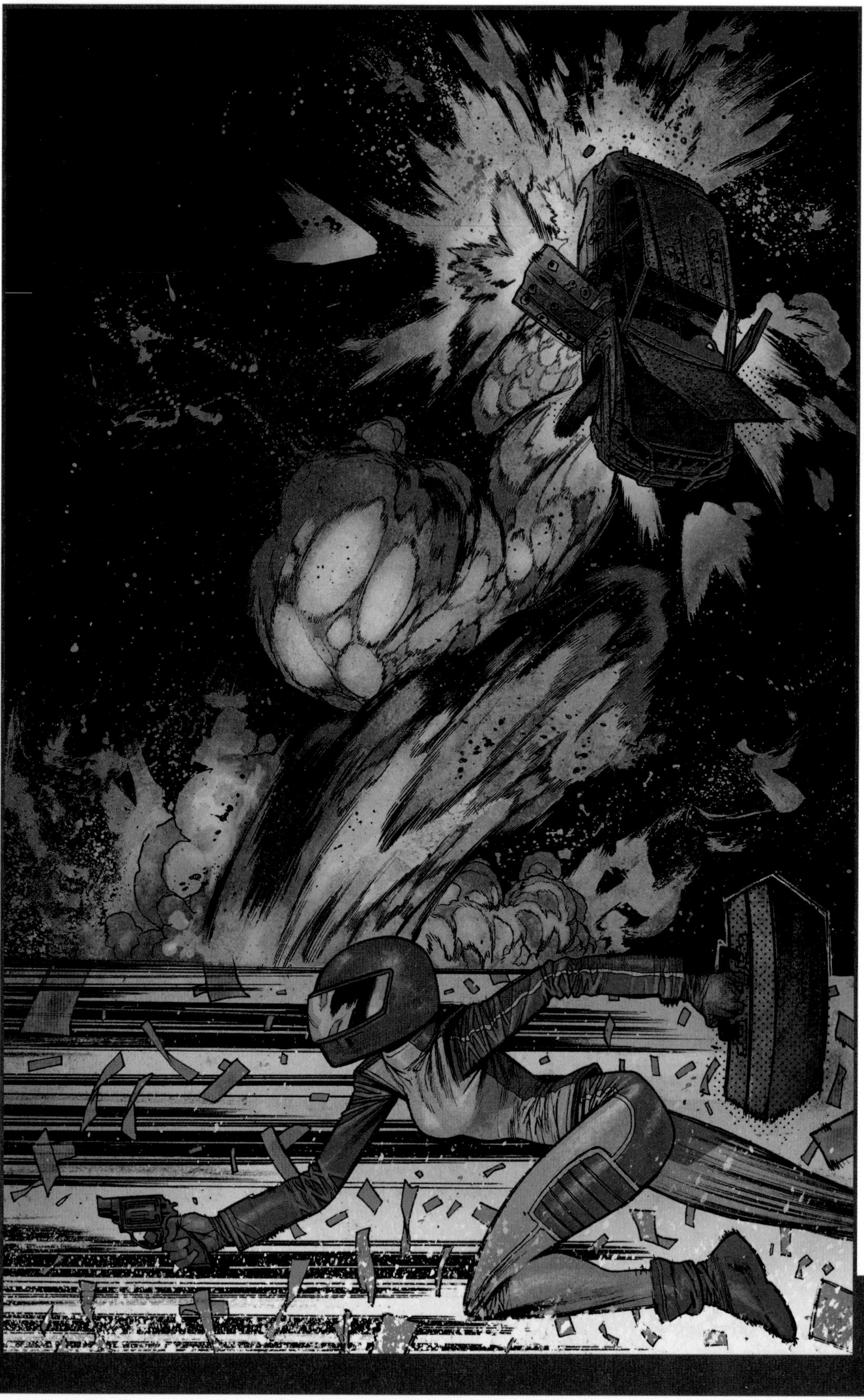

#1 VARIANT BY **JAMES HARREN**

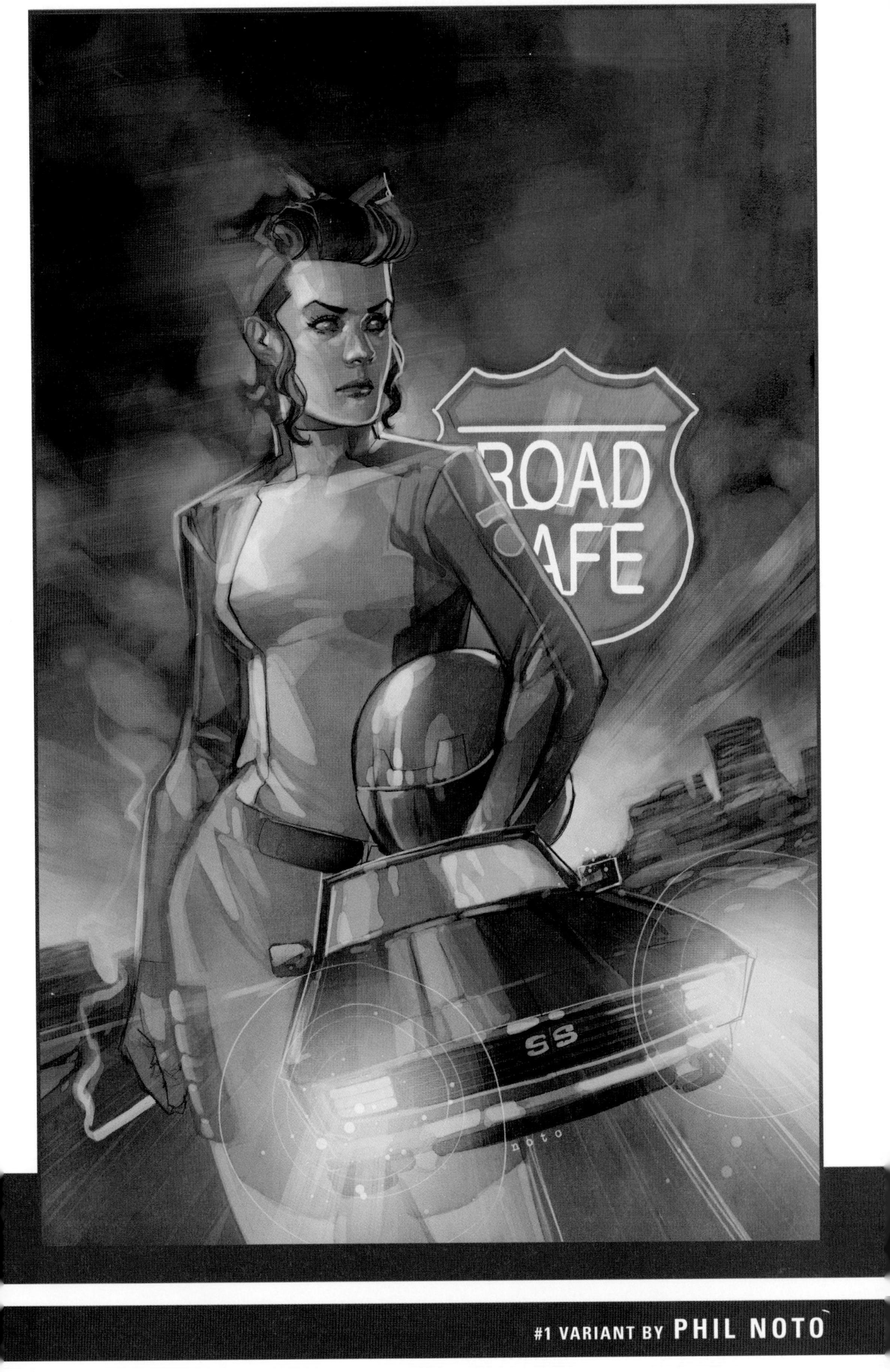
ROAD
AFE
SS
noto

#1 VARIANT BY **PHIL NOTO**

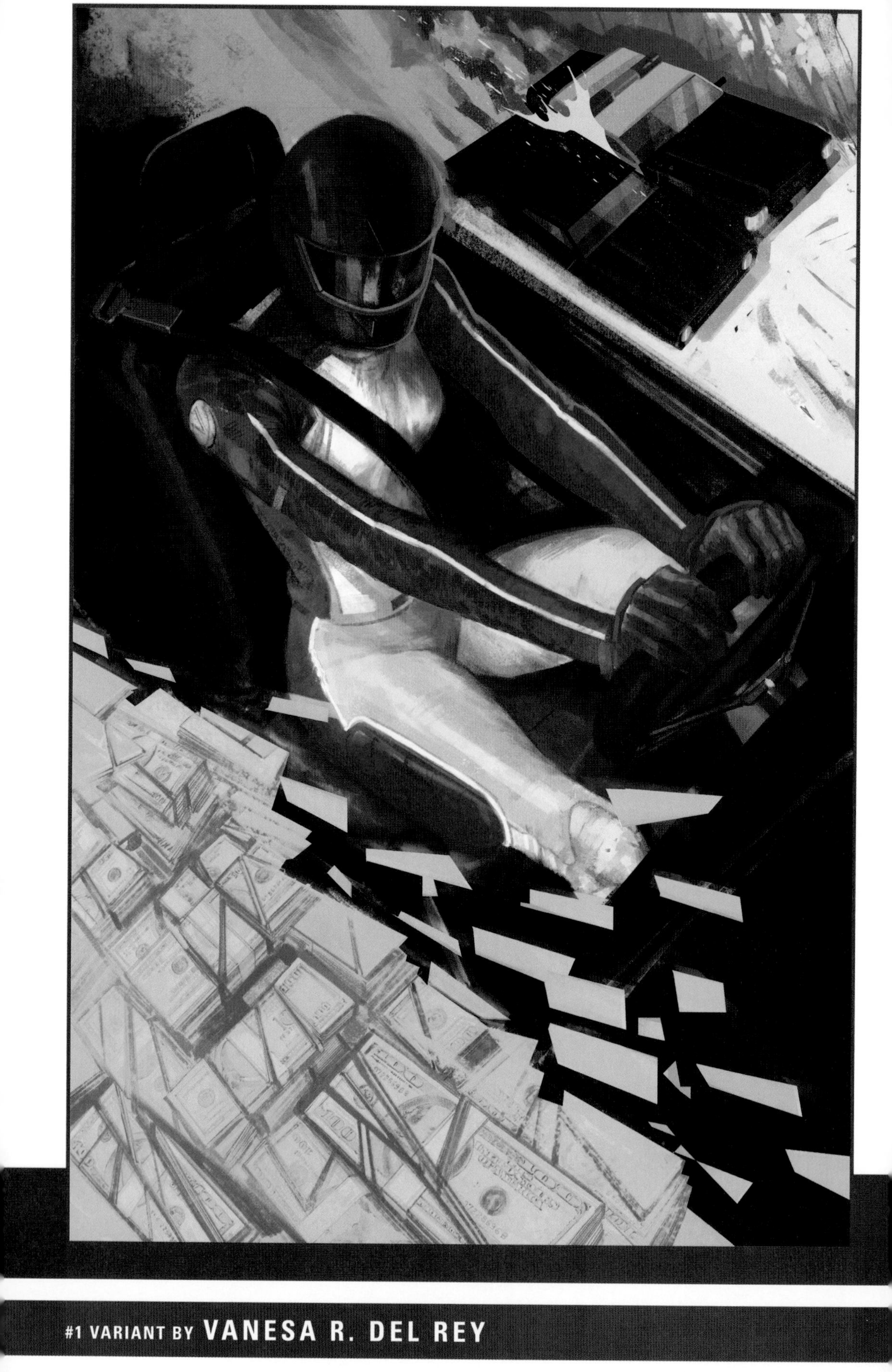

#1 VARIANT BY **VANESA R. DEL REY**

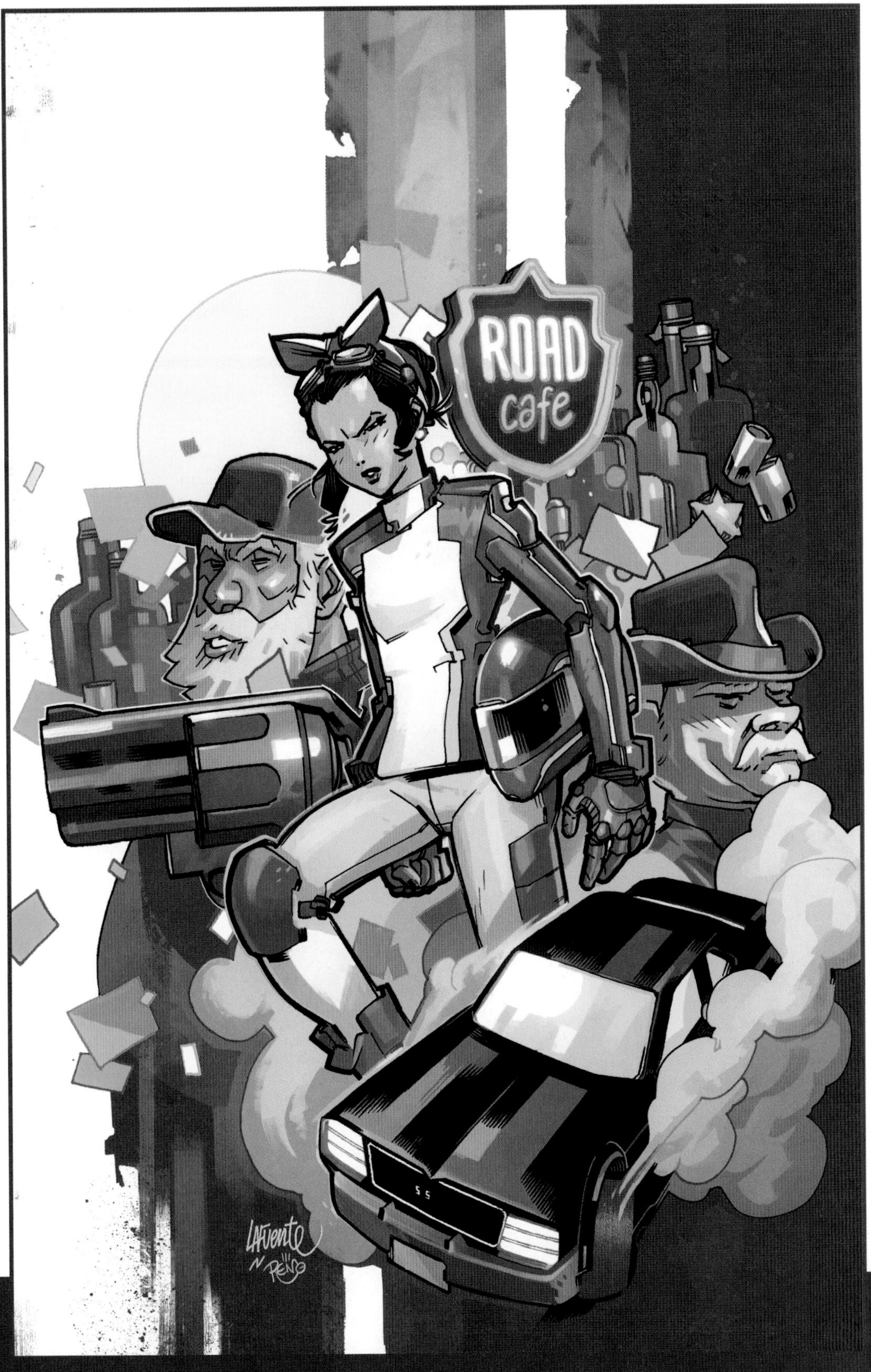
ROAD
cafe

#1 VARIANT BY **DAVID LAFUENTE & MORENO DINISIO**

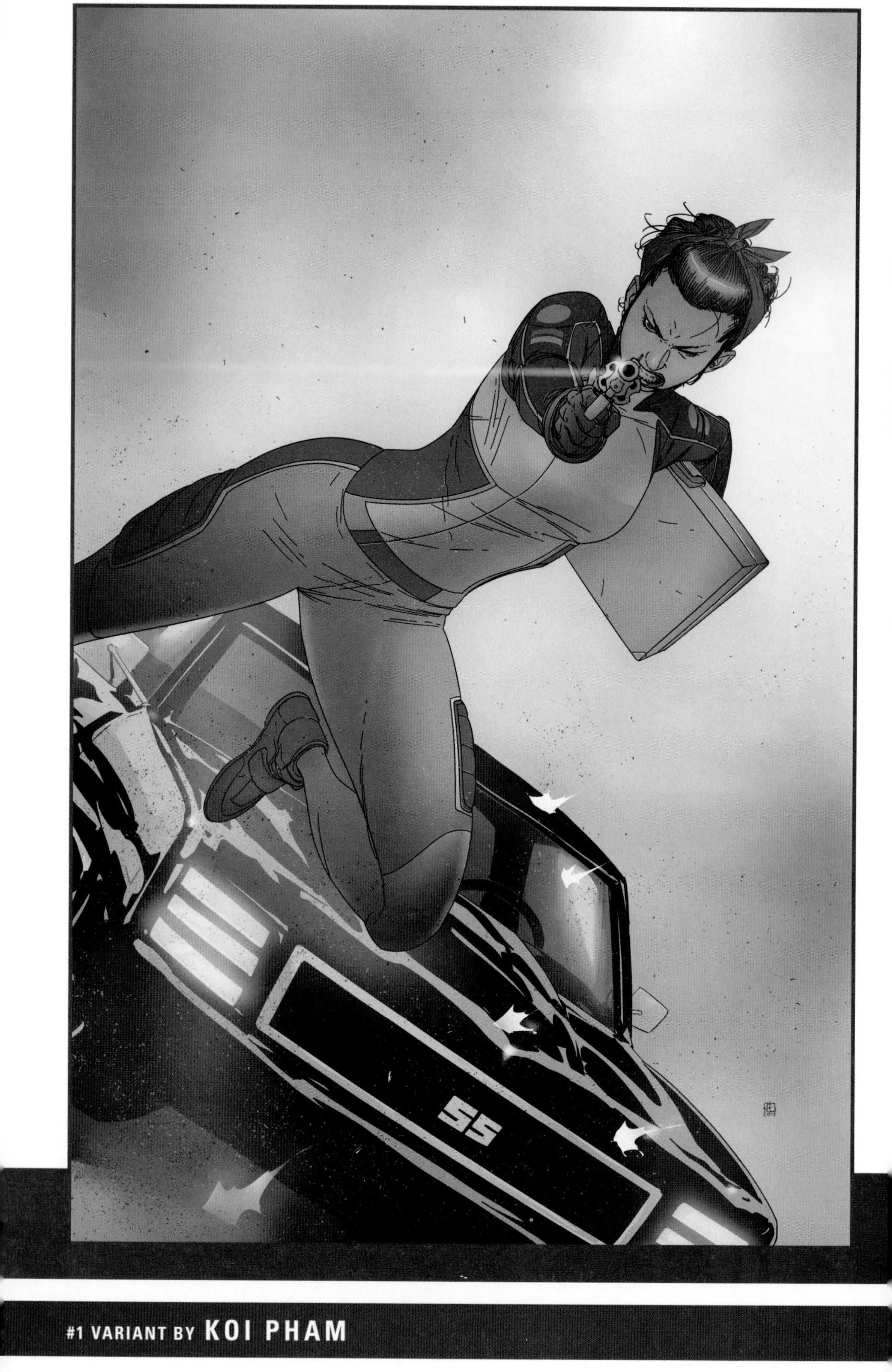
SS

#1 VARIANT BY **KOI PHAM**

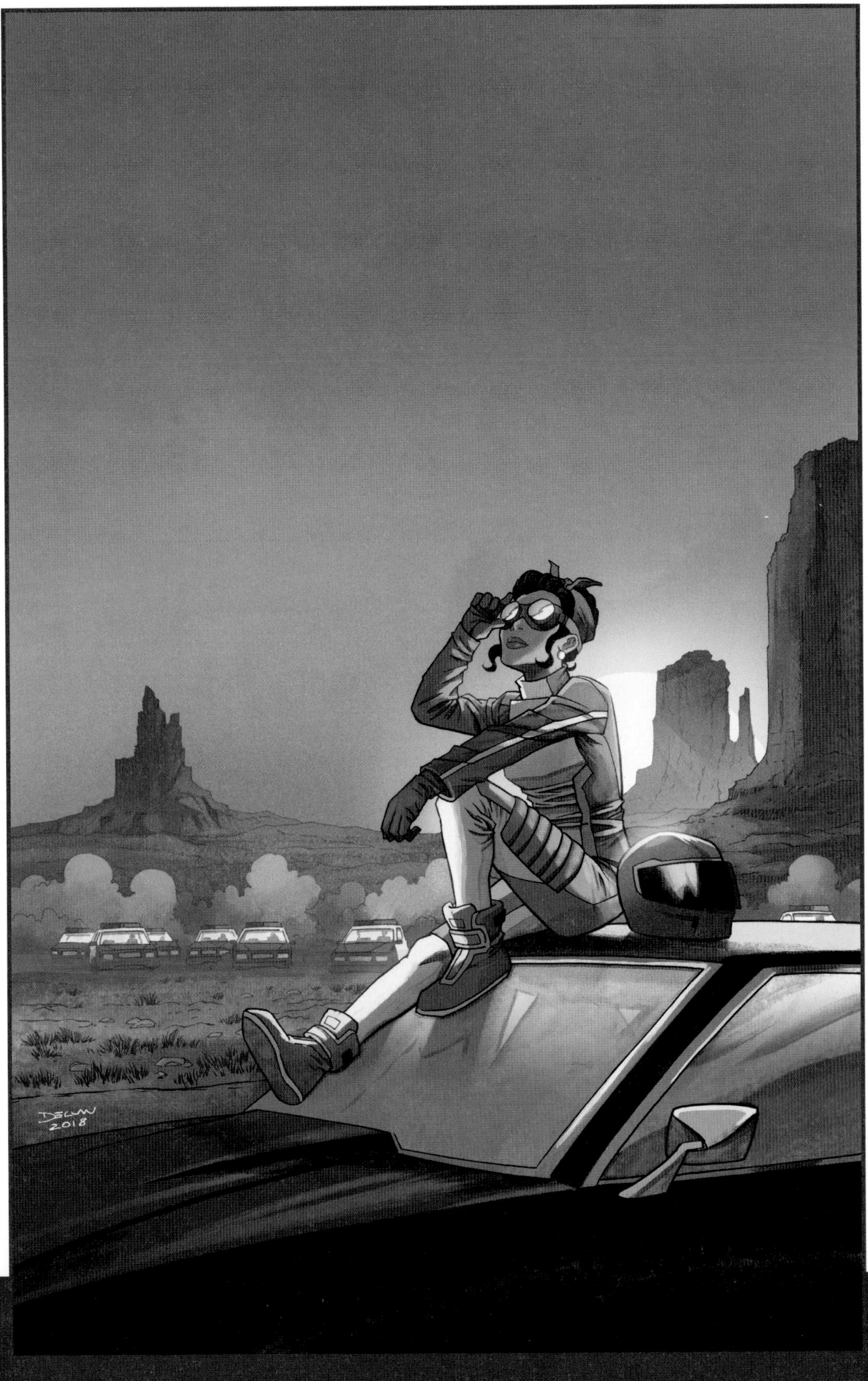

#1 VARIANT BY **DECLAN SHALVEY & TRIONA FARRELL**

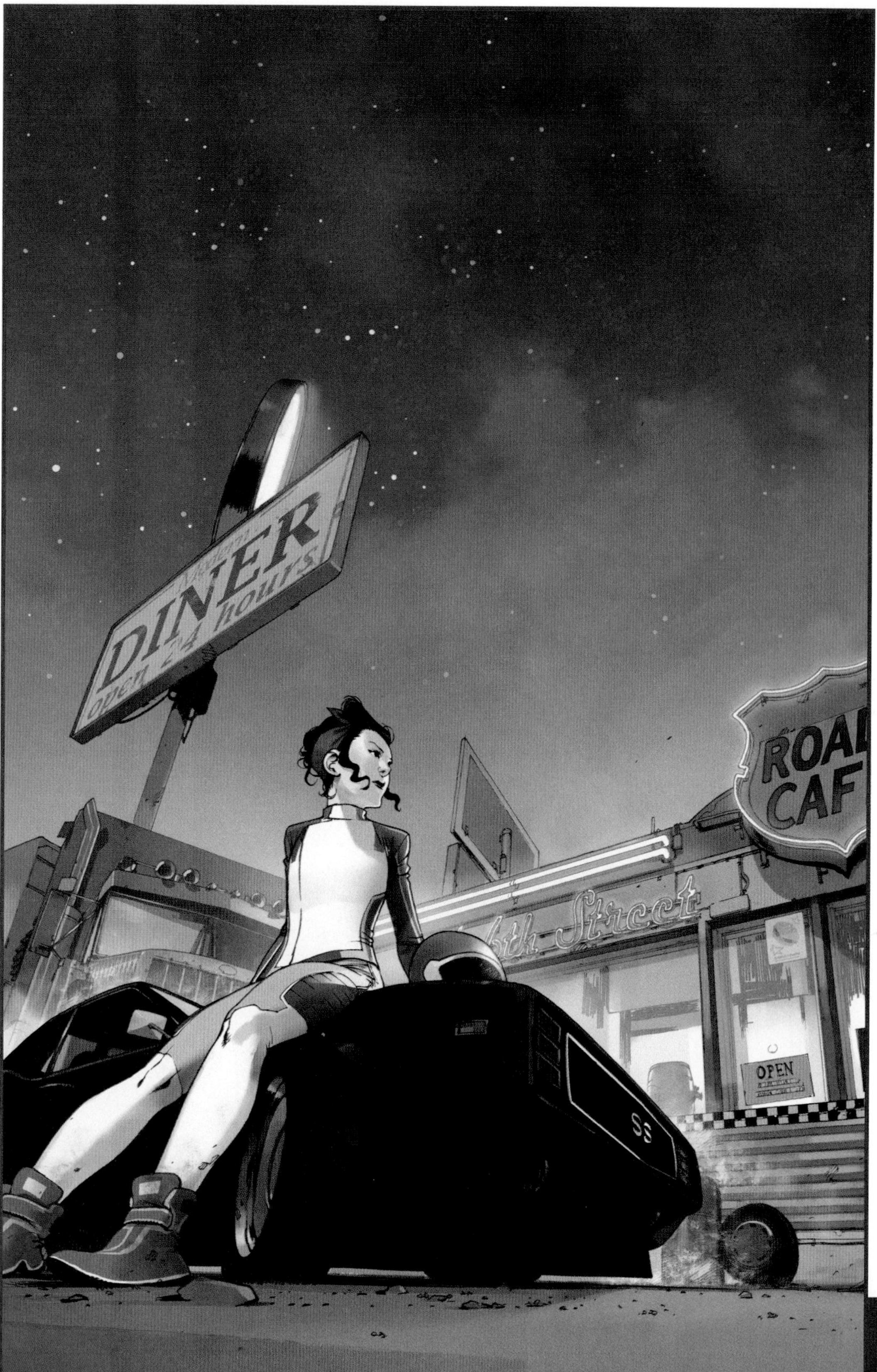
DINER
open 24 hours
ROAD
CAF
OPEN
SS

#1 2ND PRINTING VARIANT BY **BENGAL**

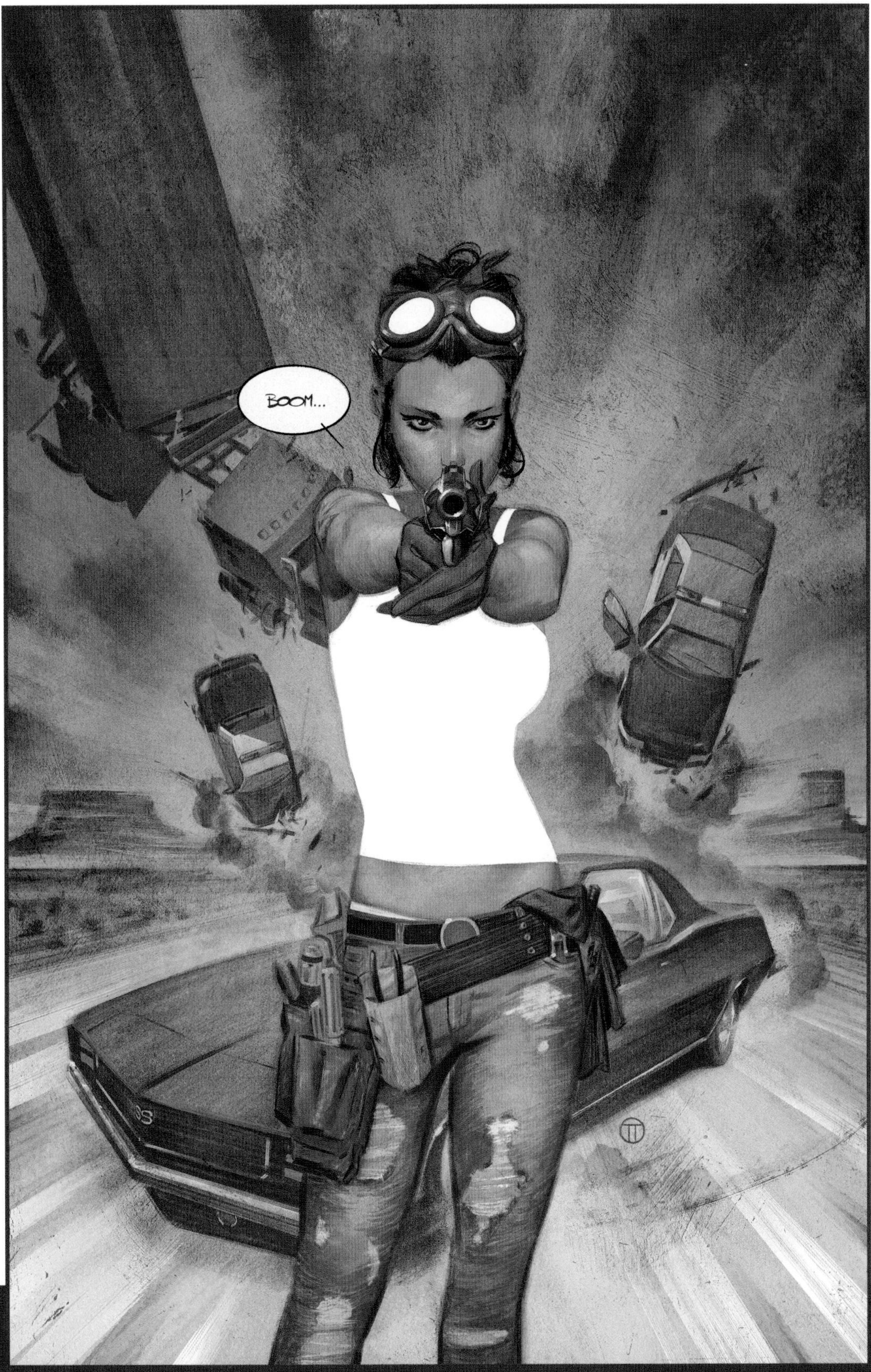
BOOM...

#2 VARIANT BY **JULIAN TOTINO TEDESCO**

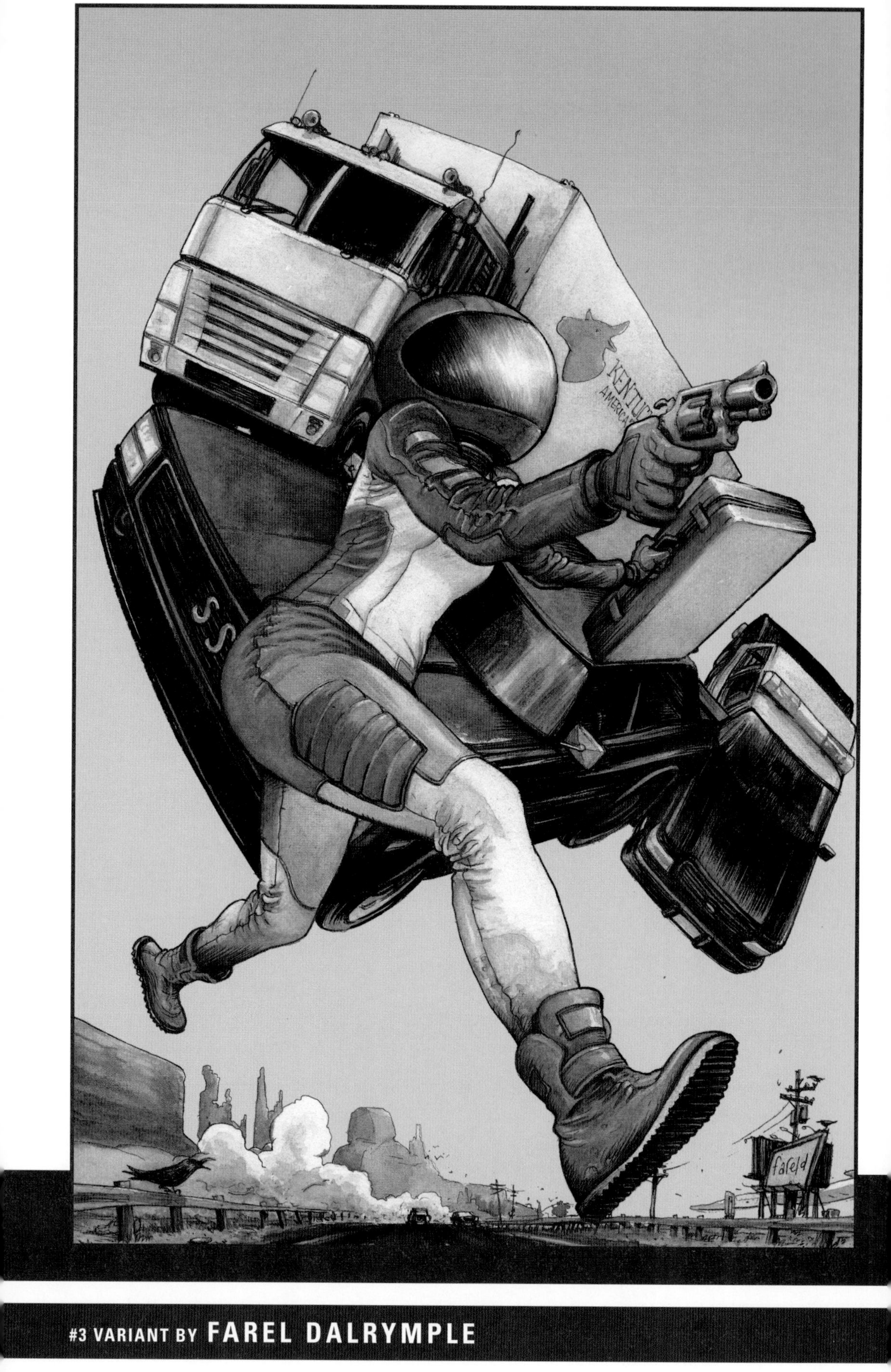
SS
faceld

#3 VARIANT BY **FAREL DALRYMPLE**

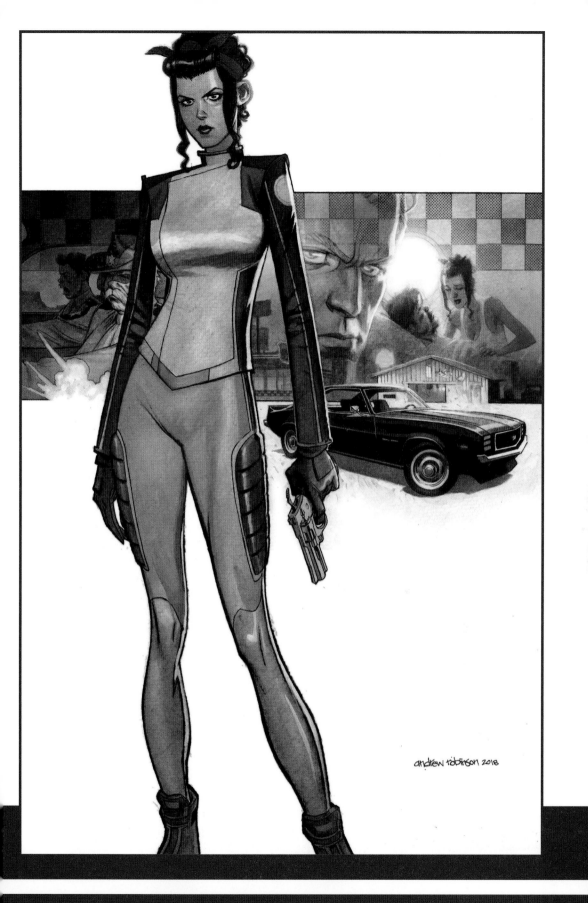

#4 VARIANT BY **ANDREW ROBINSON**

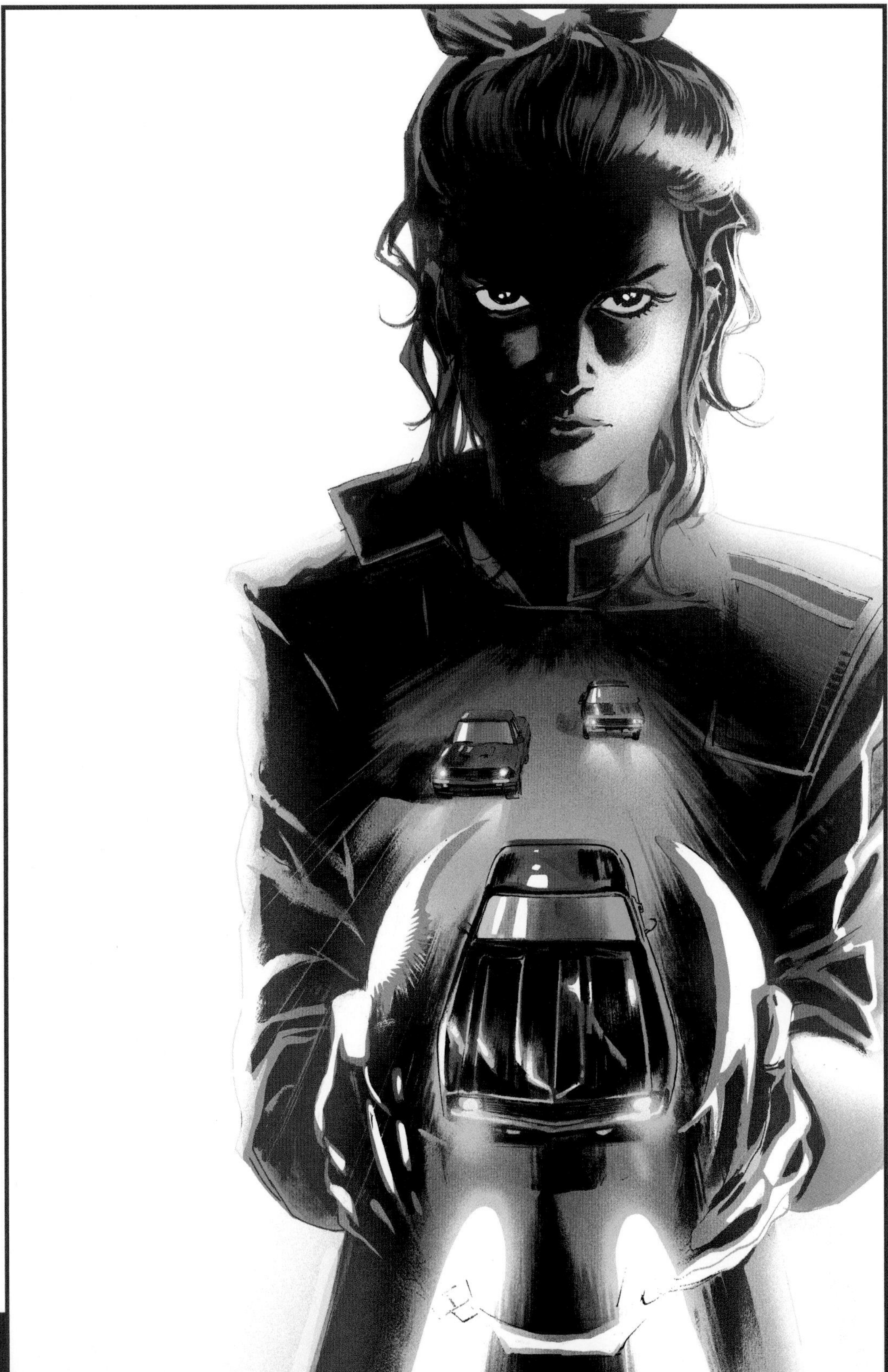

#5 VARIANT BY **RAFAEL ALBUQUERQUE**

CONCEPT ART
AND DESIGNS
BY BENGAL

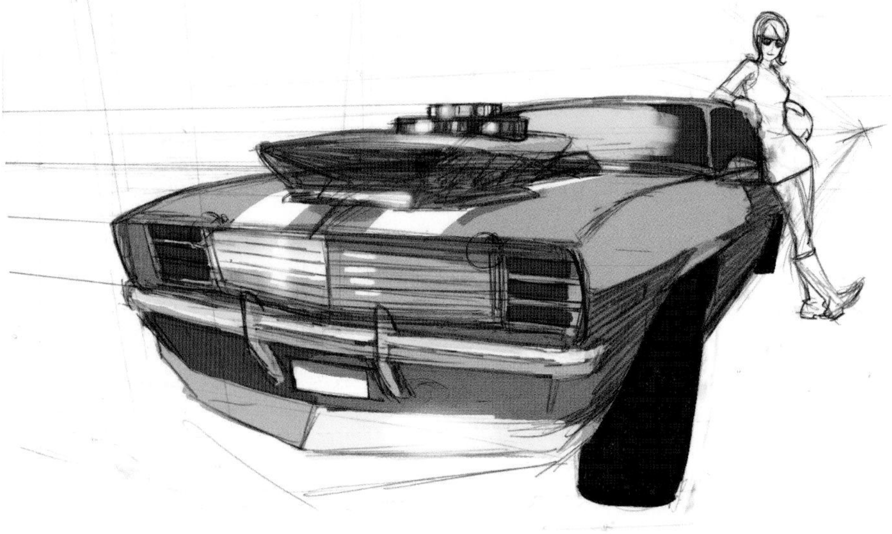
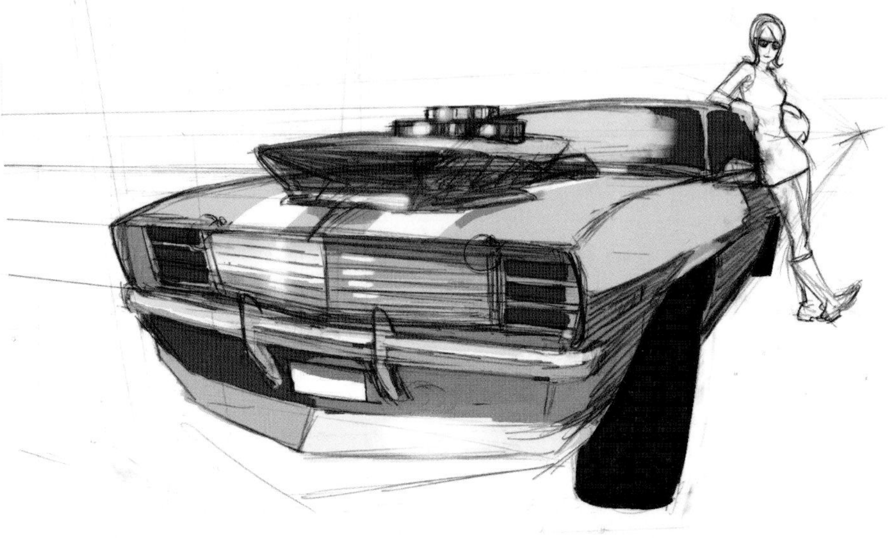
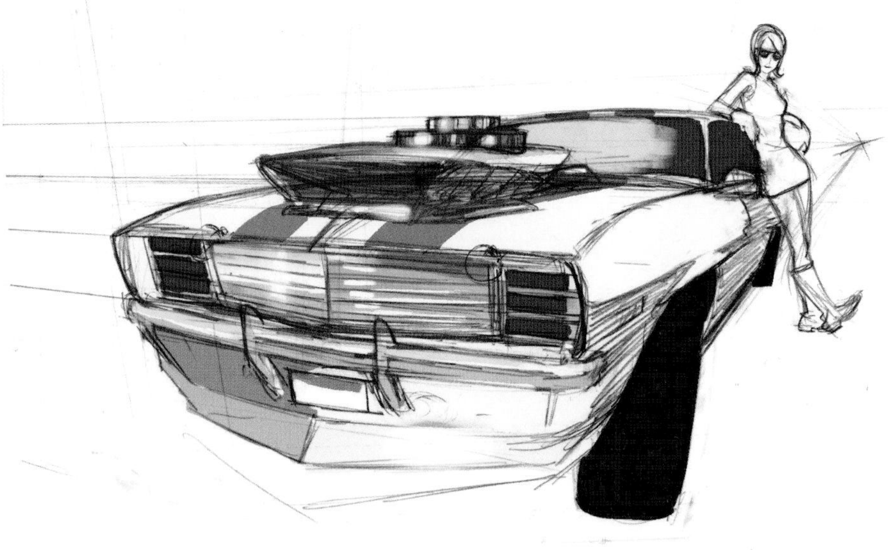

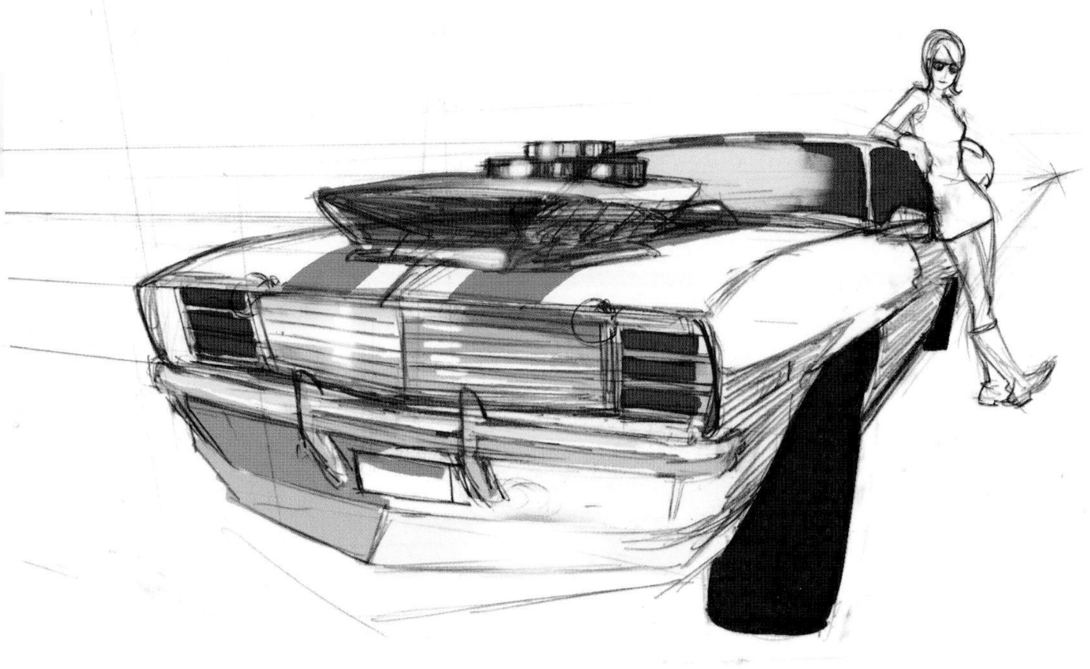

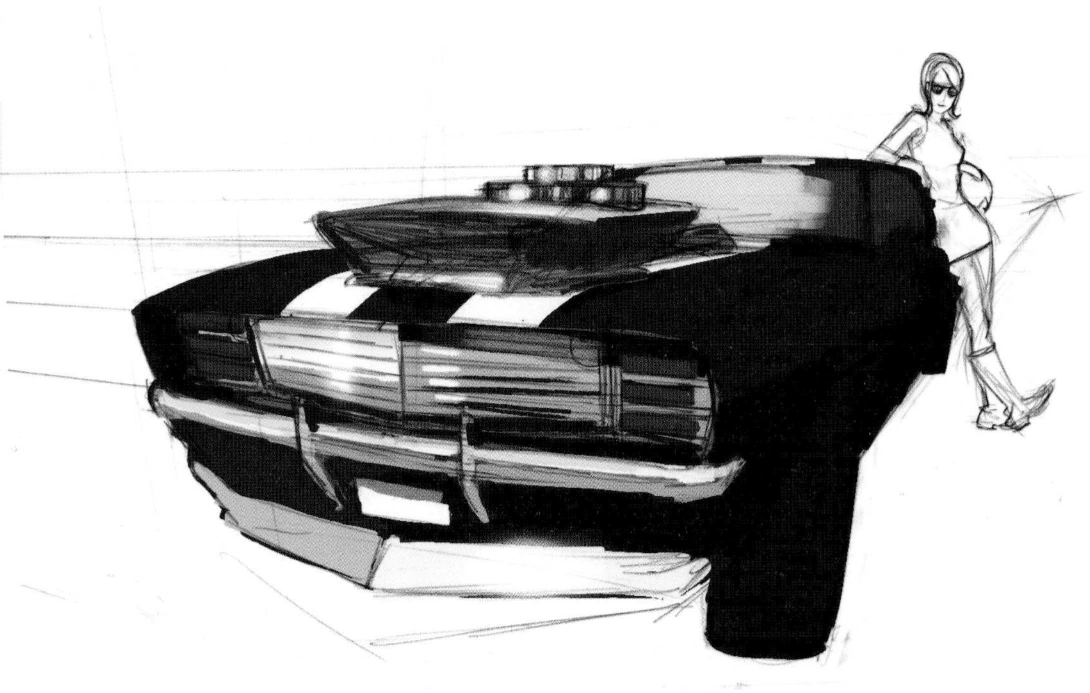

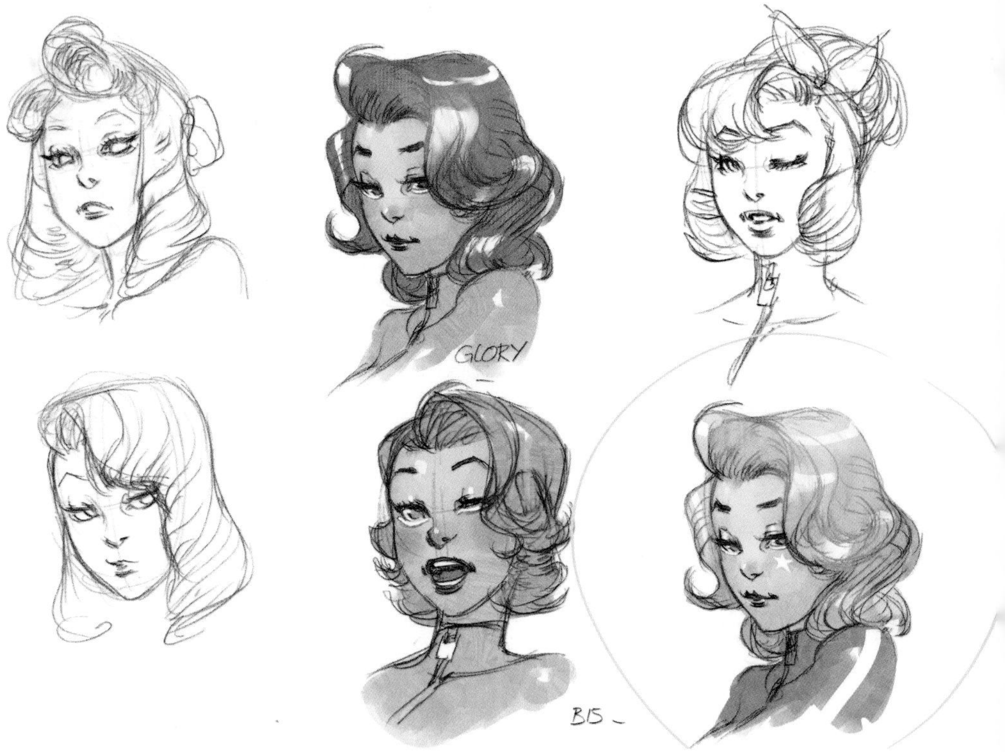
GLORY
B15 -

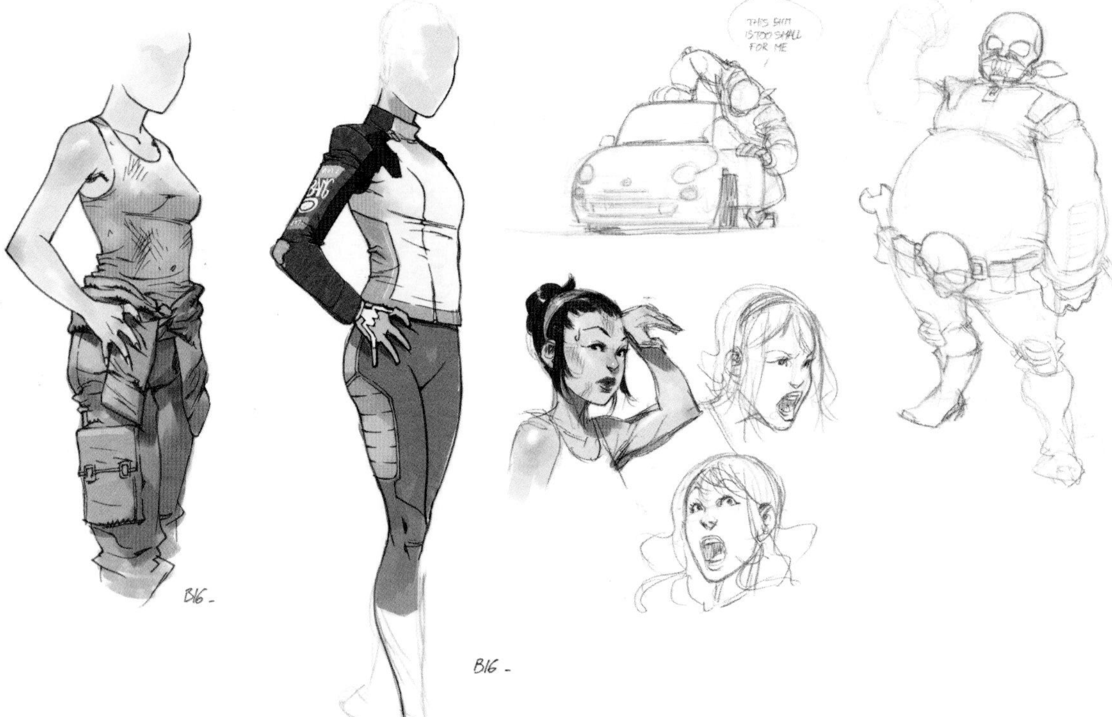
THIS SHIT IS TOO SMALL FOR ME
B16 -
B16 -

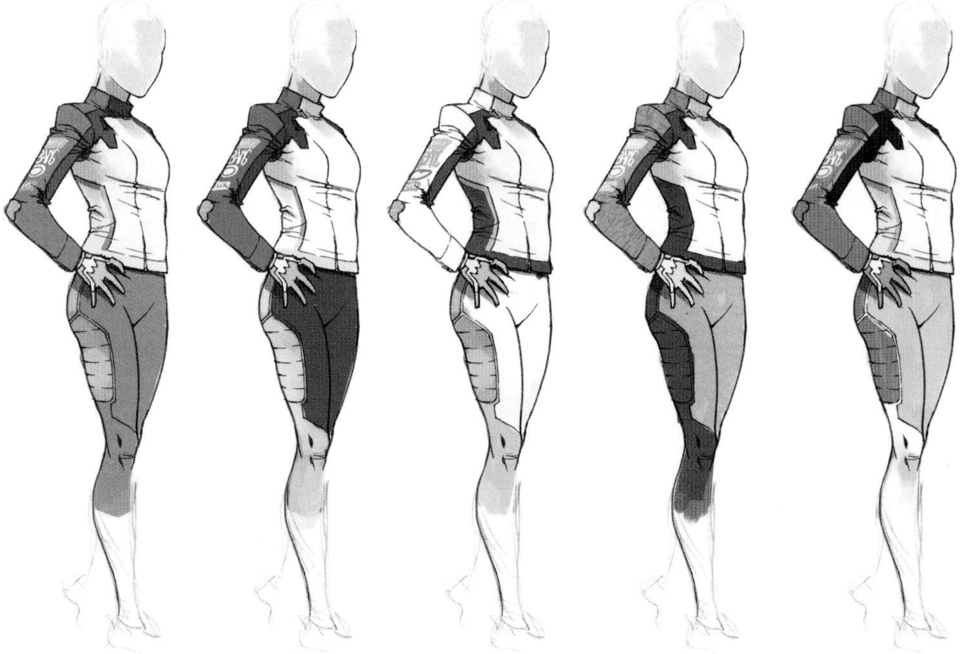

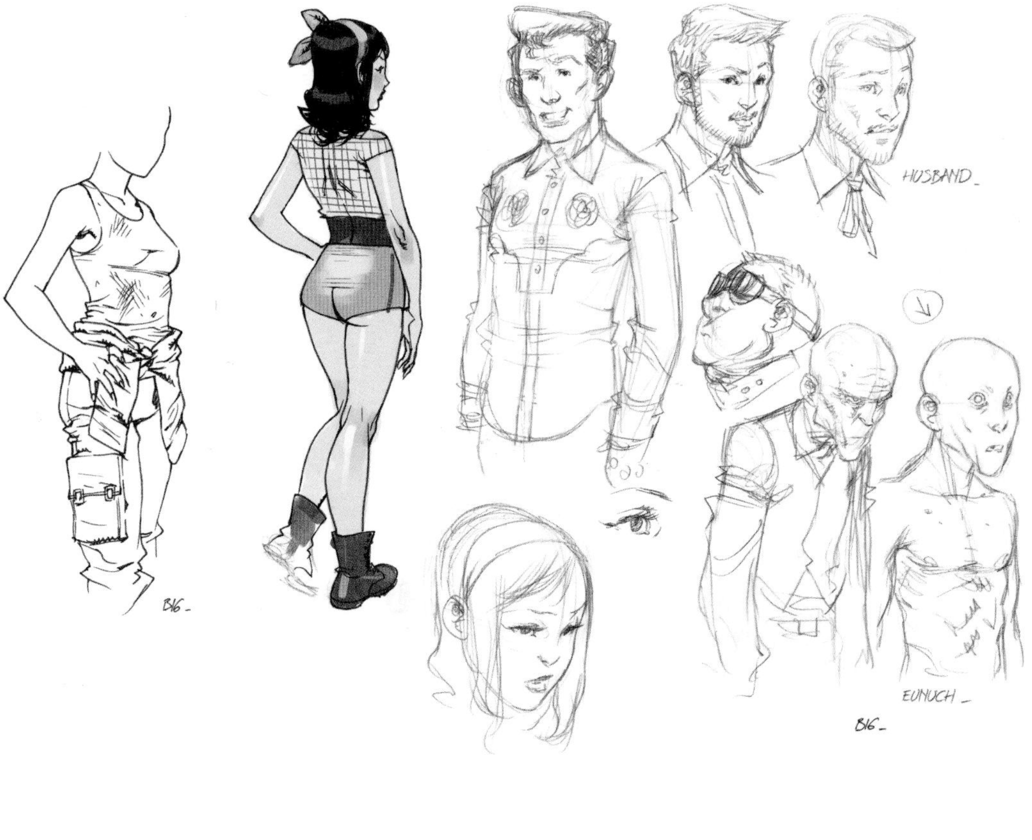
HUSBAND_
BIG_
EUNUCH_
BIG_

RICK REMENDER is the writer/co-creator of comics such as DEADLY CLASS, FEAR AGENT, BLACK SCIENCE, SEVEN TO ETERNITY, and LOW. During his years at Marvel he wrote *Captain America, Uncanny X-Force, Venom* and created *The Uncanny Avengers*. Outside of comics he served as lead writer on EA's *Bulletstorm* game and the hit game *Dead Space*. Prior to this he ran a satellite of Wild Brain animation, worked on films such as *The Iron Giant* and *Anastasia,* and taught sequential art and animation at San Francisco's Academy of Art University.

He currently curates his own publishing imprint, Giant Generator, at Image Comics while serving as lead writer/co-showrunner on SyFy's adaption of his co-creation DEADLY CLASS.

After being an author for over a decade for the European comics market, **BENGAL** got the opportunity to start doing covers and interiors for DC Comics & Marvel in 2014 and started working regularly and exclusively for the American industry, on several characters such as *Supergirl, Spider-Gwen, All-New Wolverine*, and many more. In the meantime, he was already developing a longer-term, creator-owned project with Rick Remender, which became DEATH OR GLORY. He's currently working on the next issues.